ABDUCTED BY ALIENS

Demon wind greeted pallid daylight with hell-howl fury: body-smashing sheets of rain and spray, the rolling concussion of thunder, the bellow of wind, and the endless keen of rigging and sodden percussion of torn canvas flailing to destruction. The vessel was doomed. *All* the ships of his expedition were doomed . . . and there was nothing Sir George could do about it.

Sir George's stumbling, exhaustion-sodden thoughts jerked to a stop. He clamped his jaws against a bellow of matching fear as the *shape* burst abruptly and impossibly through the savage backdrop of cloud and rain.

He couldn't grasp it, at first. It was too huge, too alien . . . too impossible. It could not exist, not in a world of mortals, yet it loomed above them, motionless, shrugging aside the fury of the gale as if it were the gentlest of zephyrs. Gleaming like polished bronze, flickering with the reflected glare of lightning, a mile and more in length. It drifted over the more distant of the cogs he'd seen earlier, and light appeared as portions of its skin shifted and changed.

No, they're _____ _____ _____ _____ ought numbly. *They're open* _____ _____ _____ _____ *bers filled with light a* _____

More sha _____ _____ _____ _____ e, but with that same u _____ _____ _____ _____ wled about them. They spread _____ _____ _____ f-foundered cog, and then—

"Holy Mary, Mother of God," the baron whispered, crossing himself slowly, almost absently, as an unearthly glare of light leapt out from the shapes which had encircled the other ship. Leapt out, touched the heaving vessel, embraced . . .

. . . and lifted it bodily from the boiling sea.

—from "Sir George and the Dragon"
by David Weber

BAEN BOOKS by DAVID DRAKE

FOREIGN LEGIONS

CREATED BY
DAVID DRAKE

BAEN

Copyright © 2001 by David Drake. "Ranks of Bronze" copyright © 1975 by UPD Publishing Corp., August 1975 *Galaxy Magazine*.

A Baen Books Original

Baen Publishing Enterprises
P.O. Box 1403
Riverdale, NY 10471
www.baen.com

ISBN: 0-7434-3560-5

Cover art by Dru Blair

First paperback printing, September 2002

Library of Congress Catalog Number 2001025187

Distributed by Simon & Schuster
1230 Avenue of the Americas
New York, NY 10020

Production by Windhaven Press, Auburn, NH
Printed in the United States of America

TABLE OF CONTENTS

Introduction:
WELL, IT HAPPENED THIS WAY ...

In 1975 I was finally able to write a story that had been knocking about in my mind for ten years. It began with an undergraduate class in Horace which started me reading (and repeatedly rereading) the whole of that wonderful poet's work. I found particularly evocative the lament which I quote in my original story:

"And Crassus's wretched soldier takes a barbarian wife from his captors and grows old waging war for them."

In a course in Chinese history a year or two later, the professor mentioned in passing a unit of troops armed like Romans which was destroyed in Central Asia in 36 B.C. at the height of Chinese westward expansion. He speculated that these were the men Horace refers to, captured by the Parthians at Carrhae in 53 B.C. and sold as mercenaries to kingdoms east of Mesopotamia.

I was trying to write sf back then, so it immediately occurred to me that there was a story there if only I could get to it. What if the folks who bought the Romans weren't Huns but rather interstellar aliens who wanted low-tech soldiers for commercial expansion (I got that notion from Andre Norton; one of many things I got from that fine writer)? And what if the alien wives were *really* alien?

The difference between an idea and a story is the difference between a wannabe and a writer; it was a long time before I was writer enough to tell that deceptively simple story. When I did I cast it in the historical present, copying the style of a passage in Sallust's *Jugurthine Wars*. This was a silly thing to do; but apart from that, I'm still pleased with the result.

The story, "Ranks of Bronze," went off to *Galaxy* magazine, edited by a fellow named Jim Baen who'd bought three other stories of mine. I was paid for the story before the magazine came out (unique in my experience of *Galaxy* at the time). As a result I was a lot less angry than I'd otherwise have been to see that the editor had added a couple hundred words to the conclusion without telling me.

I'm glad I didn't get angry, because if I had I'd also have had to apologize to Jim later, since he was absolutely correct in adding the exposition there. The story in *Galaxy* (and in every reprint) is a collaboration between Drake and Baen. (Jim and I continue to mesh well together, but we do so with fewer sparks nowadays.)

Jim really liked "Ranks of Bronze"; so much so that when he started his own publishing house, Baen Books, the first thing he asked me to write for him was a novelization of that story. I agreed, though at the time I didn't know how I was going to do it.

The writing turned out to be easier than I'd expected

(not least because I'd done an enormous amount of research for the short story, including reading the whole of Vegetius in Latin). I had things to learn about my craft (and still do today), but a lot of the bits came together right on this one.

The novel, also *Ranks of Bronze*, was a Novel of Education—a *Bildungsroman*, to use the normal German term for such a work. I started out with a young boy and ended with him having grown to manhood. Both Jim and I were very pleased with the book.

That's where the trouble started: Jim wanted a sequel. I was flabbergasted—you can't have a sequel to a *Bildungsroman*. What was I supposed to do? Take my character from adulthood to senility in the second volume?

Jim kept asking. I kept saying no. (I'm not good at saying no to friends, but on this one I was adamant.) Finally he got sneaky and suggested that I let three writers (whom he picked) do novellas in the Ranks of Bronze universe, and that these novellas be bound in with the original novel. I agreed, since I wasn't going to have to do any work myself and the project would get Jim off my back about doing a sequel.

Hope springs eternal. Or, alternatively, there's a sucker born every minute. . . .

What you see is a self-standing volume with some excellent new stories built around my original (well, Andre's original) concept, but with no other criteria. I told the writers they could do what they pleased. Eric wrote the sequel Jim was begging for, while Steve used the characters from my novel in a campaign I hadn't described. Dave and Mark did something completely different within the basic parameters. And I used Crassus's legion but not any of the characters I'd written about in the original novel.

So . . . it's been a long road but an interesting one. And after all, the road for the original survivors of Crassus's legions was longer yet.

Dave Drake
david-drake.com

RANKS OF BRONZE

David Drake

The rising sun is a dagger point casting long shadows toward Vibulenus and his cohort from the native breastworks. The legion had formed ranks an hour before; the enemy is not yet stirring. A playful breeze with a bitter edge skitters out of the south, and the tribune swings his shield to his right side against it.

"When do we advance, sir?" his first centurion asks. Gnaeus Clodius Calvus, promoted to his present position after a boulder had pulped his predecessor during the assault on a granite fortress far away. Vibulenus only vaguely recalls his first days with the cohort, a boy of eighteen in titular command of four hundred and eighty men whose names he had despaired of learning. Well, he knows them now. Of course, there are only two hundred and ninety-odd left to remember.

Calvus's bearded, silent patience snaps Vibulenus back to the present. "When the cavalry comes up, they told me. Some kinglet or other is supposed to bring up a couple of thousand men to close our flanks. Otherwise, we're hanging. . . ."

The tribune's voice trails off. He stares across the flat expanse of gravel toward the other camp, remembering another battle plain of long ago.

"Damn Parthians," Calvus mutters, his thought the same.

Vibulenus nods. "Damn Crassus, you mean. He put us *there*, and that put us *here*. The stupid bastard. But he got his, too."

The legionaries squat in their ranks, talking and chewing bits of bread or dried fruit. They display no bravado, very little concern. They have been here too often before. Sunlight turns their shield-facings green: not the crumbly fungus of verdigris but the shimmering sea-color of the harbor of Brundisium on a foggy morning.

Oh, Mother Vesta, Vibulenus breathes to himself. He is five foot two, about average for the legion. His hair is black where it curls under the rim of his helmet and he has no trace of a beard. Only his eyes make him appear more than a teenager; they would suit a tired man of fifty.

A trumpet from the command group in the rear sings three quick bars. "Fall in!" the tribune orders, but his centurions are already barking their own commands. These too are lost in the clash of hobnails on gravel. The Tenth Cohort could form ranks in its sleep.

Halfway down the front, a legionary's cloak hooks on a notch in his shield rim. He tugs at it, curses in Oscan as Calvus snarls down the line at him. Vibulenus makes a mental note to check with the centurion after the battle. That fellow should have been issued a replacement shield before disembarking. He glances at his own. How many shields has he carried? Not that it matters. Armor is replaceable. He is wearing his fourth cuirass, now, though none of them have fit like the one his father had bought him the day Crassus granted him a tribune's slot. Vesta . . .

A galloper from the command group skids his beast to a halt with a needlessly brutal jerk on its reins. Vibulenus recognizes him—Pompilius Falco. A little swine when he joined the legion, an accomplished swine now. Not bad with animals, though. "We'll be advancing without the cavalry," he shouts, leaning over in his saddle. "Get your line dressed."

"Osiris's bloody dick we will!" the tribune snaps. "Where's our support?"

"Have to support yourself, I guess," shrugs Falco. He wheels his mount. Vibulenus steps forward and catches the reins.

"Falco," he says with no attempt to lower his voice, "you tell our deified Commander to get somebody on our left flank if he expects the Tenth to advance. There's too many natives—they'll hit us from three sides at once."

"You afraid to die?" the galloper sneers. He tugs at the reins.

Vibulenus holds them. A gust of wind whips at his cloak. "Afraid to get my skull split?" he asks. "I don't know. Are you, Falco?" Falco glances at where the tribune's right hand rests. He says nothing. "Tell him we'll fight for him," Vibulenus goes on. "We won't let him throw us away. We've gone that route once." He looses the reins and watches the galloper scatter gravel on his way back.

The replacement gear is solid enough, shields that do not split when dropped and helmets forged without thin spots. But there is no craftsmanship in them. They are heavy, lifeless. Vibulenus still carries a bone-hilted sword from Toledo that required frequent sharpening but was tempered and balanced—poised to slash a life out, as it has a hundred times already. His hand continues to caress the palm-smoothed bone, and it calms him somewhat.

"Thanks, sir."

The thin-featured tribune glances back at his men. Several of the nearer ranks give him a spontaneous salute. Calvus is the one who spoke. He is blank-faced now, a statue of mahogany and strap-bronze. His stocky form radiates pride in his leader. Leader—no one in the group around the standards can lead a line soldier, though they may give commands that will be obeyed. Vibulenus grins and slaps Calvus's burly shoulder. "Maybe this is the last one and we'll be going home," he says.

Movement throws a haze over the enemy camp. At this distance it is impossible to distinguish forms, but metal flashes in the virid sunlight. The shadow of bodies spreads slowly to right and left of the breastworks as the natives order themselves. There are thousands of them, many thousands.

"Hey-*yip*!" Twenty riders of the general's bodyguard pass behind the cohort at an earthshaking trot. They rein up on the left flank, shrouding the exposed depth of the infantry. Pennons hang from the lances socketed behind their right thighs, gay yellows and greens to keep the lance heads from being driven too deep to be jerked out. The riders' faces are sullen under their mesh face guards. Vibulenus knows how angry they must be at being shifted under pressure—under his pressure—and he grins again. The bodyguards are insulted at being required to fight instead of remaining nobly aloof from the battle. The experience may do them some good.

At least it may get a few of the snotty bastards killed.

"Not exactly a regiment of cavalry," Calvus grumbles.

"He gave us half of what was available," Vibulenus replies with a shrug. "They'll do to keep the natives off our back. Likely nobody'll come near, they look so mean."

The centurion taps his thigh with his knobby swagger stick. "Mean? We'll give 'em mean."

All the horns in the command group sound together, a cacophonous bray. The jokes and scufflings freeze, and only the south wind whispers. Vibulenus takes a last look down his ranks—each of them fifty men abreast and no more sway to it than a tight-stretched cord would leave. Five feet from shield boss to shield boss, room to swing a sword. Five feet from nose guard to the nose guards of the next rank, men ready to step forward individually to replace the fallen or by ranks to lock shields with the front line in an impenetrable wall of bronze. The legion is a restive dragon, and its teeth glitter in its spears; one vertical behind each legionary's shield, one slanted from each right hand to stab or throw.

The horns blare again, the eagle standard slants forward, and Vibulenus's throat joins three thousand others in a death-rich bellow as the legion steps off on its left foot. The centurions are counting cadence and the ranks blast it back to them in the crash-jingle of boots and gear.

Striding quickly between the legionaries, Vibulenus checks the dress of his cohort. He should have a horse, but there are no horses in the legion now. The command group rides rough equivalents which are . . . very rough. Vibulenus is not sure he could accept one if his parsimonious employers offered it.

His men are a smooth bronze chain that advances in lock step. Very nice. The nine cohorts to the right are in equally good order, but Hercules! there are so few of them compared to the horde swarming from the native camp. Somebody has gotten overconfident. The enemy raises its own cheer, scattered and thin at first. But it goes on and on, building, ordering itself to a blood-pulse rhythm that moans across the intervening distance, the gap the legion is closing at two steps a second. Hercules! there is a crush of them.

The natives are close enough to be individuals now: lanky, long-armed in relation to a height that averages greater than that of the legionaries. Ill-equipped, though. Their heads are covered either by leather helmets or beehives of their own hair. Their shields appear to be hide and wicker affairs. What could live on this gravel waste and provide that much leather? But of course Vibulenus has been told none of the background, not even the immediate geography. There is some place around that raises swarms of warriors, that much is certain.

And they have iron. The black glitter of their spearheads tightens the tribune's wounded chest as he remembers.

"Smile, boys," one of the centurions calls cheerfully, "here's company." With his words a javelin hums down at a steep angle to spark on the ground. From a spearthrower, must have been. The distance is too long for any arm Vibulenus has seen, and he has seen his share.

"Ware!" he calls as another score of missiles arc from the native ranks. Legionaries judge them, raise their shields or ignore the plunging weapons as they choose. One strikes in front of Vibulenus and shatters into a dozen iron splinters and a knobby shaft that looks like rattan. One or two of the men have spears clinging to their shield faces. Their clatter syncopates the thud of boot heels. No one is down.

Vibulenus runs two paces ahead of his cohort, his sword raised at an angle. It makes him an obvious target: a dozen javelins spit toward him. The skin over his ribs crawls, the lumpy breadth of scar tissue scratching like a rope over the bones. But he can be seen by every man in his cohort, and somebody has to give the signal. . . .

"Now!" he shouts vainly in the mingling cries. His arm and sword cut down abruptly. Three hundred throats give a collective grunt as the cohort heaves its own massive spears with the full weight of its rush behind them. Another light javelin glances from the shoulder of Vibulenus's cuirass, staggering him. Calvus's broad right palm catches the tribune, holds him upright for the instant he needs to get his balance.

The front of the native line explodes as the Roman spears crash into it.

Fifty feet ahead there are orange warriors shrieking as they stumble over the bodies of comrades whose armor has shredded under the impact of the heavy spears. "At 'em!" a front-rank file-closer cries, ignoring his remaining spear as he drags out his short sword. The trumpets are calling something but it no longer matters what: tactics go hang, the Tenth is cutting its way into another native army.

In a brief spate of fury, Vibulenus holds his forward position between a pair of legionaries. A native, orange-skinned with bright carmine eyes, tries to drag himself out of the tribune's path. A Roman spear has gouged through his shield and arm, locking all three together. Vibulenus's sword takes the warrior alongside the jaw. The blood is paler than a man's.

The backward shock of meeting has bunched the natives. The press of undisciplined reserves from behind adds to their confusion. Vibulenus jumps a still-writhing body and throws himself into the wall of shields and terrified orange faces. An iron-headed spear thrusts at him, misses as another warrior jostles the wielder. Vibulenus slashes downward at his assailant. The warrior throws his shield up to catch the sword, then collapses when a second-rank legionary darts his spear through the orange abdomen.

Breathing hard with his sword still dripping in his hand, Vibulenus lets the pressing ranks flow around him. Slaughter is not a tribune's work, but increasingly Vibulenus finds that he needs the swift violence of the battle line to release the fury building within him. The cohort is advancing with the jerky sureness of an ox-drawn plow in dry soil.

A windrow of native bodies lies among the line of first contact, now well within the Roman formation. Vibulenus wipes his blade on a fallen warrior, leaving two sluggish runnels filling on the flesh. He sheathes the sword. Three bodies are sprawled together to form a hillock. Without hesitation the tribune steps onto it to survey the battle.

The legion is a broad awl punching through a belt of orange leather. The cavalry on the left stand free in a scatter of bodies, neither threatened by the natives nor making any active attempt to drive them back. One of the mounts, a hairless brute combining the shape of a wolfhound with the bulk of an ox, is feeding on a corpse his rider has lanced. Vibulenus was correct in expecting the natives to give them a wide berth; thousands of flanking warriors tremble in indecision rather than sweep forward to surround the legion. It would take more discipline than this orange rabble has shown to attack the toad-like riders on their terrible beasts.

Behind the lines, a hundred paces distant from the legionaries whose armor stands in hammering contrast to the naked autochthones, is the Commander and his remaining score of guards. He alone of the three thousand who have landed from the starship knows why the battle is being fought, but he seems to stand above it. And if the silly bastard still has half his bodyguard with him—Mars and all the gods, what must be happening on the right flank?

The inhuman shout of triumph that rises half a mile away gives Vibulenus an immediate answer.

"Prepare to disengage!" he orders the nearest centurion. The swarthy noncom, son of a North African colonist, speaks briefly into the ears of two legionaries before sending them to the ranks forward and back of his. The legion is tight for men, always has been. Tribunes have no runners, but the cohort makes do.

Trumpets blat in terror. The native warriors boil whooping around the Roman right flank. Legionaries in the rear are facing about with ragged suddenness, obeying instinct rather than the orders bawled by their startled officers. The command group suddenly realizes the situation. Three of the bodyguard charge toward the oncoming orange mob. The rest of the guards and staff scatter into the infantry.

The iron-bronze clatter has ceased on the left flank. When the cohort halts its advance, the natives gain enough room to break and flee for their encampment. Even the warriors who have not engaged are cowed by the panic of those who have; by the panic, and the sprawls of bodies left behind them.

"About face!" Vibulenus calls through the indecisive hush, "and pivot on your left flank. There's some more barbs want to fight the Tenth!"

The murderous cheer from his legionaries overlies the noise of the cohort executing his order.

As it swings, Vibulenus runs across the new front of his troops, what had been the rear rank. The cavalry, squat-bodied and grim in their full armor, shows sense enough to guide their mounts toward the flank of the Ninth Cohort as Vibulenus rotates his men away from it. Only a random javelin from the native lines appears to hinder them. Their comrades who remained with the Commander have been less fortunate.

A storm of javelins has disintegrated the half-hearted charge. Two of the mounts have gone down despite their heavy armor. Behind them, the Commander lies flat on the hard soil while his beast screams horribly above him. The shaft of a stray missile projects from its withers. Stabbing up from below, the orange warriors fell the remaining lancer and gut his companions as they try to rise. Half a dozen of the bodyguards canter nervously back from their safe bolthole among the infantry to try to rescue their employer. The wounded mount leaps at one of the lancers. The two beasts tangle with the guard between them. A clawed hind leg flicks his head. Helmet and head rip skyward in a spout of green ichor.

"Charge!" Vibulenus roars. The legionaries who can not hear him follow his running form. The knot of cavalry and natives is a quarter mile away. The cohorts of the right flank are too heavily engaged to do more than defend themselves against the new thrust. Half the legion has become a bronze worm, bristling front and back with spear-points against the surging orange flood. Without immediate support, the whole right flank will be squeezed until it collapses into a tangle of blood and scrap metal. The Tenth Cohort is their support, all the support there is.

"Rome!" the fresh veterans leading the charge shout as their shields rise against the new flight of javelins. There are gaps in the back ranks, those just disengaged. Behind the charge, men hold palms clamped over torn calves or lie crumpled around a shaft of alien wood. There will be time enough for them if the recovery teams land—which they will not do in event of a total disaster on the ground.

The warriors snap and howl at the sudden threat.

Their own success has fragmented them. What had been a flail slashing into massed bronze kernels is now a thousand leaderless handfuls in sparkling contact with the Roman line. Only the leaders bunched around the command group have held their unity.

One mount is still on its feet and snarling. Four massively-equipped guards try to ring the Commander with their maces. The Commander, his suit a splash of blue against the gravel, tries to rise. There is a flurry of mace strokes and quickly-riposting spears, ending in a clash of falling armor and an agile orange body with a knife leaping the crumpled guard. Vibulenus's sword, flung over-arm, takes the native in the throat. The inertia of its spin cracks the hilt against the warrior's forehead.

The Tenth Cohort is on the startled natives. A moment before the warriors were bounding forward in the flush of victory. Now they face the cohort's meat-axe suddenness—and turn. At sword-point and shield edge, as inexorable as the rising sun, the Tenth grinds the native retreat into panic while the cohorts of the right flank open order and advance. The ground behind them is slimy with blood.

Vibulenus rests on one knee, panting. He has retrieved his sword. Its stickiness bonds it to his hand. Already the air keens with landing motors. In minutes the recovery teams will be at work on the fallen legionaries, building life back into all but the brain-hacked or spine-severed. Vibulenus rubs his own scarred ribs in aching memory.

A hand falls on the tribune's shoulder. It is gloved in a skin-tight blue material; not armor, at least not armor against weapons. The Commander's voice comes from the small plate beneath his clear, round helmet. Speaking in Latin, his accents precisely flawed, he says, "You are splendid, you warriors."

Vibulenus sneers though he does not correct the alien. Warriors are capering heroes, good only for dying when they meet trained troops, when they meet the Tenth Cohort.

"I thought the Federation Council had gone mad," the flat voice continues, "when it ruled that we must not land weapons beyond the native level in exploiting inhabited worlds. All very well to talk of the dangers of introducing barbarians to modern weaponry, but how else could my business crush local armies and not be bled white by transportation costs?"

The Commander shakes his head in wonder at the carnage about him. Vibulenus silently wipes his blade. In front of him, Falco gapes toward the green sun. A javelin points from his right eyesocket. "When we purchased you from your Parthian captors it was only an experiment. Some of us even doubted it was worth the cost of the longevity treatments. In a way you are more effective than a Guard Regiment with lasers; outnumbered, you beat them with their own weapons. They can't even claim 'magic' as a salve to their pride. And at a score of other job sites you have done as well. And so cheaply!"

"Since we have been satisfactory," the tribune says, trying to keep the hope out of his face, "will we be returned home now?"

"Oh, goodness, no," the alien laughs, "you're far too valuable for that. But I have a surprise for you, one just as pleasant I'm sure—females."

"You found us real women?" Vibulenus whispers.

"You really won't be able to tell the difference," the Commander says with paternal confidence.

A million suns away on a farm in the Sabine hills, a poet takes the stylus from the fingers of a nude slave girl and writes, very quickly, *And Crassus's wretched soldier takes a barbarian wife from his captors and grows old waging war for them.*

The poet looks at the line with a pleased expression. "It needs polish, of course," he mutters. Then, more directly to the slave, he says, "You know, Leuconoe, there's more than inspiration to poetry, a thousand times more; but this came to me out of the air."

Horace gestures with his stylus toward the glittering night sky. The girl smiles back at him.

SIR GEORGE AND THE DRAGON

David Weber

Demon wind greeted pallid daylight with hell-howl fury. It was no true daylight, although somewhere above the clouds of seething black the sun had heaved itself once more into the heavens. It was only the devil's own twilight, slashed with body-smashing sheets of rain and spray, the rolling concussion of thunder, the bellow of wind, and the endless keen of rigging and sodden percussion of torn canvas flailing to destruction.

Sir George Wincaster, Third Baron of Wickworth, clung to a stay, feeling it quiver and groan with strain while he kept to his feet by raw, hopeless force of will alone. The lifeline the vessel's captain had lashed about him when the hideous gale burst upon them yesterday morning had ringed his chest in bruises, salt sores stung his lips, and rain and spray had soaked into his very marrow. He felt as if heavy horses had charged over him and back again, and despair was a leaden fist about his heart. He had been too ignorant to understand the captain's terror when first the weather broke, for he was a soldier, not a sailor. Now he understood only too well, and he watched almost numbly as the battered cog, creaking and groaning in every frame and stringer, corkscrewed down yet another mountainous, slate-gray wave, streaked with seething bands of spray and foam, and buried its round-cheeked prow deep. Water roared the length of the hull, poison-green and icy as death, plucking and jerking at his limbs and groping after every man on the staggering ship's deck. The hungry sheet of destruction smashed over Sir George, battering the breath from him in yet another agonized grunt, and then it was past and he threw his head up, gasping and hacking on the water which had forced itself into nostrils and eyes.

The cog fought her way once more up out of the abyss, wallowing as the water cascaded off her deck through buckled rails. Broken cordage blew out, bar-straight and deadly as flails on the howling torrent of wind, and he heard the hull crying out in torment. Sir George was a landsman, yet even he felt the ship's heavier motion, knew the men—and women—laboring frantically at the pumps and bailing with buckets, bowls, even bare hands, were losing ground steadily.

The vessel was doomed. *All* the ships of his expedition were doomed . . . and there was nothing he could do about it. The unexpected summer gale had caught them at the worst possible moment, just as they were rounding the Scilly Isles on their way from Lancaster to Normandy. There had been no warning, no time to seek shelter, only the desperate hope that they might somehow ride out the storm's violence on the open sea.

And that hope had failed.

Sir George had seen only one ship actually die. He was uncertain which, but he thought it had been Earl Cathwall's flagship. He hoped he was wrong. It was unlikely any of them would survive, but Lord Cathwall was more than the commander of the expedition. He was also Sir George's father-in-law, and they held one another in deep and affectionate respect. And perhaps Sir George *was* wrong. The dying ship had been almost close enough to hear the shrieks of its doomed company howl as it was pounded into the depths, even through the storm's demented scream, but the darkness and storm fury, broken only by the glare of forked lightning, had made exact identification impossible.

Yet even though it was the only ship he had seen destroyed, he was grimly certain there had been others. Indeed, he could see only one other vessel still fighting its hopeless battle, and he ground his teeth as yet another sea crashed over his own cog. The impact staggered the ship, and a fresh chorus of screams and prayers came faintly from the men and women and children packed below its streaming deck. His wife Matilda and their son Edward were in that dark, noisome hellhole of crowded terror and vomit, of gear come adrift and washing seawater, and terror choked him as he thought of them once again. He tried to find the words of prayer, the way to plead with God to save his wife and his son. He did not beg for himself. It was not his way, and his was the responsibility for bringing them to this in the first place. If God wanted his life in exchange for those so much dearer to him, it was a price he would pay without a whimper.

Yet he knew it was a bargain he would not be permitted. That he and Matilda and Edward would meet their ends together, crushed by the soulless malice and uncaring brutality of sea and wind, and deep within him bitter protest reproached the God who had decreed that they should.

The cog shuddered and twitched, heaving in the

torment of overstrained timbers and rigging, and Sir
George looked up as the ship's mate shouted something. He couldn't make out the words, but he knew
it was a question, and he shook himself like a sodden
dog, struggling to make his mind function. For all his
ignorance of the sea, he had found himself doomed
to command of the ship when a falling spar killed the
captain. In fact, he'd done little more than agree with
the mate's suggestions, lending his authority to the
support of a man who might—*might!*—know enough
to keep them alive a few hours more. But the mate
had needed that support, needed someone else to
assume the ultimate responsibility, and that was Sir
George's job. To assume responsibility. No, to *acknowledge* the responsibility which was already his. And so
he made himself look as if he were carefully considering whatever it was the mate wanted to do this time,
then nodded vigorously.

The mate nodded back, then bellowed orders at his
exhausted, battered handful of surviving sailors. Wind
howl and sea thunder thrashed the words into mean-
ingless fragments so far as Sir George could tell, but
two or three men began clawing their way across the
deck to obey whatever the mate had decreed, and Sir
George turned his face back to the sea's tortured
millrace. It didn't really matter what the mate did, he
thought. At worst, a mistake would cost them a few
hours of life they might otherwise have clung to; at
best, a brilliant maneuver might buy them an hour or
two they might not otherwise have had. In the end,
the result would be the same.

He'd had such hopes, made so many plans. A
hard man, Sir George Wincaster, and a determined
one. A peer of the realm, a young man who had
caught his monarch's favor at the siege of Berwick
at the age of twenty-two, who'd been made a knight

by Edward III's own hand the next year on the field of Halidon Hill. A man who'd served with distinction at the Battle of Sluys eight years later— *although*, he thought with an edge of mordant humor even now, *if I'd learned a bit more then of ships, I might have been wise enough to stay home* this *time!*—and slogged through the bitterly disappointing French campaign of 1340. And a man who had returned with a fortune from Henry of Denby's campaign in Gascony five years later.

And a bloody lot of good it's done me in the end, he thought bitterly, remembering his gleaming plans. At thirty-five, he was at the height of his prowess, a hard-bitten, professional master of the soldier's trade. A knight, yes, but one who knew the reality of war, not the minstrels' tales of romance and chivalry. A man who fought to *win* . . . and understood the enormous changes England and her lethal longbows were about to introduce into the continental princes' understanding of the art of war.

And one who knew there were fortunes to be made, lands and power to be won, in the service of his King against Philip of France. Despite the disappointments of 1340, last year had proved Edward III his grandfather's grandson, a welcome relief after the weakness and self-indulgence of his father. *Longshanks would have approved of the King*, Sir George thought now. *He started slow, but now that Denby's shown the way and he's chosen to beard Philip alone, the lions of England will make the French howl!*

Perhaps they would, and certainly Edward's claim to the throne of France was better than Philip VI's, but Sir George Wincaster would not win the additional renown—or the added wealth and power he had planned to pass to his son—at his King's side. Not now. For he and all the troops under his command would find another fate, and no one would ever know where and when they actually perished.

The corpse light of storm-wracked afternoon slid towards evening, and Sir George realized dully that they had somehow survived another day.

He was too exhausted even to feel surprised . . . and though he tried to feel grateful, at least, a part of him was anything but. Another night of horror and fear, exhaustion and desperate struggle, loomed, and even as he gathered himself to face it, that traitor part wanted only for it to end. For it to be over.

To rest.

But there would be rest enough soon enough, he reminded himself. An eternity of it, if he was fortunate enough to avoid Hell. He hoped he would be, but he was also a realist—and a soldier. And the best of soldiers would face an arduous stay in Purgatory, while the worst . . .

He brushed the thought aside, not without the wistful wish that he and Father Timothy might have argued it out one more time, and made himself peer about. The second ship was still with them, further away as darkness gathered, but still fighting its way across the heaving gray waste, and he could actually see a third vessel beyond it. There might even be one or two more beyond the range of his sight, but—

Sir George's stumbling, exhaustion-sodden thoughts jerked to a stop, and his hand tightened like a claw on the stay. A cracked voice screamed something, barely audible over the roar of wind and sea yet touched with a fresh and different terror, and Sir George clamped his jaws against a bellow of matching fear as the *shape* burst abruptly and impossibly through the savage backdrop of cloud and rain.

He couldn't grasp it, at first. Couldn't wrap his mind

about it or find any point of reference by which to measure or evaluate it. It was too huge, too alien . . . too impossible. It could not exist, not in a world of mortals, yet it loomed above them, motionless, shrugging aside the fury of the gale as if it were but the gentlest of zephyrs. Gleaming like polished bronze, flickering with the reflected glare of lightning, a mile and more in length, a thing of subtle curves and gleaming flanks caparisoned in jewellike lights of red and white and amber.

He stared at it, too amazed and astonished to think, the terror of the storm—even his fear for his wife and son—banished by sheer, disbelieving shock as that vast *shape* hung against the seething cloud and rain.

And then it began to move. Not quickly, but with contemptuous ease, laughing at the gale's baffled wrath. It drifted over the more distant of the cogs he'd seen earlier, and more light appeared as portions of its skin shifted and changed.

No, they're not "changing," Sir George thought numbly. *They're opening. And those lights are coming from inside whatever it is. Those are* doors, *doors to chambers filled with light and—*

His thoughts stuttered and halted yet again as more shapes appeared. Far smaller this time, but with that same unnatural stillness as the storm howled about them. Some were cross shaped, with the grace of a gliding gull or albatross, while others were squat cones or even spheres, but all were of the same bronze hue as the huger shape which had spawned them.

They spread out, surrounding the half-foundered cog, and then—

"Sweet Jesu!"

Sir George turned his head, too shocked by the lies of his own eyes to wonder how Father Timothy had suddenly appeared there. The snowy-haired Dominican

was a big man, with the powerful shoulders of the
archer he'd been before he heard God's call decades
before, and Sir George released his death grip on the
stay to fasten fingers of iron on his confessor's arm.

"In the name of God, Timothy! *What* is *that thing?!*"

"I don't know," the priest replied honestly. "But—"

His voice chopped off abruptly, and he released his
own clutch on the cog's rail to cross himself urgently.
Nor did Sir George blame him.

"Holy Mary, Mother of God," the baron whispered,
releasing Father Timothy and crossing himself more
slowly, almost absently, as an unearthly glare of light
leapt out from the shapes which had encircled the
other ship. Leapt out, touched the heaving vessel,
embraced it . . .

. . . and lifted it bodily from the boiling sea.

Someone aboard Sir George's own vessel was gib-
bering, gobbling out fragments of prayer punctuated
by curses of horrified denial, but the baron himself
stood silent, unable to tear his eyes from the impossible sight. He saw streams of water gushing from the
ship, draining straight down from its half-flooded hold
as if in a dead calm, only to be whipped to flying spray
by the fury of the wind as they neared the sea below.
Yet the shapes enfolded it in their brilliance, raising
it effortlessly towards the far vaster shape which had
birthed them, and he winced as someone aboard that
rising vessel, no doubt maddened by terror, hurled
himself bodily over the rail. Another body followed, and
a third.

"Fools!" Father Timothy bellowed. "Dolts! *Imbeciles!*
God Himself has offered them life, and they—!"

The priest broke off, pounding the rail with a huge,
gnarly fist.

The first plunging body struck the water and vanished without a trace, but not the second or third.

Additional shafts of light speared out, touched each falling form, and arrested that fall. The light lifted them once more, along with the cog, bearing them towards those brilliantly lit portals, and Sir George swallowed again. A mile, he had estimated that shape's length, but he'd been wrong. It was longer than that. *Much* longer, for the cog's hull finally gave him something against which to measure it, and the cog was less than a child's toy beside the vast, gleaming immensity that rode like a mountain peak of bronze amidst the black-bellied clouds of the gale's fury.

"*Were* they fools?" He didn't realize he'd spoken—certainly not that he'd spoken loudly enough for Father Timothy to hear through the crash of the sea and the wind-shriek, but the priest turned to him once more and raised an eyebrow. Even here and now, the expression brought back memories of the days when Father Timothy had been Sir George's tutor as he was now Edward's, but this was no time to be thinking of that.

"*Were* they fools?" Sir George repeated, shouting against the storm's noise. "Are you so certain that that . . . that *thing*—" he pointed a hand he was vaguely surprised to note did not tremble at the shape "—was sent by God and not the Devil?"

"I don't *care* who sent it! What matters is that it offers the chance of life, and while life endures, there is always the hope of God's mercy!"

"Life?" Sir George repeated, and Father Timothy shook his head, as if reproaching his patron and old student's slowness.

"Whatever its ultimate purpose, it clearly means for now to rescue that ship, and possibly all of us who remain alive."

"But . . . *why?*"

"That I do not know," Father Timothy admitted. "I've known enough of God's love to hope it is of His mercy, and seen enough of man's evil to fear that it is not. Whatever its purpose, and whoever sent it, we will find out soon enough, My Lord."

Sir George's cog was the last to be lifted from the sea.

He had regained at least the outward semblance of his habitual self-control and hammered a shaky calm over the others aboard the vessel by the time the lesser shapes surrounded the ship. Now he stood at the rail, gazing at the greater shape with his wife and son beside him. It might strike some as less than heroic to cling to his wife, and he tried to look as if the arm wrapped so tightly about her sought only to comfort *her*, but the two of them knew better. As always, Matilda supported him, pressing her cheek proudly against his shoulder even as he felt her tremble with terror, and he turned his head to press a kiss into her sodden, wind-straggled hair. For fourteen years she had stood beside him, one way or another, always supporting him, and a vast, familiar tenderness swelled within him as he drew strength from her yet again.

He kissed her hair once more, then returned his eyes to the vastness hovering above them. His people knew that he knew no more about what they faced than they did, but the habit of obedience ran deep, especially among the men of his own household and their families, and the need to find some fragment of çalm in *pretending* their liege knew what he was doing ran still deeper. He felt their eyes, locked upon him as the light flooded down and the scream of the wind and the thunder of the sea were abruptly shut away. There was no sense of movement, and he kept his own gaze fastened on the huge shape awaiting them rather than let himself look over the rail and watch the sea dropping away in the sudden, unnatural silence. He dared not look, lest the sight unman him at the moment when his people most needed him.

Their uncanny flight was rapid, yet their passage sent no breeze across the deck. It was as if the air about the ship had been frozen, locked into a stillness and quiet which had no place in the natural world. Sheets of rain continued to lash at them, yet those sheets burst upon the edges of that tranquil stillness and vanished in explosions of spray.

For all its swiftness, the journey seemed to take forever, and Sir George heard the rapid mutter of Father Timothy's Latin as they soared above the tumbling waves. But then, abruptly, it was their turn to pass through the opened portal, and Sir George swallowed as he saw the other cogs sitting like abandoned toys in the vastness of the cavern inside the huge shape.

There were a total of nine ships, including his own. That was more than he'd dared hope might have survived, yet little more than half the number which had set out for France, and he clenched his jaw. Whether or not it had been Earl Cathwall's ship he had seen die, the earl's vessel was not among those in the cavern.

The cog settled on the cavern floor, and Sir George tightened his grip on the rail, expecting the ship to list over on its rounded side when the light released it. But the vessel did nothing of the sort. It sat there upright, still quietly gushing water from its sodden interior, and he made himself release the rail.

"Let's get a ladder over the side," he told the mate.

"I don't—" the man began, then stopped himself. "Of course, My Lord. I'll have to rig something, but—"

He broke off again, this time with an undignified squeak, and Sir George had to lock his jaws to withhold an equally humiliating bellow as some unseen

hand lifted him from his feet. His arm tightened about
Matilda, and he heard Edward's gasp of sudden terror, but neither shamed him by crying out, and his
heart swelled with pride in them both.

The invisible hand was as gentle as it was irresistible, and he drew a deep, shuddering breath of relief
as it set them on their feet once more. Everyone else
from the ship followed, floating through the air like
ungainly birds, all too often flapping arms or legs in
panic as they floated, until all stood beside the beached
cog, bewildered and afraid and trying not to show it
while they stared at Sir George in search of guidance.

"You will walk to the green lights on the inboard
bulkhead," a voice said, and, despite himself, Sir George
twitched in astonishment.

"Witchcraft!" someone gasped, and Sir George
fought the urge to cross himself in agreement, for the
voice had spoken in his very ear, as if its owner stood
close beside him, yet there was no one to be seen! And
there was something very strange about the voice itself.
A resonance and timbre such as he had never
heard . . . and one which, he realized from the expressions about him, had spoken in *every* ear, and not his
own alone.

"Witchcraft or angelic powers, we seem to have little
choice but to obey, for now at least," he made himself say as calmly as possible. He offered Matilda his
arm, glanced at their son, and then turned to survey
the others from the ship. "And since that seems to be
the case, let us remember that we are Christians and
Englishmen."

"Well said, My Lord!" Father Timothy rumbled, and
then bestowed a fierce smile—one much better suited
to the archer he once had been than the pacific man
of God he had since become—upon his companions.
"If it be witchcraft, then God and His Mother will

surely protect our souls against it. And if we face some force of the mortal world, why, what mortal force has there ever been that *Englishmen* could not overcome?"

Several voices muttered agreement—no doubt as much in search of self-reassurance as Sir George himself at that moment—and the baron led the way towards the green lights blinking ahead of them.

It was a lengthy walk, and almost despite himself, he felt his pulse slow and some of his own undeniable terror ease. In part, he knew, that stemmed from the distraction of his inveterate curiosity. He couldn't stop himself from looking about, marveling—and wondering—at all he saw.

The gleaming floor was some strange sort of alloy, he decided, although he doubted any smith had ever even dreamed of such a huge expanse of metal. It wasn't the bronze it resembled, he felt certain, yet it rang gently under his boot heels and had the smooth, polished sheen found only on metal. It was preposterous, of course. He was only too well aware of the expense of a chain hauberk or a cuirass. It was absurd to even suggest that something as vast as the shape within which they found themselves could truly be made of metal, and yet that was the only conclusion he could reach.

The lights were equally strange, burning with a bright steadiness which was profoundly unnatural. Whatever provided their illumination, it wasn't burning oil or tallow. Indeed, there was no sign of *any* flame, as if the builders of the shape had somehow captured the light of the sun itself to release when they required it.

He blinked, wondering why he was so certain that the shape had been "built." Surely witchcraft—or, perhaps, the hand of God—was a more reasonable explanation than that any mortal being could have constructed such a wonder. Yet for all his confusion and remaining fear, Sir George discovered that he had become somehow convinced that all of this was, indeed, the work of hands neither demonic nor divine.

It was a conviction which found itself abruptly challenged when they reached their destination.

The passengers from the other cogs were already gathered there. Like Sir George, all of the knights and most of the men-at-arms clearly had snatched up their personal weapons before they left their ships. Many of the archers carried their bow staves, as well, but none had strung them. Hardly surprising, given the state their bowstrings must be in. Yet even without the bows, there were weapons in plenty in evidence among the crowd of men which had coalesced between the "bulkhead" and the expedition's women and children. That should have been a source of some comfort to Sir George, he supposed.

It wasn't.

His hand tightened on the hilt of his own sword, and his nostrils flared as he came close enough to see what held all the rest of the English frozen.

So much for "mortal hands," he told himself with a queer sort of calm, and made himself release his hilt and straighten his shoulders.

The . . . beings lined up along the bulkhead were not human. Far from it, in fact. The shortest of them must have stood at least a foot taller than Sir George's own five feet and ten inches, and Sir George was one of the tallest men in the expedition. Yet that was the smallest, least significant difference between them and any man Sir George had ever seen.

All of them went on two legs and possessed but two arms each, but that was the end of their similarity to men. Or to one another, really. Indeed, the creatures were so utterly alien that their very strangeness had prevented him from immediately realizing that there were two different sorts of them.

The first was clad in armor-plate which certainly looked like steel rather than the combination plate and mail Sir George wore—and armed with huge, double-bitted axes. Despite their height, they were almost squat for their size, and the opened visors of their helmets showed huge, bulging eyes and a depressed slot. The slot was set far too high in their faces to be called a nose, although there was nothing else it *could* be, and fringed on either side with hairlike fronds which stirred and crawled uncannily with their breathing. The wide, froglike slit of a mouth below the nose-slot and eyes was almost reassuringly homey compared to the rest of the ugly, orange-skinned and warty face in which it was set.

The second sort wore seamless, one-piece garments, predominately deep red in color, but with blue sleeves and legs. Those garments covered them from throat to toe and shoulder to fingertip but could not hide the fact that they had too many joints in the arms and legs they covered. It was as if God—or the Devil—had grafted extra elbows and knees into the creatures' limbs, and their hands and feet were larger in proportion to their bodies than those of any human. But there was worse, for the garments stopped at their throats. They offered no covering or conceal-ment for the gray-green hide—the glistening, *scale-covered* gray-green hide—of the creatures' faces, or the vertical, slit-pupilled eyes, or the lizardlike crests which crowned their snouted, reptilian heads. Yet for all their grotesqueness, they lacked the somehow malevolent air of menace which clung to their wart-faced companions.

"Demons!" someone behind Sir George gasped, and the baron swallowed hard. His hand clamped tighter on his hilt, and it took all his self-control to keep the blade sheathed, but—

"Dragons!" someone else exclaimed, and Sir George drew a deep breath and nodded hard.

"Aye, dragons they are, like enough!" he said loudly enough to be sure all of those about him heard it . . . and choosing not to look too closely at the wart-faces. The label was probably wrong even for the scale-hides, of course. At the very least, dragons were born of Earth, and he felt a deep, sudden and instinctive assurance that wherever or whatever these creatures sprang from, it was *not* Earth. Yet, however inaccurate, the label was also correct.

And the men may be less prone to panic over "dragons" than "demons," he thought with something like detachment.

He drew another breath, sensing the fragile balance between terror, discipline, caution, and ignorance which held the armed men about him precariously still. In many ways, he was astounded such a balance could have held even for a moment, for these were trained fighting men. Trained, *English* fighting men, soldiers every one of them.

But this threat was so far outside their experience that even Englishmen might be excused for uncertainty and hesitation, he told himself . . . and thank God for it! Whatever else those wart-faces and dragon-men might be, they were obviously part and parcel of whatever power had created the shape in which they all stood. Assuming they truly were mortal, Sir George never doubted that his men could swarm them under, despite the wart-faces' armor, but he had no illusions about the efficacy of edged steel against the other defenses such a power could erect to guard itself.

For that matter, we have no reason—as yet—to think our rescuers might be hostile in any way. After all, they

*were under no obligation to pluck us from the sea. If
they wished us ill, they had only to leave us there. We
would all have been dead soon enough.*

He felt the silence stretch out as those from his own
cog joined the rear ranks of the crowd. He gave
Matilda a final hug, then stepped forward.

Men who had stared fixedly at the grotesque creatures started and looked over their shoulders as they
sensed his approach, and he heard more than a few
muttered prayers (and curses) of relief as he was
recognized. He was as stained and ragged as any of
them, but his dark spade beard and the scar down his
right cheek were well known, almost famous, even
among those who had followed Earl Cathwall or Sir
Michael rather than Sir George. More to the point,
perhaps, Earl Cathwall was dead, and Sir Michael was
awaiting them in Normandy . . . where even the slow-
est must realize they were unlikely to arrive. Which
meant every one of those men looked to Sir George
Wincaster for leadership and guidance.

Now they drew apart, opening a path for him. One
or two, bolder than the others, actually reached out
to touch him as he passed, whether to lend him
reassurance or to draw confidence of their own from
him he didn't know.

Sir Richard Maynton stood at the very front of the
crowd, and his head turned sharply as Sir George
stepped up beside him. With the losses their command
structure had taken, Sir Richard had almost certainly
become Sir George's second in command, which was
unfortunate, in a way, for Sir George knew him less
well than he might have liked. On the other hand, he
couldn't misread the relief in Sir Richard's eyes.

"Thank God!" the other knight said quickly. "I feared
you, too, had perished, My Lord!"

"Aye?" Sir George managed a chuckle. "I can

understand that well enough. *I* thought I had perished a time or two, myself!" Several others chuckled at his feeble joke, and he clapped the other knight on the shoulder.

"Indeed," Sir Richard agreed. "In fact, My Lord, I—"

The knight closed his mouth with an almost audible click, and a chorus of muffled exclamations rippled through the crowd facing the dragon-men and wart-faces as a brighter light flashed. An opening appeared in the bulkhead, snapping into existence so abruptly that the eye almost missed the way the panel which formed it *flicked* aside, and another being stood within the sudden doorway or hatch.

If the wart-faces and dragon-men were alien, this being was even more bizarre, although, in many ways, it seemed more comical than menacing. Its garment was the same deep red as the dragon-men's, but its garb was *solely* red, without the blue sleeves and legs, and a gleaming pendant hung about its neck to dangle on its chest. It was also short, its head rising little higher than Sir George's chest, and the exposed portion of its face and throat was covered in plushy purple fur. Like the others, it went on two legs and had two arms, but though its hands had only three fingers, each had been given an extra thumb where a man would have had his little finger. All of that was odd enough, but the creature's face was more grotesque than a mummer's mask. It was broad and flat, with two wide, lipless mouths—one above the other—and no trace of a nose. Worse, it had three golden eyes: a single, large one centered in the upper part of its face, and two smaller ones set lower, flanking it to either side. And, as if to crown the absurdity of its appearance, its broad, squat head was topped by two enormous, foxlike ears covered in the same purple fur.

Sir George stared at it, shocked as even the wart-faces and dragon-men had not left him. They, at least, radiated a sense of watchfulness, even threat, he felt he understood, but *this* creature—! It might as easily have been a demon or a court jester, and he wondered whether he ought to smile or cross himself.

"Who leads this group?"

The voice was light, even delicate, with the piping clarity of a young child's. It spoke perfect English, and it appeared to emerge from the upper of the demon-jester's two mouths, although the lipless opening didn't move precisely in time with the words. Hearing it, Sir George was tempted to smile, despite all that had happened, for it seemed far more suited to the jester than to a demon. But the temptation was faint and brief. There was no expression in that voice at all, nor, so far as he could tell, did any hint of an expression cross that alien face. Yet that was the point—it was an *alien* face, and that was driven brutally home to Sir George as he realized that, for the first time in his life, he could not discern the smallest hint of the thoughts or wishes or emotions of the being speaking to him.

"I do," he replied after a long still moment.

"And you are?" the piping voice inquired.

"I am Sir George Wincaster, Baron of Wickworth, in the service of His Majesty Edward III, King of England, Scotland, Wales, and France." There was a hint of iron pride in that reply, and Sir George felt other spines straighten about him, but—

"You are in error, Sir George Wincaster," the piping voice told him, still with no hint of expression. "You are no longer in the service of any human. You are now in the service of my Guild."

Sir George stared at the small being, and a rumbling rustle went through the men at his back. He opened his mouth to respond, but the demon-jester went on without so much as a pause.

"But for the intervention of my vessel and crew, you all would have perished," it said. "We rescued you. As a result, you are now our property, to do with as we choose." An inarticulate half-snarl, fueled as much by fear as by anger, rose behind Sir George, but the demon-jester continued unperturbed. "No doubt it will take you some time to fully accept this change in status," its expressionless voice continued. "You would be wise, however, to accustom yourself to it as quickly as your primitive understanding permits."

"*Accustom* ourselves—!" someone began furiously, but Sir George's raised hand cut the rising tide of outrage short.

"We are Englishmen . . . sir," he said quietly, "and Englishmen are *no one's* 'property.' "

"It is unwise to disagree with me, Sir George Wincaster," the demon-jester said, still with that calm, total lack of expression. "As a group, you and your fellows are—or may become, at any rate—a valuable asset of my Guild. None of you, however, is irreplaceable as an individual."

Sir George's jaw clenched. He was unaccustomed to being threatened to his face, and certainly to being threatened by a half-sized creature he could have snapped in two one-handed. Yet he made himself swallow it. The wart-faces and dragon-men behind the demon-jester were ominous evidence of the power which backed him. Even worse, Sir George was achingly aware of the presence of his wife and son.

"Unwise or not," he said after a long, still moment, "it is I who command these men. As such, it is my duty to speak for them. We are all grateful for our rescue, but—"

"I do not want your gratitude. My Guild and I desire

only your obedience," the demon-jester interrupted. "We require certain services of you—services you should find neither difficult nor distasteful, since they are the only ones you are truly trained or equipped to provide."

Sir George's hand clenched once more on the hilt of his sword, but the demon-jester ignored the movement, as if the very notion that something as childish as a sword might threaten *it* was ludicrous.

"We require only that you fight for us," it went on. "If you do, you will be well treated and rewarded. Your lives will be extended beyond any span you can presently imagine, your health will be provided for, your—" The three eyes looked past Sir George, and the creature seemed to pause for a moment, as if searching for a word. Then it continued without inflection. "Your mates and young will be cared for, and you will be granted access to them."

"And if we choose *not* to fight for you?" Sir George asked flatly.

"Then you will be compelled to change your minds," the demon-jester replied. "Analysis indicates that such compulsion should not prove difficult. You are, of course, primitives from a primitive and barbaric culture, so simple and direct methods would undoubtedly serve best. We might, perhaps, begin by selecting five or six of your mates and young at random and executing them."

A ball of ice closed upon Sir George's stomach. The threat was scarcely unexpected, yet he had not counted on how the emotionlessness—the total lack of interest or anger—in the demon-jester's piping voice would hone the jagged edges of his fear. He forced himself not to look over his shoulder at Matilda and Edward.

"If such measures should prove insufficient, there are, of course, others," the demon-jester continued.

"Should all else fail, we could attempt complete personality erasure and simply reprogram you, but that would probably prove excessively time consuming. Nor would there be any real point in it. It would be much more cost effective simply to dispose of all of you and collect a fresh force of fighters. One group of barbarians is very like another, after all."

"But *these* barbarians are under arms, sirrah!" another voice barked.

Sir George's head snapped around, and he felt a stab of dreadful certainty at what he would see. Sir John Denmore was barely twenty years old, young and hot-blooded, with more than his fair share of arrogance, and he punctuated his fierce statement with the steely slither of a drawn blade. His sword gleamed under the unnaturally brilliant lights, and he leapt forward with a vicious stroke.

"God and Saint G—!"

He never completed the war cry. His sword swept towards the demon-jester, but the creature never even moved. It simply stood there, watching with its alien lack of expression, and the young knight's shout died in shock when his sword struck some invisible barrier, like a wall of air. It flew out of his hands, and he gaped in disbelief as it spun end over end away from him. Then he shook himself, snarled, and snatched at his dagger.

"Hold!" Sir George shouted. "Put up your—"

But he was too late. This time the demon-jester made a small gesture, and Sir John gurgled and stopped dead. His eyes bulged wildly, his expression one of raw terror as rage turned into panic, but he could not even open his mouth. He was held as though in a giant, unseen spider's web, dagger half-drawn, utterly helpless, and the demon-jester gazed at Sir George.

"It is well for you that you attempted to stop him

rather than joining in his stupidity," it informed the baron, "but I see you truly are primitives and so require proof of your status. Very well. I will give it to you."

"There is no need—" Sir George began.

"There is whatever need I say there is," the demon-jester piped, and held out a two-thumbed hand to the nearest dragon-man. The dragon-man's eyes touched Sir George for just a moment, but then it reached to its belt and drew a strange device from a scabbard. It extended the thing to the demon-jester, and the shorter creature adjusted a small knob on the device's side.

"You only think you are armed, Sir George Wincaster. Your swords and arrows do not threaten me or any member of my crew. Our own weapons, on the other hand—"

It raised the device in Sir John's direction almost negligently, and then Sir George cried out in horror. He couldn't help himself, and neither then nor later did he feel the shame he perhaps ought to have. Not when the terrible ray of light, like lightning chained to the demon-jester's will, crackled from the device and smote full upon Sir John Denmore's breast.

Its touch was death . . . but not simply death. The young man's chest cavity blew apart as if from the inside, and heart and lungs exploded with it. A grisly storm front of blood and shredded tissue flew over those about him, a stink of burning meat filled the air, and men who had seen the most horrible sights war could offer recoiled with cries of horror. But worst of all, Sir George realized later, was the dead man's silence. The fact that even as the hell weapon was raised, even as his expression twisted—first with terror, and then in agony—the young knight never made a sound. Was unable even to writhe or open his mouth. He could only stand there, frozen, more helpless than any lamb before the butcher, while the demon-jester calmly blew his body open.

Even after death, Sir John was not allowed to fall. His corpse stood upright, face contorted with the rictus of death, blood flooding down from his ruptured chest to puddle about his feet.

Had it not been for the proof that no one could touch the creature, Sir George would have attacked the thing himself, with his bare hands, if necessary. But he had that proof . . . and he had his responsibilities, and his duty, and his wife and son stood behind him. And so he did something much harder than launch a hopeless attack.

He made himself stand there, with the blood of a man under his command dripping down his face, and did nothing.

His motionless example stilled the handful of others who would have attacked, and the demon-jester regarded them all for a long, deadly silent time. Then it reached out and, without taking its triple-eyed gaze from Sir George, handed the lightning weapon back to the dragon-man.

"I trust this lesson is not lost upon your warriors, Sir George Wincaster," it piped then. "Or upon you, either. You may speak for these men, and you may lead them in combat, but you are no longer their commander. I am. Unless, of course, someone wishes to challenge that point."

It made a gesture, and the mutilated corpse which once had been an arrogant young knight thudded to the metal floor like so much dead meat.

At least this ship's decks didn't pitch and dance like the decks of those never to be sufficiently damned cogs.

The thought wended through a well-worn groove in Sir George's mind as he leaned forward to stroke Satan's shoulder. The destrier shook his head, rattling the mail crinnet protecting his arched neck, then stamped his rear off hoof. The shoe rang like thunder on the deck's bronze-tinted alloy, and Sir George smiled thinly. He and the stallion had been through this all too many times since that horrific storm. By now both of them should be accustomed to it, and he supposed they were. But neither of them was *resigned* to it.

The warning gong sounded, and Sir George rose in the stirrups and turned to regard the men behind him. A score of orange-skinned wart-faces stood beyond them, lining the bulkhead separating this cargo hold from the rest of the ship, once again armed and armored, but their function was not to support the Englishmen. It was to drive them forward if they hesitated, and to strike down any who attempted to flee.

Not that any of Sir George's men were likely to flee . . . or to require driving.

Many of the men behind him had once been sailors, but that had been before they found themselves with precisely the same choices—or *lack* of them—as Sir George's soldiers. By now there was no real way to distinguish them from any of the professional troops who had been their passengers. After all, *they* were professionals now—professionals who had seen more battles than any soldier who'd ever served an Earthly master.

Their experience showed in their expressions—not relaxed, but calm and almost thoughtful as they recalled their prebattle briefings and waited to put them into effect. The mounted men-at-arms and handful of knights sat their mounts closest to him, forming a protective barrier between the still-closed wall of metal and the more vulnerable archers. Some of those archers were more heavily armored than they had been, but even the most heavily protected wore only helmets, short chain hauberks, and, here and there, a steel breastplate. Protection was welcome, but they knew as well as Sir George that their true protection lay in mobility, the devastating fire of the longbow, and the wardship of his more heavily armored knights and men-at-arms.

And they trusted those knights and men-at-arms as totally as they had come to trust their commander. So they stood now, their faces showing grim confidence, not uncertainty, and returned Sir George's regard with level eyes.

"All right, lads." He didn't raise his voice to a bellow as he would have back home. There was no need, for their masters' magic carried his voice clearly, as if he were speaking into each man's private ear. "You know the plan . . . and Saint Michael knows we've done it often enough!" His ironic tone won a mutter of laughter, and he gave them a tight grin in reply. "Mind yourselves, keep to the plan, and we'll be done in time for dinner!"

A rumble of agreement came back, and then there was the very tiniest of lurches, the metal wall before Sir George hissed like a viper and vanished upward, and he looked out upon yet another of the endless alien worlds he and his men were doomed to conquer.

The sky was *almost* the right shade, but there was something odd about it—a darker, deeper hue than the blue he remembered (and Sweet Mary, but *did* he remember? or did he simply *think* he did?) from home—and the sun was too large by half. The "trees" rising in scraggly, scattered clumps were spidery interweavings of too-fine branches covered with long, hairy streamers for leaves, and leaves and grass alike were a strange, orangish color like nothing anyone had ever seen in any world meant for men.

Not that there *were* any men in this world. Not

born of it, at any rate. An army of not-men, too tall, too thin, and with too many limbs, had drawn up in a ragged line well beyond bowshot of the ship. They carried large wicker shields and spears, and most wore leather helmets. Aside from that, they were unarmored, and only a very few bore any weapon other than their spears or quivers of javelins. He saw maces and a handful of swords, but no decent pikes or other true polearms, and none of the not-men were mounted. Square placards on poles rose above them at ragged intervals—banners, he realized—and he wondered how long they'd been gathered. Clearly they were there to fight, but had they come for an open battle, or simply to besiege the ship? He remembered the first time *he* had seen the ship, hovering motionless in a storm-sick sky, and barked a bitter, humorless laugh. Surely the thing was huge enough to be mistaken for a castle, albeit the most oddly formed one any man—or not-man—could ever imagine!

Whatever had brought them hither, a stir went through them as the side of the ship opened abruptly. Spears were shaken, a handful of javelins were hurled, although the range was too great for that to be anything more than a gesture, and he had no need of magically enhanced hearing to recognize the sound of defiance. It was a thready, piping sound beside the surf roar a human army might have raised, but it carried the ugly undertone of hate.

Strange, he thought. *How can I be so certain it's hate I hear? These aren't men, after all. For all I know, they might be shouting cries of joyous welcome!* He grimaced at his own fanciful thought. *Of course it's hate. How could it be else when our* masters *have brought us here to break them into well-behaved cattle?*

But this was no time to be thinking such thoughts. And even if it had been, a nagging inner honesty pointed out, subduing these not-men wasn't so terribly different from what he'd planned to do to Frenchmen—who, whatever their other faults, at least went about on a mere two legs, not three, and were fellow Christians and (provisionally) human.

He scanned them one more time, confirming his masters' briefing, and snorted much as Satan had. He and his men were outnumbered by at least ten-to-one, and the wart-faces would do nothing to change those odds. *Their* job was to insure that none of this world's not-men eluded Sir George's men and entered the ship through the open hold. Which wasn't going to happen.

Sir George drew a deep breath, feeling the not-men's hatred and sensing the confidence they felt in their superior numbers.

Pity the poor bastards, he thought, then slammed the visor of his bascinet, drew his sword, and pressed with his knees to send Satan trotting forward.

It hadn't really been a battle, Sir George reflected afterward, tossing his helmet to Edward and shoving back his chain mail coif as he dismounted beside one of the mobile fountains. The metal creature was half the size of an ox but wide for its length, and the merry chuckle of the water splashing in the wide catcher basin made a grotesque background for the wailing whines and whimpers coming from the enemy's wounded. There were few moans from his own wounded. Partly because there'd been so few of them, compared to the not-men's casualties, but mostly because the hovering metal turtles—the "air cars," as their masters called them—had already picked up most of his injured. And all of the handful of dead, as well, he thought with a familiar chill. How many of them would *stay* "dead" this time, he wondered? Father Timothy had pondered the matter at length, and prayed at even greater length, before he pronounced that the men who had been seemingly returned from death were not, in fact, the demons or devils some of their fellows had feared. Sir George trusted the priest's judgment in matters religious implicitly, and he'd supported Father Timothy's pronouncement to the hilt, yet even he found it a bit . . . unsettling to see a man who had taken a lance through the chest sit down to supper with him.

He put the thought aside—again. It was easier than it once had been, despite his lingering discomfort. Partly because he'd learned to accept that much of their masters' magic was, in fact, no more than the huge advancement in matters mechanic that the Commander claimed, but even more because he was too grateful to have those men back to question the agency of their resurrection, or healing, or *whatever* it was. Any decent field commander did anything he could to hold down his casualties, if only to preserve the efficiency of his fighting force, but Sir George had even more reason to do so than most. His men—less than a thousand, all told, including the smiths and farriers and fletchers, as well as his soldiers and knights—were all he had. In a sense, they were all the men who would ever exist in the universe—or in Sir George's universe, at least—and that made every one of them even more precious than they would have been had he and they ever reached Normandy.

He snorted, shook himself, and thrust his head into the fountain. The icy water was a welcome shock, washing away the sweat, and he drank deeply before he finally raised his head at last to draw a gasping breath of relief. His right arm ached wearily, but it had been more butcher's work than sword work at the end. The not-men had never imagined anything like an English bowman. That much had been obvious. Even the Scots at Halidon Hill had shown more caution than the not-men, and not even French knights would have pressed on so stubbornly—and stupidly—into such a blizzard of arrows.

But the not-men had.

Sir George sighed and turned from the fountain, surrendering his place to Rolf Grayhame, his senior captain of archers, as he surveyed the field.

There had been even more of the not-men than he'd first thought, not that it had mattered in the end. Each of his six hundred archers could put twelve shafts in the air in a minute and, at need, hit picked, man-sized targets at two hundred paces. Their broadheaded arrows inflicted hideous wounds at any range, and their needle-pointed pile arrows could penetrate chain or even plate at pointblank ranges. Against foes who were totally unarmored, that sort of fire produced a massacre, not a battle. The only true hand-blows of the entire affair had come when Sir George and his mounted men charged the broken rabble which had once been an army to complete its rout, and he grimaced at the thought of what that charge had cost.

Only two of his mounted men had been seriously wounded, and neither of them too badly for the magical healing arts of their masters to save them, but they'd lost five more priceless horses. All too few of their original mounts had survived the brutal storm from which their masters had plucked them. Satan had been one of them, praise God, but there had been far too few others to meet Sir George's needs. At least the Commander had seemed to grasp their importance, however, for his ship's metal minions had raided a half dozen manors somewhere in France for almost two hundred more of them, and he had instructed the healer—the "Medic"—aboard the ship to breed them. But few of the horses so acquired had been destriers; most were suitable only for light or perhaps medium horse, and unlike humans, horses took poorly to the long periods of sleep their masters imposed. Nor did they reproduce well under such conditions, and whatever arts brought dead archers or men-at-arms back to life seemed unable to do the same for them. There were fewer of them for every battle, and the time would come when there were none.

The thought did not please Sir George, and not simply because Satan had been with him for so long and borne him so well. Sir George was no fool. His grandfather had been the next best thing to a common man-at-arms before he won Warwick under Edward I, and neither his son nor his grandson had been allowed to forget his hard-bitten pragmatism. A professional soldier to his toenails, Sir George knew that a mounted charge against properly supported archers was madness. *Well, against* English *archers, at any rate,* he amended. True, the shock of a horsed charge remained all but irresistible if one could carry it home, but accomplishing that critical final stage was becoming more and more difficult. Although he'd never faced them, Sir George had heard of the pikemen produced in distant Switzerland, and he rather wished he had a few of them along. A pike wall, now, formed up between his archers and the enemy . . . *that* would put paid to any cavalry charge! There was no way to know what was happening back home, of course, but surely by now even the French and Italians must be discovering the cold, bitter truth that unsupported cavalry was no longer the queen of battle.

Yet for all that, he was a knight himself, and perhaps the proudest emblems of any knight were his spurs. The day when the horse finally did vanish forever from the field of battle would be a terrible one, and Sir George was thankful he would never live long enough to see it.

*Or perhaps I will live long enough . . . now. Assuming
I might ever see Earth again. Which I won't.*

He snorted again and rose to his full height, stretch-
ing mightily. For all his inches, his son Edward bade
fair to overtop him with a handspan and more to spare
when he reached his full growth. The young man stood
beside him, still holding his helmet, and Sir George
eyed him with unobtrusive speculation. That Edward
was with him—yes, and Edward's mother, praise
God!—was one of the few things which made this
endless purgatory endurable, yet he wondered at times
how old his son truly was. He'd been thirteen when
they sailed to join King Edward in France, but how
long ago had that been?

Sir George had no answer for that question. The
Commander had spoken nothing but the truth when
he promised to extend their life spans. His claim that
it was to reward their loyal service, on the other hand,
failed to fool even the most credulous of Sir George's
men. It was merely simpler to extend the lives of the
men they had rather than spend the time to return to
Earth to catch still more of them. Not that voyages to
Earth were the only way their masters could secure
more manpower, the baron thought sourly.

He'd concluded long ago that only coincidence had
caused the Commander to sweep up their womenfolk
and children with them. Whatever else the Commander
was, he had no true understanding of the humans
under his command. No, perhaps that was unfair. He'd
gained at least *some* understanding of them; it was
simply that he had never—and *would* never—see them
as anything more than animate property. He didn't even
feel contempt for them—not truly—for they weren't
sufficiently important to waste contempt upon. They
were exactly what he'd called them: barbarians and
primitives. Valuable to his Guild, as he'd said, but lesser

life forms, to be used however their natural superiors found most advantageous.

Sir George refused to make the mistake of regarding the Commander with responsive contempt, yet neither was he blind to the peculiar blindnesses and weaknesses which accompanied the Commander's disdain. For example, the Commander had come to Earth solely to secure a fighting force (though it had taken Sir George a long, long time to begin to understand why beings who could build such marvels as the ship should need archers and swordsmen). The baron had no doubt that the Commander would have preferred to secure *only* a fighting force, unencumbered by "useless" women or children. But like any expeditionary force of its time, the Englishmen he'd actually stolen had been accompanied by dozens of women. A few, like his own Matilda, were the wives of knights or other officers. Others were the wives of common soldiers or archers, and still more had been the wives of convenience and outright prostitutes found among any army's camp followers.

Sir George was certain that the Commander had seriously considered simply disposing of those "useless" mouths, and he thanked God that the alien had at least recognized the way in which wives and children could be used to insure the obedience of husbands and fathers. What the Commander had been slower to recognize was that the presence of women and the natural inclinations of men offered the opportunity to make his small fighting force self-sustaining. Although Sir George's age had been frozen at the thirty-five he had been before he'd been snatched into servitude, many of the youngsters who'd been taken with him had grown into young manhood and taken their place in the ranks, and still more children had been born . . . no doubt to follow them, when the time came.

By Sir George's reckoning, he and his men had spent something close to fifty years awake and aware, but the time had been less for their families. All of them were returned to their magical slumber between battles, of course. Voyages between worlds, Sir George had gathered from conversations with the Commander, took years, and it was simpler to wrap them in sleep while the huge ship sailed among the stars. But their families were not always awakened when the soldiers were. Much depended upon how long they would remain on any given world before their masters were satisfied with their control of it, but the Commander had also learned to dole out reunions as rewards . . . or to withhold them as punishment.

The result was that far less time had passed for Matilda and the other women than for Sir George and his troops, and for many years, Edward had been kept to his mother's calendar. He was old enough—or physically mature enough—now to take his place on the field as his father's squire, and now he woke and slept with the rest of the men. Sir George was glad to have the boy with him, yet he knew Matilda was in two minds. She didn't miss her son when she slept, but not even their alien masters could heal all wounds. They had lost men, slowly but in a steady trickle, ever since they had been stolen away from hearth and home forever, and she did not want Edward to become one of those they lost.

Nor did Sir George. But they had no choice—less even here than they might have had at home. They fought, or they perished. That was their reality, and it was unwise to think of other realities, or how things might have been, or to long to return, however briefly, to the world of their birth.

He knew all that, yet he sometimes wondered how long had truly passed since he and his men had set sail. What year was it, assuming that the years of Earth had any meaning so far from her?

He had no idea. But he suspected they were far, far away from the twelfth day of July in the Year of Our Lord Thirteen Hundred and Forty-Six.

The silent dragon-man stopped and stood aside as they approached the glowing wall, and Sir George glanced sideways at the creature. He'd seen enough of them to know that they, like the wart-faces, were flesh and blood, for all their oddness in human eyes, and not simply more of his masters' mechanical devices, but even now, he had never heard one of the dragon-men make a single sound. The wart-faces, yes. He hadn't learned a word of their language of grunts and hoarse hoots—in large part because his masters clearly didn't *want* the English to be able to converse with them—but he and his men had been given ample proof that the wart-faces at least *had* a language.

Not the dragon-men. The wart-faces were properly called "Hathori," or that, at least, was what the Commander called them, and they had far more contact with the English than the dragon-men did, for they were the Commander's whip hand. They were the prison guards, charged with driving and goading the English outside the ship, and there had been some ugly incidents in the early days. At least one of them had been killed by the Englishmen they guarded . . . and half a dozen of Sir George's men had been slain by the Commander's order as retribution. There was no love lost between the English and the Hathori—which, Sir George suspected, was precisely what the Commander wished—and the wart-faces were almost as stupid as the Commander seemed to think the English were. Indeed, the Hathori were exactly what they seemed: brutal, incurious enforcers, smart enough to obey orders and individually powerful, but with no interest in anything *beyond* their orders. Which, Sir George had concluded, was the reason the Commander had needed his own Englishmen. As individuals, the wart-faces were formidable killing machines, but they lacked the cohesion, the discipline and ability, to fight as *soldiers*.

But the eternally silent dragon-men, he suspected, were a very different matter indeed. He had no idea what they called themselves—if, in fact, they called themselves anything at all—and the Commander never even mentioned them directly. They were simply always there, looming in the background, and unlike the axe-wielding Hathori, armed with their deadly lightning weapons and guarding the Commander and the crew of the huge vessel.

Now the dragon-man returned Sir George's glance impassively, motionless as a lizard on a stone and with the same sense of poised, absolute readiness. The glowing wall sealed the English into their own portion of their ship prison, and none of them had yet been able to discover how the portal through it was opened or closed. They had discovered a great deal about other controls in their quarters, ways to turn devices on and off, and Sir George and Father Timothy were certain that the glowing wall must be controlled in some similar—or at least comparable—fashion, yet they'd never been able to detect how it was done.

Which was as well for their masters, Sir George thought grimly, and nodded to the dragon-man as he stepped past him into the corridor beyond the wall. As always, the towering creature did not react in any way to the human gesture, but somehow Sir George felt certain the dragon-men recognized it as an acknowledgment and a courtesy of sorts. Whatever else they were, they were obviously capable of thought, or the Commander's Guild *would* have replaced them with more of its clever mechanical devices. Equally obviously, it regarded both the Hathori and the dragon-men much as it did the English: as more or less domesticated, moderately dangerous, useful beasts of burden, although the Commander clearly placed greater faith in the loyalty of the dragon-men.

Sir George had often wondered how the dragon-men regarded the English. Did they, like the Commander's kind, regard them as primitives and barbarians, beneath their own notice? Certainly they possessed and used more of the wondrous tools of their masters, but that didn't seem to make them their masters' equals. So did they see the English as companions in servitude? Or did they cling to the need to look down upon the humans as a way to make themselves appear less wretched by comparison?

It seemed unlikely to make a great deal of difference either way, as neither Sir George, nor Father Timothy, nor any other human had ever discovered a way to communicate with the dragon-men. Their masters gave them precious little opportunity to experiment, but it was impossible to completely eliminate all physical contact between humans and dragon-men. Not if the dragon-men were to be useful as guards *against* the humans, at any rate. Most of the other humans had completely abandoned the task, but Father Timothy continued to try, and Sir George shared his confessor's hopes, although he lacked the priest's patience and dogged faith.

Not even Father Timothy, on the other hand, still sought to communicate with the Hathori.

Sir George snorted at his own cross-grained nature as he followed the guiding light down the empty passageway. He shared Sir Timothy's hopes yet lacked the other's faith, a contradiction if ever he'd heard of one.

Yet he couldn't quite turn off that tiny sprig of hope, and he often found himself dreaming of the dragon-men. Indeed, he'd dreamed of them more often during the last few periods of wakefulness than in quite some time.

His thoughts broke off as the guide light reached another hatch and stopped. It bobbed there imperatively, as if impatient with his slow progress, and he grinned wryly. Such guides were necessary, for the architecture of the ship could be bewildering, especially to one who spent virtually all of his time aboard it locked into the portion assigned to the English. He couldn't be positive, but he was privately certain that the layout of the rest of the ship changed between his infrequent visits here, as if it were not fixed and his masters rearranged it with casual ease whenever they tired of the current arrangement. He had been told by the Commander that the guide lights were only another of the endless mechanisms available to his masters, and he supposed he believed the alien. Yet he often wondered, especially at times like this, when the lights twitched so impatiently, scolding him for dawdling and eager to be off about some fresh business of their own.

He stepped through the indicated hatch, and the light whisked off with a final bob and dodge. He watched it go, then stepped back as the hatch closed.

The chamber was no different from the one to which the lights had guided him the last time the Commander summoned him, although they'd followed nothing remotely like the same path to reach it. It was octagonal, with hatches in each wall, and perhaps fifteen feet across. A glowing table at its center supported one of the marvels his masters called a "light sculpture." Sir George had no idea how the things were made, but they always fascinated him. All were beautiful, though the beauty was often strange to human eyes—so strange, sometimes, as to make one uneasy, even frightened—and almost always subtle. This one was a thing of flowing angles and forms, of brilliant color threaded through a cool background of blues and greens, and he gazed upon it in delight as its soothing presence flowed over him.

There are times, he thought dreamily, *when I could almost forgive them for what they've done to us. Our lives are longer, our people healthier, than they ever would have been at home, and they can create such beauty and wonders as this. And yet all the marvels we've received are nothing but scraps from the table, dropped casually to us or—worse!—given only because it benefits them for us to have them. To them, we are less important, although not, perhaps, less valuable, than the things they build of metal and crystal, and—*

"You did well. But then you English always do, don't you?"

Sir George turned from the light sculpture. He hadn't heard the hatch open, but one rarely did aboard this ship. The main hatches, big enough for a score of mounted men abreast, yes. Not even their masters seemed able to make something that large move without even a whisper of sound, but the smaller hatches within the ship proper were another matter.

Not that most of his men would know that from personal experience. Only he, Sir Richard Maynton, and—on very rare occasions—Matilda had ever been permitted inside the portion of the vast ship reserved for their masters and their masters' nonhuman henchmen. Even then, they must come totally unarmed and submit to the humiliation of a search before they passed the glowing wall between their section of the ship and the rest of its interior.

Now he cocked his head, gazing at the Commander,

and tried to gauge the other's mood. Despite the years
of his servitude, he still found the task all but hopeless. That was immensely frustrating, and it was also
dangerous. But the Commander's piping voice remained
a dead, expressionless thing, and the three-eyed face
remained so utterly alien as to make reading *its*
expression utterly impossible. Certainly Sir George had
never seen anything he could classify as a smile or a
frown. And the fact that the Commander didn't truly
speak English (or Latin, or French) complicated things
still further. Father Timothy and Dickon Yardley, Sir
George's senior surgeon, had concluded that the upper
of the Commander's two mouths was exclusively a
breathing and speaking orifice, but as Sir George had
noticed the very first day, that mouth didn't move in
time with the words the Commander "spoke." Instead,
the Commander spoke in his own tongue—whatever
that was—and one of the many mechanisms of the ship
translated that into a language Sir George could
understand and made it *appear* to be coming from the
Commander.

Sir George had often wondered whether that arti-
ficiality was the true reason the voice sounded so
expressionless. He couldn't be certain, but he *had*
concluded that the Commander's failure—or refusal—
to learn the language of his captive troops was another
indication of his sense of utter superiority to them. It
was, however, a foolish decision, unless whatever translated his words into English did a far better job of
communicating nuance and emotion when it translated
English into his own language.

But however ridiculous the demon-jester might still
look, and despite the foolishness of any decisions the
Commander might make, Sir George would never
underestimate him. He dared not, for his own life, but
even more for the lives of the men and women for

whom he was responsible, and that was the true reason he found his inability to read the Commander's mood so maddening. He must watch his words with this creature far more closely than he'd ever watched them with any other commander, yet he was never quite free of the fear that he would choose the wrong one simply because he'd misunderstood or misinterpreted the Commander.

Still, he knew he'd made some progress, and at least the Commander appeared to choose his words with care, as if seeking to make his meaning completely clear through what he said since he couldn't communicate fine shades of meaning by *how* he said it.

And, of course, there's also the fact that we're valuable to him and to his "trading guild." Very valuable, if he's to be believed. And I rather think he is, given the lengths they went to to steal us all away.

Sir George would never be so stupid as to assume that that value would preserve any human foolish enough to anger or appear to threaten their masters. Sir John Denmore's fate on that very first day would have been enough to prevent that, but there had been a handful of other deaths over the years. Two men who'd attempted to desert on a beautiful world of blue skies and deep green seas, another who'd simply refused one day to leave the ship, the six executed for the wart-face's death, another who'd gone berserk and attacked the dragon-men and the Commander himself with naked steel . . . All had been slaughtered as easily as Sir John, and with as little apparent emotion. Yet the Commander's actions and normal attitude (as well as Sir George could read the latter) were those of a being well pleased with his investment . . . and aware that his own masters were equally pleased. He would shed no tears (or whatever his kind did to express sorrow) over the death of any single human, but he

valued them as a group and so took pains to avoid
misunderstandings which might require him to destroy
any of them.

Or any *more* of them, at any rate.

Sir George realized the Commander was still gazing at him, waiting for a response, and gave himself
a small shake.

"Your pardon, Commander," he said. "The aftermath
of battle lingers with me, I fear, and makes me somewhat slow of wit. You were saying?"

"I said that you English had done well today," the
Commander said patiently. "My guild superiors will be
pleased with the results of your valiant fighting. I feel
certain that they will express that pleasure to me in
some material form quite soon, and I, of course, wish
to express my own pleasure to your men. Accordingly,
I have instructed the Medic to awaken your mates and
children. We will remain on this world for at least
another several weeks while the details of our agree-
ments are worked out with the natives. It may be that
I shall need your services once again—or to trot a few
of you out to remind the natives of your prowess, at
least—during my negotiations. Since we must keep you
awake during that period anyway, and since you have
fought so well, rewarding you with the opportunity for
a reunion seems only just."

"I thank you, Commander." Sir George fought to
keep his own emotions out of his voice and expression.
The fact that he was unable to read the Commander's
feelings didn't mean the Commander or one of his
fiendishly clever devices couldn't read Sir George's. He
doubted that they could, but he might be wrong, and
so he throttled back the mixture of elation, joy, hatred,
and fury the news sent racing through him.

"You are welcome, of course," the Commander piped
back, and gestured for Sir George to seat himself on

the human-style chair which had suddenly appeared beside the table of glowing light. Sir George took the chair gingerly, unable even after all this time to completely hide his discomfort with furnishings which appeared and disappeared as if out of thin air. Nor did he much care for the table. He had no idea how it had been created, but he knew its top was actually as immaterial as the air about him. It was indisputably there. He could lay a hand upon it and feel . . . *something*. Yet he could never have described that something. It supported anything set upon it, but it was as if he couldn't quite place his hand on its actual surface, assuming it had one. It was more as if . . . as if he were pressing his palm against a powerful current of water, or perhaps an equally powerful current of air itself. There was a *resistance* as his hand approached what ought to be the surface of the table, yet there was no sense of *friction*, and he always seemed on the brink of being able to push just a little further, just a bit closer.

He put the thought aside once more and watched another of the ship's small metal servitors move silently into the compartment and deposit a crystal carafe of wine and an exquisite goblet before him. Another goblet and carafe, this time filled with some thick, purple-gold, sludgelike liquid was placed before the Commander, and Sir George managed not to blink in surprise. The Commander had offered him what amounted to a social meeting only five times before, and as closely as he could estimate, each had followed on the heels of some particularly valuable coup which the English had executed for the Guild. Which seemed to suggest that the hapless not-men Sir George and his troops had slaughtered the day before must be the source of some commodity vastly more valuable than he would have believed this

world could offer to anyone with the capabilities of
his masters.

"You are wondering what brings us to this world,
are you not?" the Commander asked, and Sir George
nodded. The Commander had learned the meaning of
at least some human gestures, and he made an alarming
sound. Sir George wasn't positive, but he'd come to
suspect it was the equivalent of a human chuckle,
although whether it indicated satisfaction, amusement,
scorn, impatience, or some other emotion was impossible to say.

"I am not surprised that you wonder," the Commander went on. "After all, these aliens are even more
primitive than your own world. It must be difficult to
grasp what such barbarians could possibly offer to
civilized beings."

Sir George gritted his teeth and made himself take
a sip of the truly excellent wine. He had no idea whether
or not the Commander realized how insulting his words
were, and the voice in which they were delivered gave
no clue. He suspected the Commander wouldn't have
cared a great deal if he *had* known, and he could even
admit—intellectually—that there was some point to the
other's attitude. Compared to the Commander's people,
humans *were* primitive. On the other hand, Sir George
had come to suspect that the Commander's Guild wasn't
actually so very different from guilds or other powerful groups of Sir George's own experience. He would
have given a great deal, for example, to see how the
Commander would have fared bargaining with a Cyp-
riot or a Venetian. Without the advantage of his "technology," he strongly suspected, the demon-jester would
be plucked like a pigeon.

"In actual fact," the Commander continued, seemingly oblivious to Sir George's silence, "this planet does
not offer us any physical commodity. Some of the

worlds which the Guild has used you to open to them have offered such commodities, although normally only in the form of resources the primitives who live upon them are too stupid to exploit themselves. In this case, however, it is the position of the world which is of such value. It will provide us with a location for . . . warehouses, I suppose you might call them, and one from which we may fuel and maintain our vessels."

He paused, looking at Sir George with that impossible to read face, then raised his goblet to tip a little of the purple-gold sludge into his lower mouth.

"You may think of it as a strategically located island or trading port," his piping voice said after a moment, issuing from his upper mouth while the lower one was busy with the goblet. "It will bring us many advantages. And of particular satisfaction to me personally, it will cut deeply into the flank of the Sharnhaishian Guild's trade network."

Sir George pricked up his ears at that. Impossible though he found it to reliably interpret the Commander's tone or expression, he'd formed some conclusions about the other's personality. He knew it was risky to draw parallels between such unearthly creatures and the personality traits of humans, yet he couldn't help doing so. Perhaps it was simply that he had to put it in *some* sort of familiar framework or go mad. Indeed, he often thought that might be the best explanation of all. But he also felt certain that he'd read at least one aspect of the Commander correctly: the thick-bodied little creature loved to brag . . . even when his audience was no more than a primitive, barbarian English slave. Perhaps even more importantly—and, again, like many boastful *humans* Sir George had known—the Commander seemed blissfully unaware of the weakness such bragging could become. A wise man, Sir George's father had often said, learns from the things fools let slip.

Fortunately, the Commander had never met Sir James Wincaster.

Sir George realized the Commander had said nothing for several seconds, simply gazing at him with that disconcerting triple stare, and he shook himself.

"I see . . . I think," he said, hoping his suspicion that the Commander wanted him to respond was correct. "I suppose it would be like capturing, oh, Constantinople and seizing control of all access to the Black Sea."

"I am not certain," the Commander replied. "I am insufficiently familiar with the geography of your home world to know if the analogy is accurate, but it sounds as if it might be. At any rate, there will be major bonuses for myself and the members of my team, which is one reason I wish to reward you. You and your kind are a very valuable guild asset, and unlike some of my guild brothers, I have always believed that valuable property should be well cared for and that assets are better motivated by reward than by punishment alone."

"I have observed much the same," Sir George said with what might charitably have been described as a smile. He managed to keep his voice level and thoughtful, whatever his expression might have briefly revealed, and he castigated himself for that teeth-baring smile, reminding himself yet again that his masters might be—indeed, almost certainly were—better versed at reading human expressions than he was at reading theirs. Unlike humans, they at least had experience of scores of other races and sorts of creatures. They must have learned at least a little something about interpreting alien emotions from that experience, and even if they hadn't, it was far better to *over*estimate a foe than to underestimate one.

"I suspected that you might have reached the same

conclusion," the Commander said with what Sir George rather thought might have been an expansive air had the Commander been human. "Yet I must confess that for me, personally, the fact that we have dealt the Sharnhaishians a blow is of even greater satisfaction than any bonus."

"You've mentioned the . . . the—" Sir George snorted impatiently. He simply could not wrap his tongue about the sounds of the alien name, and the Commander made that alarming sound once again.

"The Sharnhaishian Guild," he supplied, and Sir George nodded.

"Yes. You've mentioned them before, Commander."

"Indeed I have," the Commander agreed. There was still no readable emotion in his voice or face, yet Sir George suspected that if there had been, the emotion would have been one of bitter hatred. "I owe the Sharnhaishians a great deal," the Commander went on. "They almost destroyed my career when they first produced their accursed 'Romans.'"

Sir George nodded again, striving to project an air of understanding and sympathy while he hoped desperately that the Commander would continue. The other had touched upon the Sharnhaishian Guild—obviously the great rival of his own trading house—in earlier conversations. The references had been maddeningly vague, yet they had made it plain that the Sharnhaishians were currently ascendent over the Commander's own guild, and their success seemed to have a great deal to do with the Romans the Commander had mentioned more than once. Sir George found it all but impossible to believe, even now, that the "Romans" in question could be what it *sounded* as if they were, but if he was wrong, he wanted to know it. It might be ludicrous to believe he could hope to achieve anything against his alien masters, yet Sir

George had seen too much of purely human struggles to surrender all hope, despite the huge gulf between their physical capabilities. There were times when a bit of knowledge, or of insight into an enemy's thoughts and plans (or fears), could be more valuable than a thousand bowmen.

And given all the marvels the Commander and his kind possess, knowledge is the only *thing which might aid me against them,* he reminded himself.

The Commander ingested more purple-gold sludge, all three eyes gazing at the "light sculpture" as if he'd completely forgotten Sir George was present, and the human had a sudden thought. The wine in his goblet was perhaps the finest vintage he'd ever sampled, and potent, as well. Was it reasonable to guess that the sludge was equally or even more potent for the Commander's kind? The more he considered it, the more possible—and probable—it seemed, and he smiled inwardly, much as a shark might have smiled.

Truth in the wine, he reminded himself, and took another sip—a very *small* one this time—from his own glass.

"It was the Sharnhaishians and their Romans who kept me from being appointed a sector commissioner long ago," the Commander said at last. He moved his eyes from the light sculpture to Sir George, and the Englishman hid another smile as he realized the flanking eyes had gone just a bit unfocused. They seemed to be wandering off in directions of their own, as well, and he filed that fact away. He could be wrong, but if he wasn't, recognizing the signs of drunkenness in the Commander might prove valuable in the future.

"How was I to know they might come up with something like the Romans?" the Commander demanded. "It must have cost them a fortune to bribe the Council into letting them buy the damned barbarians in the first place." Sir George cocked his head slightly, and the Commander slapped a double-thumbed hand on the table top. On a normal table, such a blow would have produced a thunderclap of sound; on *this* table, there was no noise at all, but the Commander seemed to draw a certain comfort from the gesture.

"Oh, yes." He took another deep sip of sludge and refilled his goblet once more. "The Federation has rules, you know. Laws. Like the one that says none of us can use modern weapons on primitive worlds. The 'Prime Directive,' they call it." He slurped more sludge, but his upper mouth never stopped speaking. "Bunch of hypocrites, that's what they are. Carrying on like the thing is supposed to protect the stupid primitives. You know what it really is?"

His large, central eye fixed on Sir George, and the Englishman shook his head.

"Fear, that's what," the Commander told him. "Stupid bureaucrats are afraid we'll lose some of our toys where the barbarians can find them. As if the idiots could figure them out in the first place."

He fell silent again, and alien though his voice and face might be, Sir George was increasingly certain that he truly was as moody as any drunken human.

"Actually, it makes a sort of sense, you know," the Commander went on finally. He gave the table another silent thump and leaned back in the oddly shaped, bucketlike piece of furniture which served his kind as a chair. "Takes years and years to move between stars, even with phase drive. One reason the ships are so damned big. Don't have to be, you know. We could put a phase drive in a hull a tenth the size of this one—even smaller. But size doesn't matter much. Oh, the mass curve's important, but once you've got the basic system—" He waved a hand, and Sir George nodded once again. He didn't have the faintest idea what a "mass curve" or a "phase drive" was, and at the moment, he didn't much care. Other bits and pieces *did* make sense to him, and he listened avidly for more.

And, he thought from behind his own masklike expression, *it doesn't hurt a bit to watch the Commander. "Truth in the wine," indeed! His voice and face may not reveal much, but his* gestures *are another matter entirely. Perhaps I've been looking in the wrong places to gauge his moods.* He filed that away, as well, and sat back in his chair, nursing his goblet in both hands while he listened attentively . . . and sympathetically.

"Thing is, if it takes decades to make the trip, better have the capacity to make the trip worthwhile, right?" the Commander demanded. "You think this ship is big?" Another wave of a double-thumbed hand, gesturing at the bulkheads. "Well, you're wrong. Lots of ships out there lots bigger than this one. Most of the guild ships, as a matter of fact, because it doesn't cost any more to run a really big ship than a little one like this. But that's the real reason for their stupid 'Prime Directive.' "

"The size of your vessels?" Sir George made his tone puzzled and wrinkled his forehead ferociously, hoping the Commander had become sufficiently well versed in human expressions to recognize perplexity, although if his estimate of the other's condition was accurate it was unlikely the Commander would be noticing anything so subtle as an alien race's expressions. But whether or not the Commander recognized his expression, it was quickly clear that he'd asked the right question.

"Of course not," the Commander told him. "Not the size, the speed. Might be fifteen or twenty of your years between visits to most of these backwater planets.

Maybe even longer. I know one planet that the Guild only sends a ship to every two and a half of your centuries or so, and the Federation knows it, too. So they don't want to take any chances on having some bunch of primitives figure out we're not really gods or whatever between visits. Want to keep them awed and humble around us. That's why they passed their 'Prime Directive' something like—" The Commander paused in thought for a few seconds, as if considering something. "Would have been something like eighteen thousand of your years ago, I think. Give or take a century or two."

He made the alarming sound again, and Sir George was certain now that it was his kind's equivalent of laughter. For just a moment, that hardly seemed to matter, however. Eighteen *thousand* years? His alien masters' civilization had existed for over eighteen millennia? Impossible! And yet—

"Even for us, that's a long time for a law to be in effect," the Commander said. His piping voice was less clear, the words beginning to blur just a bit around the corners as he leaned towards Sir George, and the baron had to fight back a chuckle of his own as he realized that whatever did the translating was faithfully slurring the translation to match the drunken original. "We don't like to change things unless we have to, you know, so once we write a law, it stays around a while, but this one's made lots of trouble for the guilds, because it's meant we couldn't just go in and rearrange things properly. Actually had to bargain with barbarians so primitive they don't have a clue of the value of the things they're sitting on top of. Couldn't violate the damned 'Prime Directive' after all, now could we?"

Another thump on the table. This time, it wouldn't have made any sound anyway, because the Commander missed the table top entirely, and Sir George began to wonder how much longer the creature would last before he passed out.

"So what did the Sharnhaishians do?" the Commander continued. "I'll tell you what. They went out and found another primitive world—one the Council didn't even know about yet—and they bought their damned 'Romans.' Never occurred to any of the rest of us. But the Prime Directive doesn't say we can't use force. All it says is that we can't use our own weapons. It just never occurred to any of us that there was anything we could do without using our weapons except negotiate and bribe."

He lowered his goblet and peered down into it for several seconds, then made a sound suspiciously like a human belch and returned his central eye to Sir George.

"Not the Sharnhaishians, though. If they want a primitive world, they just send in their Romans. Just as primitive as the local barbarians, so the Council can't complain, and I'll say this for the Romans. They're tough. Never run into anything they couldn't handle, and the Sharnhaishians've used them to take dozens of backwater worlds away from the other guilds. Whole trade nets, cut to pieces. Strategic commodities sewn up, warehousing and basing rights snatched out from under us, careers ruined. And all because the Sharnhaishians acquired a few thousand primitives in bronze armor."

He fell silent for a long time, swirling sludge in his goblet and peering down into it, then looked back up more or less in Sir George's direction.

"But they're not the only ones who can play that game. They thought they were. The other guilds got together to complain to the Council, and the Council agreed to take the matter under consideration. It may even decide the Sharnhaishians have to stop using their

Romans entirely, but that may take centuries, and in the meantime, Sharnhaishian is shipping them from one strategic point to another and taking them away from the rest of us. And they slipped someone on the Council a big enough bribe to get your world declared off-limits for all the rest of us."

Sir George stiffened, and hoped the Commander was too drunk to notice. He wasn't surprised that the other guild could have bribed the Council the Commander was yammering about. Bribing a few key rulers was often more efficient—and cheaper—than relying on armies. *Although if His Majesty had spent a little more money on his army and a little less on trying to buy allies in his first French campaign he might have been on the throne of France by its end!*

But if the Commander was telling the truth, if the Council to which he referred had the authority to declare that contact with Sir George's home world was no longer permitted and had done so, then the Commander's Guild must have violated that decree in order to kidnap Sir George and his troops. And if that was the case—if their servitude was unlawful in the eyes of what passed for the Crown among these creatures—then they were in even more danger than he had believed.

"It took me two or three of your centuries just to figure out where your world was," the Commander went on, and now Sir George seemed to sense an air of pride. "Some of the other guilds recruited their own primitive armies, like the Hathori. But none of them have been able to match the Romans. I still remember the first time we sent the Hathori in against a bunch of natives." The Commander stared down into his goblet, and his ears flattened.

"Damned aborigines cut them to pieces," he said after a long moment. "Cost them a lot of casualties at first, but then they swarmed right over the Hathori. Butchered them one by one. I doubt we got one in twenty of them back alive at the end, but that wouldn't have happened against the damned Romans. Those aren't just warriors—they're demons that carve up anything they run into. So it occurred to me that what we needed were Romans of our own, and I managed to convince my creche cousin to convince his sector commissioner to speak to the guild masters for me. I needed all the help I could get, thanks to the Sharn-haishians and their Romans. Of course, it helped that by then they'd done the same thing to dozens of other guildsmen, and not just in our guild, either. So they gave me a chance to reclaim my career if I could find where the Romans came from, get past the Council ban, and catch us some Romans of our own. And I did it, too."

This time his slap managed to connect with the table top again, though it was still soundless, and he threw himself untidily back in his chair.

"But we're not Romans," Sir George pointed out after a moment. He was half afraid to say another word, for if the Commander remembered any of this conversation—and realized all he was letting slip—at a later date, there would be one very simple way to rectify his error.

"Of course not," the Commander said. "Good thing, too, in a way. It surprised me, of course. I never expected to see so much change on a single planet in such a short period. Couldn't have been more than eight or nine hundred of your years between you and the Romans, and just look at all the differences. It's not decent. Oh," he waved a hand again, "you're still primitives, of course. Haven't changed that. But we got there in just the nick of time. Another five or six of your centuries or so, and you might actually have been

using true firearms, and we couldn't have that. Unlikely,
I admit, but there you were, already experimenting with
them." The Commander eyed Sir George. "I have to
wonder how you stumbled on the idea so soon. Could
the Sharnhaishians have slipped up and suggested it
to you?"

"The idea of 'firearms'?" Sir George frowned.

"Pots de fer, I believe you call them," the Commander said.

"Fire pots?" Sir George blinked in genuine consternation. "But they're nothing but toys, Commander!
Good for scaring horses and people who never encountered them, perhaps, but scarcely serious weapons.
Even bombards are little more than noisy nuisances
against anyone who knows his business! Why, my
bowmen would massacre any army stupid enough to
arm itself with such weapons. *Crossbows* are more
effective than they are!"

"No doubt they are—now," the Commander replied.
"Won't stay that way, though. Of course, you've still got
another thousand years or so to go before anyone
develops truly effective small arms. Still, I suppose it's
a fairly good example of why they passed the Prime
Directive in the first place. If the Sharnhaishians hadn't
somehow contaminated your world, you never would
have come up with gunpowder at all—not so quickly."

He took another deep swallow, and Sir George
decided to stay away from the question of where
gunpowder came from. He himself knew only a very
little about the subject—such weapons had become
available in Europe only during his own lifetime and,
like most of his military contemporaries, he'd had little
faith that they would ever amount to much as effective field weapons. Certainly such crude, short-ranged,
dangerous devices would never pose any threat to the
supremacy of his bowmen! Yet the Commander seemed

to find their existence deeply significant and more than a little worrying. It was almost as if the fact that humans had begun experimenting with them was somehow threatening, and Sir George had no intention of suggesting that the Sharnhaishians hadn't had anything to do with the development. Besides, how did he *know* the rival guild hadn't?

"Anyway," the Commander said, the words more slurred than ever, "it's a good thing we found you when we did. Couldn't have used you at all if you'd been armed with firearms. Would've been a clear violation of the Prime Directive, and that would've gotten questions asked. People would've noticed, too, and the Council would start asking questions of its own."

He leaned back towards Sir George again, and this time he patted the Englishman on the knee with what would have been a conspiratorial air from another human.

"As it is, nobody really cares. Just another bunch of primitives with muscle-powered weapons, nothing to worry about. None of the Council's inspectors even knows enough about humans to realize you and the Romans are the same species, and if any of them ever do notice, we know where to put the bribes to convince them they were mistaken. Besides," another pat on the knee, "you're all off the books." Sir George frowned, puzzled by the peculiar phrase, and the Commander thumped his knee a third time. "No document trail," he said, the words now so slurred that Sir George found it virtually impossible to understand them even as words, far less to grasp the concept behind them. "Grabbed you out of the middle of a storm. Everybody on your stupid planet figures you all drowned—would have without us, too, you know. But that means even if the Council investigates, they won't find any evidence of contact between us and your world, because aside from picking you out of the water and grabbing a few horses in the middle of the night, there wasn't any. So we've got our own little army, and unless some inspector does get nosy, nobody will ever even ask where you came from."

The Commander leaned back in his chair once more and reached out for his goblet. But his groping hand knocked it over, and he peered down at it. His central eye was almost as unfocused as the secondary ones now, and his strange, sideways eyelids began to iris out to cover them all.

"S' take that, Sharnhaishian," he muttered. "Thought you'd wrecked my career, didn' you? But who's going to . . ."

His voice trailed off entirely, his eyes closed, and he slumped in his chair. His upper mouth fell open, and a whistling sound which Sir George realized must be his kind's equivalent of a snore came from it.

The human sat in his own chair, staring numbly at the Commander, until the door opened silently once more. He looked up quickly then and saw one of his masters' guardsmen in the opening. The dragon-man beckoned imperatively with one clawed hand, and Sir George noted the way that its other hand rested on the weapon scabbarded at its side.

Could that be what the Commander actually meant by "firearms"? he wondered suddenly. *Not even a true dragon could hurl hotter "fire" than they do . . . and they're certainly far more dangerous than any stupid fire pot!*

The dragon-man beckoned again, its meaning clear, and Sir George sighed and rose. Of course they wouldn't leave him alone with the senseless Commander. No doubt they'd been watching through some sort of spyhole and come to collect him the instant the Commander collapsed. But had they paid any attention

to the Commander's conversation *before* he collapsed?
And even if they had, had they guessed that Sir George
might realize the significance of what the Commander
had told him?

He hoped not, just as he hoped the Commander
wouldn't remember all that he'd let slip. Because if the
others had guessed, or the Commander did remember, Sir George would almost certainly die.

After all, it would never do for their pet army's
commander to realize that if anyone from the
Council—wherever and exactly whatever it was—*did*
begin to question that army's origins, the entire army
would have to disappear.

Forever . . . and without a trace that could tie the
Commander's Guild to a planet which the "Council"
had interdicted.

"Are you certain, my love?"

Lady Matilda Wincaster reclined against the cush-
ion under the brightly colored awning and regarded
her husband with a serious expression. Despite the
difficulty in reading alien moods, the Commander's
incredulity had been obvious the first time Sir George
requested permission for the English to set up tents
outside the hull of the vast ship. That had been long
ago, on only the third world to which they'd been
taken, and the Commander had regarded Sir George
very closely as he warned against any thought that the
English might be able to slip away and hide from their
masters. Sir George hadn't doubted the warning, and
he'd taken steps to impress it equally strongly on his
subordinates. He'd also been able to understand why
the Commander might be astounded by the notion that
anyone could prefer a tent in the open to the always
perfect temperature and luxurious marvels of the ship.
To be sure, the English undoubtedly had far fewer of

those luxuries than their masters did, but what they did have surpassed anything any king or emperor might have boasted back on Earth.

They were well aware of the wonders, and, despite their captivity, they weren't so stupid as to reject them. But they also had an inborn hunger for open skies and natural air . . . even the "natural air" of planets which had never been home to any of their kind. In clement weather, many of them actually preferred to sleep amid the fresh air and breezes, the sounds of whatever passed for birds on a given planet, and the chuckling sounds of running water. And even those who invariably returned aboard ship for the night enjoyed the occasional open air meal. Indeed, the picnic feasts often took on the air of a festival or fair from Earth, helping to bind them together and reinforce their sense of community.

And they *were* a community, as well as an army. In many ways, they were fortunate that there were so few gently born among them, Sir George had often thought. He himself was the only true noble, and aside from himself and Maynton, only one other knight, Sir Henry de Maricourt, could claim any real highborn connection. The rest of his men were of common birth . . . and so were their wives. Which meant that, especially with Lady Matilda to lead the way, they had decided to overlook the dubious origins of many of the unwed camp followers who'd joined them in their involuntary exile. Most of those camp followers, though by no means all, had acquired husbands quite speedily. A few had chosen not to, and Father Timothy had agreed, under the circumstances, not to inveigh against them. There were a great many more men than women, and the one thing most likely to provoke trouble among them was that imbalance in numbers. No doubt Father Timothy would have preferred for all of the women to be respectfully wedded wives, but he, too, had been a soldier in his time. He understood the temper of men who still were, and he was able to appreciate the need to adapt to the conditions in which they found themselves forced to live.

As a result, not even those women who continued to ply their original trade were ostracized as they might have been, and a tightly knit cluster of families formed the core of the English community. The steadily growing number of children (both legitimate and bastard) helped cement that sense of community even further, and for all the bitterness with which Sir George chafed against his servitude, even he had to admit the awe he felt that not a single one of those children had perished in infancy. That was undoubtedly the most treasured of the "luxuries" their masters had made available to them. The *strangest*, however (though it was hard to pick the single most strange), was the fact that so few of those children's mothers remembered their births. It had caused some consternation and even terror and talk of "changelings" at first, but as time passed, the women had adjusted to the fact that their babies were almost always born during one of their sleep periods. The Medic had explained the process, pointing out that it only made sense to get such time-consuming worries as pregnancies out of the way when they were asleep anyway, and after an initial period of extreme uneasiness, most of the women had come to agree. Led in almost every case, Sir George had been amused (but not surprised) to note, by the women who had birthed the most babies the "old-fashioned" way.

He smiled even now, at the memory, but his attention was on his wife's question. One of the real reasons he'd requested freedom from the ship for his people was his certainty that anything which was said *aboard* the ship would be overheard by one of their masters' clever mechanical spies. It was probable that those same spies could eavesdrop upon them outside the ship, as well, but he hoped it would at least be a bit harder. And he rather suspected that even the most clever of mechanisms would find it difficult to keep track of several hundred individual conversations out in the open against the background noise of wind and water. Which meant such excursions were the only time he felt even remotely safe discussing dangerous matters.

Although even then, he reflected, the only person with whom he truly discussed them was Matilda.

"Yes, I'm certain," he said at last, meeting her gray eyes as he answered her question. *God, she's beautiful*, he thought with a familiar sense of wonder and awe. Seven years younger than he—or seven years younger back on Earth, at least—her huge eyes and the golden glory of her hair had delighted him from the moment he laid eyes upon her. She was better born than he, but his own soldier grandfather and father had been thrifty men, and Wickworth had been the sort of manor to please any nobly born father.

Their marriage had been one of political advantage, yet it had also been more, which had been one reason for the warm relationship with Earl Cathwall which Sir George had treasured so highly. The earl had been a doting father. He had refused to marry his daughter off for his own advantage, for he'd wanted her to marry for love, and he had been satisfied that she'd done just that as he watched her with his son-in-law.

He had also actively encouraged his daughter's pursuit of an education, which was almost unseemly, and Sir George was devoutly grateful that he had. Matilda's love was the core of his own strength, but she'd also become his wisest and most trusted advisor, as well.

"I don't think he realizes he revealed so much," the baron went on now, raising a wine goblet to hide the movement of his lips and speaking very quietly, "but I'm certain of it. More certain than I like."

"But surely there's no longer any doubt that we truly are as valuable to his Guild as he's suggested," Lady Matilda pointed out. "They would not lightly discard a tool whose worth they hold so high."

"Um." Sir George set the goblet aside, then stretched in an ostentatious yawn. He smiled at his wife and moved to lay his head in her lap, smiling up at her as she tickled the tip of his nose with a stalk of local grass. To the casual eye, they were but two people—people miraculously young and comely—in love, but his eyes were serious as he gazed up at her.

"We *are* valuable," he agreed, "but we're also the very thing you just called us: a tool. You haven't spent as many hours with him as I have, love. I wish *I* hadn't, but I have. And in the spending, I've learned that we have absolutely no value to him *except* as tools. He sees us as we might see a horse, or a cow. Certainly with less affection than I hold for Satan!"

"Because we aren't of his kind?" Lady Matilda murmured, her expression troubled, and Sir George shrugged.

"In part, perhaps, but I think not entirely. At least he loves to boast, and I've gleaned what bits and pieces I can from his bragging. As nearly as I can tell, there are several kinds of creatures in the 'Federation' of which he speaks. His own kind is but one sort of them, and there are great physical differences between them. But they seem much alike in spirit and outlook. All consider themselves 'advanced' because of the machines and other devices they build and control, just as they consider *us* 'primitives' because we lack the knowledge to construct such devices. And to the Federation, primitives are less than French serfs. As primitives, we have no rights, no value, except as tools. We aren't remotely their equals, and most of them wouldn't as much as blink at the thought of killing us all. So if our value in the field should suddenly find itself outweighed by the potential discovery that the Commander's Guild violated a Federation edict—"

He shrugged again, and she nodded unhappily, glorious eyes dark. He felt the fear she tried to hide and smiled ruefully as he reached to pat her knee.

"Forgive me, dear heart. I should never have burdened you with the thought."

"Nonsense!" She laid a small hand across his mouth and shook her head fiercely. "I am your wife, and you are not a god to carry all the weight of our fate upon your shoulders alone. There may be nothing I can do to help beyond listening, but that—and sharing your burden—I *can* do, at least!"

"Perhaps," he agreed, reaching up to caress the side of her face. She leaned down to kiss him, and he savored the taste of her lips. She broke the kiss and started to say something more, but he shook his head and drew her gently down beside him, pillowing her head on his shoulder as they lay on the cushions, gazing up at the sky.

She accepted his unspoken injunction to change the subject and began to talk more lightly of their children—first of Edward, and then of the four younger children born to them aboard their masters' ship. As far as Matilda was concerned, that was the greatest wonder of all, for back in Lancaster, she'd been unable to conceive again after Edward's birth, and her children were the one unblemished joy of their captivity. They were Sir George's, as well, and so he listened with smiling, tender attentiveness, gazing at her face and never once, by even so much as a glance, acknowledging the presence of the dragon-man who had drifted out of the spidery trees. The creature paused for a long moment near the awning under which the baron and his lady lay. It stood there, as if listening intently, and then, as slowly and silently as it had come, it drifted back into the forest and was gone.

The Commander seldom appeared among the men of "his" army, but the demon-jester made a point of summoning them all before him in his own portion of the huge vessel on the day after they'd won yet another victory for his Guild. In turn, Sir George had made a point of seeing to it that none of those men ever revealed how they felt about those summonings, for the Commander would have reacted poorly to their scorn and soul-deep anger. The baron had never been able to decide how even the Commander could be so utterly ignorant of the men who fought and died for him because they had no choice, but that he was seemed undeniable. Who but a fool who knew nothing of Englishmen would appear before those he'd stolen from their homes as his slaves to praise them for their efforts in his behalf? To tell them how well they had served the Guild they'd come to hate with all their hearts and souls? To promise them as the "reward" for their "valor" and "loyalty" the *privilege* of seeing their own wives and children?

Yet that was precisely what the Commander had done on other occasions, and it was what he did today . . . while dragon-men surrounded him protectively and armored wart-faces stood stolidly along the bulkheads of the huge, octagonal chamber, watching frog-eyed through the slots in their visors. Sir George gritted his own teeth until his muscles ached as that piping, emotionless voice wound its monotonous way through the endless monologue. He felt the invisible fury rising from his men like smoke and marveled once more that any creature whose kind could build wonders like the ship and all its marvelous servitors could be so stupid. It was as if the Commander had read some treatise which insisted a commander of barbarians must inspire his troops with flattering words and was determined to do just that.

" . . . reward you for your courage and hardihood," the piping voice went on. "I salute your loyalty and bravery, which has once more carried our Guild's banner to victory, and I hope to grant you the rewards you so richly deserve in the very near future. In the meantime, we—"

"Reward I deserve, hey?" Rolf Grayhame muttered. He stood beside Sir George, his voice a thread, leaking from the side of his fiercely moustachioed lips. "Only one reward *I* want, My Lord, and that's a clean shot. Just one."

Sir George elbowed the archer sharply, and Grayhame closed his mouth with an apologetic glower. He knew Sir George's orders as well as any, but like his baron, he felt only contempt for the Commander. The demon-jester was far from the first arrogant lordling Grayhame had seen in his career, but he was arguably the stupidest. Secure in the superiority of his mechanisms and guards though he might be, he was still witless enough to infuriate fighting men by dragging them out to hear this sort of crap. Not even a Frenchman was *that* stupid!

"Sorry, My Lord," the archer captain muttered. "Shouldn't have said it. But not even a *Scot* would—"

He clamped his jaw again, and Sir George gave him a stern look that was only slightly flawed by the smile twitching at the corners of his mouth. That small lip twitch emboldened Grayhame, and his gray-green eyes glinted for just a moment. Then he shrugged his shoulders apologetically and returned his attention to the Commander.

" . . . and so we will spend several more of your weeks here," the demon-jester was saying. "The craven curs you have whipped to their kennels will offer no threat," he seemed completely oblivious to how foolish his rhetoric sounded to human ears delivered in his piping, emotionless voice, "and you and your mates and children will have that time to enjoy the sunlight and fresh air you so treasure. Go now. Return to your families, secure in the knowledge that you are valued and treasured by our guild."

Sir George started to follow his men out, but a gesture from the Commander stopped him. Grayhame and Maynton paused as well, their eyes meeting Sir George's questioningly, but a tiny shake of his head sent them on after the others. He watched them leave, then turned to his master.

"Yes, Commander?"

"Not all of this planet's primitives have been sufficiently cowed by your defeat of the local clans," the Commander said. "They appear to grasp that their local colleagues' forces have been utterly destroyed, but they do not seem to believe the same could be done to their own. Apparently they feel that those you have defeated were poorly led and motivated—unlike, of course, their own warriors. While cautious, they have not yet accepted that they have no choice but to do as we bid them or be destroyed in their separate turns."

He paused, his three-eyed gaze fixed on Sir George's face, and the human tried to hide his dismay. Not from concern over what might happen to his own men, but because the thought of butchering still more of the local not-men for the benefit of the Commander's guild sickened him.

"I see," he said at last. "Will it be necessary for us to destroy their forces in the field, as well?"

"It may," the Commander replied in that emotionless voice, "but I hope to avoid that. We would be forced to move the ship in order to transport your troops into reach of their warriors. That would be inconvenient. Worse, it might actually encourage them to resist. Such primitive species have exhibited similar behavior in the past, particularly when they believe their numbers are greatly superior. My own analysis suggests that moving the ship from point to point, thus emphasizing the fact that we have but one of it and but a limited number of you English, might encourage some among them to overestimate their ability to resist us. In the end, of course, they would be proven wrong, but teaching them that lesson might require us to spend much longer on this single world than my superiors would like."

"I see," Sir George repeated, and this time he truly did. Before he had fallen into the hands of the Commander's Guild, he, too, had sometimes found himself looking over his shoulder at superiors who insisted that he accomplish his tasks with near-impossible speed. Not that understanding the Commander's quandary woke any particular sympathy within him.

"No doubt you do," the Commander replied. "I hope, however, to avoid that necessity by demonstrating their inferiority to them. Accordingly, I have summoned all of the principal chieftains from within reasonable travel distance from our current location. They will begin arriving within the next two local days, and all should be here within no more than twelve. While your bows are clumsy and primitive in the extreme, the locals have nothing which can compare to them in range and rate of fire. When the chieftains arrive, you will demonstrate this fact to them, and the leaders of the clans you have already defeated will explain to them how your weapons allowed you to annihilate their own troops. With this evidence of their inferiority before them and demonstrated before their own eyes, they should be forced to admit that they cannot, in fact, withstand you in open combat and so have no choice but to accept my terms."

He paused once more, waiting until Sir George nodded.

"Very well. I will leave the details of the demonstration up to you. Be prepared to describe them to me in two days' time."

The Commander turned away without another word, and most of his dragon-man guards closed in around him. One remained behind, obviously to escort Sir George from the ship, but the baron ignored the alien creature, hot eyes fixed on the Commander's arrogant back as the wart-faces fell in behind the demon-jester and his entourage.

Plan a demonstration, is it? Sir George thought venomously. *Jesu, but I know what I'd like to use as a target! The sight of your precious hide sprouting arrows like peacock feathers ought to impress the "local lordlings" no end!*

He snorted bitterly at the thought, then drew a deep breath and turned to the dragon-man as the hatch closed behind the Commander. The towering alien looked down at him, then gestured for Sir George to accompany him from the ship.

Sir George obeyed the gesture, not without a fresh flicker of anger. Yet there was no point in resenting the dragon-man, and he tried to put his emotions aside as the dragon-man steered him out of the unfamiliar portion of the ship.

To Sir George's surprise, however, the alien did not stop when they reached the huge cargo deck which stood open to the local environment. Instead, the dragon-man actually followed him from the ship, as if it meant to accompany him all the way to the pavilion which had been set up for Sir George and Lady Matilda.

The baron paused, surprised by the departure from normal practice, but the dragon-man only gestured him onward. He hesitated a moment longer, then shrugged ever so slightly and resumed his progress.

The two of them passed the screen of shrubbery separating the English camp from the ship, and Sir George smiled as he caught sight of Matilda, waiting for him. He raised his hand and opened his mouth to call her name . . .

. . . and found himself lying on the ground with no memory at all of how he had gotten there.

He blinked, head swimming, and peered up as a small hand stroked his brow anxiously. Matilda's worried face peered down at him, and beyond her he saw Father Timothy, Dickon Yardley, Sir Richard, Rolf Grayhame, and a dozen others. And, to his immense surprise, he saw the dragon-man, as well, still standing behind the circle of far shorter humans and gazing down at him over their heads.

"My love?" Matilda's voice was taut with anxiety, and he blinked again, forcing his eyes to focus on her face. "What happened?" she demanded.

"I—" He blinked a third time and shook the head he now realized lay in her lap. It seemed to be still attached to his shoulders, and his mouth quirked in a small, wry smile.

"I have no idea," he admitted. "I'd hoped that perhaps *you* might be able to tell *me* that!"

Her worried expression eased somewhat at his teasing tone, but it was her turn to shake her head.

"Would that I could," she told him, her voice far more serious than his had been. "You simply stepped around the bushes there and raised your hand, then collapsed. And—" despite herself, her voice quivered just a bit "—lay like one dead for the better part of a quarter-hour." She looked anxiously up at Yardley, who shrugged.

"It's as Her Ladyship says, My Lord," the surgeon told him. Yardley lacked the training and miraculous devices of the Medic, but he'd always been an excellent field surgeon, and he'd been given far longer to learn his craft than any other human battle surgeon. Now he shook his head. "Oh, she exaggerates a little— you were scarcely 'like one dead.' I fear we've seen all too many of *those*, have we not?" He smiled grimly, and one or two of the others chuckled as they recalled men who most certainly *had* lain "like one dead" until their masters' marvels restored them to life and health. "Your breathing was deeper than usual, yet not dangerously so, and your pulse steady. But for the fact that we couldn't wake you, you might simply have been soundly asleep. Have you no memory of having tripped or fallen?"

"None," Sir George admitted. He pushed himself experimentally into a sitting position and patted Matilda's knee reassuringly when he felt no sudden dizziness. He sat a moment, then rose smoothly to his feet and raised one hand, palm uppermost.

"I feel fine," he told them, and it was true.

"Perhaps you do, but you've given *me* more than enough fright for one day, Sir George Wincaster!" Matilda said in a much tarter tone. He grinned apologetically down at her and extended his hand, raising her lightly, and tucked her arm through his as he turned to face his senior officers once more.

"I feel fine," he repeated. "No doubt I did stumble

over something—my thoughts were elsewhere, and any man may be clumsy enough to fall over his own two feet from time to time. But no harm was done, so be about your business while I—" he smiled at them and patted his wife's hand where it rested on his elbow "—attempt to make some amends to my lady wife for having afrighted her so boorishly!"

A rumble of laughter greeted his sally and the crowd began to disperse. He watched them go, then turned his gaze back to the dragon-man.

But the dragon-man was no longer there.

Matilda watched him closely for the rest of that long day, and she fussed over him as they prepared for bed that night, but Sir George had told her nothing but the simple truth. He did, indeed, feel fine—better, in some ways, than in a very long time—and he soothed her fears by drawing her down beside him. Her eyes widened with delight at the sudden passion of his embrace, and he proceeded to give her the most conclusive possible proof that there was nothing at all wrong with her husband.

But that night, as Matilda drifted into sleep in the circle of his arms and he prepared to follow her, he dreamed. Or thought he did, at least . . .

"Welcome, Sir George," the voice said, and the baron turned to find the speaker, only to blink in astonishment. The voice sounded remarkably like Father Timothy's, although it carried an edge of polish and sophistication the blunt-spoken priest had never displayed. But it wasn't Father Timothy. For that matter, it wasn't even human, and he gaped in shock as he found himself facing one of the eternally silent dragon-men.

"I fear we have taken some liberties with your mind, Sir George," the dragon-man said—or seemed to, *although his mouth never moved.* "We apologize for that. It was both a violation of your privacy and our own customs and codes, yet in this instance we had no choice, for it is imperative that we speak with you."

"Speak with me?" Sir George blurted. "How is it that I've never heard so much as a single sound from any of you, and now . . . now this—"

He waved his arms, and only then did he realize how odd their surroundings were. They stood in the center of a featureless gray plain, surrounded by . . . nothing. The grayness underfoot simply stretched away in every direction, to the uttermost limit of visibility, and he swallowed hard.

"Where are we?" he demanded, and was pleased to hear no quaver in his voice.

"Inside your own mind, in a sense," the dragon-man replied. "That isn't precisely *correct*, but it will serve as a crude approximation. It is our hope to be able to explain it more fully at a future time. But unless you and we act soon—and decisively—it is unlikely either your people or ours will have sufficient future for such explanations."

"What do you mean? And if you wished to speak with me, why did you never do so before this?" Sir George asked warily.

"To answer your second question first," the dragon-man answered calmly, "it was not possible to speak directly to you prior to this time. Indeed, we aren't 'speaking' even now—not as your species understands the term."

Sir George frowned in perplexity, and the dragon-man cocked his head. His features were as alien as the Commander's, yet Sir George had the sudden, unmistakable feeling of an amused smile. It came, he realized slowly, not from the dragon-man's face, but rather from somewhere inside the other. It was nothing he *saw; rather it was something he felt. Which was absurd, of course . . . except that he felt absolutely no doubt of what he was sensing.*

"This is a dream," he said flatly, and the dragon-man responded with a very human shrug.

"*In a sense,*" *he acknowledged.* "*You are most certainly asleep, at any rate. But if this is a dream, it's one we share . . . and the only way in which we could communicate with you. It is also—*" *the sense of a smile was even stronger, but this time it carried a hungry edge, as well* "*—a method of communication which the Commander and his kind cannot possibly tap or intercept.*"

"*Ah?*" *Despite himself, Sir George's mental ears pricked at that. No doubt it was only a dream, and this talkative dragon-man was no more than his own imagination, but if only—*

"*Indeed,*" *the dragon-man reassured him, and folded his arms across a massive chest.* "*Our kind do not use spoken speech among ourselves as most other races do,*" *he explained.* "*In fact, we are not capable of it, for we lack the vocal cords—or equivalent—which you and other species use to produce sound.*"

"*Then how do you speak to one another?*" *Sir George asked intently.* "*And, for that matter, what do you call your kind among yourselves?*"

"We are what others call 'telepaths,'" the dragon-man replied. "It means simply that we cast our thoughts directly into one another's minds, without need of words. And no doubt because we do so, we do not use individual names as other species do. Or, rather, we don't require them, for each of us has a unique gestalt—a taste, or flavor, if you will—which all others of our kind recognize. As for what we call ourselves as a species, the closest equivalent in your language would probably be 'People.' Since meeting you humans, however, and especially since establishing a contact point in your mind, we aboard this ship have been rather taken by your own descriptions of us." The dragon-man's amusement was apparent. "The notion of playing the part of one of your 'dragons' against the Commander is extremely attractive to us, Sir George."

Sir George smiled. "In that case, we will no doubt continue to call you dragons," he said, and the dragon-man projected the sense of another fierce grin as he nodded.

"We would find that most acceptable," he said. "Yet the need for you to give us a name because we've never developed one is another example of the differences between your kind and us which result from the fact of our telepathy. Despite several of your millennia as the Federation's slaves, we have still to evolve many of the reference points most other species take for granted. Indeed, it was extremely difficult for our ancestors to grasp even the concept of spoken communication when the Federation discovered our world. They took many years to do so, and only the fact that we had independently developed a nuclear-age technology of our own prevented the Federation from classifying us as dumb beasts."

" 'Nuclear-age'?" Sir George repeated, and the dragon-man shrugged again, this time impatiently.

"Don't worry about that now. It simply means that we were considerably more advanced technically than your own world . . . although the Federation was even more relatively advanced compared to us than we would have been compared to your world.

"Unfortunately," the alien went on, and his "voice" turned cold and bleak, "we were too advanced for our own good—just enough to be considered a potential threat, yet not sufficiently so to defend ourselves—and the Federation declared our world a 'protectorate.'

They moved in their military units 'for our own good,' to 'protect' us from ourselves . . . and to insure that we never became any more advanced than we were at the moment they discovered us."

"Because they feared competition," Sir George said shrewdly.

"Perhaps," the dragon-man replied. "No, certainly. But there was another reason, as well. You see, the Federation is entirely controlled by species like the Commander's. They are far more advanced than our own race—or yours—and they regard that as proof of their inherent superiority."

"So I've noticed," Sir George said bitterly.

"We realize that, yet we doubt that you have fully realized what that means," the dragon-man said, "for you lack certain information."

"What information?" Sir George's voice sharpened and his eyes narrowed.

"Explaining that will take some time," the dragon-man replied, and Sir George nodded brusquely for him to continue.

"Life-bearing worlds are very numerous," the dragon-man began. "They're far less common, statistically speaking, than nonlife-bearing or prebiotic worlds, but there are so very many stars, and so very many of them have planets, that the absolute number of life-bearing worlds is quite high."

The creature paused, and Sir George blinked as he realized he actually understood what the other was talking about. Ideas and concepts he had never imagined, even after all his years in his masters' service, seemed to flood into his mind as the dragon-man spoke. He didn't fully understand them—not yet—but he grasped enough to follow what he was being told, and he was vaguely aware that he should have been frightened by the discovery. Yet he wasn't. That curiosity

*of his was at work once more, he realized, and some-
thing else, as well. Something the dragon-man had
done, perhaps.*

*And perhaps not. He shook himself, grinning lop-
sidedly at the stretched feeling of his brain, and nodded
for the dragon-man to continue.*

*"While life-bearing worlds are numerous," the alien
said after a moment, "intelligent life is very rare.
Counting our own species, and yours, the Federation
has encountered less than two hundred intelligent races.
While this sounds like a great many, you must recall
that the Federation has possessed phase drive and
faster-than-light travel—the ability to voyage between
stars and their planets—for more than one hundred
thousand of your years. Which means that they have
discovered a new intelligent species no more than once
every five hundred years."*

*Sir George swallowed hard. The Englishmen's
experiences in their masters' service had half-prepared
him for such concepts, but nothing could have fully
prepared him. Still, much of what the dragon-man was
saying wasn't terribly different from concepts he and
Matilda and Father Timothy had been groping towards
for years. In fact, the priest had proved more ready
than Sir George to accept that Mother Church's teach-
ings and Holy Scripture's accounts of things such as
the Creation stood in need of correction and revision.
Not that even Father Timothy had been prepared to
go quite so far as this!*

"Of all the species the Federation has encountered,
only thirty-two had developed the phase drive themselves, or attained an equivalent technological level,
when they were encountered. Those races, more
advanced than any others, are full members of the Federation. They sit on its Council, formulate its laws, and
enjoy its benefits. The rest of us . . . do not.

"In the eyes of the Federation, less advanced races have no rights. They exist only for the benefit of the Federation itself, although the Council occasionally mouths a few platitudes about the 'advanced races' burden' and the Federation's responsibility to 'look after' us inferior races. What it means in practical terms, however, is that we are their property, to be disposed of as they will. As you and your people have become."

The dragon-man paused once more, and Sir George nodded hard. He could taste the other's emotions—his hatred and resentment, burning as hot as Sir George's own—and a distant sort of amazement filled him. Not that he could understand the other, but that under their utterly different exteriors they could be so much alike.

"Some of the subject species, however, are more useful to the 'advanced races' than others," the dragon-man resumed after a long, smoldering moment. "Yours, for example, has proven very useful as a means to evade the letter of their prime directive, while ours—" the dragon-man seemed to draw a deep breath "—has proven equally valuable as bodyguards and personal servants."

"Why?" Sir George asked. The question could have come out harsh, demanding to know why the dragon-men should be so compliant and submissive, but it didn't. There was too much anger—and hatred—in the dragon-man's "voice" for that.

"Our species is not like yours. We are not only telepaths—among ourselves, at least—but also empaths. While we are not normally able to make other species hear our thoughts, nor able to hear their thoughts, we are able to sense their emotions, their feelings. This makes it very difficult for anyone who might pose a threat to one we have been assigned to guard to slip past us.

*"But those aren't the only differences between us.
Your kind has but two sexes, male and female. Our
species has four: three which are involved in procre-
ation, and a fourth which might be thought of as our
'worker' caste."*

"In the same way as bees?" Sir George asked, and
the dragon-man paused, gazing intently at him. For a
moment, his brain felt even more stretched than before,
and then the alien nodded.

"Very much like your 'bees,'" the dragon-man told
him. "All of our kind aboard this ship are from that
worker caste, which also provides our warriors. We are
neither male nor female, as you use the terms, but we
are the most numerous sex among our kind. And, like
your world's 'bees,' we exist to serve our 'queen.'" The
dragon-man paused and cocked his head once more.
"It's actually considerably more complex than that.
There are nuances and— Well, no matter. The analogy will serve for the moment."

It seemed to refocus its attention upon Sir George.

"The point is that, unlike your kind, our kind are
not entirely what you would think of as individuals. We
are more than simple parts of a greater whole, and each
of us has his—or her, depending upon how one chooses
to regard us—hopes and desires, yet we see into one
another's minds and emotions with such clarity and
depth that it's almost impossible for us to develop a
true sense of 'self' as you nontelepathic species do.

*"More than that, our 'queens' dominate our lives.
According to our own histories—or those the Federation hasn't completely suppressed, at any rate—that
domination was far less complete before the Federation encountered us. The development of our own
advanced technology and the society which went with
it had apparently inspired our reproductive sexes to
extend a greater degree of freedom—of equality, one*

might say—to the worker caste. But the Federation quickly put a stop to that, for it is the queen's very domination which makes us so valuable.

"You see, Sir George, unlike your species, our young receive their initial educations from direct mind-to-mind contact with their parents . . . and queens. And during that process, the queen is able to direct us—to 'program' us—in order to direct and constrain our behavior. We believe this was once a survival trait of the species, but it is now the thing which makes us so valuable to the Federation, for guilds like the Commander's 'recruit' us from our home world. For all intents and purposes, they buy us from our queens, and our queens have no choice but to sell us, for the Federation controls our world completely and we continue to exist only at the Federation's sufferance."

"This 'programing' of which you speak," Sir George said very carefully. "Of what does it consist?"

"Of mental commands we cannot disobey," the dragon-man said softly. "The guilds specify what commands they wish set upon us, and our queens impress those orders so deeply into our minds that we cannot even contemplate disobeying them. And so, you see, the Federation regards us—rightly—as even more suitable for slaves than your own kind."

"And yet . . ." Sir George let his voice trail off, and again he received that impression of a fierce and hungry grin.

"And yet we have now communicated with you," the dragon-man agreed. "You see, our queens are most displeased at the manner in which they are forced to sell their children into slavery. And they are aware that the guilds buy us primarily to be used as the Commander uses us—as security forces for exploration and trade vessels. Even with phase drive, a few ships are lost in every decade or so, of course, but we suspect

*that not all of them have been lost to, ah, natural
causes."*

"Ah?" *Sir George looked at the dragon-man with
sudden, deep intensity, and the alien's mental chuckle
rumbled deep in his brain.*

"Our queen programmed us *exactly as the Commander demanded when he bought us for this expedition," the dragon-man told him. "We must obey any
order he may give, and we may not attack or injure
our masters. But that is* all *we must do. We feel quite
certain that the Guild* also *wanted us programmed to*
protect *our masters at all times, but that wasn't the
way the Commander phrased their demands. Nor did
he demand that we be programmed so as to be unable
to watch* others *harm them without intervening. We
believe—hope!—that over the centuries some of our
kind have found ways to turn similar chinks in their
programming against their masters. Just as we now
hope to turn this against* our *masters."*

"Ah," *Sir George said again, and this time his voice
was dark and hungry.*

"Indeed. And that brings us to your *species, Sir
George. You see, your kind are unique in at least two
ways. Most importantly, in terms of our present needs,
your minds operate on a . . . frequency quite close to
our own. We realized that from the beginning, though
our masters did not ask us about it, and so we weren't
required to tell them. It is far from a perfect match,
of course, and to communicate with you as we are
doing required the linked efforts of several of our kind.
Nor could we do it while you were awake without
immediately alerting our masters. Simply establishing
the initial contact point rendered you unconscious for
twelve of your minutes, and we had not previously
dared risk causing such a thing to happen."*

"But now you have," *Sir George said flatly.*

"For two reasons," the dragon-man agreed. "One was that we were able to do so when neither the Commander, the Hathori, any other guildsmen, nor any of the ship's remotes were in position to observe it. Such a situation had never before arisen."

Sir George nodded slowly, and the dragon-man continued.

The second reason is that, for the first time, it may be possible for us to win our freedom from the Guild . . . if you will act with us." The alien raised a clawed hand as if he sensed the sudden, fierce surge of Sir George's emotions—as no doubt he had—and shook his head quickly. *"Do not leap too quickly, Sir George Wincaster! If we act, and fail, the Commander will not leave one of us alive. Not simply you and your soldiers, but your wives and children, will perish, as will all of our own kind aboard this ship."*

Sir George nodded again, feeling a cold shiver run down his spine, for the dragon-man was certainly correct. The thought of freedom, or even of the chance to at least strike back even once before he was killed, burned in his blood like poison, but behind that thought lay Matilda, and Edward, and the younger children . . .

"Before you decide, Sir George, there is one other thing you should know," the dragon-man said softly, breaking gently into his thoughts, and the baron looked up. There was a new flavor to the dragon-man's feelings, almost a compassionate one.

"And that thing is?" the human asked after a moment.

"We said that two things made your people unique," the dragon-man told him. *"One is our ability to make you hear our thoughts. The second is the terrible threat you represent to the Federation."*

"Threat? Us?" Sir George barked a laugh. "You say

your kind were far more advanced than ours, yet you were no threat to them!"

"No. But we are not like you. To the best of my knowledge, no other race has been like you in at least one regard."

"And that is?"

"The rate at which you learn new things," the dragon-man said simply. "The Commander's Guild regards you as primitives, and so you are . . . at the moment. But we have seen inside your minds, as the Commander cannot. You are ignorant and untaught, but you are far from stupid or simple, and you have reached your present state of development far, far sooner than any of the Federation's 'advanced' races could have."

"You must be wrong," Sir George argued. "The Commander has spoken to me of the Romans his competitors first bought from our world. My own knowledge of history is far from complete, yet even I know that we've lost the knowledge of things the men of those times once took for granted, and—"

"You've suffered a temporary setback as a culture," the dragon-man disagreed, *"and even that was only a local event, restricted to a single one of your continents. Do not forget—we were aboard this ship when the Commander carried out his initial survey of your world, and it is well for your species that he did not recognize what we did. Compared to any other race in the explored galaxy, you 'humans' have been—and are—advancing at a phenomenal rate. We believe that, from the point your kind had reached when you were taken by the Guild—"*

"How long?" It was Sir George's turn to interrupt, and even he was stunned by the sheer ferocity of his own question. "How long has it been?" he demanded harshly.

"Some six hundred and sixty of your years, approximately," the dragon-man told him, and Sir George stared at him in shock. He'd known, intellectually, that he'd slept away long, endless years in the service of his masters, but this—!

"Are . . . are you certain?" he asked finally.

"There is some margin for error. We are not trained in the mathematics to allow properly for the relativistic effects of the phase drive—" not even the dragon-man could make the dimly sensed concepts that went with that terminology comprehensible to Sir George "—and the guildsmen do not share such information with us. But they do speak among themselves in front of us, and they frequently forget—in their arrogance—that while we cannot speak as they do, we can hear. Indeed, that our kind has been forced to learn to understand spoken languages so that we can be ordered about by our 'betters.'"

"I . . . see," Sir George said, then shook himself. "But you were saying . . . ?"

"I was saying that even after so brief a period as that, we would estimate that your kind has certainly advanced at least to steam power and electrical generation by now. It is even possible you have developed the earliest forms of radio communication and atmospheric flight. But even if you have come only so far as inefficient steam engines and, perhaps, effective artillery and small arms, you will have advanced at more than double the rate of any of the so-called 'advanced' members of the Federation. If you are left alone for only a very little longer—perhaps another four or five of your centuries—you will have discovered the phase drive for yourselves."

"We will have?" Sir George blinked in astonishment at the thought.

"That is our belief. And it is also what makes your

species so dangerous to the Federation. Compared to any human institution, the Federation is immensely old and stable—which is another way of saying 'static'— and possessed of an ironbound bureaucracy and customary usages. By its own rules and precedents, it must admit your world as a co-equal member if you have developed phase drive independently. Yet your kind will be a terribly disruptive influence on the other races' dearly beloved stability. By your very nature, you will soon outstrip all of them technologically, making them inferior to you . . . and so, by their own measure, justifying your people in using them as they have used us. Even worse—though we think they will be slower to recognize this—your race, assuming that you and your fellows are representative—will not take well to the pyramid of power the Federation has built. Within a very short period of time, whether by direct intervention or simply by example, you will have led dozens of other species to rebel against the 'advanced races,' and so destroyed forever the foundation upon which their power and wealth—and comfortable arrogance—depends."

"You expect a great deal from a single world of 'primitives,' my friend."

"Yes, we do. But should the Federation, or another guild, learn that you, too, are from Earth and return there too soon, it will never happen. They will recognize the threat this time, for they will have a better basis for comparison . . . and will probably be considerably more intelligent and observant than the Commander. They can hardly be less, *at any rate!"* The mental snort of contempt was unmistakable, and Sir George grinned wryly. *"But if they do recognize it, they will take steps to deflect the threat. They may settle for establishing a 'protectorate' over you, as they did with us, but you represent a much more serious threat*

*than we did, for we did not share your flexibility. We
believe it is far more likely that they will simply order
your race destroyed, once and for all."*

Sir George grunted as if he had just been punched
in the belly. For a long, seemingly endless moment, his
mind simply refused to grapple with the idea. But
however long it seemed, it was only a moment, for Sir
George never knowingly lied to himself. Besides, the
concept differed only in scale from what he'd already
deduced the Commander would do if his violation of
the Council's decrees became public knowledge.

"What . . . what can we do about it?" he asked.

"About your home world, nothing," the dragon-man
replied in a tone of gentle but firm compassion. "We
can only hope the Federation is as lethargic as usual
and gives your people time to develop their own
defenses. Yet there is something you may do to protect your species, as opposed to your world."

"What?" Sir George shook himself. "What do you
mean? You just said—"

"We said we could not protect your home world. But
if your kind and ours, working together, could seize
this ship, it is more than ample to transport all of us
to a habitable world so far from the normal trade
routes that it would not be found for centuries, or even
longer. We here aboard this ship are unable to reproduce our kind but, as you, we have received the longevity treatments. You have not only received those
treatments but are capable of reproducing, and the
medical capabilities of the ship would provide the
support needed to avoid the consequences of genetic
drift or associated problems. Moreover, the ship itself
is designed to last for centuries of hard service. It
would provide a nice initial home for both of our races,
as well as a very advanced starting point for our own
technology. With human inventiveness to back it up,*

no more than a century or two would be required to
establish a second home world for your kind. One that
would certainly *provide the threat we have projected*
that your original home world may *someday pose."*

"And why should you care about that?" Sir George
demanded.

"For two reasons," the dragon-man replied imper-
turbably. "First, there would be our own freedom. We
would, of course, quickly find ourselves a tiny minor-
ity on a world full of humans, but at least we would
be freed from our slavery. And, we believe, we would
have earned for ourselves a position of equality and
respect among you.

"But the second reason is even more compelling. If
we are correct about the impact your species will have
upon the Federation, then you offer the best—perhaps
the only—chance our home world will ever have to win
its freedom."

"Ummm . . ." Sir George gazed at the other, his
thoughts racing, and then he nodded—slowly, at first,
but with rapidly increasing vigor. If the dragon-man
was telling the truth (and Sir George felt certain that
he was), all he had just said made perfect sense. But—

"Even assuming that all you say is true, what can
we possibly do?"

"We have already told you that we believe we have
a chance—a slim one, but a chance—to gain our freedom. If we succeed in that, then all else follows."

"And how can we hope to succeed?"

"Assume that you English had free access to the
ship's interior and to your weapons," the dragon-man
replied somewhat obliquely. "Could you take it from
its crew?"

"Hm?" Sir George rubbed his beard, then nodded.
"Aye, we could do that," he said flatly. "Assuming we
could move freely about the ship, at least. Even its

*largest corridors and compartments aren't so large as
to prevent swords—or bows—from reaching anyone in
them quickly. Of course, our losses might be heavy,
especially if the crew would have access to weapons
like your fire-throwers."*

"They would," the dragon-man said grimly. "Worse,
they might very well have access to us, as well."

"What do you mean?"

"We told you that we have been conditioned to obey
orders. As it happens, the Commander personally
purchased us for this mission, and his demand was that
we obey him. He may have intended that to apply to
his entire crew, but that was not the way he phrased
himself. Even if he realized that at the time, however,
we believe he has long since forgotten, since we have
always been careful to obey any order any guildsman
gave us. By the same token, we were never conditioned
not to attack the Hathori, who are no more guildsmen
or proper crewmen than you or we. The Hathori,
unfortunately, truly are almost as stupid and brutish
as the Commander believes. Whatever happens, they
will fight for the Guild like loyal hounds . . . but as you
have seen on the field of battle, they are no match for
you Englishmen with hand-to-hand weapons. And they
are certainly no match for our own energy weapons."

The sense of a smile in every way worthy of a true
dragon was stronger than ever, and Sir George laughed
out loud. But then the dragon-man sobered.

"Yet all of this hinges upon what happens to the
Commander at the very outset. If he should have the
opportunity—and recognize the need—to order us to
crush you, we would obey. We would have no choice,
and afterward, our deeper programming would prevent
us from attacking any surviving guildsmen."

"I see." Sir George regarded the dragon-man
thoughtfully. "On the other hand, Sir Dragon, I doubt

that you would have spent so long explaining so much if you had not already considered how best to deal with those possibilities."

"We have. The key is the Commander. He wears the device which controls the force fields which keep your people sealed outside the core hull of the ship on a chain about his neck." Sir George nodded, recalling the gleaming pendant the Commander always bore with him. "That is the master control, designed to override any opposing commands and open any hatch or force field for whoever possesses it. The programming can be altered from the control deck, assuming one has the proper access codes, but the process would take hours. By the time it could be completed, the battle would be over one way or the other."

"So we must find some way to capture or kill the Commander as the first step," Sir George mused. The dragon-man nodded, and the baron shrugged. "Well, that seems to add little extra difficulty to an already impossible task."

"True," the dragon-man agreed gravely, yet a flicker of humor danced in his voice, and Sir George grinned crookedly.

"So how do we capture or kill him?"

" 'We' do not," the dragon-man replied. "You do."

"Somehow I had already guessed that," Sir George said dryly. "But you still haven't explained how."

"It has to do with his weapons-suit," the dragon-man said, and ran his own clawed hand over the red-and-blue garment he wore. "He has great faith in its protective capabilities, and under most circumstances, that faith would probably be justified. Alas!" Another, hungry mental grin. "Certain threats are so primitive, so unlikely to ever face any civilized being from an advanced race, that, well—"

Again that very human shrug, and this time Sir George began to grin in equal anticipation.

In the event, it proved far simpler to become allies than for their alliance to carry out the dragon-men's plan. The basic strategy was almost breathtaking in its simplicity and audacity, but Sir George lacked the secret means of communication the dragon-men shared among themselves.

His newfound allies confirmed his own suspicion that the Commander and his fellows were able to eavesdrop on virtually any human conversation. Fortunately, after so long the crewmen responsible for monitoring those conversations—who shared the Commander's arrogant contempt for all "primitive" races to the full—had become overconfident, bored, and lax. They paid only cursory attention to their duties, and it had been many years since they'd reexamined the patterns in which they'd placed their mechanical spies. Worse, they had even more contempt, in many ways, for the dragon-men than for the humans. Absolutely confident in their subservience, and with no suspicion that it was even physically possible for dragon to communicate with human, the guildsmen made no effort to conceal the placement of their spies from their bodyguards.

All of which meant that if Sir George was very careful, it was possible to speak to his subordinates in places where the Guild could not overhear him. But those conversations must be very brief, lest the watchers note that he had abruptly begun spending a suspicious amount of time in the "dead zones" not covered by their spies.

And it was difficult, Sir George soon discovered, to plan a desperate rebellion, even with men who'd known and served with one for decades, when that planning could be carried out only in bits and pieces. Especially when the entire plan had to be completed and in place in no more than twelve days.

Matilda came first, of course. He'd feared that she would believe his dream had been just that—only a dream—and he could hardly have blamed her. After all, *he* had more than half-believed it one when he awoke. But she only gazed deeply and intently into his eyes as they stood in a small hollow beside the river, temporarily safe from eavesdroppers. Then she nodded.

"I understand, my love," she said simply. "Who shall we tell first?"

Matilda's belief made things much simpler. All of Sir George's officers had long since come to recognize her as his closest advisor and confidante, as well as his wife. They weren't precisely accustomed to receiving orders directly from her, for she had always been careful to remain in the background, but they neither felt surprised nor questioned her when she *did* inform them that she spoke for her husband.

With her assistance, Sir George found it relatively simple to inform those most necessary to working out and executing the plan. Father Timothy was crucial, not least because the Commander had accepted his role as a spiritual counselor. The demon-jester might scoff at "primitive superstition," but clearly he had thought better of attempting to interfere with it. Sir George suspected that the Commander actively encouraged the faith among his human slaves in the belief that it kept them more pliable, but that was perfectly acceptable to the baron, for Father Timothy's pastoral duties gave him an excellent excuse to be out and about among them. His ability to speak to any human without arousing suspicion, coupled with the imprimatur of his moral and religious authority in the eyes of those to whom he spoke, made him of enormous value as a plotter.

Rolf Grayhame was the next most important member of the cabal. The burly archer went paper-white when Sir George first broached the subject, for, despite his hatred for the Commander, Grayhame—more than any other among the English, perhaps—had had the lesson of the guildsmen's inviolability driven into his head. Indeed, Sir George had done a great deal of the driving himself, for it had seemed far more likely that the archers might decide they could reach the Commander than that one of the knights or men-at-arms who must somehow come within arm's reach might decide the same thing.

But despite his initial shock, Grayhame recovered quickly, and his smile was ferret-fierce—and hungry—when Sir George explained his part in the plan.

"Said it was the only reward I really wanted, now didn't I, My Lord?" the archer demanded, his voice little more than a harsh, whispered mutter despite Sir George's assurance that no spies were placed to hear or see them at the moment. "Can't say the notion of relying so much on the dragon-men will make me sleep sound of nights, but for the rest—*pah*!" He spat on the ground. "I'll take my chances, My Lord. Oh, aye, *indeed* will I take my chances!"

Sir Richard Maynton completed the uppermost tier of the conspiracy, and, in some ways, his was the hardest task of all. Grayhame needed to enlist only a dozen or so of his men; Maynton's task was to prepare *all* of their men, archers and men-at-arms alike, for the brutal hand-to-hand combat certain to rage within the hull of the ship. And he had to do it in a way which would not warn the Commander. Which meant he also had to do it without actually warning any more than a tiny handful of his own subordinates.

In many ways, that was the aspect of the plan which most disturbed Sir George. He felt more than a little guilty for involving not simply his men but their families and children in a mutiny which could end only in victory or death without even warning them, yet he had no choice. Once he and the dragons had established communications, the aliens "spoke" with him every night while he seemed to sleep dreamlessly beside his wife, and each of those conversations served only to reinforce the baron's own earlier conclusions about the Commander. Whatever happened to Earth, and however much the Commander might praise Sir George and his men, the time was virtually certain to arise when the English would become a potential embarrassment for the Commander's Guild . . . and when that happened, they would all die.

And so Sir George and his officers made their plans and prayed for success.

"Good afternoon, Commander," Sir George said courteously as the demon-jester's air car floated to a stop at the meticulously laid out lists and the vehicle's domed top retracted.

"Good afternoon," the Commander piped back. He pushed up out of his comfortable, form-fitting seat to stand upright in the air car, and Sir George held his breath. The Commander had approved the plan the baron had presented for their demonstration, but there was always the possibility that he might change his mind at the last moment. Now the demon-jester glanced around for another long moment, studying the tall rows of seats the English had erected for the local not-men's chieftains. The "seats" were actually little more than long, bare poles, but they served the three-legged aliens well enough, and the chieftains sat with barbarian impassivity. It was, of course, impossible to read their mood from their expressions, but their total motionlessness suggested a great deal to Sir George.

The Commander gazed at them without comment, but Sir George could almost taste the demon-jester's satisfaction. He had eagerly embraced the baron's suggestion that they might also organize a joust and melee to follow the archery competition and demonstrate the advantages which the Englishmen's armor bestowed upon them in close combat, as well. The fact that organizing the melee meant that Maynton and Sir George, the leaders of the competing sides, would each have a small but fully armed and armored force under his immediate command, clearly had not occurred to the demon-jester. Of course, the implications hadn't occurred to most of the Englishmen, either . . . but a handpicked few among them knew precisely what their commanders intended.

"You have done well," the Commander said now, and Sir George smiled broadly as the alien stepped out of the air car at last.

"Thank you, Commander. It's always easier to over-awe a foe into surrender than to defeat him in the field."

"So I also believe," the Commander agreed, and started up the wooden stairs to the special box the English had built for him. It was rare, though not completely unheard of, for him to leave his air car in the field. But this time there was a difference. Before, Sir George had never known that his invisible barriers—the force fields, as the dragon-men described them—protected him from all physical contact only aboard the ship or within the confines of the air car. Now, thanks to the dragon-men, he did know, and his smile grew still broader as the Commander ascended to his place.

His personal escort of six dragon-men followed with no more sign of expression or excitement than they had ever shown, and Sir George's smile faded as he gazed upon them. They remained as alien, as unearthly—in every sense of the word—as ever to his eye, but he no longer knew them by eye alone. Truth to tell, the subtler internal differences between them and humans were almost more alien than their outer appearances, yet those differences now struck him as intriguing, almost exciting, rather than grotesque or repellent. The joint sense of existence which always led them to use "we" or "us" rather than "I" or "me" in communication, the calm with which they accepted their own inability to reproduce or their inevitable separation from the ongoing growth and change of their own race, the manner in which they accepted contact—and other-induced change or constraint—at the very deepest level of their beings . . . all of those things were truly and utterly alien to Sir George. But they were not threatening. They were not . . . evil. Whatever the dragons' outer shape and form, Sir George had decided, however different their perceptions and methods of communication, and despite the fact they could never father or bear children, they were as much "men" in every important sense of the word as any Englishman he had ever met.

Indeed, far more so than most, for the six dragons "guarding" the Commander went knowingly and willingly to their own deaths as they followed the Commander up the steps to his box.

Neither Matilda nor Father Timothy had cared at all for that portion of the plan. Grayhame had been unhappy with it, but had grasped its necessity, while Maynton had objected only mildly, as if because he knew it was expected. Sir George suspected that was largely because the other knight had a limited imagination. Despite all else that had happened, only Sir George had ever actually "spoken" with the dragons. The others were willing to take his word for what had happened because for over fifty years he had never lied to them, never abused their trust in him, but they had not themselves "heard" the dragons speak. And because Maynton had never heard them, they remained less than human to him. He continued to regard them, in many ways, as Sir George continued to regard the Hathori: as roughly human-shaped animals which, however clever or well-trained, remained animals.

But they were not animals, and Sir George knew he would never be able to see them as such again, for it had been they who insisted that their fellows with the Commander must die.

Their logic was as simple as it was brutal. If the Commander could be enticed out of his air car and taken alive, he could be compelled to order the remainder of his crew to surrender. Like so much else of the vaunted Federation, the Guild's hierarchical command structure was iron bound. If their superior officer ordered them to surrender, the other guildsmen would obey . . . and the Commander, for all his readiness to expend his English slaves or slaughter the inhabitants of "primitive" planets possessed nothing remotely resembling the human—or dragon—quality of courage. With a blade pressed to his throat, he would yield.

But to get close enough to apply that blade had required, first, a way to get him out from behind his air car's force fields and, second, that someone get within arm's reach. The fashion in which Sir George had structured the "demonstration" for the local chieftains had accomplished the former, but no one could accomplish the latter until the Commander's guards— Hathori and dragon alike—were neutralized. The Hathori would defend him no matter what; the dragons would have no choice but to do the same if they were commanded to, and no one could doubt that such a command would be given if they did not spring forward on their own immediately.

Neither Sir George nor his senior officers were particularly concerned about the Hathori. Not in the open field, at least. They had seen the bulge-eyed wart-faces in action, and were confident of their ability to destroy them with longbow fire or swarm them under quickly here. Once aboard ship, in the narrow confines of its corridors and chambers, it would be another matter, unless they could win their way into its interior before the Hathori could be armed and armored by the guildsmen.

The dragons and their "energy weapons" were another matter entirely, and they had been relentless in their conversations with Sir George. It was entirely possible that the Commander's personal guards would be able to cut a way at least as far as the air car with their personal weapons, especially if the Hathori kept the English busy, and once he was behind his force fields and once again invulnerable, the Commander would be ruthless in destroying any and all possible threats. Which meant, the dragons insisted, that no chances could be taken. Capturing the Commander alive was the one move they could be certain would succeed; at the very best, any other gambit would almost certainly cost the English far heavier casualties by requiring them to fight their way into the ship. For those reasons, the Commander's personal guards must die, and they had hammered away at that point until Sir George was forced to promise to accept their plan. Which didn't mean he liked it.

Now he watched the Commander reach his position on the canopied platform. The demon-jester crossed to the thronelike chair constructed especially for him, and Sir George could almost taste the thick-bodied little creature's satisfaction as he gazed down at all about him. The elevation of his position, establishing his authority over the chieftains he had summoned here, had been a major part of the baron's argument for the arrangement of the stands, and Sir George smiled a much harder, hungrier smile as he watched the Commander bask in his superiority to the despised primitives clustered about his feet in all their abject inferiority.

The Commander gazed down at Sir George for another moment, then nodded regally for the demonstration to begin, and Sir George, in turn, nodded to Rolf Grayhame.

The archery captain barked an order, and two dozen archers, helmets and metalwork brightly polished for the occasion, garments washed and bright with color, marched briskly to the firing line. Sir George had longed to call for a larger number of them, but he'd concluded that he dared not. Twenty-four was more than sufficient to provide the demonstration the Commander desired. To ask for more bows to be issued might have aroused suspicion, or at least caution, and the Commander might have decided to remain safely in his air car after all.

The archers stopped in formation and quickly and smoothly bent and strung their bows, and the Commander, like the gathered chieftains, turned to gaze at the targets just over a hundred yards down range. Most of those targets were shaped like humans, but some among them were also shaped like natives of this world, and all were "protected" only by the large wicker shields the natives used in battle. The sort of shields longbow arrows would pierce as effortlessly as awls.

Grayhame barked another order, and twenty-four archers nocked arrows and raised their bows.

"Draw!" Grayhame shouted, and twenty-four bowstaves bent as one.

"*Loose!*" the captain bellowed . . . and twenty-four

archers turned on their heels, and twenty-four bow-strings snapped as one. Two dozen arrows flew through the bright sunlight of an alien world, glittering like long, lethal hornets and crashed into their targets with devastating force.

Eighteen of those arrows carried deadly, needle-pointed pile heads. At such short range they could pierce even plate, and they smashed into the Hathori on the Commander's raised dais like hammers. Five bounced harmlessly aside, defeated by the angle and the Hathori's armor; thirteen did not, and all but two of the bulge-eyed aliens went down. Not all of those felled were dead, but all were out of action at least for the moment.

And so were the two who were unwounded, for the remaining six arrows had done their own lethal work. Every one of them had slammed home in the Commander's body, and the brilliant red garment which would have shrugged aside fire from the dragons' terrifying "energy weapons" was no help at all against clothyard shafts at a range of under ten yards. They drove clean through the creature's body, spraying bright orange blood, and then deep into the back of the Commander's thronelike chair.

The demon-jester never even screamed—couldn't even tumble from the chair to which the arrows had nailed it—and the two surviving Hathori gaped at their master's feathered corpse in shock. That shock seemed to hold them forever, although it could not actually have been more than the briefest span of seconds, but then they turned as one, raising their axes as they charged the nearest humans.

They never reached their targets. The archers were already nocking fresh arrows while the handful of knights and men-at-arms who had known what was to happen charged forward, but many of the men—and women—who hadn't had the least idea what was planned were in the way. As surprised as the Hathori themselves and completely unarmed, all they could do was flee, and their bodies blocked the archers' shot at the surviving Hathori.

But it didn't matter. The Hathori had moved no more than two strides when half a dozen lightning bolts literally tore them apart.

The air was full of human shouts and screams of consternation and shock as the enormity of what had just happened smashed home, and the alien chieftains had vaulted from their places and disappeared with commendable quickness of mind. Sir George had watched them vanish, and now he made a mental note to keep an eye out for their return, in case they should sense an opportunity to strike at all the hated off-worlders while those invaders fought among themselves. But almost all of his attention was focused elsewhere, and he charged up the stairs towards the Commander's body. Maynton and three other picked knights accompanied him, helping to drive through the confusion, and his own sword was in his hand by the time he bounded onto the platform. It wasn't needed—the dragons had already dispatched the wounded Hathori with ruthless efficiency—and he leaned forward to jerk the bright, faceted pendant from around the neck of the corpse. He held the precious device in his hand, his heart flaming with exultation as he gazed down at it, and then something touched his armored shoulder.

He spun quickly, only to relax as he found himself gazing up into the eyes of one of the dragons. The towering alien regarded him for several long seconds and then waved at the carnage about them, pointed to the dead Commander, and cocked his head in unmistakable question. The baron followed the gesturing hand with his eyes, then looked back up at his huge, alien ally, and grinned fiercely.

"Your folk may have been willing enough to die, Sir Dragon—aye, and brave enough to do it, as well! But it is not the English way to murder our own, and with this—" he raised the pendant "—we'll not need that piece of meat to take his precious ship, now will we? And with us to hunt the guildsmen, and your folk to hunt Hathori, well—"

His grin bared his teeth as he and the mute dragon stood eye to eye, and then, slowly, the dragon showed its own deadly looking fangs in a hungry grin of its own and it gave a very human nod.

"Then let's be about it, my friend!" Sir George invited, reaching up to clap the huge alien on the back, and the two of them started down the platform stairs together.

LAMBS TO THE SLAUGHTER

David Drake

A trumpet called, giving the go-ahead to a detachment leaving by one of the other gates of the Harbor. Half of Froggie's bored troopers looked up; a few even hopped to their feet.

The century's band of local females roused, clucking like a hen-coop at dinner time and grasping the poles of the handcarts holding the troopers' noncombat gear. Slats, the six-limbed administrator who Froggie was escorting out to some barb village the gods knew where, clambered into his palanquin and ordered his bearers to lift him.

"Everybody sit down and wait for orders!" Froggie said in a voice that boomed through the chatter. "Which will come from me, Sedulus, so you can get your ass back into line. When I want you to lead the advance, I'll tell you."

That'd be some time after Hermes came down and

announced Sedulus was the son of Jupiter, Froggie guessed.

Three days after Froggie was born, his father had lifted him before the door of their hut in the Alban Hills and announced that the infant, Marcus Vibius Taena, was his legitimate son and heir. He'd been nicknamed Ranunculus, Froggie, the day the training centurion heard him bellow cadence the first time. Froggie's what he'd been since then; that or Top, after he'd been promoted to command the Third Century of the Fourth Cohort in one of the legions Crassus had taken east to conquer Parthia.

Froggie'd continued in that rank when the Parthians sold their Roman prisoners to a man in a blue suit, who wasn't a man as it turned out. A very long time ago, *that* was.

The girls subsided, cackling merrily. Queenie, the chief girl, called something to the others that Froggie didn't catch. They laughed even harder.

The barbarians in this place were pinkish and had knees that bent the wrong way. They grew little ruffs of down at their waists and throat, and the males had top-knots of real feathers that they spent hours primping.

Froggie's men didn't have much to do with the male barbs, except to slaughter enough of them the day after the legion landed that the bottom lands flooded from the dam of bodies in the river. As for the girls—they weren't built like real women, but the troopers had gotten used to field expedients; and anyway, the girls were close enough.

"Don't worry, boys," Froggie added mildly. "We'll get there as soon as we need to."

And maybe a little sooner than that. Froggie didn't understand this operation, and experience had left him with a bad feeling about things he didn't understand.

Commanding the Third of the Fourth didn't give

Froggie much in the way of bragging rights in the legion, but he'd never cared about that. Superior officers knew that Froggie's century could be depended on to get the job done; the human officers did, at least. If any of the blue-suits, the Commanders, bothered to think about it, they knew as well.

Froggie's men could be sure that their centurion wasn't going to volunteer them for anything, not even guard duty on a whore house, because there was always going to be a catch in it. And if the century wound up in the shit anyway, Froggie'd get them out of it if there was any way in Hell to do that. He'd always managed before.

The howl of the Commander's air chariot rose, then drummed toward the gate. Froggie stood, using his vinewood swagger stick as a cane.

"*Now* you can get your thumbs out, troopers!" he said in a roar they could hear inside the huge metal ship that the legion had arrived on. Froggie was short and squat—shorter than any but a handful of the fifty-seven troopers in his century—but his voice would have been loud in a man twice his size.

The troopers fell in with the skill of long practice; their grunts and curses were part of the operation. Men butted their javelins and lifted themselves like codgers leaning on a staff, or else they held their heavy shields out at arm's length to balance the weight of their armored bodies as their knees straightened.

They wore their cuirasses. They'd march carrying their shields on their left shoulders, though they'd sling their helmets rather than wear them. Marching all day in a helmet gave the most experienced veteran a throbbing headache and cut off about half the sounds around him besides.

Froggie remembered the day the legion had marched in battle order, under a desert sun and a

constant rain of Parthian arrows. They all remembered
that. All the survivors.

Besides his sword and dagger, each trooper carried
a pair of javelins meant for throwing. Their points were
steel, but the slim neck of each shaft was soft iron that
bent when it hit and kept the other fellow from pulling it out and maybe throwing it back at you. After
you hurled your javelins it was work for the sword, and
Froggie's troopers were better at that than anybody
who'd faced them so far.

Slats stood on his two legs with his four arms crossed
behind his back. He'd travelled in the same ship as the
legion for the past good while. Slats wasn't a Commander any more than Froggie was, but he seemed
to have a bit of rank with his own people. Like all the
civilians who had to deal with the barbs, Slats wore a
lavaliere that turned the gabble from his own triangular mouth into words the person he was talking to
could understand.

"The bug's been around a while, right?" murmured
Glabrio, a file-closer who could've had more rank if
he'd been willing to take it. Though Slats looked a lot
like a big grasshopper, he had bones inside his limbs
the same as a man did.

"Yeah, Slats was in charge of billeting three campaigns ago," Froggie said. "He's all right. He'd jump
if a fly buzzed him, but seems to know his business."

Glabrio laughed without bitterness. "That's more'n
you could say about some Commanders we've had,
right?" he said.

"Starting with Crassus," Froggie agreed.

Froggie'd stopped trying to get his mind around the
whole of the past; time went on too far now. Little bits
of memory still stuck up like rocks in a cold green sea.
One of those memories was Crassus, red-faced with
the effort of squeezing into his gilded cuirass, telling

the Parthian envoys that he'd explain the cause of the war at the same time as he dictated terms in the Parthian capital.

The Commander's flying chariot came over a range of buildings. The guards in the gate tower here, a squad from the Ninth Cohort, leaned over the battlements to watch. One of them made a joke and the others laughed. Glad they weren't going, Froggie guessed.

The Harbor, the Commander's city across the river from what had been the barb capital, had started as a Roman palisade thrown up half a mile out from the huge metal ship from which the legion had landed. The open area had immediately begun to fill with housing for civilians: those from the metal ship and also for barbs quick to take allegiance with the new masters whom Roman swords had imposed.

Glabrio must've been thinking the same thing Froggie was, because he eyed the barbs thronging the streets and said, "If anybody'd asked me, I'd have waited till I was damned sure the fighting was over before I let any of the birds this side of my walls. The men, I mean. They strut around like so many banty roosters."

"Next time I'm having dinner with the Commander," Froggie said sourly, "I'll mention it to him."

The flying chariot settled majestically onto the space left open for it beside the gate. Froggie felt the hair on the back of his arms rise as it always did when the machines landed or took off nearby. This was a big example of the breed. It carried the Commander and his driver; two of the Commander's huge, mace-wielding toad bodyguards; Pollio, the legion's trumpeter; and five of the male barbs who'd joined the Commander's entourage almost from the moment he'd strode into the palace still splashed with the orange blood of the barb king.

The top barb aide was named Three-Spire. Froggie had seen him before and would've been just as happy never to see him again.

The troopers clashed to attention. Froggie crossed his right arm over his cuirass in salute, sharply enough to make the hoops clatter.

"Sir!" he boomed. "Third Century of the Fourth Cohort, all present or accounted for!"

The Commander stood up, though he didn't bother to get out of his chariot. The barbs sharing the vehicle with him—all this Commander's aides were barbs, the first time Froggie remembered that happening— continued to talk among themselves.

"Very good, warrior," the Commander said. He wore a thin, tight suit that might have almost have been blue skin, but his face was pale behind the enclosing bubble of a helmet. His garb was protection of some sort, but he wouldn't need the huge bodyguards if he didn't fear weapons. "Don't let sloth degrade your unit while you're on this assignment. No doubt my Guild will have fighting for you in the future."

Even without using the chariot for a reviewing stand, the Commander would be taller than any trooper in the legion. Back in the days before Crassus, though, Froggie had seen Gauls who were even taller, as well as heavier-bodied than the blue-suited race.

The Commander turned to Slats and spoke again; this time the words that came from the lavaliere around the Commander's neck sounded like the squeak of twisted sinews: they were in Slats' language, not Latin or any other human tongue. The administrator spread his six limbs wide and waggled submissively, miming a bug flipped on its back.

Fixing Froggie with a pop-eyed glare that was probably meant to be stern—language could be translated; expressions couldn't—the Commander resumed, "Obey the orders of the administrator I've provided you with as though his orders were mine. You have your duty."

Three-Spire said something to the Commander. The barb wore one of the little translator plates and must have spoken in the Commander's own language, instead of speaking barb and letting the Commander's device translate it.

The Commander flicked his left arm to the side in his equivalent of a nod. "I'll be checking up on you," he added to Froggie. "Remember that!"

"Yes, sir!" Froggie boomed, his face impassive. "The Third of the Fourth never shirks its duty!"

Three-Spire looked at the girls with dawning comprehension; his topknot bristled with anger, bringing its three peaks into greater prominence. "You! Warrior!" he said. "Where's the leader of these females?"

"Hey, Queenie!" Froggie said—in Latin. He could've called the chief girl in a passable equivalent of her own language, but he didn't think it was the time or place to show off. The troopers didn't have lavalieres to translate for them, but they'd had a lot of experience getting ideas across to barbs. Especially female barbs.

Queenie obediently stepped forward, but Froggie could see that she was worried. Well, so was he.

"No, not a female!" Three-Spire said. The lavaliere wouldn't translate a snarl, but it wasn't hard to figure there should've been one. "I mean the male who's leading this contingent!"

The Commander looked from Queenie to his aide, apparently puzzled. He didn't slap Three-Spire down the way Froggie expected. Hercules! Froggie remembered one Commander who'd had his guards smash a centurion to a pulp for saying the ground of the chosen campsite was too soft to support tent poles. The legion had slept *on* its tents that night, because spread like tarpaulins the thick leather walls supported the troopers enough that they didn't sink into the muck in the constant rain.

"We take care of that ourself, citizen," Froggie said, more polite than he wanted to be. Something funny was going on here, and Froggie'd learned his first day in the army that you usually win if you bet "unusual" meant "bad."

"That's not permitted!" Three-Spire said. "Sawtooth here will accompany you."

He spoke to the barb beside him, then opened a bin that was part of the chariot and handed the fellow a lavaliere from it. Sawtooth walked toward the girls clustered around the carts. He didn't look any too pleased about the assignment.

"What's this barb mean 'not permitted'?" Glabrio said in a ragged whisper. "If he don't watch his tongue, he's going to lose it!"

"Take your own advice," Froggie said out of the side of his mouth. Loudly, facing the Commander, he said, "Yes, *sir!*" and saluted again. "Century, form marching order and await the command!"

The Commander blinked inner eyelids that worked sideways the way a snake's do. He spoke to Pollio, who obediently stood and raised his trumpet.

"You're going to take this from a barb?" Glabrio demanded.

Pollio blew the long attention call, then the three quick toots for Advance. He looked past the tube of his instrument at his fellow troopers, his eyes troubled.

"March!" Froggie called. The century was too small a unit to have a proper standard to tilt forward, so Froggie swept his swagger stick toward the open gateway instead. To Glabrio, in a voice that could scarcely be heard over the crash of boots and equipment, he added, "For a while, sure. Look what Crassus bought by getting hasty, trooper."

✧   ✧   ✧

Before his Third Squad was out of the gate, Froggie heard the chariot lift with a frying-bacon sizzle. A moment later he saw it fly over the palisade, heading for the next gate south where the Fifth of the Fourth waited to escort another administrator out into the sticks. Pollio looked down at the troops; none of the others aboard the vehicle bothered to.

Froggie stepped out of line, letting Lucky Castus of the first squad lead. Sunlight winked on the battle monument which the legion had set up outside the main gate of the Harbor: a pillar of rough-cut stonework, with captured armor set in niches around it and a barb war chariot filled with royal standards on top.

The barbs used brass rather than bronze for their helmets and the facings of their wicker shields. Polished brass shone like an array of gold, but verdigris had turned this equipment to poisonous green in the three months since the battle.

A lot of things had gone bad in the past three months. Froggie'd be glad to get out of this place. If it could be done alive.

The girls came through the gate, pushing the carts. Froggie'd heard Sawtooth shouting, "March! March! March!" for as long as the Commander's chariot was visible, but the barb was silent now.

Queenie saw Froggie watching. She twitched the point of her shoulder in Sawtooth's direction. Froggie smiled and moved his open hand in a short arc as though he were smoothing dirt.

That was a barb gesture. For men with damage to the spine or brain that even the Commanders' machines couldn't repair, the legion continued the Roman practice of cremating corpses. The barbs here buried their dead in the ground.

Slats came through the gate after the last cart,

swinging in his palanquin. His four girls handled the weight all right, but they didn't seem to have much sparkle. Well, that'd change when they started eating army rations along with the century's girls.

As soon as Slats saw Froggie, he desperately beckoned the Roman to him. Froggie didn't care for anybody calling him like a dog, but there wasn't much option this time. As clumsy as Slats was, he'd probably break his neck if he tried to climb out of the palanquin hastily. Froggie sauntered over and walked beside the vehicle. That wasn't hard; the carts were setting the pace.

"Centurion Vibius," the administrator said, "I'm pleased to see you. I have studied your record. There is no unit whose escort on this expedition I would prefer to yours."

Froggie thought about that for a moment. You'd rarely go wrong to assume whatever your officers told you was a lie . . . but Slats wasn't exactly an officer. Also, Froggie'd gotten the impression back when Slats was billeting officer that his race of bugs couldn't tell lies any better than they could fly.

"If we're going to be stuck in the middle of nowhere for however long," the centurion said, "then you may as well learn to call me Froggie. And I'm not sorry we're with you, Slats, if we've got to be out here at all."

Pollio's trumpet called again, ordering Postumius and his boys into the back of beyond. Three centuries from each cohort, half the strength of the legion, had been sent off these past two days on individual escort missions.

"Exactly!" said Slats. He spoke through his mouth— not every race serving the Commanders did—but he had three jaw plates, not two, and he looked more like a lamprey talking than he did anything Froggie wanted to watch. "*If* we have to be here. What do you think of the expedition, Centurion Froggie?"

Froggie thought it was the worst idea he'd heard since Crassus marched into Parthia with no guides and no clue, but he wasn't going to say that to *any*damnbody. Aloud he said, "I would've thought that maybe waiting till this place was officially pacified so you guys could move in your burning weapons and so forth . . . that that might be a good idea."

The First Squad with Glabrio in front was entering the forest. It niggled Froggie that he wasn't up with them, though he knew how sharp Glabrio's eyes were. The file-closer had served as the unofficial unit scout ever since Froggie got to know him.

"Exactly!" Slats repeated. "It is extremely dangerous to treat the planet as pacified when it is *not* pacified. What if the Anroklaatschi—"

The barbs; Froggie never bothered to learn what barbs called themself. Most times you couldn't pronounce it anyway.

"—attack the Harbor in force as they attacked when we landed? They could sweep right over the few troops remaining, could they not?"

Froggie thought about the question. The barbs came riding to battle on chariots. One fellow with only a kinked sword drove while two warriors with long spears and full armor stood in the back. The driver held the "horses" behind the lines while his betters stomped forward in no better order than a flock of sheep wearing brass.

The barbs had gotten a real surprise when—instead of spending half the afternoon shouting challenges— the legion had advanced on the double, launched javelins, and then waded in for the real butcher's work with swords. That surprise couldn't be repeated, but so long as whoever was in command of the understrength legion kept his head . . .

"Some folks' swordarms are going to be real tired by the time it's over," Froggie said judiciously, "but I guess they'd come through all right."

The smooth-barked trees in this place were tall, some of them up to two hundred feet. The branches came off in rows slanting up the trunks to end in sprays of tassels like willow whips instead of proper leaves.

Froggie hadn't seen real trees since he'd marched into Mesopotamia. He'd seen a date palm there and wondered what he was doing in a place so strange. He'd been right to worry.

Slats and the Commander called this place a planet, just like the Commanders did every place they took the legion to. The only thing "planet" meant to Froggie was the stars that he used to watch move slowly across the sky while he tended sheep before he enlisted. Hercules! but he wished he was back in the Sabine Hills now.

"Well, all right, the Harbor may hold," Slats said peevishly, "but what about you and I, Centurion Froggie? What chance do we have if the Anroklaatschi attack?"

"Well, Slats . . ." Froggie said. "That depends on a lot of things. I'd just as soon it didn't happen, but me and the boys'll see what can be done if it does."

Froggie and the palanquin reached the shade of the forest. This wasn't a proper road but it was a lot more than an animal track. Two and generally three men could march abreast, though their outside knees and elbows brushed low growth which looked like starbursts from a peglike stem.

Tassels closed all but slivers of the sky overhead, and the trunks cut off sight of the Harbor. Froggie knew the Commander had ways to see through trees or even solid rock, but he still relaxed a little to have the feeling of privacy.

"I'm wondering . . ." Slats said. He spoke softly and seemed to be afraid to meet Froggie's eyes. "I'm wondering if perhaps the Commander is sending us and the others out to give him warning if the Anroklaatschi are planning an attack? They would hit us first, and of course I would call a warning to the Harbor."

He waggled a little rod that Froggie had taken for a writing stylus.

Froggie sighed. "Well, I tell you, Slats," he said. "A long time ago I gave up expecting what officers did to make a lot of sense. But I gotta say, as a plan that'd *really* be a bad one. He's weakening his base too much."

"Nothing about this planet makes sense!" Slats burst out. "None of the products are of real value to the Guild. Oh, in the long term, certainly—but nothing worth the loss of warrior slaves as valuable as you are, Roman. And to lose my life as well over this wretched planet! Oh, what a tragedy!"

"I can see you'd feel that way about it," Froggie said. "Well, you worry about your business, Slats, and me and the boys'll worry about ours."

He stepped aside and let the column tramp on by him. He'd see how Verruca, his number two, was making out at the end of the line; then he'd go up with Glabrio again where he belonged.

It didn't make Froggie feel good that the administrator was just as worried about this business as he was, but sometimes it's nice to know that you can trust your instincts *even* when they're telling you you're stepping into a pool of hog manure.

After all, you had to trust something.

Froggie looked at the sun, a hand's-breadth past zenith. He thought the days here were about the same length as those in Italy—that wasn't true a lot of places the legion had been—but home was too long ago for him to be sure.

A few big trees sprang from the protection of a limestone outcrop, but only saplings grew in the rest of the broad floodplain. At the moment the river was well within its channel.

"Queenie!" Froggie said. The chief girl, older than the others by a ways, didn't actually push one of the carts. She trotted over to him. "River there—much water come down? Quick quick happen?"

Half his words were Latin, most of the rest were in Queenie's chirps or as close as Froggie could come to the sounds. Trooper pidgin had bits and pieces of other tongues, too, some of them going back to the Pahlevi the legions had picked up marching into Parthia.

Queenie glanced at the river, using Froggie's gestures as much as his words to figure out what he was asking. Some troopers had a knack for jawing with barbs. Froggie didn't, but he could make out. It wasn't like they were going to be talking philosophy, after all.

"No way, boss-man!" Queenie said. "Sky get cold first, then get warm, then *hoosh!* sweep all shit downstream. Long time, boss-man."

Then, hopefully, "We camp here?"

"We camp here," Froggie agreed. The century had already halted and the men were watching him; it wasn't like they were recruits who couldn't figure out what was going to happen next.

"Fall out!" Froggie said. "First and Third Squads provide security, Second digs posts every twelve feet—" for a marching camp there was no need to set every timber of the palisade in the ground, the way you'd do for a more permanent structure "—and the rest of you start cutting timber. I want this complete before sunset, and I *don't* mean last light."

Verruca and Blasus already had the T-staff and measuring cord out. Any of the troopers could survey a simple camp by now, and with the right tools Blasus could've set an aqueduct.

He'd never have occasion to do that, of course. The Guild didn't use the legion for that kind of work. Well, Blasus was a good man to have at your side with a sword, too.

Troopers unlimbered axes, saws and shovels from the leading cart. The first job was to remove trees from the campsite, but they'd need to clear a wider area to complete the palisade. There wasn't a high likelihood that the barbs would try anything, but—

"Hey, Froggie!" Galerius called. "You know it's a waste of time to fort up in the middle of a nowhere like this. Ain't the blisters on our feet enough for today that we got to blister our hands, too?"

"Yeah, Froggie," Laena said. "Give it a rest for tonight, why don't you? We all know you're boss—you don't got to prove it."

There was a chorus of agreement, though Froggie was glad to notice the grumblers continued to pick up their tools. "You're damned right I don't have to prove it!" Froggie said. "And if you don't start working your shovel instead of your tongue, Laena, you're going to have four shifts of night watch on top of the post-holing!"

"By Hercules!" Laena said as he strode toward the line the surveyors were laying out. "One of these days I'll get some rank myself so I can stand and watch other guys sweat!"

It was the same thing every halt, whether they were operating as the whole legion or in detachments like now: the centurions ordered the troopers to fortify the camp and the troopers complained. *Every* damned time!

And the troopers went ahead and fortified the camp anyway, with palisades, turf walls, drystone, or even fascines of spiky brush. Whatever there was that'd make a wall, that's what the legion used.

The troopers didn't obey because they were afraid of Froggie. Oh, he was tough enough—but Froggie'd seen Laena strangle a barb half again his own size in a place where the grass grew to the height of a small tree.

They obeyed, Laena and the rest, because they knew Froggie was right: that one of these nights they'd bed down in a spot just as empty as this one, and the walls Froggie had forced them to build would be the difference between seeing the dawn and having barbs cut all their throats. But they'd still complain and fight the orders, just like Froggie had before he got promoted.

The girls were starting cookfires and getting ration packs out of the third cart. The barbs here used wooden pistons to light wads of dry moss, quicker and at least as easy as striking sparks off steel with a flint. Queenie'd called something to Slats' porters, who obediently put him down.

The barb aide, Sawtooth, trotted over to Froggie. "You, warrior!" he said, his words coming out of the translator on his chest. "Why are we stopping?"

Glabrio put a hand on his swordhilt. Froggie waved him to calm down and walked over where Slats was cautiously stepping out of his vehicle. Sawtooth continued to jabber, but Froggie ignored him.

"Slats, this is a good place to set up," Froggie said. "When we get out of this bottom the trees'll be too big for us to build a stockade with the manpower we got. Besides, I don't want to work the girls too hard. This is a damned poor road for carts."

"Do not be concerned for the females," Sawtooth said. His barb chattering was an overtone to the accentless Latin coming out of the lavaliere. "We must push on till dark. Then we will reach Kascanschi by tomorrow!"

"Another thing, Slats," Froggie said without turning to look at the aide. "I wish you'd tell that barb who got wished on us that all he has to do to live a long, happy life is to keep his mouth shut and let me forget he's around. If he can't do that, then there's going to be a problem and he ain't going to like the way it gets solved."

"What?" said Sawtooth. "What do you mean? Three-Spire gave me complete authority over the females!"

"But Centurion Froggie . . . ?" Slats said. The translated words were without inflection, but the way the bug flicked his middle arms to the side indicated puzzlement. "Sawtooth has a translator. He has heard your words directly."

"No fooling?" said Froggie. He turned and tapped the barb's nose with his left index finger. Sawtooth yipped and jumped backward. "Well, I hope he was listening. I hate trouble."

"All right," Froggie ordered. "One man from each squad stands wall guard, and the rest of you are dismissed for dinner. Squad leaders, set up a roster for the night watches."

The stockade wasn't fancy—you could stick your arm between posts in a lot of places—but it'd slow down a barb attack in the unlikely event that there was one. Froggie eyed it with approval. His boys hadn't forgotten how to work during the past three months in the Harbor.

The tents were up. Normally there'd have been six big ones holding a squad apiece, plus a pair of little bell tents with Slats in one and the other for Froggie and Verruca together. Slats still was separate, but

Froggie'd traded the other little one for three more squad tents. He and Verruca would bunk down with the men—that was a better idea anyway, when you were out in the back of beyond with only a century— and the girls didn't have to make their own shelters.

One tent was for the unattached girls; the rest bunked with the soldiers they'd paired off with. If you wanted privacy you shouldn't have joined the army, but the extra tents provided a little elbow room when otherwise things would've been pretty crowded.

Froggie wondered where Sawtooth thought he was going to sleep. The question didn't concern him; he just wondered.

Because he wasn't especially hungry, Froggie paused for a moment on the low fighting step that let the troopers look over the top of the six-foot palisade. Glabrio walked over to him.

"The tree tassels are going yellow," Glabrio said. "They were dirty blue when we landed, do you remember?"

Froggie shrugged. "You think it's turning Fall?" he said. "I sure haven't noticed it getting colder."

The sky still looked bright, but the cookfires illuminated circles of ground. The green wood gave off clouds of smoke that looked oily but didn't smell too bad. Girls dipped stew into troopers' messkits, then sat beside them on split-log benches to share the food.

There was a lot of laughter. Froggie didn't like this operation one bit, but even he had to admit that it felt good to get away from the Harbor and the eyes of hundreds of bureaucrats.

Slats watched them from across the encampment, his upper and middle arms twitching to separate rhythms. Froggie nodded toward the administrator. To Glabrio he murmured, "The poor bastard's probably lonely. This can't be a picnic for him either."

There was a high, clucking scream. Sawtooth burst into the circle around the First Squad's cookfire and began to shriek at Queenie. Froggie sighed and strode over to the commotion. He'd been as clear as he could be, but some people—and some barbs—just wouldn't listen.

"What's the problem?" Froggie demanded, not shouting but making sure that Sawtooth and Queenie both would hear him over their gabble. He couldn't make out a word of it, they were talking so quick and angry.

"These sluts were proposing to eat meat!" the barb aide shouted, through the lavaliere now because he was speaking to Froggie. "They have no right to meat!"

"Is everything all right, Centurion Froggie?" Slats demanded nervously. He barely poked his head around the edge of one of the tents where he was hiding from the threat of violence.

"All's fine, Slats," Froggie called. Because Froggie was on top of things, the troopers kept a bit back. They were all steaming, though, and more than one man had his hand on his swordhilt.

"Look, buddy," Froggie said to the barb aide. "I decide who eats what here. The girls do better work with a little sausage in their mush, and—"

"They are not breeders!" Sawtooth shouted. He struck the mess tin out of Queenie's hand, spraying the savory brown stew across the ground in an arc. "I will not permit them to eat meat!"

"Top?" said Glabrio. He was standing right behind the barb.

"Yeah," said Froggie, "but you have to clean it up."

"What do you—" Sawtooth said. Glabrio grabbed his topknot with his left hand and pulled the barb's head back.

Most troopers used their daggers for the odds and

ends of life in the field: trimming leather for bootsoles, picking a stone out of a draft animal's hoof, that sort of thing. Glabrio often carried only the dagger when he went scouting and didn't want the weight and clatter of full equipment. He kept a working edge on one side of the blade, but the other was honed to where he could slice sunbeams with it.

It was the sharp edge that he dragged across Sawtooth's throat, cutting through to the spine. The barb's blood was coppery in the firelight.

Glabrio twisted and flung Sawtooth on the ground behind him to finish thrashing. Bending, he wiped the daggerblade on the barb's kilt. Over his shoulder he asked, "Is the river all right, Froggie?"

"Dis, no! the river's not all right!" Froggie said. "I want him buried deep enough nobody's going to find him till we've shipped out of this place. I want the ground smooth so you don't see there's a grave there, too!"

Glabrio stood and sheathed his dagger with a clack of the guard against the lip of the tin scabbard. "Sounds good to me, Froggie," he said.

Froggie grimaced. "Caepio and Messus," he said to the pair of men nearest, both of them members of the First Squad. "Get your shovels out and give him a hand."

Queenie stepped over to Froggie and held his hands as she touched cheeks, the right one and then the left. That was what the barbs did instead of kiss; they didn't really have lips, just a layer of skin over their mouth bones.

"You great boss-man!" she said. "We proud we be in your flock!"

Froggie patted her. "Hey, Marcellus!" he said to the guard from the Fourth Squad who was watching the excitement. "All of you who've got the duty—you think the barbs are going to pop up out of the campfires? Turn your heads around or you'll find 'em decorating somebody's lodgepole!"

Glabrio chose a patch of ground without many roots and started breaking it with his mattock; the rest of the squad was getting its tools out, not just the two troopers who'd been told off for the job. That was more people than you needed to dig a hole, but they were making a point that Froggie could appreciate.

Slats had vanished. Very slowly, he raised his triangular face around the edge of the tent again. Froggie smiled, raised his hands to show that they were empty, and walked over so he could talk to the administrator without shouting. Slats trembled, but he didn't run screaming toward the back gate the way Froggie half expected him to do.

"I was . . ." Slats said. "I . . ."

The bug turned his head around so that he was looking over his left shoulder, then repeated the gesture in the other direction. As if that had been his way of clearing his throat, he resumed, "Centurion Froggie, was that action necessary?"

"Yeah," Froggie said, "it was. Or anyway, it was going to be necessary before long. I figured it was better to take care of it out here where there wasn't anybody to watch. Right?"

"Hey, Top?" Glabrio called. "What about this?"

He held up Sawtooth's lavaliere, dangling on the tip of his finger. It winked in the firelight, except where tacky blood covered the metal.

"Hercules, bury it with him!" Froggie said. "If the barb deserted, he wasn't going to give us his gadget first, was he?"

He turned to the administrator again. "How about it, Slats?" he said. He didn't touch his swordhilt or do anything that might be taken as threatening; the poor bug was set to shake himself apart already. "Do you agree?"

"Centurion Froggie," Slats said finally, "I trust you to keep us all safe if it is possible to be safe. But the next time, the next time . . ."

He did his spin-your-head-around-twice trick again.

"The next time, Centurion Froggie, please warn me so that I know not to be watching!"

Tatius and Laena were talking in low voices at the corner where their guard posts met. They heard the crunch of Froggie's boots and moved apart, each down his own stretch of palisade. Froggie didn't mind the guards chatting on duty if it didn't get out of hand.

Which it wouldn't, so long as Froggie made a pass around the posts once or twice each night. He didn't even have to speak.

A couple—or maybe it was a pair of the girls—sat in the shelter of the carts and shared a mug of something. Guild rations were pretty good, but the troopers had learned to supplement them from whatever was available locally. The wine here was first-rate, though the barbs made it from a root that looked like a beet.

The fires had burned down. Slats' tent was leather like all the rest, but the cold light that the Guild bureaucrats used leaked out the seams and underneath the tent walls. It didn't look like the administrator was going to make trouble over the business this evening. Froggie knew there'd been a risk in killing Sawtooth, but Hercules! he just couldn't feel in his heart that one barb more or less made a difference.

"Hey, boss-man!" Queenie called in a fluting whisper from the tower protecting the front gate. "Come up, we talk-talk."

Froggie looked at the night sky. He missed having a moon. In all the places the legion had been, there'd only been half a dozen where the moon was as big and bright as it ought to be. There was no moon at all here.

"Yeah, sure," Froggie said. He wriggled the pole that served as a ladder, making sure it was solid, then climbed. They'd trimmed a young tree, leaving stubs of branches on alternating sides for steps. The sap of the trees here dried hard and as smooth as glass.

Calling a platform with a waist-high parapet "the gate tower" was bragging a bit, but this was a damned impressive marching camp for a single century to lay out. The Third of the Fourth would survive this business if anybody could.

Of course, they might be in for nothing but a short march and a few days of boredom. Froggie'd been a soldier too long to complain about being bored. There was lots worse that happened.

"This bad shit, boss-man," Queenie said as she offered Froggie a skin of wine. "We watch out or we get chopped, right?"

"You can break your neck stepping off the curb, Queenie," Froggie said. Hercules, did *everybody* think they were all marching off a cliff? He squirted a stream of wine into his mouth like he was milking a ewe.

The girls and the troopers had gotten together pretty quick after the legion stood down from the battle; within a few hours, mostly. A lot of them were widows and orphans, but not by any means all. Females turned to strength as sure as the sun rises in the east; and when the legion was in town, strength spoke Latin.

Queenie spat over the parapet. She said, "Three-Spire a—" Froggie didn't catch the word, but she mimed squishing something against the platform. "A little bug, you know? He nasty bug serving king, he same-same nasty bug now. You chop him like you chop Sawtooth, boss-man?"

Froggie shrugged and passed the wine back. "No

chance, Queenie," he said. "King boss-man, the blue guy, him love Three-Spire. Me just little boss-man."

Queenie patted him. "You find way, boss-man. You find way."

Far off in the night an animal gave a long, rising shriek. It wasn't a cry of pain because nothing that hurt so much could live to finish the call.

"New girls virgin," Queenie said unexpectedly. "Feed 'em up meat, they be ready in one day, two day. Want me save them for you, boss-man?"

"What?" said Froggie. Frowning, he took the offered wine and drank deeply. "Oh, Slats' porters, you mean. So it's the meat that warms 'em up, huh?"

He hadn't known that, but he'd seen that the girls on army rations had a lot more life in them than those eating mush in labor teams bossed by male barbs. Sometimes he wondered—he always wondered, every place they went where there were girls—what happened when the legion pulled out for the next campaign. Froggie'd met a cute little Armenian girl in Samosata while Crassus was getting ready to march east. . . .

Froggie sighed. "Naw, me no care, Queenie," he said.

Queenie finished the wine and clucked contentedly. She turned and fixed Froggie with eyes larger than a human's and perfectly round. "You no want me, boss-man?" she said. "Queenie too old?"

Froggie thought about it, then reached for the girl. "Naw, Queenie first rate," he said.

After all, with what they were getting into, he didn't know how many more chances he'd be getting.

"What do you think of Kascanschi, Centurion Froggie?" Slats asked. He'd climbed out of his palanquin as soon as they came into sight of the walls.

"I've seen worse towns," Froggie replied. "It'll do, I guess."

The village was a whole lot bigger than Froggie'd figured. If the barbs lived as tight together as they did in the old capital, there must be nigh onto three thousand of them here. They weren't all warriors, and a lot of what warriors there'd been had probably joined their king for the battle. Most of *those* had been feeding the eels for the past three months.

It was still a damned big place for one century to garrison.

The troops remained in marching order, but everybody wore his helmet with the crest mounted. Froggie's crest was transverse and twice as wide as those of the common troopers. Originally they'd been made of bleached horsehair. These most recent replacements weren't from a horse's tail—Froggie hadn't seen a real horse since Parthia—but they did the job.

The village gates were hung from towers made of irregularly shaped stones mortared together. A mound with a timber stockade on top surrounded the rest of the village. The posts were thicker than those of the troopers' marching camps, but the wall wasn't in good repair.

"It looks very strong, Centurion Froggie," Slats said. "Does it not?"

Froggie snorted. "Give us two hours to build a siege shed and we'll bore through that sorry excuse for a wall in another ten minutes," he said.

That was bragging; it'd take a bit longer. Though if wet rot had eaten the posts as bad as it just might have done . . .

After the battle in the bow of the river, the barb king had escaped inside the thick stone walls of his capital. It had taken the legion just two days to undermine them, replace the pilings with props of dry timber, and then set the timbers ablaze. The barbs ran around like a stirred-up anthill when smoke started coming out of the ground, but even then they didn't seem to realize that the walls were going to collapse into a fiery pit along with everybody who was on the battlements at the time.

The Fourth Cohort was the lead unit through the breach. The barbs were too stunned by the disaster to put up much of a fight, but the troopers still had to kill like a plague to show what'd happen anytime the barbs didn't do just what the Guild said. The muscles of Froggie's right shoulder still twinged at the thought of how he'd lifted his sword again and again and again.

The gates of Kascanschi were open. From inside, barbs clacked the flat blocks of wood they used instead of trumpets. A procession of males came out: the six village elders, like enough, and a section of forty soldiers. Froggie felt his muscles tighten, but he hoped nothing showed on his face.

Slats stepped forward and started jawing the village chief, using his lavaliere. Glabrio edged toward Froggie and slid his shield out of the way so he could whisper. He saw it too. Dis, they all did, they were all veterans.

And so were the soldiers who'd just come through the gates.

They weren't big. One by one they were shorter than the warriors the legion had slaughtered three months before. These troops didn't *move* one by one, though: they moved like a team, like disciplined soldiers, and that was all the difference between being sheep and being the butcher.

"They're a funny color pink," Glabrio said. "And look, they got axes instead of spears."

The knives Froggie had seen previously in this place

were of brittle iron that he wouldn't have used for a plow coulter back in Latium. These short-hafted axes had blades of real steel, and the iron-strapped wooden bucklers were a lot solider than the brass-faced wicker that the royal army had died with.

Slats returned to Froggie. "The chief bids us welcome," he said. Because of the translator, it was hard to tell if Slats was as worried about the situation as he ought to be. "They've prepared housing for us in the village temple, the big building just inside the gate."

Froggie looked around instead of immediately answering Slats or giving the troops an order. For most of the past mile they'd been marching between fields of broad-leafed root vegetables, each growing in a little mound of compost. The area for nearly a bowshot outside the walls wasn't planted. At one time it must have been cleared for defensive purposes, but for at least a decade it'd grown up in brush.

"Glabrio," Froggie said, "you come with me. The rest of you wait for orders."

Slapping his swagger stick into his left palm, he strode through the gate with Glabrio at his side. Queenie trotted along two paces behind, which was fine. Slats rotated his head in desperation, then scuttled after Froggie like a nervous cockroach.

Four of the barb axemen came too, which was no more than Froggie expected. Close up, the pink of their skins had a lot more blue and less red than the village elders did. They looked tough and no mistake.

"That's the temple, huh?" Froggie said, eyeing the structure. It was impressive, all right: sixty feet at least to the top of the main spire. Ten or a dozen lesser peaks sprang from other parts of the wooden roof. The walls were built up from staves, not heavy timbers, and every finger's breadth of the pieces had been carved with the images of plants and animals before they were pegged together.

"According to my briefing cube . . ." Slats said, facing Froggie very deliberately so that he could pretend that the four funny-looking barbs weren't standing close holding their axes. " . . . the chiefs are also priests just as the king is the high priest. This would be the chief's residence as well as the temple."

The temple's lines were all up and down, but it covered a fair stretch of ground besides. There'd be room for the century to fit inside even if the height wasn't divided into several floors.

"It looks impressive, doesn't it?" Slats said nervously.

"It looks like a bloody firetrap!" said Glabrio, who'd come from Sicily a long time ago. "I'd sooner bunk in Etna than there!"

"Right," said Froggie. "Slats, we're not going to billet inside the walls, but it won't be any problem—"

"Company coming!" Verruca called from the other side of the gate. "The bluebird's returning to our happy meadows."

"Seems the Commander's paying us a visit, Slats," Froggie said. "What do you suppose he's got in mind?"

"If he were ordering us home," Slats said in obvious disquiet, "he would call me instead of coming out here. It must be a tour of inspection."

Froggie walked out and caught the wink of sunset on metal as the Commander's chariot came over the eastern horizon. When the sun's angle was just right, the light twisted as though Froggie were seeing the vehicle through the clear water of a pond.

Usually when barbs saw a flying chariot for the first time, they threw themselves face-down and prayed— the ones who didn't run off screaming. The village elders looked scared, no mistake, but the axemen stood rock solid. In fact when the chief turned like he planned to run, the guard with gold wristlets—the others wore black—caught him and faced him around with a firm grip. It made you wonder who was really in charge of things.

The flying chariot hissed to the ground alongside where Slats had spoken to the village chief. The vehicle was the same one that had seen the century out of the Harbor, but the only ones aboard were the driver, the Commander and his two bodyguards, and Three-Spire.

"Is he sick?" Glabrio whispered. The Commander had a glassy expression and didn't move when the chariot landed.

My guess'd be drunk, Froggie thought, but he didn't let those words or any touch his lips.

While the Commander remained in his comatose half-sprawl, Three-Spire stood in the chariot and spoke to the village chief. The elders bent their heads back in a gesture of submission.

Their posture reminded Froggie of Sawtooth's last moments, so he was smiling when Three-Spire turned and spoke to Slats. The administrator replied and, to Froggie, said, "Three-Spire says we are to enter our assigned quarters at once and dismiss the porters. Sawtooth will lead them back to the Harbor, Three-Spire says. He speaks with the authority of the Commander, who is indisposed. Three-Spire says."

"I guess you'll want to assure the Commander that you'll inform your escort and other interested parties," Froggie said. This wasn't the perfect time to explain where Sawtooth was at, but Froggie wouldn't have gotten as old as he was if he counted on perfection. "We'll find a way to deal with the girls ourselves in the absence of Sawtooth."

"What?" said Three-Spire, his translator croaking in Latin. He hopped out of the chariot and stepped so close to Froggie that the centurion had to look up if he wanted to see anything above the barb's neckline. "Where is Sawtooth? He should be—"

Changing tack in the middle of the question, Three-Spire cawed a demand at Queenie. Before she could speak—not that Froggie was worried about Queenie forgetting the story they'd worked out together—Froggie said, "Sawtooth went off last night with one of the girls, citizen. The others tell me he'd been feeding her meat from army rations."

That set the barb back like Froggie'd caught him at throat level with a shield-rim—an image which'd been going through Froggie's mind, sure enough. "Sawtooth did that?" Three-Spire said.

This time Queenie answered, speaking slowly enough that Froggie caught the word for disgrace. She even squatted down and raised her hips, the way the girls here did to honor a man.

Three-Spire's translator shot a question at Slats. The administrator answered just as smooth and polite as he would've the Commander. *Speaking* of Blue-Suit, he'd stuck a finger in his mouth and was rolling it around like a pestle in a handmill.

The aide bobbed his head, indicating a complete lack of understanding. To Froggie he said, "Well, the females must return on their own, then. They won't need food—it's a short journey since they no longer have burdens."

"Ah . . ." said Froggie. It griped his soul to have to treat this barb like he was real people, but whatever was going on was deeper waters than Froggie was ready to swim in yet. "I guess the girls can stay with us. We'll need cooks and, and washing done, so—"

Three-Spire's crest twitched, sticking straight up and then spreading out like a drop of water splashing on bone-dry ground. Instead of talking to Froggie, he turned and flung another load of gabble at Slats through the lavaliere. Slats twice tried to reply, but the barb snarled him down before he got out more than a few clicking words. When Three-Spire finally finished, he glared at Froggie.

Slats spread his limbs in acceptance. Very carefully he said to Froggie, "Three-Spire, speaking in the Commander's name, says that the females cannot remain within Kascanschi because they are not of this tribe. He says that would cause offense—"

The administrator flicked his middle limbs out minusculely.

"—although my briefing cube failed to note this cultural peculiarity. Furthermore, Three-Spire rejects my suggestion that we could camp outside the walls as we did on the way here. That would be a rejection of the villagers' hospitality that again would give offense, Three-Spire says. Speaking for the Commander."

In Latin Three-Spire said, "The Commander wishes to inform you that if you do not carry out his orders at once, his terrible weapons will burn all you warriors to ash for mutiny. To ash!"

"I see," Froggie said. He looked over his troopers. Verruca had lined them up five squads abreast with the carts behind them and the Sixth Squad acting as a rear guard and reserve. "Century, mount up! We'll be billeted in that big-ass building right inside the gates until we hear different. By squads, march!"

In truth Froggie didn't see very much, but at least he knew for sure where he stood. He'd met plenty of Three-Spire's type, politicians who always landed on their feet. By now all of that sort had been weeded out of the legion. No matter how well you sucked up to the high command, in a battle there was a lot of stuff happening. Sometimes javelins flew from a funny direction.

Glabrio joined his fellows as they clashed off on their left feet. He gave Froggie a hard glance from beneath the brim of his helmet.

The Commander had slumped down onto the chariot's floor. The bodyguards remained stolidly motionless but the driver was peering over his seat-back at the Commander, her scaly hide turning mauve in concern.

The Guild had long ago made sure the legion knew about those weapons that could find a man wherever he hid and burn him alive through solid rock. It was interesting that a barb aide knew about them, though. Froggie wasn't about to bet that those weapons wouldn't be used on him and his boys, even though the Commander didn't look in much shape to give orders.

"Slats," Froggie said aloud, "please inform our Commander that I hear him talking."

Some things translate, others—with luck—don't. Nodding to Three-Spire, Froggie turned and strode into the village behind his last squad.

The temple or whatever was built even stranger on the inside, but it was comfortable enough if you avoided thinking of it as the setup for the world's biggest funeral pyre. You could look up to the open sky from the central court. At the back of the ground floor was a sanctum set off by heavy doors; inside was a black stone on a plinth. At six levels above the ground were rooms for sleeping and storage, reached by stairs that snaked up both sides of the walls.

Froggie was overseeing the squad that stowed the century's gear when one of the pair of guards at the entrance called, "Hey Top? The bug wants to come in."

"Well, let him in, Calamus," Froggie said with a touch of irritation in his tone. He strode toward the door, his feet drumming thump/*squeal* on floor timbers. "He's our commanding officer, remember."

"Right, Froggie," a trooper called from halfway up the open staircase. "And I'm Venus rising from the seafoam!"

Froggie really hadn't meant Slats when he said not to let any but their own people into the billets even if that meant putting twelve inches of steel through a few of them. He'd damned well meant it about the barbs, though. He guessed he ought to be glad Slats wasn't the sort who'd try to push through a door when a guard stopped him.

Slats entered, his middle limbs quivering. "Centurion Froggie," he said, "the village chief says—"

He turned, apparently expecting to see the barb following him. Instead, the guards had locked their shields across the entrance. The chief jumped back like he'd stepped on a hot griddle, but the four axemen who tagged along might have been inclined to try something.

Calamus and Baldy both had their swords drawn; door-guard was no job for javelins. The barb soldiers backed away, looking angry but not afraid.

"Slats, tell the barbs that this building is now Guild territory," Froggie said. "Tell them that any attempt to enter it while we're billeted here is an attack on the Guild, to which we'll respond with all necessary force."

"Well, really, Centurion Froggie," the administrator said. "I don't think—"

"Tell them!" Froggie said.

Slats spread his limbs, then clicked to the barbs through his translator. The chief twisted his throat back. His bodyguards' faces didn't change a bit, but Froggie figured those boys had understood the deal before they were told.

Slats turned to Froggie. He went into his submissive posture again and said, "The chief informs me that your men are constructing a camp outside the walls. The Commander—we must accept that it was the Commander speaking—was explicit that you warriors and I live within Kascanschi. *Please*, Centurion Froggie!"

"Sirmius?" Froggie called to the squad leader. Poor Slats was scared enough to turn into a pile of the little green pellets he shit. "Finish up here. I'm going to take our leader on a tour of the make-work I've got the other squads doing."

He put his arm around the administrator and walked him into the evening. There were a lot of women and children in the town; they'd come out a few at a time and headed for the fields when they saw the century was settling into a routine that didn't include rape and slaughter. Now they were returning.

There weren't many males, though, except for the forty axemen who'd escorted the chief and elders. Those were keeping pretty much out of the way since they and the century had sized each other up. The four shepherding the chief in the wake of Froggie and Slats were the only ones in sight now.

"You see, sir," Froggie said to the administrator as they walked through the gate, "I've got to keep the men busy. You'll recall the Commander gave me specific orders about that when he sent us out. I've got the boys building a fort in this waste ground, just for the exercise. They've got a good start, wouldn't you say?"

"You're not going to live there?" Slats said in desperate hope. His triangular head moved back and forth in quick jerks, the way a human might have done with his eyes alone. "I thought . . ."

Froggie had left Verruca to deal with the fort because he was more worried about the way the temple had been constructed. The wall was well begun already. The ground cover here didn't bind the soil the way grass did, so the squads were trading off on the task of weaving brush into rough baskets to hold dirt.

This sort of construction would keep out prying eyes better than a stockade. Besides, when the troopers had time in a day or two to wet and tamp the soil, the result'd be as good as a turf wall.

The men had stripped off their helmets and body armor, but they still wore their sword belts. Four fully-equipped troopers guarded the gear of the others in the center of the rising fort. No point in taking chances.

"But the female barbarians?" Slats said. "They have remained, against the Commander's clear orders."

"Huh!" Froggie said. "I guess you're right. Who'd have thought it?"

Most of the girls were helping with the work, but a pair were coming back from the stream with buckets of water for the evening meal. They waved gaily to Froggie. Queenie came out from behind the barrier that protected the fort's gateway and walked over.

"But they must leave," Slats said in frightened animation. "You must order them to leave!"

"Oh, I did," Froggie said. He'd said the words to Queenie, true enough. He'd sooner not tell a lie if he could avoid it, and a long career in the army had taught him lots of ways to avoid it. "Maybe you should try yourself, Slats."

The administrator rotated his head toward the approaching girl. Froggie patted Slats on the back and said, "Go ahead. Maybe you'll have better luck."

And maybe pigs would fly. The troopers had seen stranger things since they'd been bought by the Guild.

Slats' translator blurted a demand that was so full of apologies you'd have thought he was talking to the Commander. Slats really didn't like saying things the listener might not want to hear.

"Go fuck tree, bug-man," Queenie said in cheerful pidgin. "We stay."

"I guess they can camp out in the fort," Froggie said. "Since it's built, after all."

"But—" said Slats. "They're supposed to go—"

The village chief spoke to Queenie. She'd known to be politic when Three-Spire was here with the Commander, but the local hick got out less than ten words when Queenie lit into him.

Queenie didn't kick the barb in the balls, but she did everything short of that. He bobbed and fluttered his arms up and down. Other girls called raucous support, and half a dozen of the nearest troopers rested their hands on their swordhilts as they smiled and watched.

Slats turned to Froggie. "She says—" he began.

Queenie whirled toward the centurion and administrator. "We no need him shitpot village!" she cried. "We stay out here, take care boss-man and great warriors like always!"

The village chief skittered back when Queenie let him go, but the captain of his guards caught him by the arm and pushed him forward again. Froggie stepped between the chief and Queenie.

"Slats," he said without looking around, "to make sure that none of the girls leave their quarters at night, I'm going to station an outpost here during the four watches."

"An outpost?" Slats said. Froggie could hear the administrator's limbs rubbing against the slick, copper-colored robe he wore.

"Just two men," Froggie said reassuringly. "Tell the chief that if he's got problems with Guild personnel and their slaves using waste ground outside his village, he'd better keep them to himself."

The administrator's lavaliere began chirping away in rapid barb. Froggie looked the head of the axemen in

"I'm going to go finish this business, Slats," Froggie said. "Want to come along?"

The administrator's body didn't move. His head swivelled, then swiveled back. "You are going to the dimensional portal," he said. "That is so?"

"That is so," Froggie said. Castus had his boys lined up. Caepio was using a broken javelin as a crutch. He'd have to stay, but they'd still be nine swords counting Froggie. That was plenty for the job.

"Yes, Centurion Froggie," Slats said. "I will come along. And we will finish the business!"

Glabrio led and Froggie was at the end of the line, since they were the two who knew the way. Froggie guessed the squad sounded like a drove of cattle—hobnails, shields clanking against cuirasses, and every couple of strides a man tripping on a root and swearing like a, well, a trooper. Slats said the folks inside the portal couldn't see or hear till it opened; that had better be true.

The administrator walked right in front of Froggie, making just as good time as the troopers. The bug's legs were plenty strong enough for his thin frame, and he seemed to see better than a man in this shadowed forest.

"We're getting close, now," Froggie said, as much to remind himself as to encourage Slats. Froggie'd come back mentally after the battle, but his body was still weaker than it'd been this morning. "It'll be right over the next rise."

Slats swivelled to look over his shoulders. He kept on walking and didn't stumble. Did he have eyes someplace besides the ones on the front of his face?

"I am still surprised that our rivals found it worth the expense of a dimensional portal," Slats said. "Though of course that is the only way they could carry out their regulation-breaking activities. The product must be of remarkable value."

"The Commander seems to think so," Froggie said. "If 'thinks' is the right word for the state he's in."

"Yes," Slats said. His words came eerily to Froggie's ears through the administrator's translator and directly to Froggie's mind, he guessed because of the lavaliere he'd taken from the barb. "The mercenary leader said the dose Three-Spire gives the Commander is a dangerously heavy one. It saps the user of all will, but our rivals were concerned that only slightly more would be fatal. The Commander's death would require a replacement and cause them problems."

Froggie caressed the hilt of his well-used sword. "They'll learn about problems," he said quietly.

Word came down the line over the shoulder of each trooper in turn. Froggie already knew what it was. "We've arrived, Slats," he said.

Lucky lined the squad up to face the spike of rock. Everybody had his sword drawn. Froggie took the key out of his pouch and handed it to the administrator.

"Open it when I tell you, Slats," he said. "Not before."

Now that the troopers' clattering equipment didn't mask it, the night was bright with animal sounds: chirps, peeps, and a *thoom, thoom,* that could almost have been a bullfrog sounding from a bog in the Sabine Hills. Froggie missed being able to wander around in the countryside at night the way he had as a kid . . . but Hercules! that was asking to get chopped in a place the legion had just conquered. Since the Guild bought him, Froggie was only going to see places just before or just after the legion had smashed the local king or chief or priestess.

"All right, boys," Froggie said. His breathing was

under control and his body ready now. His sword was the only one still sheathed. "When Glabrio and me was here before it was just a guy in a blue suit—he's not our Commander, don't worry—"

"Who was worried?" Glabrio muttered.

" . . . along with two bodyguards and that barb Three-Spire from the Harbor," Froggie continued. "These bodyguards look like monkeys, but they're big and they've got spiked gloves."

A trooper spit on the ground and grinned.

"There was two axemen besides from the town," Froggie added with a gesture back the direction they'd come, "but they won't be there this time."

"There may be messengers from the other locations, however," Slats said. "This same portal can serve many local sites. I would expect our rivals to keep in touch with all thirty locations to which detachments from your legion were sent."

Froggie shrugged. "Regardless," he said. "There's not room inside for more than maybe a dozen people, and they won't be expecting us. Glabrio and I lead in, then the rest of the squad by pairs till the job's done. Lucky, you watch our rear. There's the off chance that a few of the barbs got loose back at the town. They could be waiting for us to get focused on what's inside the cave before they weigh in."

"Pollux, Froggie!" Lucky said. "I ought to be in front with you. It's my squad!"

"Lucky," Froggie said, "if I thought you had anything to prove, you wouldn't be here. Now, carry out my orders or it *won't* be your squad."

Lucky nodded. "Sorry, Top," he said through tight lips.

Froggie drew his sword and walked close enough to the rock that he could touch it with the outstretched blade. He hefted his shield, making sure that the heavy oblong was balanced to swing or smash. A shield was a better weapon than a sword, often enough.

"All right, Slats," he said calmly. "Do it!"

Solid basalt dissolved into a cave. The vanishing rock gave Froggie an instant of vertigo: his mind told him he'd plunged over a cliff. He strode forward.

The Commander looked up angrily and said, "You're off your sched—"

His face blanked. He shrieked and dived behind his bodyguards.

Three-Spire was talking to the barbs behind the Commander. Two were axemen like the batch who'd been running things at Kascanschi, but the third was a real local with strings of quartz and coral beads woven through his topknot. He was taking a cake of tarry-looking stuff from the sack he held.

A guard drove a spiked fist at Froggie. Froggie raised his shield a hand's-breadth and twisted his body out of the line of impact.

It was like being punched by a battering ram. Froggie heard two boards of the outer lamination split; the shield's lower edge rocked up, using Froggie's grip as a fulcrum and absorbing the force of the blow. Froggie thrust at the ape's knee, feeling the thin armor over the joint separate an instant before gristle and spongy bone did.

The ape bellowed. He swung with his other fist but he was already toppling toward his crippled leg. The spike that brushed Froggie's helmet gouged through the bronze and even nicked the leather harness within.

Bald Lucius, a pace behind Froggie, stabbed for the ape's head. His blade sparkled into the upright of the helmet's T opening, grinding on teeth and then the creature's spine. Baldy put his right boot on the helmet and tugged his sword free with both hands.

Glabrio was down but twisting as he grappled with

the other guard. Two troopers stood over the pair, chopping at joints in the ape's backplate. Three more troopers had sprinted past that part of the melee to get at the mercenaries beyond. Velio blocked an axe with his shield as his two companions hacked at the barb from either side.

At Froggie's feet, the Commander tried to squirm around a console of translucent blue ice. Froggie grabbed him by the throat and pulled him upright.

"You cannot—" the Commander shrilled. Froggie punched his sword home, all the way to the hilt. He felt ribs grate, then a snap! and a shock that numbed his arm. He'd driven his point into the ice beyond.

The Commander's eyes rolled up. The blood that spewed from his mouth was as red as a man's.

Froggie couldn't grip his sword. Ice was boiling away from where the steel pierced it; the Commander's staring body toppled backward, no longer supported by the blade.

All the barbs were down. A trooper was helping Glabrio get out from under the bodyguard. The hilt of his dagger stuck from beneath the ape's chin like a hazelwood beard.

Everybody was all right, everybody who counted. Slats hopped over the litter of bodies with the bag the local—his head now sitting on the stump of his neck with a startled expression—had brought to show.

"Get out!" Slats screamed. "The wormhole generator has been damaged!"

Something had been damaged, sure enough. The ice into which Froggie'd pinned the Commander had burned completely away, and the hissing scar was spreading across the floor. Froggie grabbed a trooper's shoulder and jerked him toward the mouth of the cave.

"Go!" he said. He reached for another man, but they were all moving in the right direction, stumbling and cursing. Glabrio bent to pick up his shield but thought again and lunged through the opening instead.

There was a smell like the air gets sometimes just *before* a thunderbolt. Froggie stamped out of the cave with only Slats behind him. "Venus Mother of Men!" he said as the forest enfolded him, blissfully cooler than the place he'd just left.

Three-Spire, unhurt and unnoticed, sprang from the sizzling, sparking portal. "I will help you—" he cried.

Slats put his four hands on the ground and kicked with both feet. The barb aide toppled backward, into the cave again. His scream stopped while he was still in the air.

The walls of the cave vanished. It was like looking into the green depths of the sea. Three-Spire fell, his body shrinking but remaining visible even when it was smaller than a gnat glimpsed through an emerald lens.

Froggie blinked. The basalt spike was before him again. His right arm ached, and the night was alive with noises of the forest.

Nobody spoke for a moment. Lucky was bandaging Messus' left forearm; it was a bad cut, definitely a job for the medics from the Harbor.

Froggie rubbed his right wrist against his thigh, trying to work the feeling back into it. His shield was scrap, but he guessed he'd carry it to Kascanschi.

"We're done here," he said. "Let's get back to the damned town and Slats can call for help. It's safe to do that now."

"Top?" said Lucky. He glanced toward where the cave had been, then straightened his head very quickly. "Is there going to be trouble? Because of, you know, what happened?"

"No," said Slats forcefully. When they left the Harbor just a few days ago, Froggie wouldn't have believed the bug had the balls to do what he'd done—

any of the things he'd done—tonight. "The event will never be reported. Our rivals have lost their considerable investment when we destroyed the dimensional portal; they will fear severe sanctions in addition if the truth comes out. We will gain credit for discovering a product of unexpected value on this planet."

"Let's go," said Froggie, slinging what was left of his shield behind him. "I'll lead."

"*We'll* gain, you say," Glabrio muttered. "The Commander gains, you mean. Third of the Fourth don't get jack shit."

"You're alive, aren't you, Glabrio?" Froggie said as he stepped off on his left foot. "You'd bitch if they crucified you with golden nails!"

The squad swung into motion behind him. Over the noise of boots and equipment Slats said, "The first thing the Commander will gain is this satchel of prepared drug which I rescued before the portal collapsed. I will present it to him myself. I estimate there are three thousand euphoric doses in it. And one fatal dose, I suspect."

Froggie chuckled. He was looking forward to seeing Queenie. After a night like this, you needed to remind yourself you were alive.

Not that it'd been a bad night. Froggie thought again about the way his sword had slid through a blue suit and the ribs beneath it.

He chuckled again. In some ways this had been the best night of Froggie's life.

A CLEAR SIGNAL

Mark L. Van Name

One month to the day after Jim's execution, the aliens showed up at my gym. It was a Tuesday morning, and, as usual, R.C. and I had the place to ourselves. R.C. was in the far rear corner of the large free-weight room, methodically pumping his way through a warm-up set of hack squats. I had just finished my last set of bench presses and was sitting on the bench, trying to decide whether to add an extra chest exercise or call it a day. When the three aliens came through the gym's steel door without setting off any of the alarms, we both reached into our gym bags and kept our hands on our weapons, waiting to see what would happen.

The aliens were taller and more buglike than the way they looked in the pictures and video I'd seen, and their skin was more of a sky blue than I would have guessed. As they walked closer, their legs moving more like those of a mantis than a man, I could see the clear, skintight suits they wore, the necklaces I knew from the news were translators, and the gill-like atmosphere conversion slits in the clear hoods that fit them like kids' Halloween masks of dead presidents.

They moved as a group, in a triangle. R.C. stood, his hand still in his gym bag, and took one step closer to them. The rear one nearer to him turned its head to follow his progress, while the other rear one kept its eyes on me; clearly, the leader walked in front. I liked that; I respected the alien in front for the choice, and I was glad to have an easy target. The leader was a little larger than the others, probably edging toward a full seven feet tall and almost as wide as a thin man; hitting him should not be a problem if it came to that. All four of the leader's hands were obviously empty; disks the shape and thickness of bagels and the color of the morning ocean off Key West were equally obvious in all four hands of each of his bodyguards.

R.C. tilted his head at them and raised an eyebrow. I shook my head slightly; he'd know I wouldn't do it, and he'd also know that I would back his play if he felt it had to go that way. He pulled out his gun, and immediately a low buzzing filled the room as the air between the aliens and R.C. shimmered briefly. R.C. went down fast, all six and a half feet and 280 pounds of him collapsing as if the air had gone out of him.

My hand was just clear of my gym bag. I dropped the gun onto the towels in the bag and pulled my empty hand very slowly away. Going cold inside, I asked, "Will he be okay?"

"Yes," the leader replied. "He should awaken in approximately one hour and experience almost no discomfort." His voice was as good as it had sounded on TV, an announcer's voice, deep and rich. It lacked only emotion, but that lack made it disconcerting, almost threatening.

I let out the breath I hadn't realized I had been holding since I asked the question, and I leaned back against the racked bar. The metal plates on the bar clanged from the impact, and the aliens paused; I wondered if their translators were trying to make sense of the noise. "So what can I do for you guys? From what I've read I thought you were meeting only with government leaders. I thought you weren't allowed to mingle with the rest of us."

My question seemed to catch the leader off guard, and he paused and waved his lower left arm slightly. "Yes, we are restricted. We are here . . . without official approval. We are seeking Matthew Stark. You are he?"

"Yes."

"You must do something for us."

I looked at R.C.'s crumpled body and knew I shouldn't say it, but if I were any good anymore at taking orders I wouldn't have ended my five years with the gang at Langley with the company version of a dishonorable discharge. "Screw you. You bypass my alarms, waltz into my gym, mess up my workout, and zap my partner; I don't have to do anything for you."

"Yes, you do. We would not have risked the negotiations with your governments if we had been able to ascertain other possibilities. You must come with us, receive your instructions, and then execute them. No other option is acceptable."

The three of them had stopped only a few feet away, and all eight of the bodyguards' hands were now pointed at me. I could feel the anger welling in me even as I fought to control it. "Sure, there are other options. One is that you and your two friends turn around, walk your skinny blue asses out of my gym, and do whatever it is that you want me to do. Or you find somebody else to do it. Try one of those options.

I choose when I work, and I choose the people I work for, and I don't choose to work for you."

After a slight pause, the leader spread all four of its arms and said, "We did consider those options, but we do not believe either would lead to success. We cannot do what we need you to do. We have already tried and failed. We do not know of anyone else with your unique qualifications. And, time is increasingly precious."

"What exactly is it that you want me to do?"

"Locate James Peterson and return him to us."

I stood up without realizing I was going to do so. Eight disk-filled hands tilted and followed my movement. I felt the rush of emotions as my sadness and anger fought, then went cold as the anger took over completely. "I can save you idiots a lot of work. Jim's dead. He's been dead for a month. It was all over the news, the first execution in North Carolina in over three years."

"No. He is not. We . . . intervened and repaired him."

"That's crap. I read the stories on the execution, and the coroner pronounced him dead on the spot."

"Yes, by your standards, for a short time he was dead. Our medical facilities are much more advanced than yours, however, and we were able to repair him before he suffered any permanent neural damage. After we restored him, he was . . . working for us. But now he has escaped."

I didn't want to listen to any more. I had not particularly wanted the state to execute Jim. If anyone was to going to kill him, I should have done it, but I had had that chance and had chosen to let it go. The state's killing him would not bring him back to what he had been, and it sure wouldn't bring Louise back. In the end, though, I had made peace with the execution; he had brought it on himself. I didn't need my own special representatives from the first confirmed alien visitors to Earth coming into my gym and picking at that wound. "If you really did steal Jim's body and bring him back to life, he's your problem. I've been done with him since they arrested him five years ago. I'm going to shower. Get the hell out of my gym."

I turned and headed for the showers. A current like the shock from a wall outlet passed through my whole body, and as I passed out I heard the buzzing.

I met Jim the summer before ninth grade, in those uncomfortable months when we were stuck between schools, between the friends we had known and the ones we hoped to meet, between the old hat of middle school and the new adventure of upper school. I had always loved watching basketball but had never been any good at it, and I had always been too afraid of failing to be willing to pursue it. On the first Monday morning of that summer vacation I promised myself I would try basketball in earnest, and I walked the half mile to the nearby community center, where I knew pickup games were always available for those brave enough to join them.

The Woodlawn community center was a large old yellow stucco building that housed a surprisingly well-equipped weight room, a torn-up pool table, a trampoline, and one real wood-floored basketball court. The air conditioning couldn't keep up with the combination of the summer heat and the energy of all the kids in the place, but it did at least manage to make the inside temperature stay well below that of the St. Pete summer outside. The basketball court was the most beautiful thing I had ever seen, the wood worn smooth by years of running feet, the glass backboards freshly marked for the summer season, the nets still white. It was also a place I could not play, because you had to either bring your own five players to queue up for a chance at the current winners on the court or be on a summer-league team scheduled to play on it.

Fortunately, a row of six concrete outdoor courts stood right next to the building. Each was full-sized and had a buffer of about ten feet between it and the next court. A few trees at one end of the row provided a little bit of shade from the sun; the best players not already indoors competed on the court nearest to those trees. The worse you were, the farther you played from those trees.

I knew my place and went to the farthest court, where two half-court games of three-on-three were in progress. I stood on the sidelines, practiced dribbling the old rubber ball I had picked up at a yard sale, and waited for a chance at joining a team. Despite several game changes and a few half-hearted attempts on my part to get the players to notice me, no one picked me for a team. As angry as that made me at them, I also really didn't blame them. I had grown up but not filled out the previous year, so though I was already a little over six feet tall and almost to my adult height, I still weighed barely a hundred and forty pounds. Despite my weight, my height would have made me attractive to potential teammates if I hadn't been so obviously uncoordinated, a guy who had trouble dribbling for more than two bounces without losing control of the ball. I could have claimed a shot at a game and picked up two other guys when my turn came, but I was afraid of the anger that would roar out of me at the humiliation I would feel when all of them turned me down.

Around lunchtime a lot of guys headed out to get food, and the games on my court shrunk to two on two. I was watching a game carefully, studying the moves of the players just as I studied the NBA stars on TV, hoping the knowledge would help me when

I finally got into a game, when up walked the only guy in the place who looked like more of a geek than I did.

He was an inch or two shorter than I, and he looked like he weighed a good thirty pounds less, a bag of small bones wrapped in sickly white, acne-scarred skin. His shorts were unfashionably short, and he wore a tee shirt that said, "Jocks suck." He came straight over to me, stuck out his hand, and said, "Hi. I'm Jim, Jim Peterson. Looking for a partner?"

I stared at him for a moment. I couldn't imagine a worse partner, but then again, any partner was a way onto the court, and I probably looked like just as bad a prospect to him. I shook his hand. "Matt."

"Gotten in yet?" he asked.

I laughed. "What do you think?"

"You're not sweating enough to have played recently, and I'm betting you're about as attractive to these Neanderthals as I am, so I'd guess no."

"You'd guess right."

"Well, we'll fix that now." He turned and yelled to the four guys playing on the half court in front of me, "My partner and I have next. What's the score?"

None of the guys looked happy about it, but one of them said, "Eight to five, us."

Jim sat with me and watched the game.

"Have you ever played here before?" I asked.

"A couple of times," he said, "though getting on without a partner is tough."

"Have you ever won?"

He laughed this time. "What do you think?"

I liked his honesty. "I'd have to guess no."

"You'd guess right."

One of the guys on the floor hit a rattling jumper from just north of the foul line, his teammate high-fived him, and the other two guys grumbled. The guy who hit the shot waved us onto the court and said, "You're up."

Jim jumped up and headed toward the foul line and the guy with the ball. "I'll take this one."

I walked to my man, Jim checked the ball, and the game started.

We could do no right. Though both of them were shorter than either of us, they shot over us, went around us like we were rooted to the ground, out-rebounded us, and generally kicked our butts. Playground rules were make-em, take-em, and they either made their shots or got the rebounds, so we barely touched the ball. The game ended eleven to one, our only point a lucky heave by Jim on a move that I think was supposed to have been a lay-up but that ended up looking like he was tripping over his own feet while running. I was hugging my sides for wind as I walked off the court.

I didn't care about losing, and I didn't care about the pain in my side. I was elated. I had come to the courts, found a partner, and gotten into a game. Jim had treated me like I was competent, even though I wasn't, and so though I failed, I at least got a chance to try. As bad as I was, I learned that day that I loved playing the game—even playing it that badly—even more than I loved watching it.

Jim and I sat together the rest of the afternoon, until I had to go home to dinner. We played every chance we got, and we talked between those chances. We talked about the players on the court. We debated the greatest moment in an NBA championship series, both of us going for classics over recent efforts: Jim argued for Michael Jordan's huge straight-from-the-sickbed performance in Utah, while I pitched a moment from ancient history, Willis Reed's injured run onto the court in the famous game in the Garden. We lost every game,

with our best effort coming in an eleven-to-four out-
ing in which a lot of lucky bounces went our way and
the other guys looked like they were barely paying
attention.

The best moment of the day, though, came when
I got up to leave. As I turned to walk away, Jim said,
"See you tomorrow?"

I smiled. "Yeah." I was sore from a day of playing—
not watching, but playing—basketball. I had a partner
and a chance to play again. Life was good. "See you
tomorrow."

As consciousness returned I fought the temptation
to move and instead stayed very still, eyes shut, trying to maintain the slow, even breathing of one asleep.
I felt a bit muzzy from whatever the aliens had hit me
with and had to work to concentrate, but I was not
in any physical pain—good news for R.C., I hoped. I
could feel a hard platform under me and bonds of
some sort around my wrists and ankles. I tensed my
muscles ever so slightly against first the wrist bonds
and then the ankle ties, but predictably none of them
gave at all. If I couldn't work the bonds I wasn't going
to gain any advantage by pretending to still be out, so
I opened my eyes and looked around.

I was in what had been an auto mechanic's garage.
As my head cleared, the smells of the room grew
stronger, more distinct: oil that had worked its way for
years into the pores of the concrete floor, grease, dust,
bits of metal, hints of mold. The room was dim but I
could clearly see the old wooden workbenches along
the side walls and the lighter spots on the walls where
racks had hung. I could also see three aliens—they
looked like the ones who had taken me, though I
couldn't be sure—standing in the same triangular formation near the foot of the unfinished worktable I was

sprawled across. To my left and slightly behind them sat a fourth alien, one a bit smaller than the original three and wearing a large breathing helmet instead of the tighter masks of the others.

The alien who had done all the talking so far picked up where it had left off, as if nothing had happened. "You must locate James Peterson and return him to us."

My throat was dry enough that it took me a few moments to be able to speak clearly. "No," I said, "I don't have to do that."

"You are our prisoner, and you must do as we instruct."

Motivation was clearly not their strong suit. I raised my head a bit and cleared my throat. "No, I don't. You can obviously knock me out and take me captive, but you can't make me do anything. It doesn't work like that."

The alien in the rear spoke for the first time. His translator must have been set differently from the other alien's, because his voice came out higher, a tenor to the other's bass. "We can kill you if you do not do as we say."

I was glad and a bit surprised to realize that aliens could be amateurs, too. They were clearly used to dealing with people who were also amateurs, people who had no ability to accurately gauge what they were really worth—or not worth—in any situation. I don't know why I was surprised, because most people—and, I had to assume, most aliens—aren't very good at what they do. I'd almost certainly end up paying in the short term for this knowledge, but it was still a source of power they didn't realize they had given me. "Of course. But if you kill me, I can't do what you want me to do."

The new speaker paused for a moment, then rose

and walked slowly over to me. Though he looked to me much like the others, his slower, more careful walk made him seem older, an elderly man forced out of a comfortable chair by an impolite guest. "You are, of course, correct. Though your life is . . . irrelevant to me, killing you would not help us achieve our goals. We do, however, have another option: We can make your lack of cooperation more painful than the choice of helping us."

I saw his upper right arm move; then the pain hit and I couldn't see anything. I made no attempt to suppress my scream; they can always make you scream, so there's no point in pretending otherwise. My whole body felt like it was pulsing with currents of pain, every inch of skin, bit of bone, and length of vein and artery a channel for the purest pain I'd known. I prayed I'd black out. The pain continued for a time I couldn't measure or even find the words to contemplate, and then I got my wish.

I'm not sure how long I was out. As I came to I tried to prepare myself for the thickheadedness and the racking residue of pain that my past similar experiences had left, but consciousness returned, as it had before, quickly, and amazingly, pain did not come with it. Either the torture device or their healing technology was very good.

The older alien was standing where he had been, so I probably hadn't been unconscious for long. When I opened my eyes, he spoke. "Are you now prepared to do as we instruct?"

I knew I'd win this game—I'd known from the moment I knew they needed me—but I also knew that playing was going to be expensive. What I didn't know was just how expensive. I was going to have to find out. "No," I said. "But—"

The pain hit just as quickly as the last time and even more forcefully, and it seemed to go on longer. I didn't even have enough control left to pray for unconsciousness, but fortunately it came on its own.

I lost count of how many times I blacked out, but I don't believe there were actually that many. In the few moments of consciousness I enjoyed between the attacks of pain I tried to focus on the goal of making the deal I knew I would have a chance to make.

Finally, the opportunity came.

As usual, the older one asked if I would help, and as usual I said no and tried to continue, expecting the pain again. This time, though, he let me go on.

" . . . but I do think we could make a deal that would meet your goals." I gulped air as I realized I had held my breath before speaking and had tried to blurt out the whole sentence before they could zap me again. When the pain didn't come, I kept going. "I know you can hurt me enough to make me say anything. You can even make me do anything—for a while. As soon as I get a chance, though, I'll end up trying to get away. So, why not make a deal instead? From what I've read about your people, you're here to discuss possible trade opportunities. Well, we can make a trade."

New sounds filled the air, sounds I realized were their voices in their own tongue. The older one and my gym visitor seemed to be doing the talking, though I couldn't be sure others didn't speak.

After a short time the older one spoke to me again. "You are right that we are primarily merchants. We do not, though, normally make trades with . . . races such as yours. We simply take the helpers we need. In this case, our goals and our arrangements with your governments make that option more expensive to pursue than normal. So, what sort of trade?"

"When I work, I do—" I paused to find the right word, a word that would appeal to them "—salvage. I find things for people, and I return those things, and the people pay me."

"How much do they pay you?"

"Half of what the thing is worth."

The alien's response was the fastest it had been. "That is absurd. No such service is worth half the value of the object in question."

"It is," I said, "if the object is difficult to find and retrieve, so difficult that normal approaches will not work, so difficult that there is significant risk and there are no other options." Anyone talking to the highest levels of all the leading governments on Earth who resorted to kidnapping a single guy rather than simply asking for government help clearly couldn't operate in the open, so I spelled it out for them, just in case. "My services are worth the fee, for example, when the buyer cannot afford to be openly searching for the lost goods."

"Of course. It is clear that you appreciate our situation. I assume it is also clear that your . . . discretion is vital in this matter."

"Of course. When I work, it's always confidential."

"And what price would you put on James Peterson that we might pay you half?"

They were serious. Jim was alive, or at least they believed he was.

"He really is alive?"

"Of course. He has been working for us since the moment we arranged his revival. I repeat: What price would you put on him and on this task?"

I could have told them that I would find Jim just so I could put him away again, but there was no point in throwing away a good opportunity.

"I assume you guys don't have anything like a normal

bank account, so I have to answer your question with another: What can you pay that I can use but that would also allow you to meet your needs for discretion?"

They chattered again for a while, then the original speaker left the room. He returned quickly with a stained brown paper bag that looked and smelled like it had been in the trash for a couple of days.

"Diamonds. We traded some very simple devices to a minor government to obtain some working capital. This bag contains enough value to easily equal the cost of a single human."

The original speaker opened the bag next to my head so I could look inside. The contents were beautiful, more diamonds than I had ever seen in one place, facets dancing in even the room's dim light, each stone easily a carat or more. He put the bag in my hand so I could gauge its weight. I'd have to revise my opinion about the aliens' skill at motivation: The bag had to weigh at least two pounds, maybe more. Even with the massive cuts we'd have to take to move the diamonds without alerting the IRS, they would buy R.C. and me a long, long break in high style before we had to work again.

The alien took the bag from my hand and put it on a workbench on the right-hand wall.

"It's enough," I said. "What do you want me to do when I find him?"

The original leader stepped back as the older alien spoke. "You do not need to do anything. He—" he pointed with his upper left arm toward the original speaker "—will accompany you. You will leave when you have found James Peterson. He will retrieve some materials that are ours and . . . deal with Peterson."

I shook my head. "That won't work. To find him, I have to talk to people. Your friend here is hardly inconspicuous, and I'm sure you don't want him to be seen wandering around in the open."

"That point is not negotiable. He must be with you."

I stared at the original leader and pictured him in a pair of pants, a sweatshirt, and a big hat. It wouldn't be enough. There was no way I could take him out in public. Perhaps, though, if he stayed out of sight, kept to the car while I worked. "Let's compromise. He can ride with me to each place I go, but he'll have to wait in the car whenever I deal with other humans."

The two of them chattered again briefly, then the older alien spoke to me. "That is acceptable."

"What assurances do I have that you will not kill me after I find him for you?"

"The same assurance we have that you will not try to kill our representative: Neither side would gain anything by such behavior."

It wasn't much, but it was what I had expected him to say, all he really could say. "Okay. Now, how about letting me go so we can get started?"

The older alien pointed an arm and the bodyguards freed me. The bonds appeared to be a sort of flexible plastic wrap. I reached for one near my ankle but the nearer bodyguard snatched it away.

"Leave now and begin your work," the older alien said. Pointing to the original leader, he continued, "He will answer the questions you will need to ask." He turned and walked toward a side door, the two bodyguards trailing him.

I got up, grabbed the bag of diamonds, and followed them. My new buddy trailed me. The side door led to what had once been the garage's office, and from there we went out into the light. It was early afternoon, the fall air still warming from the sun, so I had indeed been gone only a few hours. My stomach began to rumble as my body relaxed and I realized I was hungry.

Two black BMW sedans with blacked-out windows were parked outside the garage, which sat well back from the road. On either side of the garage and on the other side of the road were fields of wild growth. A road sign just visible from where I stood told me I was only a few miles outside of Pittsboro, so they had taken me less than an hour from the gym. Moving surprisingly quickly now that he was out in the open, the older alien folded himself into the passenger seat of one of the cars. The bodyguards crammed themselves into the car with him and quickly drove off.

"You were expecting spaceships?" asked my companion.

When I realized he was trying to make a joke, I stared at his face for a sign I could use in the future. I found nothing. If their expressions changed, it was in ways I was unable to discern. Then I noticed that his lower right arm was twitching slightly; I'd have to watch those arms.

"No. It makes sense that with your particular needs you'd try to keep a low profile."

His lower left arm reached into his suit and briefly disappeared; the suit appeared transparent the entire time. The arm reappeared holding the car's keys.

"How about I drive?" I asked.

"I would prefer that," he said. "Your automobiles are not well suited to us."

"I would also prefer it." I took the keys and headed to the car. The seat was all the way back and leaning two-thirds of the way down, so it took me a few moments to adjust it. The alien folded quickly into the car, but he definitely didn't look comfortable. That was fine by me; we'd be in the car a lot, and after this morning's episode I didn't mind at all that he suffered. "We're going to be together for a while, so I need to know what to call you. I go by Matt; what's your name?"

"In my language it is—" the translator let out a burst of the chattering noises I had heard earlier "—but the translator cannot find equivalents in your language for our names."

"Okay, I'll name you." I looked at him crammed into the seat, arms everywhere, a giant blue bug reclined almost on its back, and I laughed. "I'd go with Gregor, but that's too much work to say. So, Greg it is."

"Greg?"

"Yup."

"It will serve. Now, you must find James Peterson."

"First, we have to go back to the gym so I can change and grab some food." I started the car and we headed out. I drove in silence, wanting the time to think, and I was pleased to find that Greg was content to ride quietly along.

By the time ninth grade ended, Jim and I were the closest of friends. Neither of us needed to study much to keep up with our homework, so we spent every evening we could at the courts. We played every two-man team we could find, we joined every larger game that would have us, and when no one else was around to play, we practiced shooting and played each other. The playing and the practice paid off, because by the end of the year we were regularly joining games on the second court from the trees. The day we were asked for the first time to play in a game on that court, we celebrated like we had jointly jammed home the winning basket in the NBA championship game.

When we weren't playing basketball, we were talking. We talked about everything. We endlessly analyzed what it would take to transform ourselves from the geeks we knew we were to the cool juniors and seniors who somehow managed to actually date girls and not merely wonder what happened on dates. We found we were both only children and speculated what it would be like to have a brother or a sister or both. We learned we both hated our fathers: I hated mine for abandoning my mother and me before I was born, and he hated his for not leaving, for staying to smack him and his mother around whenever the guy had a bad day. We confessed our big, ill-formed dreams; Jim loved science and wanted to win the Nobel Prize in something, while I wanted to somehow change the world, to make a big difference.

We were brothers.

We began the new summer with two goals: To play our way onto the wood floor before school started again, and to put some muscle on our skinny frames. To reach our goals, we created a ritual of work and swore we'd make each other keep to it until the summer ended.

We started each morning by hitting the center right when it opened so we could get a jump on the weight benches. We worked out most of each morning, until we were too sore to continue. Then we'd eat an early lunch, stretch a bit, and hit the courts. We'd play until dinner, go to one or the other of our houses to eat, then head back to the courts and more games until the outside lights cut off at ten. By the time we got home it was all we could do to collapse into bed until the next morning.

The gym was where we discovered just how hard we could push one another, and where I found for the first time a constructive way to express the anger that was always roiling inside me.

We were at the end of our Thursday leg workout, a particularly brutal routine in which we did twenty-rep leg sets with heavy weights: first extensions, then squats, and finally leg presses. I was on the incline leg-press machine, in my third and final set of twenty heavy reps, fighting a weight I had been stuck on for a month. Each time I had tried this weight, I had grunted out the first two sets, but I had failed to make the third. I couldn't even come close. I'd never made it past fifteen reps on that set, and the exercise now loomed as a demon in the gym, a dragon that always slayed me.

Jim had gone first and pounded out his third set, setting a personal best. He was sitting on the bench next to the machine as I strapped myself in. "You can do this, Matt," he said.

"I know I can," I lied. I didn't know it at all. Sure, my head knew it was possible, but in my heart I could already feel the incredible pain that hit around the tenth rep, already see the image of myself getting up from the machine having failed yet again.

"No," he said. "You don't know it, you don't believe it, but you're wrong. You can do it, but have to believe it and you have to pay the price."

I nodded, took a couple of deep breaths, and started the set.

The first nine reps were good and relatively painless, my body a machine, my legs pistons the weight could not stop. The tenth was everything I had feared, as much a blast of pain as the previous nine had been routine. I paused after it, legs extended, sucking air.

"Push it," I heard Jim say.

I pounded out two more reps without pause and then had to rest for air. I looked at my legs and was surprised to find they were shaking. I shook my head no.

"Bull," Jim said. "Don't you give up."

I nodded yes and ground out the thirteenth and fourteenth repetitions, then stopped again for air. It was over. My legs knew it. My head knew it. My heart knew it. I might get the fifteenth, though even that was doubtful, but I surely wouldn't get another. It was over.

"No!" Jim shouted in my ear. "You are *not* giving up! Not this time." Out of the corner of my eye I saw him stand. "Hey," he yelled, "you guys want to see a real wimp? This loser's been stuck on this same rep for a month and he's about to wuss out again."

I sucked air and shook my head at him, anger filling me faster than air. In the mirrors on the side walls I saw a few guys stop what they were doing and look at us. I hated them for it, hated them for all the crap they and others like them had given me, hated them for having fathers they could go home to, hated them for all the times they knew how guys were supposed to behave and I didn't, hated them for already having the kind of body I wanted, hated them for everything I wasn't and didn't have.

"Go ahead, Matt," Jim said. "Fail. Just get out of there fast so somebody else can use the machine."

I wanted to kill him. The rage formed into a single word, first in my brain and then in a hiss from my lips: "No." I beat my head against the back support, hit it and hit it and hit it again until the pain in my head overwhelmed the pain in my legs, and then I let the weight down and slammed it back up, then down again, no pause, my legs almost throwing the weight. The rep numbers appeared in red in my mind. Fifteen. Sixteen. Seventeen. Eighteen. Nineteen. Twenty. I couldn't stop, couldn't give them the satisfaction of doing only the minimum. Twenty-one. That would show them. I pushed the twenty-second rep up so hard the weights actually left contact with my feet for just a second, slammed up the supports, and unstrapped my hands as the weight fell back onto the supports. I jumped up, seeing only red, ready to kill, anger with no goal or target, just anger.

"Good job, Matt," Jim said from somewhere not far away.

The anger receded like the tide flowing away from the beach, leaving me breathing hard, legs shaking, the back of my head pounding, and I sat down hard on the bench where Jim had been.

"I could have killed you," I said between gasps.

"Nah," Jim said. "You couldn't have caught me, not with those legs after that monster set."

We both laughed. Even though I didn't think I could stand I felt so good, so happy to have cracked that barrier, so free of any anger—for the first time, even if only for just that moment—that I laughed again, and Jim laughed with me.

I parked the BMW in back of the gym near the employees-only entrance, next to R.C.'s enormous truck. I put down the window to give R.C. a good look at me; after this morning, he'd have all the defenses activated and be monitoring the security cameras, ready for bear and heavily armed.

"I have one of them with me," I said. "I also have these." I held the bag out the window in my left hand and twisted my body so I could pull out a diamond with my right. "I'm working."

The gym's metal security door clicked three times and popped open. I got out of the car and Greg followed, unfolding more quickly than I would have thought he could. We walked inside, and the door closed automatically, leaving us in total darkness. I stood while R.C. finished the scans and satisfied himself that all was well, then the door a few feet in front of me opened to our office. R.C. was off to the side, his eyes and a shotgun trained on the alien.

I handed R.C. the diamonds. He took them but kept his eyes on Greg.

"What's the job?" he asked.

"Apparently, Jim really is alive. I have to find him, and then Greg here will take him and some stuff of theirs away."

R.C. raised an eyebrow and asked, " 'I'?"

I watched Greg's arms, but nothing moved. Their translators had worked well enough so far that I had to assume he was following everything now. "Yes," I said. "I have to do this on my own. I think Greg here and his people would be a lot more comfortable that way."

"That is correct," Greg said.

I looked R.C. in the eyes. "You need to stay here and cover the business. The gym's been busy enough that you'll have plenty to do." Our gym had over two thousand square feet of workout space, another three thousand square feet of living space, all the latest fitness equipment, thousands of pounds of free weights, and more than twenty-five hundred members on its books. It also sat nearly empty almost all of the time, a convenient cash business. All but a few of its members were just names we bought from friends at local hotels, out-of-state travelers who had passed through Raleigh at one time or another. R.C. and I were the only people with permanent access cards, though from time to time we would give temporary cards to others working on jobs with us. R.C. would be covering something, but it would be my back, not the business.

He nodded, grabbed the bag of diamonds, and left through the door opposite the one we had entered. I knew he'd monitor the room until I left, and that from then on he'd be there if I needed him—but I also knew I'd never see him, and neither would Greg.

"Tell me about what Jim was doing for you guys," I said, "and about how he escaped and when."

"I cannot discuss that," Greg replied.

I pulled over a chair and sat down in front of him. I motioned to another chair, but he didn't take it. Instead, he folded his legs and sank slowly to the floor.

"If you don't," I said, "finding him will take a lot more time. Your leader said you wanted to get both him and some materials back. The most logical assumption is that those materials are related to what he was doing. Right?"

"That is correct."

"If he took them, it was almost certainly either to sell them or to continue the work you were doing that involved them and then sell the result of that work. Otherwise, he'd have no reason to take them. If I don't know what he was doing for you guys, I can't know whether he's likely to be looking to sell something or to hole up for a while, and so I can't know how to track him. Understand?"

"Yes." Greg paused long enough that I wondered if I'd have to push him again to get him to talk. Finally, though, he resumed. "Our race belongs to a trade guild that includes many other races. The guild's rules are quite strict and very expensive to disobey. They limit the technologies guild members can use and the products they can offer when they operate on nonguild planets, such as yours. The overt mission of our visit to this planet is in accordance with those rules; we and others have guild permission to begin preliminary trade talks. The project for which we took James Peterson is not, however, in accordance with those rules. Thus our increased need for discretion and my unwillingness to answer your questions."

"So you were smuggling?"

"If I understand the term correctly, the answer is, somewhat. It is not that simple."

"Then cheer up, Greg, because I don't care about smuggling." I pulled my chair a bit closer. "What I do care about is earning those diamonds, which means I have to find Jim, which means I need to know what he was doing. So, one more time: What was he doing?"

"We chose you for this job because he mentioned you."

I had assumed they knew about me from Jim's police records, but I should have known better than to make assumptions. "What did he say?"

"That he was looking forward to seeing you again. He laughed when he said it. Were you friends? Did he laugh from happiness?"

"Yes, we were friends once. Not any more." The anger I felt rising inside me, the anger I always felt when I thought of Jim, was not going to help me now, so I pushed it back. "No, I doubt he was laughing from happiness." I still needed to know what Jim had been doing, and I didn't want to keep dancing with Greg. "How you found me doesn't matter now. What matters now is what Jim was doing for you and when and how he escaped."

"You are aware of his work in nanotechnology."

"Of course. He loved it and was really good at it, right up to the end." Even then he was as good as anyone, just not good enough, and certainly not entitled to do what he did. I had to look away from Greg because this time the flush of anger was almost overpowering. As I so often did, I wondered what it would be like not to be made of anger, not to have it always just under the surface, a river washing over and through me and ready to boil over at any time. I know most people aren't this way, and I'm glad, but I can't really imagine what it's like inside their skins. And, of course, it was irrelevant, because I was built the way I was built, and that wasn't going to change now, if ever. "So what he was doing for you involved nanotech?"

"Yes. We had adapted a technology of ours for use

here. We were unable to complete the adaptation without certain aspects of your environment that we could not get without being here. Guild rules would not allow us to bring a research team here or to test here, so we smuggled samples of the technology and recruited James Peterson to complete it for us."

Nanotech research meant an electron microscope, one or more controlling computers, and some very specialized nano-machine building tools. "How much equipment did he have?"

"Perhaps ten pieces. I am not sure. I was not involved in its procurement or setup."

"Where did he get it?"

"We gave him diamonds, as we did you, and I believe he traded them at local universities for the equipment he needed."

That made sense. He had been a researcher at UNC, and he knew every nanotech research lab in the area. A few bribes and a panel truck, and he'd be set.

"Did he transport the equipment in a truck?"

"Yes, a large white one he purchased."

"Did he take the truck when he escaped?"

"Yes."

"I don't suppose you know the truck's license number or make or anything like that?"

"No. It was white and old and tall enough inside for us to be able to sit like this but not tall enough for us to be able to fully stand without bending."

It was probably a used delivery truck. Possibly useful to know, but nothing I was going to be able to trace easily. Besides, he was smart enough to pick up another one just to be safe. "Where was he working?"

"In a warehouse not far from where we took you earlier. He arranged the use of the building."

"Was there a basketball hoop near it?" I pointed to one of my prize possessions, a framed signed poster of Dr. J dunking in the last All-Star game he had played in while still in the ABA. He was retired long before I was ever watching basketball, but in the hours and hours of videos I had studied I had always found him to be one of the most graceful players ever. "A metal rim, like that, on a pole."

"Yes. Behind the building. He threw a ball at it every day for quite some time, until we forced him to return to work. We found this activity senseless, but he insisted on repeating it."

Jim, like me, had always been a creature of habit. I was glad his time in jail hadn't worked this habit out of him, because it would help me find him.

"After you brought him back after his execution, was one of you always with him?"

"Until his escape, yes."

"Good. Did he ever go anywhere other than this building and the places he bought the equipment?"

"No. We would not allow it."

"Good. Now, back to my two remaining original questions: When did he escape, and how?"

"He left in the early morning eight days ago." Greg's lower left arm twitched slightly. "It took us a very long time to locate you."

I realized Greg was embarrassed. If I was right, a lower left arm twitch noted embarrassment, a lower right, humor.

"How did he escape?"

"We cannot be sure, because none of our people with him survived. We believe he created a solvent from some of the chemicals he acquired for his work, because the suits of all four of his guards were partially decomposed. Our suits provide us with both a breathable atmosphere and skeletal support; without them, this planet is almost immediately fatal to us." Greg touched his suit with his upper right arm. "In the last week we have changed some of the materials in the suits. I am wearing one of the newer versions." The lower right arm twitched again.

I laughed. "Don't worry; I have no desire to kill you. If I had wanted you dead, R.C. would have killed you before you made it from the car to the gym. We've made a deal, and I'll honor my part."

I stood and pushed back the chair. "Right now, though, I'm going to grab a bite to eat and take a shower. Then we'll start looking for Jim. Can I get you anything?"

"No," Greg said. "The suit provides for my nutritional needs."

I headed for the kitchen. As the door into the rest of the gym was shutting and locking, I yelled, "Stay there, and you'll be fine. I'll be back in about an hour."

Louise Mason entered our lives in the second semester of our junior year of high school, a mid-year transfer whose father's business had brought her family from North Carolina to St. Pete for a three-year stint. Jim and I were in a lot of the same classes, and Louise was in every one we shared: AP math, AP English, third-year programming, marine biology, and creative writing. She was bit of a geek—barely over five feet tall, rail-thin, glasses, a tendency to laugh too loudly and too easily—but she had a brilliant smile and an always tangled mane of shoulder-length curly brown hair that drew your attention and made you smile every time you saw her bounce into a room. Every smart guy in the school noticed her and, if the hallway chatter was any indicator, wanted her.

Earlier that year, Jim had broken through the dating wall, and he was now going out regularly with a girl named Margie who was also in most of our shared classes. Margie befriended Louise, and I used that friendship as a way to meet and then, with Margie's nudging, ask Louise to join the three of us for dinner and a movie at the mall. To my surprise, Louise accepted.

In the course of the evening we discovered we had none of the usual things in common. She came from a rich Raleigh family and was determined to go back to North Carolina to college so she could be near them. My mother and I were poor, and I wanted to go to college somewhere else, anywhere else, that I could make a fresh start. Louise hated sports, and basketball and the gym provided the best moments of most of my days. She was an ovo-lacto vegetarian, and I loved red meat and ate it every chance I got.

A dumb comment of Jim's brought Louise and me to our first piece of common ground. We were sitting on benches outside the theater, people-watching while we waited for the previous film to end. A mother and father were taking turns pushing their young son, a kid who couldn't have been more than six or seven, along the main walkway of the mall. The boy was crying, but they kept pushing him. Every now and then his father would slap the back of his head and whisper angrily at him.

"Some people shouldn't have kids," Margie said.

We all nodded in agreement.

"We shouldn't *allow* them to have kids," Jim said.

"What do you mean?" Louise asked.

"Just what I said," Jim answered. "We should not allow people who aren't competent to have kids to breed. We should sterilize them."

Louise looked at him and shook her head. "Who's going to decide who's competent to have kids and who's not?" she said.

"I have to agree with Louise," I said. "I'm with you,

Jim, in not wanting people like that to have kids, but I can only wish those people would make that choice. I sure don't want somebody else having that much control over anybody."

"Well, I do," Jim said. "I think the people who are smart enough should make the choice." He waved his arm to take in the four of us. "People like us."

"No way," I said. "I don't want that kind of power over anybody else, and I sure don't want other people having that kind of power over me. I'd be happy just being able to make my own decisions."

"Definitely," Louise said. "People have to make their own decisions, and as long as those decisions don't interfere with the rights of others, we have to respect them."

"I don't," Jim said. "I don't respect them at all. If they aren't going to be decent parents, we shouldn't let 'em breed. It's just that simple."

We all knew there was no point in arguing further, so we dropped the topic and moved on.

After the movie, I gave Louise a ride home. On the way we ended up talking about individual rights, the limits of personal freedom and responsibility, what we each thought good governments should do, and on and on. We kept talking in her living room, long into the night, and when our hands accidentally touched around two A.M., we held them tightly. I had never known how much power could come from one small hand until that moment. I was on fire, almost giddy from that small touch. Louise's mother came down and kicked me out a little while later.

Louise and I didn't kiss that night, but as I looked her in the eyes at the door, I knew one day we would. It took a whole month more for me to work up the courage, a month in which I found an excuse to sit alone with her for at least a few minutes almost every day. By the time we kissed, we knew we belonged together.

After my shower, I threw a few days' worth of clothes into my duffel bag, which by default I kept loaded with my toiletries kit, a specially encrypted cell phone, a leather indoor/outdoor basketball, and some workout clothes in a smaller gym bag that fit inside the duffel. I added some color printouts of photos of Jim the papers had run in the days right before the execution. Last to go in was an old favorite, an over-and-under, sawed-off Winchester shotgun I hoped I wouldn't need. R.C. was already gone. I gathered up Greg, and we headed out.

The Raleigh-Durham-Chapel Hill area of North Carolina had for decades been merging into a single population center, and today almost every major link between the cities showed the typical artifacts of modern American suburban sprawl: well-maintained roads, clumps of fast-food restaurants yelling for your attention, malls spaced so you were never far from one, and the occasional outlet stores claiming unheard-of bargains. Every such sprawl also has its darker arteries, where everything takes a step down and the businesses cater to the appetites that every such area inevitably both has and feels obliged to deny. The center of the run along the top of the triangle between Durham and Raleigh was one such route. Here you could still find car lots that would accept cash and forget to report the transaction, restaurants with truly cheap food for those brave enough to eat it, discount gas you'd put only in cars you didn't plan to keep long, check-cashing places with rates that would embarrass loan sharks and a shotgun always in sight behind the wire mesh, and older ranch homes set back from the road with neon signs noting they were open until two A.M. and offered all-girl companionship.

When we stopped at the first one, a white clapboard joint with no name I'd ever known and simply a red neon "Massage" sign out front, Greg asked, "Why are we stopping at this place?"

"What's the first thing a man will want when he gets out of jail?" I said.

"I do not know. We fed Peterson and provided him shelter."

"Have you ever dealt with large groups of males stuck with only males for long periods of time?"

"Of course," Greg said. "Sex. We failed to provide it. We take care of this appetite between engagements with the legions we use on other planets, but we failed to do so with Peterson."

"Exactly. Jim wouldn't want to show his face to anyone who might turn him in, but he would want to get laid."

Unfortunately, he hadn't been at the first place I tried, so we moved down the road to the next one. It was also a bust.

The third was an old brick ranch with a sputtering orange neon sign that showed an outline of a cat and the words "The Cat House" below it. Small ceramic cats filled the interior space between the windows and the blackout curtains behind them. A woman named Shirley ran the business for the Durham biker gang that controlled the low-rent half of the prostitution business in the area. I had done some work for her when she lived in a monstrosity of a house on a golf course in Cary with a husband who was a bigger monster than the house. R.C. and I had found their teenage daughter and returned her before we learned why she ran away. The next time they called us to find their daughter, we never called back. The time after that it was just the husband calling, and this time he was seeking Shirley. For her, not for him, we went looking and found her at Duke Medical, tubes down her throat to help her breathe while she healed from the repairs to her shattered cheekbones and broken nose. We never told him where she was, but we didn't have to; she went back on her own. When she grew old enough and damaged enough, he left her and she ended up here. Nothing new about the story, but nothing good about it, either.

"How are you, Shirley?" I asked after they buzzed me in and she took me back to the office, a smoke-filled room where a TV always ran and the women dozed or doped between visitors.

"You know, Stark," she said. "Same old thing." She plopped into an overstuffed chair that had last been comfortable around the time I was born. She lit up a cigarette. "That Beemer you're driving tells me you haven't sunken low enough to be shopping here, so what can I do for you?"

I showed her the picture of Jim. "Has he been here in the last week or so?"

She didn't even look at it. "You know I don't care about stuff like that. They're all just men. The faces don't matter."

I walked to her and bent over her chair so I could whisper. With my right hand I held the picture in front of her face, and with my left I fanned out five hundreds. "I can afford to be generous here, Shirley. Have you seen this guy?"

She stared at the money longer than she looked at the picture, but she did finally look at it. "Yeah," she said as she grabbed the half of the bills not in my hand, "he was here."

I held onto my half as our hands touched. Her hand was cool and dry. "When?"

"A week ago today. He bought a couple of sessions, one with two girls. Generous." She looked up at me. "Like you, right?"

I let go of the bills and she quickly tucked them into a pocket in her grayish housedress. "Right," I said. "Now, I need one more thing."

"What's that?"

"I need to see your parking lot videos for that day." The bikers who ran the place didn't invest much in the girls or the building, but the steelwork over the doors and the surveillance gear that ringed the building and sat in some of the nearby trees were both solid. Their places were never successfully raided, because by the time the cops could get inside everyone was just watching dirty movies and talking.

"You know I'm not supposed to even look at those, Stark."

I held out five more hundreds. "I know. But I need to spend some time with those videos. I'll do it here so the disks never even need to leave the building."

She grabbed the money. "You know, Stark, with this and maybe a little more, I could get out of here, start over, maybe even find that daughter of mine again."

I knew it would never happen, but what the hell, Greg and his friends were paying. "Show me the videos, and I'll give you another grand when I'm done with them."

She nodded and took me back to the camera room. It had once been a nice-sized closet, but now it was so crowded with gear and supplies that my shoulders touched the shelves on either side when I sat in its lone chair. Shirley grabbed a box of disks off a shelf, rifled through them, and handed me one. She pointed to the only empty player. "Knock yourself out."

I started the disk and the little monitor above the player came to life with a soundless image of the rear parking area. I hit fast forward and watched long stretches of empty ground broken occasionally by cars speeding up and men jumping out of them and running out of this camera's view and to the rear door of the house. Finally, one of the men was Jim. I reversed and took it slowly until I had the moment when he drove up. I paused on the best shot of his vehicle coming down the drive. It was an old yellow panel truck, the paint doing a good enough job of covering whatever its sides had once said that I couldn't read the words but a bad enough job that I was sure there had been words. I moved the images forward slowly until I got a clear shot of the rear of the truck as Jim parked it and was getting out, then paused the image.

Jim had been careful, careful enough to throw off almost anyone who would be looking for him, but he was not so careful that I couldn't get what I wanted. Mud covered the license plate numbers, but not completely, so you couldn't read the numbers but the mud would still look like a legitimate accident should anyone stop him. Clearly visible, however, was the state name and symbol: Florida. I knew he would steal plates from where he wanted to be, because the theft would get reported here in North Carolina but take a while to find its way to the local cops, and in the meantime the vehicle would blend in where he was headed.

He was going home.

I ejected the disk and took it back to Shirley. I handed it to her with another ten hundreds sitting on top of it. "Thanks, Shirley."

She put the money into the pocket along with the earlier bills. "No problem, Stark."

I stopped in the doorway of the office as I was heading out. "You could get out, Shirley. You know that, don't you?"

"Yeah, I know. This might be what it takes."

I looked at her and knew that her head might know what she could do but that her spirit had never known, would never know. I didn't mind the money, though; I'd love to be wrong, to see a miracle one day. "Sure thing, Shirley."

Out in the car I called R.C. He picked up on the first ring but said nothing; had he spoken, I would have known something was wrong. I told him to look for warehouse rentals in St. Pete and gave him the description of the truck.

"What is St. Pete?" Greg asked.

"A city in Florida," I said. "Where Jim and I grew up. Where I believe Jim is now. And, where we're going."

Louise and I were in the second to last month of our senior year at the University of North Carolina in Chapel Hill when we got the news about Jim's parents. Jim and I had kept in touch by e-mail since he went to Florida State and I followed Louise to UNC, but we had visited rarely. Louise was staying over at my apartment—she wasn't willing to upset her parents by actually living with me—so we were both caught off-guard when he showed up at my place.

When I let him in, Jim collapsed onto some pillows on the floor in my small living room. "Have you heard?" he said.

I looked at Louise to see if she knew something I didn't, but she shook her head. She still had the same mass of hair I'd noticed in high school, and I still loved the way it danced when she shook her head.

"No," I said. "Heard what?"

"My Mom and Dad are dead," Jim said.

I knelt down beside him. "What happened?"

He wouldn't look at me. He just kept staring straight

ahead. "The funeral was this morning, and then I drove all day to get here. I didn't want to be there anymore."

"What happened, Jim?" I asked again.

He finally looked at me. "I was in Tallahassee when the police there found me. They pulled me out of class. I thought I was in trouble, but I couldn't figure out for what. Other than spending too much after-hours time with the 'scope and the other lab gear messing around with my own nano-machine projects, I couldn't think of anything I'd done even remotely wrong." He looked away again, off into the space in front of him.

Louise moved to his other side and reached to touch him, but I shook my head no and she backed off.

"As near as they can tell, he beat her to death, Matt." He balled his hands and hit the sides of his head a couple of times. "He hit her too hard or too many times or something—I don't know—but something broke inside her. They might have been able to save her if he'd just called for help, but the jerk shot himself first. One bullet from a pistol right through the brain; he got that right." He looked at me. "No one called the police for days. I was at school, Matt. If I'd been home I could have stopped him, or at least gotten her to a doctor. I could have saved her."

"You can't blame yourself for that, Jim," I said. "There's no way you could have known to pick that particular time to drive all the way home from Tallahassee. No way. He did it, and it's his fault."

Matt stood. "Yeah, right!" he yelled. "I couldn't have known that he was going to beat her to death that particular day. But what I *could* have known is that it was going to happen someday, that he was going to go too far one day and kill her! I could have taken him out first. I could have, and I should have."

"No, Jim, you shouldn't have. That would have been murder, and that would have been wrong."

"Wrong? More wrong than my mother being beaten to death by that animal I had to have for a father?"

"I can't say what would be more wrong. I don't think it works like that. What I can say is that your mother was the one who had to make the choice. She had to leave. *She* had to make that choice, not you."

"You think she *deserved* this?" he said. His hands were in fists and he looked like he might hit me.

"No," Louise said quietly, so quietly I don't think Jim heard her.

"No," I agreed. "She didn't deserve it." I stood and faced him. "I'm not saying that at all, and I don't for a second believe she deserved this. I'm just saying that she had to make the choice to leave, and nobody—not you, not anybody—could make that choice for her."

"Well if I had, she'd still be alive," Jim said.

"It's not your fault, Jim," I said.

He stared at me for a bit, but I don't think he was seeing me. Finally, he said, "You mind if I crash here tonight?"

"No problem. You want the bed or the sofa?"

He looked at Louise like he was seeing her for the first time. "Hi, Louise," he said. "Sorry about showing up like this. You guys keep the bed. I'll just sit here for a while."

We went into the bedroom. When I came out a few minutes later to get a glass of water, Jim was curled in a ball on the sofa, fast asleep. I threw a sheet over him and went back to the bed and Louise.

We talked until almost four A.M. that night, Jim's tragedy making us both feel the need to stay awake, to stretch the day, to cling to another as if we needed proof we were still alive. We talked about our life after college, and I told Louise about the men who had visited me in my latest political science class, about the offers they made of a chance to really make a difference, to channel all my frustrations and energy into working to change the system. I told her the job would mean training in Virginia for a year or two, then moving around the world for a while. She didn't want to leave the area and intended to get her Ph.D. in math at UNC and teach or do research if she could find a job. We agreed to worry about all this later and fell asleep curled tightly together.

When we awoke in the late morning, Jim was gone. Louise asked me again about what I had planned, and though I tried to say nothing was set, she knew what I was going to do, and so did I. I had always wanted to be somebody special, to do something special, something that would matter, and this seemed to be the best shot I'd get. I thought of Jim's mother and desperately did not want to be someone who had never made the choice to make the changes his life needed. I had no idea what I was really getting into, but at that age, who does?

By the time we graduated, Louise had slowly taken all of her stuff out of my apartment, and though we were still dating only each other, you could almost see the space between us. Jim and I talked a couple of times a week for the first couple of weeks after the funeral, but then the calls faded away. A week after graduation, Louise and I said good-bye, I called Jim to let him know I was moving, and I headed for Langley.

Greg and I rode without talking until we were almost through South Carolina, and then I decided to try again. "What was Jim doing for you guys?" I asked.

"That is not relevant," Greg said.

"Yes, it is. You've told me it involved nanotech, so I know what sort of gear we're looking for, but I don't know how we'll spot these materials you want back."

"I am to locate them."

"Are you sure you'll be able to do that?" I said. "Do you know what form they'll be in? Whether Jim might have copied them? How he might have stored them? Whether he'll be in a public place when we find him?"

Greg was silent for several minutes before answering. "I find myself in an awkward situation. You are right that I may not succeed in that part of my mission without sharing the information you have requested, but I am also not to discuss it. Some of my more . . . aggressive colleagues have gone beyond the rules others of us advised them to follow, and now we must remove all traces of those transgressions. James Peterson's work is such evidence."

"What form will the evidence be in?"

"I do not know. Small, sealed containers are likely, of course; that is the form in which we gave him the original nano-machines."

Greg paused again for long enough that I assumed he was done and switched on some music.

Halfway through a song, he turned off the music and resumed talking. "It is also possible that the machines will be in one or more human subjects," he said.

I was glad traffic was light and I had the cruise control on, because I swerved slightly as I whipped my head to the side to look at him. "He's putting your nano-machines in people?"

"Not exactly. His job involved the adaptation of our machines to humans in this environment. So, what he would put in humans would more precisely be his own machines, built from our initial prototypes."

I forced my voice to be calm. Nothing about this sounded good, but I wasn't going to get anything from Greg by appearing too anxious. "What do these nano-machines do?"

"That is not relevant."

"Maybe not. What certainly is relevant is why you needed Jim, because if I know that I may be able to guide our search better." I didn't need that info, because merely knowing the type of equipment and where Jim was headed was a good enough start, but I was hoping Greg wouldn't realize that. "Was it because you couldn't make the machines work in humans without his help?"

"No. We have our own supply of humans in other locations. The machines definitely work in humans."

"Your own supply?" This time my voice rose slightly before I got it under control. "What does that mean?"

"That is not relevant."

I took a slow, deep breath before continuing. For the first time in my life, I seriously wondered if the alien abduction stories were true. "Okay. But what did you need Jim to do if you knew the machines would work in people? I mean, once you knew they worked, you were done, right?"

"No," Greg said. "We knew they worked in humans in other locations. They would not work correctly in this location, on your planet. Conditions here were interfering with the machines, stopping them from functioning properly. We do not know exactly what those conditions are, so we could not at any reasonable cost duplicate them elsewhere. Guild rules do not allow us to set up our own laboratory here. As we explained, the guild would also not allow us to openly pursue the product line this more aggressive faction led us to create. Hence our need for James Peterson."

The realization hit me hard enough that I had to stay quiet or risk giving it away, so I made myself drive in silence for another half hour before I said, "One more question. How far along was Jim in his research when he escaped?"

"I do not know."

"Was he yet using human subjects? If so, it would help me find him to know that he needed a place that could hold additional people."

"No," Greg said, "he had not yet progressed to that point. However, the day before he escaped he told us that he would need to obtain subjects soon."

"What if he has tested the nano-machines in people, or if he's testing them in people when we find him?"

"Then we must retrieve those people as well as any other containers of the machines."

Crap. Now I had to find Jim or risk either him hurting more people, the aliens taking those people away, or both. I nudged the cruise control a few miles per hour higher and forced myself to focus again on the road.

For a little over two years after I left the company, I traveled and worked odd jobs when I found them or they found me. As the specter of turning thirty became more real, I decided it was time to settle in one place, even if only to have a base of operations for a while. The Chapel Hill area was the logical choice. My mother had died in my second year at Langley, so there was nothing to take me back to St. Pete. I'd kept up with Jim and Louise via the Web, and I knew they were both working at UNC, Jim as a nanotechnology staff researcher and Louise as a math post-doc. Though part of me wasn't sure seeing Louise again was the best idea, another part was eager to see her. More importantly, she and Jim were the closest thing to family that I had. R.C. and I had just started working together, and where we were based didn't really affect the kind of work we did, so he agreed to move to North Carolina as well.

We spent the first year there setting up our gym and doing a couple of small jobs for old clients so we could have a bit of a nest egg, and I wondered when I'd get around to calling Jim and Louise. I meant to do it many times, but I kept finding excuses to put it off. Finally, I called. They both seemed happy to hear from me, so I proposed that the three of us get together.

At my suggestion, we met on neutral ground at a neutral time, for lunch at a Mexican restaurant in a shopping center in the middle of Research Triangle Park. I got there first and grabbed a booth in the back with a clear view of the front door. They came in only a few minutes apart, Jim first, then Louise. Jim looked like he still played some ball but wasn't hitting the gym much, thinner than he had been during college but still carrying more muscle than when we first met. Louise was remarkably unchanged, perhaps a bit heavier but with the additional weight only filling out her figure and making her look even better than she had. We were all pretty awkward at first, but when I got them talking about their work, the conversation flowed easily.

"The use of nanotech in medicine is in its infancy," Jim said. "Drugs can take you only so far. Cloned parts are okay if the host body can handle the shock of the transplant surgery and if you can afford the cloning. Only nanotech can go right in and actually rebuild organs that aren't working well, destroy bad cells, and basically make you a literally new person."

"I didn't think the FDA had cleared any nanotech testing on humans yet," Louise said.

"It hasn't," Jim said. "The stupid government would rather make us twiddle our thumbs with animals than give us access to a decent group of subjects. It's not like it would be hard to find subjects, and everyone knows we won't be able to make real progress until we do. Yet the government won't even lift a finger to help. Do you have any idea how many prisoners would jump at the chance to risk one of our tests in exchange for an early release?"

Louise looked furious. "What if the tests go wrong? And even if the tests were to work out, what about the prisoners' rights? Wouldn't that kind of offer amount to coercion?"

"Sure," Jim said, "the tests could go badly. Some of the prisoners might die; I acknowledge that risk. It's not like we're talking about the cream of the crop of humanity here, Louise." He took a sip of his drink. "As for it being coercion, maybe, in some cases, it would be. In most cases, though, I think the prisoners would truly volunteer happily. More importantly, though, so what if it is coercion? For Christ's sake, they're prisoners; it's not like they didn't earn whatever happens to them."

I saw the fight brewing and though I was on Louise's side I didn't want to sit through it. "Louise, what is your research in?" I asked.

She glared at Jim but took the opportunity to change the subject. "I'm investigating possible uses of a type of math known as negative probabilities—it's primarily German, never really caught on here—in algorithms to mimic human vision. I'm working with a couple of people in the computer science department and a cognitive scientist in the psych department, and we think we're onto some pretty exciting stuff. Take our work, add it to some of the recent advances in direct neural feeds, and we might really be able to feed visual pattern data even to people without optic nerves so they could effectively see."

Jim shook his head. "Why use your giant machines to feed that data down some wire into a dead nerve, when with just a little slack from the government we could learn what it would take to make nano-machines that could rebuild all the missing parts, from the nerve on out? The ability to make that kind of repair doesn't have to be far off, you know."

Jim and Louise went back and forth for a while, until Louise said, "We've been talking about our work, Matt. What have you been up to? Are you still working with the same people?"

I looked her in the eyes as I spoke, hoping to see . . . I don't know what, maybe some sign that my having left would be important to her, or that she'd be interested in trying again. "No. I left a couple of years ago. A friend of mine and I opened a gym together, and we do odd jobs to make a little extra money." I didn't see whatever it was I was seeking, but I couldn't tell if that was because it wasn't there or because I looked away too quickly, embarrassed at lying to them but not willing to tell the truth, not there, not yet.

"That sounds like fun," she said.

Despite her words, Louise's body language convinced me she felt I was a total failure. Or maybe it was all inside me, maybe I just felt like a total failure simply because I wouldn't tell her everything I did. I couldn't tell the difference, couldn't separate the words she said from the way I expected her to feel about them.

The lunch ran out of steam quickly after that. Jim asked if he could come by and shoot some hoops and grab a workout some time, and I said sure and gave him my number. Louise said she'd keep in touch, and I knew she wouldn't.

When I got back to the gym I worked the squat rack until my legs were shaking and I felt the old rush of cleansing anger as all the mess-ups and dumb choices of the past seven years washed away in the purifying red haze. I did set after set until I couldn't do any more and I felt like I was going to throw up, and then I just sat on the floor, wishing things were different but not having a clue how to make the wishes come true. I'd made the choices I'd made, and I could go only

forward, not back. Looking forward, I couldn't see how
or even why Louise and I could be together again, but
still I missed her and wondered over and over what
my life might have been if I had stayed.

Way past midnight, I pulled the BMW into the
parking lot of a motel near the ocean outside Savan-
nah. It was very late, and the city was buttoned down
for the night. At first I was too wired to sleep, so I
walked to the beach and sat on the sand. Greg insisted
on following, so I made him wrap a towel around his
head and a bedspread from one of the two motel beds
around his body. It was late enough and dark enough
that I figured no one was likely to spot him, and anyone
who did would just see a very tall, very thin man
wrapped in a blanket against the slightly chilly evening.

I called R.C. and asked him to reach out to some
of our police friends and see if there were any recent
increases in missing-person reports in St. Pete or
Tampa. As usual, he had nothing to say. I knew I'd hear
from him when he had any information he felt we
needed to discuss.

For a few minutes I tried to figure out just what
was going on, what Jim was doing for the aliens, but
after a while I finally accepted the simple fact that in
the end the answer did not matter because it would
not change what I had to do, that the details of whatever was going on would not stop me or change my
mission. The sooner I found Jim, the sooner all of it
ended. Time and again I've found myself in situations
where I was desperate to understand the why of it all,
the reasons for everything that was going on, and every
single time I ended up having to act without all the
knowledge I wanted. You learned what you could, but
in the end, whether you understood everything or not,
you did what you should.

I gave myself over to the sound of the waves. Growing up on the Gulf side of Florida, I had always found waves to be a special prize, a treat nature brought only when a storm disturbed the normal flatness of the Gulf of Mexico. That this treat was almost always available in the Atlantic was something I had never learned to take for granted, and waves never failed to calm and center me. When I realized my chin had hit my chest for the second time, I clung to the drowsiness and the calm and headed back to the motel, Greg in tow.

We slept well but still got a reasonably early start. We rolled into St. Pete late in the afternoon of a beautiful, cloud-free day. I was itchy for activity, an animal corralled in too tight a space for too long. We stayed on the freeway until we hit the middle of town, then I exited and parked in a lot near Haslam's, one of the city's few surviving private bookstores. I called R.C. to see what he had found. This time, after I identified myself, he spoke.

"The old Woodlawn community center."

"Are you sure?"

"It's now a warehouse for the county. The truck is parked under cover out back. It's him."

R.C. knew it was my play and he was backup, so I was sure he wouldn't go in before me.

"Thanks. I'm on the way." I started to hang up but realized he should have hung up first and hadn't. "What?"

"He's not this stupid. He kept the truck. He came here. He's expecting you."

It didn't change a thing, but I was still embarrassed for not realizing it earlier. "Yeah."

"I'm here," R.C. said, and then the phone went dead. I smiled; for R.C., that was a positively tender moment.

"Do you know where James Peterson is?" Greg asked.

"I think so," I said.

"Then drive me there," Greg said, "and we will take him and the materials we require." Greg stuck the upper arm on each side into his suit and withdrew in each one of the bagel-sized weapon disks. "Your job will then be done."

"No. I have to go there to be sure. If he is there, I'll need a little time alone with him to learn where the materials are. Then he's yours." I pointed at the weapons. "You've got the firepower to take us both. A little time won't hurt you, and it might make the difference between getting back the materials and having Jim leave them where someone else—maybe others from your guild—could find them."

I waited while Greg thought about it.

At length, he said, "That is acceptable."

I nodded, then got my bag out of the trunk and crawled into the backseat. I changed into a pair of shorts, a sleeveless sweatshirt, two pairs of socks, and my high-tops.

"What are you doing?" Greg asked.

"Jim's expecting me. The most comfortable ritual for us is to shoot—" I realized how Greg might misinterpret that just as I said it and quickly corrected myself "—play some basketball, so I figured I might as well be comfortable. It also gives me an excuse to carry a bag." I put the stubby shotgun in the gym bag, then covered it with a couple of small sweat towels and the basketball. I left the gym bag in the backseat, tossed the duffel back into the trunk, and climbed into the front.

I turned to face Greg. "What will you do with Jim when I give him to you?"

"As we have discussed," Greg said, "we are operating beyond the guild rules. That fact must not come to the guild's attention. So we must not allow James Peterson to be accessible."

"Let's talk about ways to make that happen," I said.

Greg listened as I talked, and when we had a deal, I headed the car up Sixteenth Street to the old community center.

After the lunch at the Mexican restaurant I didn't see Louise or Jim again until she surprised me by calling and asking me to join Jim and her for dinner at her place. Her home was a small but lovely old brick ranch house not far off Franklin Street in Chapel Hill. I knew no post-doc paid enough for her to afford the place, so I figured her parents were still helping her out. I felt the same mixture of disdain and envy I always experienced when I learned that other people's parents were helping them pay their way.

I arrived on time. Jim pulled in behind me just as I was getting out of my car. We walked up to the door together and knocked.

When Louise answered we were both so visibly shocked that she had to speak to get us to move. "Will you two stop staring and come in, please? I'm not contagious or anything like that."

Louise looked like a skeleton wrapped in parchment. Gone was the hair I had always adored, her scalp now completely bare. Her cheeks and eye sockets were sunken, and she moved slowly, carefully. I had thought she was thin in high school, but compared to now she had been plump then.

She led us to a living room with a sofa, a couple of chairs, a granite-topped fireplace, and framed photos on all the walls. I recognized many of the people in the photos, found myself in quite a few, and also noticed some with her and men I didn't know. I knew I had no right to the quick flash of jealousy and suppressed it.

After we all sat, I asked, "What's wrong, Louise?"

"That depends on what you're talking about," she said. "If you're talking about the way I look, the answer is the combination of radiation, chemo, and drug therapies I've been taking for the last four months. If you're talking about what's really wrong, it's the cancer."

"What kind do you have?" Jim asked.

She laughed. "I wish it were only one kind. The doctors don't know what came first or why, but I have both ovarian and renal cell."

She leaned forward, her elbows on her knees, and she looked so frail I was afraid her arms would crumble under her own weight. "I don't want to make a big deal out of this. I'm at peace with it, or at least I'm at peace with it most of the time. I've already stopped the therapies because I couldn't bear them any more. I didn't want to spend however many more days I have going to the hospital for therapy and then feeling sick afterward. I called you guys because I didn't want you to find out later, and because I wanted to see you while I was sure I could still have a decent time."

I wanted to scream, but I didn't know exactly why or at what. Instead, I felt myself go cold inside, the way I had trained myself to do when I was working, and I asked, "How long?"

"The doctors say that if I'm lucky, I might have as much as three more months. I'm more likely, though, to have only three or four more weeks. I've done a living will and worked everything out with my doctors and my family, because once my brain is gone I want them to let me go."

Jim appeared lost, staring into space, not able to look directly at her. "Have you tried everything?" he said.

"Everything I'm willing to try," she said. She stood. "And that's all I want to say about that. Now, if you can stand to be with the world's thinnest hairless woman, I've ordered some tasty Chinese take-out, and we can eat. I'm really enjoying my food now that the drugs and chemo have worn off, though my throat is still sore. I definitely don't worry about calories anymore."

I don't remember much about that dinner. I know I didn't eat much, and for all her talk of enjoying food, Louise ate even less. Louise and I did most of the talking, and Jim either listened or pretended to listen as he stared off into space. We talked about her house, about places I'd seen, about old times, and when she got tired, Jim and I cleaned up for her and headed for our cars.

He stopped me at the door to my car, grabbed my arm as I was reaching for the door handle. "Are you just going to let her die?" he asked.

The question uncorked the rage I'd bottled when she first told us, and I wanted to scream at him and hit him. Instead, I kept my voice level and asked, "What else can we do?"

"We can make her try more treatments, keep fighting, not give up," he said.

"No," I said, "we can't. We could try to talk her into it, but you heard her: she's endured all she's willing to take, and none of it has done any good. She's made her choice, and she's at peace with it, and that's it, that's all there is."

He threw my arm aside in disgust. "I cannot believe you're just giving up like that," he said. "You want to watch her die because you blew it with her and she dumped you? Is that it?"

I grabbed him by the throat and took him down to the road before he could even raise a hand to stop me. I fought to keep myself from crushing his larynx and quickly released my grip. "Jim, you know better than that, and you're lucky, very lucky, that I know you know better. Yeah, I blew it with her, but I've never wished her harm, and I never will. I don't have any choice but to respect her choice—and neither do you." I got into my car and drove off.

The truck I had seen in the security video at The Cat House was right where R.C. had said it would be, so I parked behind it and sat for a moment.

"Don't blow this, Greg. Wait for me, and I'll come back."

"And if you do not?"

"Then do what you want with him. The only way I won't come back is if I can't."

The truck was tucked under an overhang that had once protected a loading dock. The wall in front of it had provided rolling doors for the loading dock, but now boards covered where the doors had been. I carried the gym bag around to the right side, where I knew some courts stood outside one of the center's side doors, and walked over to the nearest hoop. I put the bag just off the court under the basket, grabbed the ball, and started shooting.

I was just beginning to work up a light sweat from some lay-up drills when Jim, dressed in some still-new gym clothes, came out of the door. He was more muscular than I remembered, but after his time in jail that only made sense. He rebounded one of my shots, dribbled out past where the foul line had once been, and took a shot. His form was as beautiful as ever: effortless leap, good extension at the ball's release, wrist held too long forward in the playground show-off mode he'd never outgrown, great rotation on the ball. Swish. I caught the ball as it was coming through and tossed it back to him. You make it, you get to take another; playground rules, the way we'd grown up.

We went back and forth that way for a while, just

like old times, each always knowing where the other's shot would go. I felt my body relax into the rhythms of the court, and I enjoyed it for a few minutes. I could almost forget why I was there, all that had happened before. Almost.

The sun was going down when Jim spoke.

"Did they pay you in diamonds, too, Matt?"

"Yeah. When did you figure it?"

"The moment I got away. Who else could they call? It's a good thing for you they didn't know enough to realize you would have done it for free."

"I suppose so," I said. "You know more about this whole mess than I do."

He tossed me the ball and stared at me.

"You don't know what this is all about, do you?"

I walked over to the gym bag, put the ball inside, and grabbed a towel. As I dried my face, I said, "Not really. I know it's about putting you back in jail. That's enough for me."

He laughed. "That's amazing. Come on; I'll show you what your new friends were up to."

I dropped the towel into the bag and pulled out the shotgun. "Hold up, Jim."

He turned and looked first at the gun, then at me.

"You couldn't kill me before. You had to rely on the cops to take me where someone else could kill me." He shook his head, then turned around again and started walking. "Bring your toy and come see just what you're rescuing."

I kept the shotgun pointed at him and followed him into the building.

The walls of the place were piled high with old sports and recreation equipment: disassembled trampolines, tumbling mats, broken-down pool tables and ping-pong tables, boxes and boxes and boxes of who knows what. Jim had cleared a sizable section of the concrete floor and set up some old pool tables as work surfaces. The computers and microscope, a few racks of labeled vials, and some odd gear I did not recognize sat on three of the tables. On the fourth was a man who looked like a derelict on a three-day binge and who smelled worse, his arms and legs spread and bound by rope to the legs of the pool table. When I got closer I could see the blood dried around his eye sockets, ears, and mouth.

"Dead?" I said.

"Yeah," Jim answered. "I thought I had this thing figured out, but my first cut at it was too much for the body. The head bleeds out as soon as the machines start working."

"Your first cut at what?"

"Ah," Jim laughed, "that is what our new blue friends are so eager to cover up, isn't it? What they have built is really quite remarkable. A lot of people must have died before they got it right. You see, their nano-machines infiltrate the brain and bond to all the sensory connections and the key emotion centers. The machines record what you see and how you feel, then transmit it in real time in compressed form to a receiver like this one—" he pointed to the piece of equipment I had not recognized "—which decodes it into a signal they can interpret and use." He patted the box. "I confess I don't have their encoding standard completely worked out yet, but I'll get it."

"What's the point of all this, Jim?"

He laughed again. "Don't you see? We're the product here, Matt. Pump these nano-machines into one of us, and we become a walking show for the amusement of the aliens and their customers. Set up receivers around the planet, fill us all with the nano-machines, and they've got seven billion channels that are always on!" He paced in front of the equipment, visibly excited by the pure tech aspects of it, all implications irrelevant in the face of the technical challenge.

"So why did they need you? If they had this all figured out, why not just release the machines?"

"Because though the nano-machines may work, the signal they produce is trash. Two-thirds of the manufactured goods on this planet contain a processor and a transmitter, and all those processors are talking all the time. Our atmosphere is positively drenched with transmissions. Wherever they tested must have had way fewer transmissions or transmissions at different frequencies, because when they tried out the prototype here the broadcasts from the nano-machines were garbled—total garbage."

He walked over to the table that held the dead man. "My job was to get them a clear signal. I thought I could do it just by boosting the power a little and shifting to a less frequently used band, but as I said and as you can see—" he patted the corpse on the table "—the power increase is more than a body can bear."

For the next few days after Louise told Jim and me about her cancer, she and I talked almost every day. She didn't want to get together in person, but she seemed to enjoy chatting on the phone. She called a couple of the days, and I called the others. We talked about old times, her work, her family—everything but the cancer. So I wasn't surprised to hear her voice when I picked up the phone one afternoon, but I was surprised at what she said.

"Something's wrong. I'm hurting in different ways than usual, ways I don't think I should be hurting."

"Did you call your doctor?" I asked.

"Not yet, because I just saw him this morning, and I was fine—I mean, as fine as I get these days." She paused and I could hear her sucking in air, fighting the pain. "Nothing unusual was wrong, nothing to explain all this pain I'm feeling in my abdomen."

"Did you do anything unusual?"

"Not really," she said. "After the doctor appointment I stopped and picked up some flowers, then I met Jim for lunch—he finally called, you see, so I figured what the heck—and then I came home."

I thought about my last meeting with Jim, about the talk the three of us had had that day at lunch, about his research, about his mother, and my heart sank.

"Call your doctor," I said. "I'm coming over."

"Okay," she said. "I don't think you need to, but right now I wouldn't mind the company either. This feels weird."

I drove as fast as I could from our gym to her house. Along the way I dug out Jim's card and finally got him on his cell phone.

"What did you do?" I asked.

"She called you," Jim said.

"Yes. What did you do?"

"I made a choice," he said, "that's all. I couldn't just sit by and let her die. Maybe you could do that, but I couldn't."

"That wasn't your choice to make, Jim. She had a few more weeks, maybe a few more months, and now you may have taken those from her."

"Or I may have saved her."

"For your sake, I hope you're right," I said. "But even if you are it wasn't your choice to make. I'm on the way there now; I'll deal with you after I see her." I hung up.

Louise didn't answer my knock on her front door, but it was unlocked so I let myself in.

I found her lying on the floor in her bedroom. Her eyes were bloodshot, blood was coming from her ears and her mouth, and she was barely conscious. I knelt beside her, wanting to hold her but fearing contact might infect me and so unwilling to risk my life, too.

She looked at me. "Matt?"

"Yeah," I said.

"I think this is it."

My face and eyes were hot. "Yeah, it probably is."

"I thought I'd get more time, but it's okay," she said, "it really is okay."

"Sure," I said, knowing it wasn't, knowing she didn't have to die now, at this time, in this way.

Her head fell to one side, and it was over. I didn't bother to check for a pulse. The flow of blood picked up unnaturally, the nano-machines continuing to work, and I backed out of the room.

Jim came through the front door just as I finished explaining the situation to the 911 operator. Ignoring the operator's instructions to stay on the line, I dropped the phone and tackled Jim, taking him down hard. I hit him in the stomach and the face, then sat on his chest and pinned his arms. He spit blood and didn't resist.

"It didn't work, Jim. You killed her."

He looked genuinely sad, but I didn't care how he felt.

"I had to try, Matt. She wasn't going to do anything, and at least this treatment had a chance of working. The nano-machines should have been able to find and destroy the cancer cells. I really thought they could do it."

"Maybe they could have, but they didn't. They also destroyed her."

"I couldn't just let her die," he said. "Can't you see that?"

"No, dammit!" I screamed. "I don't see that at all. It was her choice, not yours."

"She was making the wrong choice," he said. "I

couldn't let her do it when I knew there was a chance I could save her."

"It was her choice," I said. "Hers!"

I grabbed his throat with my left hand and began to squeeze. He tried to buck out from under me, but I kept him pinned, kept slowly increasing the pressure. I wanted to kill him, and I wanted to do it slowly.

"I'm the one holding you down, Jim, so I think I'm the one who gets to make the choice right now. How do you like it?"

I squeezed more, and I could see in his eyes that the lack of air was starting to really hurt him. I wanted so much to finish it, to crush his throat and kill him for what he did, but I didn't. I forced myself to let go of his throat, and then I stayed on top of him until the police arrived.

I looked again at the dead man and shook my head. "Why help them, Jim? What's in it for you?"

"I suppose I could say I helped them because they saved my life," he said, "but you'd know better than that." He leaned against the pool table that held the dead man. "I helped them because I knew I'd get a chance to steal this technology. Do you have any idea how valuable this technology will be once I perfect it? How much it could do for us? Imagine the possibilities. Want to know what your lover is really feeling? This can let you. Want to know what it's like to play in the NBA All-Star game? Now you can, even if you'll never be that good."

"What about the people you infect with these things?"

"Once I get it working, they won't suffer at all. I doubt they'll even know."

"That's not the point, Jim, and you know it. You can't

just take control of other people's lives like this. They get to decide; not you."

"No, Matt, they don't. None of us gets to decide much of anything. Haven't you learned that yet? Governments decide to fight wars, and people go off and die. Companies that leave toxic materials where their employees work and ultimately cause the deaths of those people decades later are making fatal decisions for those people—and the people never even know it. Drivers who aren't paying attention kill other drivers who never had a choice in their fate. It happens all the time. This technology will be just one more way some people won't get to make choices."

I raised the gun. "No, Jim, it won't. It's wrong. I can't stop all the ways that people don't get to choose, but I can stop this. And I will."

He pushed off the table and walked toward me. He stopped six feet away.

"What are you going to do, Matt? You couldn't kill me before, and you can't kill me now. Oh, I believe you can kill, but you can't kill me because I won't fight back and because we're brothers, two of a kind."

"No. We were brothers. We haven't been that for a long time."

"Maybe not, but you still can't kill me, and you can't stop me without killing me." He turned his back on me and headed over to the table that held the computer. "Get out of here. Go tell them you couldn't find me, and let me get back to work."

"Jim."

He stopped and turned. "What?"

I pointed the shotgun at the ground in front of him. "You may be right that I can't kill you, but that doesn't matter. I don't have to kill you to stop you."

He opened his mouth to speak, but I could not hear what he said over the sound of the shotgun blast. The shot tore up the concrete in front of him, ripped small holes through his legs, and threw him backwards. He lay on the ground, his legs a pulpy mass, bleeding heavily, screaming.

I yelled over the screams. "You'll only suffer for a while, Jim. The aliens will fix you up; they've done it before. And when they're done, they'll take you away, because they can't afford to have anyone working on this stuff on Earth anymore. They may be back with this technology, but that's tomorrow's problem, and we'll have time to prepare." Shock was clearly setting in, and Jim had stopped screaming and was now whimpering in pain. "You'll be working for them for a very long time."

I grabbed a couple of vials from the rack, retrieved the gym bag from under the basket, wrapped the vials in the sweat towels, and put them and the shotgun in the bag. Our best hope was that the alien guild rules would keep this technology away long enough that we could figure out how to deal with it. I knew some researchers, some former colleagues of Jim's, whom I thought might be trustworthy enough to try. It wasn't a great chance, but it was a chance.

Greg was lying facedown on the ground beside the car, all of his arms spread, R.C. standing over him and holding a very large shotgun against his neck. Both of the disk weapons were on the ground behind R.C.

"Feel better?" I said to him.

R.C. smiled. "Much."

"Good. Now let him go."

R.C. raised an eyebrow.

"He and I have a deal. Don't we, Greg?"

"Yes," Greg said.

R.C. backed away, and Greg righted himself.

"Jim is inside. Call your people now, because he's hurt and you'll need to repair him."

"What about our materials?" Greg asked.

"Everything is inside."

"Did he succeed?"

"No. He said he still hadn't made it work. There's a dead man in there whose body is proof that Jim's telling the truth. You need to get rid of that body, too."

"Did James Peterson tell you what he was doing for us?"

"No," I said. I handed him the weapons. "Now, keep your part of the deal and get him out of here."

Greg put the weapons back in his suit and went silent for a moment. "A small ship is on the way and should be here momentarily. Though we dislike landings, we must conclude this affair quickly. You are done. You should leave."

"You'll take him away? You can take him anywhere you want, as long as it's not on this planet, but you will repair him and take him away?"

"Yes," Greg said. "We have found humans useful in many situations. Even though we cannot use him on this planet to continue his work, I am confident we will find a use for him elsewhere for a very long time."

I nodded and turned to R.C. Greg headed toward the building where Jim lay bleeding, and R.C. and I walked off to his truck. I felt the disturbance in the air before I heard the ship's very quiet approach, but I didn't look back to watch it land. I'd done what I could and what I should, and for now that had to be enough.

THE THREE WALLS—32nd CAMPAIGN

S. M. Stirling

"Sir," Gnaeus Clodius Afer said. "Exactly which bunch of these *fucking* wogs are we supposed to be fighting, anyway?"

Gaius Vibulenus squeezed his hand on the mail-clad shoulder of the man who commanded the Tenth Cohort. Clodius Afer wore a red transverse crest across his helmet; he carried a staff of hard twisted wood rather than the two javelins the enlisted men bore, and his short stabbing sword was slung on the right from a baldric rather than the left side of his military belt: a centurion's gear. Gaius Vibulenus's Attic helmet had a white plume, and he wore a back-and-breast armor of cast bronze hinged at the shoulders. The Hellenic-style outfit marked him as an officer, a military tribune.

At least, it had when the legion sailed out of Brundisium to join Crassus's glorious conquest of Parthia. He'd been able to wear it because his family were wealthy landowners in Campania and politically well-connected; one more gentry sprig gaining a little military experience to help him with the *cursus honorum* to office, and hopefully a share of the plunder. Militarily he'd been a joke. The actual work of the unit was done by men like Clodius Afer. Since then, things had changed.

Hercules, but they've changed, Gaius Vibulenus thought, looking down the hillside where the Romans stood at ease and waited for the aliens who'd bought them from their Parthian captors to decide what they were going to do.

I'd like to know in more detail too. Usually they just march us out of the ship, we kick arse, and then we march back. He didn't like it when things got more complicated than that. The last time they'd gotten really complex . . . that had been the siege. The siege had been very bad. . . .

To blank out the memory of ton-weights of stone grinding through his body Gaius Vibulenus looked over his shoulder, towards the group who would send the legion into action. The hulking presence of the Guild Commander was half a hundred paces away, surrounded by his monstrous toadlike guards mounted on their giant hyenalike mounts. The seven-foot spiked maces the guards bore glinted in the light of a sun paler than that the Roman had been born under, with a pinkish tinge to its yellow. The banded iron armor they wore creaked on its leather backing, and the scale-sewn blankets that protected their mounts rustled and clicked. The Commander—this Commander, there had been a dozen of as many different types—was himself as large as his hideous bodyguards, and dressed in the inevitable blue jumpsuit with the shimmer of a force-screen before his face. His hands dangled nearly to his back-acting knees, and when he was nervous claws like so many straight razors unfolded from the insides of his fingers. They were thin and translucent and looked sharp enough to cut the air.

Compared to him, the natives of this low-technology world were positively homelike, much more so than most the legion had fought in the service of the . . . creatures . . . who'd bought them. The group around the Commander were fairly typical. Almost homelike . . . if you ignored the fact that they had greenish feather fronds instead of hair, and huge eyes of a deep purple without whites, and thumbs on either side of their three-fingered hands. About half the delegation arguing with the Commander were females, their breasts left bare by the linen kilts that were their only garments—four breasts each.

One of the guard detail standing easy behind the tribune pursed his lips. "You know, some of them wog bitches, they're not bad looking," he murmured. "Wonder what they're shaped like under those kilts?" A couple of the naked attendants with collars around their necks, probably slaves, were male and equipped the same way as someone from Campania.

"Silence in the ranks!" Afer barked. In a conversational voice: "Sir?"

"It's a little more complex than usual, Centurion," Vibulenus said. "The . . . Guild—" he'd always wondered if that Latin word was precisely what the creatures who'd brought them *meant* "—is supporting the rulers of a kingdom southeast of here. *They're* in the process of conquering this area we're in, and they're facing a rebellion that they can't put down."

If the Guild used its *lasers* and flying boats, putting an end to the uprising would take about thirty minutes. For some reason Vibulenus had never even begun to understand, the Federation the trading guild served forbade the use of weapons more advanced than those of the locals of any given area. If the natives used hand-weapons of iron, the slave-mercenaries of the Guild had to do likewise. That was why they'd bought the Romans; the legion was very, very skilled with those tools, and had the discipline to slaughter many times their number of those who were less so.

"And *we're* supposed to pull it out of the pot for them, right," Afer said. "Well, that's familiar enough." His eyes lifted over the ranks of the Roman legionaries appraising the local help they'd be working with. "That'll be their lot, eh?"

Vibulenus nodded; the remark had been a conversational placeholder. The legion often had to work with local auxiliaries and it usually wasn't any pleasure . . . but it was as necessary here as it had been back in the lands around the Middle Sea, since Rome produced little in the way of cavalry or light missile-infantry. For instance, under Crassus they'd depended on Celtic auxiliary cavalry from Gaul to keep the Parthians away while they marched through the desert of Ctesiphon.

"And *that* didn't work all that well, the *gods* know," he murmured.

Afer nodded, understanding him without need for further words. They both remembered it more vividly than most things since: the dust and the thirst, the glitter of the mail and lances of the Parthian cataphracts whose presence forced them into tight formation . . . and the horse-archers darting in, loosing their clouds of shafts. Shafts thrown by their horse-and-sinew composite bows with enough force to slam the point right through the leather and plywood of a shield, forcing you back a pace with the whipcrack impact and leaving the triangular head of the arrow on the inside of your shield. If you were lucky; right through your mailcoat if you weren't, and your body lay with all its blood running out on the alkaline clay of Mesopotamia. . . .

Vibulenus shrugged off the memory and looked at the locals. Many of them drove chariots, not much different from the ones immortal Homer had described, except that the pair of beasts which drew them had feathers rather than fur, and blunt omnivore fangs instead of a horse's grass-cropping equipment. They looked like big dogs or slim bears with the skins of pigeons, or at least that was as close as you could come to describing them in Latin. Each cart carried three of the beasts, a driver in a kilt, a spearman in a long coat of iron or bronze scales and carrying a big rectangular shield, and an archer. There were more feathery plumes on the helmets of all three. Their infantry . . .

Well, that's what we're here for, he thought. The infantry were a rabble, some of their spears only fire-hardened wood at the business end, none of them with much in the way of armor. The slingers and archers might be of some use.

"Gaius Vibulenus Caper," the Commander called.

Vibulenus sighed and adjusted his helmet. "Time to get the word," he said, and strode towards the toad-guards.

"Hasn't it ever occurred to these dickheads to *ride* the bloody things?" someone snarled.

Apparently not, Vibulenus thought.

The enemy were a huge shambling clot pouring out of the distant woods and across the lowlands. Their crest was cavalry—a line of chariots, not much different from the ones the Romans'—the trading guild's—allies used.

Gaudy, though, Vibulenus thought critically, looking at the enemy vehicles. Two of them collided as they swept in one-wheel-down circuits that were probably designed to show off the driver's skill. *And I've seen better coordination in a tavern brawl.*

The allied war-carts sweeping in from the flanks to meet the enemy were fairly uniform, and they moved in squadrons of four and larger units to horn and flag signals. Those of the enemy were decorated with feathers and paint, plumes and gilded bronze and silver, whatever their owners fancied or could afford—and the skulls of enemies past nailed to their railings. The skulls looked less human than the faces of the locals did alive.

Arrows flickered out. Vibulenus's eyebrows rose. A good two or three hundred yards, and they hit hard when they landed—that was almost as good as the Parthians. Chariots tumbled into splintered wreck, their passengers flying out like rag dolls with their limbs flapping until the bone-crunching impact. Others careened away driverless, or stopped as their beasts were injured—unlike horses, the local draft animals seemed inclined to fight when they were hurt, not run away. It was all as distant and safe as matched pairs in an arena in Capua; a few of the troops were even calling out *hoc habet* and making gestures with their thumbs.

"Looks like our wogs are thrashing their wogs, sir," After said after a moment. "Leastways with the chariots."

Vibulenus nodded. *But that isn't going to be what settles this fight*, he thought. The enemy infantry was still spilling out of the woods, and while the allied chariots were getting the better of the melee they still weren't free to range up and down shooting them to pieces. *Not many missile infantry*, he noted. Spearmen with seven-foot stabbing weapons and shields, and swordsmen with long leaf-shaped slashing weapons, the few slingers and archers were to the rear where they couldn't do much good. The local wogs were bigger than the Guild's allies, and their feathery head-tufts had a reddish or yellow tinge to the green. They painted their naked bodies in patterns as gaudy as the chariots of their lords; some of them wore strings of hands or disconcertingly humanlike genitalia around their necks, while others had torques of pure soft gold.

"Noisy buggers," Afer added after a minute.

Vibulenus nodded again. They were chanting in high-pitched squealing voices as they came, hammering their weapons on their shields and prancing with a high-stepping gait like trained horses. That changed to a flat-out run as they came within range of the chariot battle; it was a little like watching heavy surf rolling on a beach. The Roman tribune's brows went up as he watched. They might be savages, but they knew their business. Dozens of them swarmed around every allied war-car, throwing clouds of short weighted darts, then dashing in to slash or stab at the chariot teams. Dozens of chariots went over in the first few minutes, or disappeared under mounds of hacking, heaving foemen. Then a trio of heads would go up on spearpoints, and the mob would move on to the next target with a loping movement like a pack of wolves. They ignored the auxiliary infantry as if they weren't there, despite a trickle of casualties from arrows and slung stones.

"They probably think everyone will run away when the chariots pull out," the tribune said in a neutral tone. "Probably has gone that way for them, until now."

The allied chariots *were* disengaging, those still able to move—drivers lashing their beasts to reckless haste, high spoked wheels bouncing over irregularities at speeds that made even a heavy tuft of grass a menace to their stability. They had to get out, though, or go down like a beetle swarmed over by ants.

"Hercules. Must be twenty, twenty-five thousand of them," someone muttered.

"Yeah, we'll all have to throw both spears and then gut one each," his file-mate replied. "Don't any of 'em have armor, and this bunch aren't nine feet tall, either, for a fucking change."

The tribune's eyes went right and left along the long mail-gray line of the legion. Sure as shit, the auxiliary infantry posted on either flank *were* running; not as fast as the chariots, but there was a lot less chance of them rallying, too. Vibulenus sighed and reached up to settle his white-plumed helmet more securely on his head.

"*Limlairabu!*" the enemy soldier screamed.

Or something like that. Gaius Vibulenus swung his round bronze-faced officer's shield up and sideways with a mindless skill born of more years experience than he cared to remember. His opponent was wielding his axe one-handed, with a small iron-rimmed buckler in the other hand. The axe handle was some springy hornlike substance, rather than wood—or maybe that was the way wood grew here—and the edge of the axe whickered through the air as it blurred towards him. The edge was good steel, and so was the spike on the other side. Either could give him a brain-deep head wound beyond even the Medic's ability to cure.

Crack. The axe took a gouge out of the rim of Vibulenus's shield, leaving creamy-white splinters and torn bronze facing in its wake. He stepped in, stamped a hobnailed foot down on the native's bare one, and stabbed underarm. The Spanish steel of his sword scarcely slowed as it went into the native's taut belly-muscles, but a sudden spasm locked flesh around the metal as he tried to withdraw it. With a wheezing curse he put a foot on the spasming body and wrenched it out, straightening up to look around. Oblong Roman shields closed around him as the first two ranks trotted past, into the unraveling enemy formation. . . .

Well, no, he thought, straining to catch his breath. *It never was a formation. More of a mob.*

Tubas snarled. *"Loose!"* he heard, and the massed javelins of the rear two ranks whistled overhead. They didn't have the densely packed shoulder-to-shoulder targets of the volley that had opened the battle, but there were still enough of the enemy crowded into the zone just behind the edge of combat that virtually every spear found a mark in a shield or in naked flesh. A frenzied mass scream went up; part of that was frustrated rage. Surviving warriors found they could neither pull the *pilum* points out of their shields nor use the javelins for a return throw if they did manage to wriggle them free, since the soft iron shanks of the weapons buckled on impact.

He was reminded of a wave breaking on a rock again, as he had been at the beginning of the battle, but this time it was the rock that advanced, crying out and stabbing. Vibulenus trotted forward, his head moving to keep the action in view as far as he could. So far it was pretty routine . . . routine for everyone except the luckless bastards the floating metal turtles were picking up. Particularly except for the ones the turtles *weren't* picking up. No matter how badly injured you were—no matter how *dead*, with a spear through the guts or your groin slashed up—if the turtles took you, you'd wake up. Weak, and crimson over most of your body, but that would pass and you'd be good as new, except for the memories. If the turtle rejected you, you were as dead as the men who'd taken a Parthian arrow under Crassus.

Sometimes he thought they'd been the lucky ones.

"Routine," he said. "But somehow I don't think so."

"Sir," Gaius Vibulenus said with desperate earnestness. "We don't *have* to storm the fortress."

The Commander had put his headquarters on a grassy knoll overlooking the valley. From here there was a clear view across a checkerboard of croplands and pasture toward the steep-sided plateau at the center of the basin. It didn't look like Campania here, but it looked a *lot* like say, Cisalpine Gaul; in a way that made it more disturbing than most of the howling wilderness the legion had been landed in. The trees that gave shade overhead weren't quite like oaks; the grain turning tawny-colored down below wasn't like wheat or barley—more like a set of kernels on a broomstick—and the grass had a subtle bluish tint beneath its green. Even the scents were *subtly* wrong, close enough to leaf mold and ordinary crushed grass that you started doubting if it really was different, or if your memories were fading. Vibulenus was aware that his perception of the environment wasn't typical, though; there had been a lot of comments on how homelike the place was. If it hadn't been for the example made of the last attempted deserters—the tribune suppressed a sudden white flash of rage at the memory of what the Guild lasers had done to those soldiers, those Romans, those *friends*—he'd have been apprehensive about men going over the hill. That object lesson had driven home two facts, though. You couldn't hide from the Guild sensors that could peer through solid rock, and you couldn't do anything about the lasers that could *burn* through solid rock.

The fort was disturbing in another way. Not that it was particularly sophisticated. He'd seen much better; that stone castle they'd besieged in the fifth campaign, for instance, the one built by the furry little wogs who looked like giant dormice. That had been like an artificial cliff. This was fifty or sixty feet of steep turf, and then a wall of huge squared logs; another log wall was built twenty feet within, tied in to the first with cross-timbers, and the intervening space filled with rubble and earth. The logs were big, forty feet to their sharpened tips, and they wouldn't burn easily—wood here didn't, for some reason, as if it had strands of glass inside it. That wasn't the problem. There were towers every fifty or sixty feet, too, full of archers and slingers and javelineers. But *that* wasn't the problem.

"Are you unable to take the fortress?" the Commander said, his voice the same neutral baritone that all the Commanders had. That was more incongruous than the bestial snarling his mouth suggested would be more natural.

"Sir, no, we can take it," Vibulenus said. *The Commander is the problem.* "A week to build catapults, then we put in a ramp and some siege towers and go over the palisade. But there are better than ten thousand of them in there, and it'll turn into a ratfight—our discipline and armor are bigger advantages in the open field than in street-fighting. We'll lose a hundred, maybe two hundred men . . . and you've told us that the Guild can't replace our losses."

The Commander pursed his lips. "That is correct," he said.

Vibulenus's stomach knotted. The Guild could make the Romans immortal—unaging, at least—and it could repair anything but a spearpoint through the braincase. But it couldn't get more Romans. *Never more Romans. Never Rome again. Never home again—*

He cut off that train of thought with practiced ease. There were easier ways to die here than a spear or a sword; thinking about home too much was one of them. Even the Medic couldn't bring you back from a really determined attempt at suicide.

Attacking the Commander, for instance.

"That is correct," the Commander went on. "But it

is essential that this rebellion be put down. If assets must be expended, then they must."

"Sir," Gaius Vibulenus went on, in a voice that must *not* shake with the anger that poured through him like boiling oil poured on a storming party. "There *are* ten thousand men in there. Each of them has to eat every day. You can see that they didn't have the time to get their harvest in, but it's nearly ripe—all their food-stocks must be low. If we invest the fortress, we can starve them out and solve the problem *economically*."

The Commander made a noncommittal sound, then blinked and looked at the fields and nodded. Vibulenus felt a slight chill. The Commander *looked* like something out of a nightmare . . . but in a way that response made him seem even more alien. He obviously hadn't thought of the harvest as something *important*.

"If you assets are encamped here, is there not a risk that the enemy will . . . I believe the term is *sally*? At night, for instance."

Vibulenus's head rose up. "Sir, we are *Romans*. I assure you that within a week, they'll no more be able to sally successfully than they could fly to Rome by flapping their arms."

"Now, *stay* there, ye bugger," the legionary grunted. The pit he'd been digging was the depth of a man's arm, slanting forward at a forty-five-degree angle. Inside it was a wooden stake only a little shorter, the upper point trimmed to a sharp point and fire-hardened. The soldier finished ramming the unhardened point into the soft earth at the base of the pit, flicked the stake to make sure that it was firmly seated, then moved on to the next pit, dragging his bundle of stakes with him.

The air smelled of freshly turned earth; from the rings of pits for the stakes, and from the square-section ditch ahead of them, twenty feet deep and neat as a knife-cut through cake. The ditch was an irregular oblong, intended to run all around the hill on which the enemy squatted; when the Romans began their siege works the ramparts had been black with watchers, but now only a normal number squatted or leaned on their spears atop the ramparts. Vibulenus cocked a critical eye at the massive excavation. The layout and initial digging had been done by the legion's soldiers, but much of the donkey-work was being handed off to local peasants rounded up by the auxiliaries. The main problem hadn't been resistance, but the simple blundering incompetence of backwoodsmen not accustomed to working in groups. Despite that the peasants were working hard—they'd been told that they could go back to their harvest when the circumvallation was complete. They even had a few tricks that the Romans hadn't run into before.

Their spades and picks were familiar enough, but instead of carrying dirt away in baskets they used a little box with a wheel in front and two handles behind— really extremely clever. *I wonder why we never thought of that?* Vibulenus wondered mildly, then turned.

Behind the rows of lilies were more rows of *stimulators*, short sticks with a pointed iron barb at one end, hammered into the dirt with the barb pointing inward towards the enemy. Behind *them* was a ditch ten feet deep, full of trees with sharpened branches making a forest of points; behind *that* was another ditch, this one to be flooded when they'd linked it to the river that ran through the valley. Behind that was the wall proper, an earthen rampart, then an upright palisade. From the base of the palisade bristling sharpened stakes pointed downward, into the space where the faces of attackers would be if they tried to scale it. Square-section towers of wooden framework reared along the growing wall, each a long javelin-cast apart. Building the rampart and towers was skilled work; the locals were just dragging up the necessary timber, and the legion's men were busy with adz and saw and hammer.

Vibulenus's mouth quirked. Nobody in the whole Roman world worked as fast and well as legionaries. Back home, work like this would be done by slaves. Not as well, and much more slowly.

Many of the legionaries were working on the fortifications; twenty-five hundred men stood to arms, in case . . .

A centurion named Pompilius Niger trotted up. He'd been a ranker when the legion left Campania for the East; a ranker, and a neighbor and friend of Vibulenus since childhood, since his father's farm adjoined the Vibulenii's estate.

"Found any honey yet?" Gaius Vibulenus asked, smiling slightly.

Niger shook his head. "No, they don't *have* any," he said in frustration. "The wogs, they crush a sort of thick reed and boil the juice. It's sweet, but it isn't honey, you know?"

The junior centurion had been trying to find materials to make proper mead since they'd left Parthia. He was a round-faced young man . . . young in appearance, at least; his eyes had little youth left in them, although objectively they hadn't altered an iota since the Guild decided that their Roman *assets* were too valuable to be left to weaken with age.

"Anyways, sir," he went on, his voice growing more formal—business, then. "I wanted to ask you something. There's a *noise* over by the northern gates."

"Noise?" Vibulenus asked.

"Yeah. Sort of a *grinding* sound. Not really like troops mustering . . . more like *traffic*. Getting louder, though. So I sent a runner to Rusticanus—" Julius Rusticanus, the legion's senior centurion, the *primus pilus*, the "first spear" "—and I thought you'd like to know, anyway."

Vibulenus nodded; he'd been at loose ends. It was unlikely that men as experienced as Niger would miss anything obvious. He and the centurion began to walk over to the area covering the northern gate of the enemy fortress; there was a road running up to it, and it even had pavement. Not the smooth blocks Romans could have laid. It was rounded rocks from the river-bed, laid close together and pounded down into a lumpy surface that he supposed was better than the bottomless mud this alluvial soil would produce otherwise. . . .

The tribune looked down at the rocks under his feet. The hobnails in his *caligulae* gritted and sparked on the flint-rich stones, and he remembered . . .

"It's a breakout!" he snapped, picking up the pace to a trot. "Sound the alarm!"

"I had seen the reports, of course," the Commander said, in his neutral too-perfect voice, the voice of a hired teacher of rhetoric or a professional of the law-courts. *Nobody* spoke Latin like that every day. "But I admit that I am impressed."

He was fucking terrified, Vibulenus thought, carefully keeping his features blank, not shaped in the derisive grin that his mind felt. He didn't *think* that the Commander could read a Roman's facial expressions, any more than the tribune could make sense of what went on behind the Commander's face shield. There was no sense in taking a chance, though.

"What was it that enabled you to anticipate the enemy's actions?" the Commander went on.

The sally had started with the abruptness of an axe dropping—a hinged section of wall that acted as a drawbridge had come down, and a wave of screaming spearmen had come tearing out behind a cloud of arrows and slung stones. *That* had been a diversion, though it might well have been a lethal one for a *sightseer* in a blue jumpsuit, if Roman cohorts hadn't already been falling in in front of him, and more grabbing up stacked shields and javelins along the wall, turning themselves from working parties into fighting men again with the smooth efficiency of a machine turning in a pivot.

From the way he'd reacted, the Commander had known it too. He'd screamed—the sound had come through as its natural guttural bellow, not being words—and crouched reflexively, the claws flashing out from his fingers like straight razors as his mouth gaped and showed rows of serrated teeth like a shark's.

The "ship" the Guild provided for its Roman assets could swallow waste, litter and spare weapons through its skin. Vibulenus wondered if the Commander's blue jumpsuit could do the same with bodily wastes released in sudden panic. Not that the smell would stand out here; the windrow of bodies where the locals' berserk onrush had met the serried ranks of the legion was two deep in places. None were Romans; their wounded were being carried back by the floating turtle or limping along with the help of friends as they walked to the Medic. There weren't any who weren't . . . repairable. If they hadn't been warned, they'd still have *won*—Rusticanus had been taking precautions, on the theory that turning out for trouble never hurt—but the butcher's bill would have been heavier. An edge of the chill pride he felt was in his voice as he replied to the Guild's officer.

"Your worship, it occurred to me that the wheels of the enemy chariots were iron-rimmed, and that the . . . the *grinding* sound reported would come from iron wheels moving over cobbles."

The infantry attack had been delivered with dreadful speed and intensity—the wogs might as well have been bloody *Gauls*, as Clodius Afer had commented—but it was only cover for the chariots behind. Those had made straight for the remaining gaps in the walls of the circumvallation. Some had gone into the ditches and pits; some had run into lilies or stimulators. The Guild's local auxiliaries had taken a fair toll of the rest. Plenty of them had made it out into open country, though, and from the watchers' reports they were scattering in every direction. The auxiliaries tailing them were reporting that each group was making for its home tribal territory.

"Well," the Commander said. "Be that as it may. Yes, apparently your . . . engineering . . ." the cool mechanical voice had a tint of well-bred amusement " . . . has alarmed them to the point of demoralization. I think we may expect them to yield soon."

"Your Worship . . ." Vibulenus said. "No, I'm afraid that's not the purpose of this breakout."

The Commander didn't have eyebrows to arch, but somehow managed to convey the same silent doubt. The Roman tribune went on:

"Sir, I don't think they could have persuaded that many of their infantry to fight that hard just to cover a bugout by their overlords. And they're not just running, they're heading for their tribal homelands."

"So?"

"Your worship, what they're doing . . . those ones in the chariots, they're the leaders, the landowners, the patricians—the men who'll be listened to. And what I think they're going to do is gather every wog in three hundred miles in every direction, every wog who can walk, and head straight here. As a relief force, to catch us and smash us against the anvil of the fortress."

He nodded to the great timber-and-earthwork fort

looming above them. "While we fight the relief force, they'll sally against us, or vice versa. That's their objective."

Beside him, First Spear Rusticanus nodded and went on: "Sir . . . Your Worship . . . them wogs is pretty densely packed around here. There's going to be a *lot* of them coming at us."

The Commander went halfway into his defensive crouch again. The mechanism that turned his voice into too-perfect Latin wouldn't let squealing fright through into the tones. "Then you must storm the fortress *at once*! The Guild will not tolerate failure!"

Meaning your ass is in a sling if we lose, Vibulenus thought. Of course, the *legion's* ass was in the same unpleasant situation, and in a far more literal sense. He looked up the steep turf of the earthwork, at the great logs of the fort, at the locals prancing and yelling on the bulwarks.

"Your Worship!" he barked, in a tone that contained all he could put into it of servile enthusiasm. "Under your leadership, we *Romans* will now show you that the Guild's confidence in us is not misplaced!"

The Commander blinked, and let his rubbery pinkish lips cover the multiple-saw layers of his teeth. "You have a plan?"

"Sir, I do," Vibulenus said. He poured strength into his voice, as he might into a wavering rank. There was none of the concern he'd have felt for men in that situation, but he had to do it nonetheless—the blue-suited figure before him could order his men, *his* men, into a suicidal frontal attack. If he thought that would secure his position with the Guild, he'd do it in a moment. "My plan is—"

He went into details. The Commander raised a hand. "Surely there isn't time for all that?" he said.

Vibulenus exchanged a brief glance with the senior

centurion, saw an imperceptible nod. "Your Worship, until now we've been assuming we had plenty of time. Now we'll show you what Romans can do in a *hurry*."

"Think they'll come, sir?" Clodius Afer said quietly. The ground in front of the outward-facing line of fortifications looked as if giant moles had been gnawing and chewing their way through it. There hadn't been time for neatness, and there wasn't a man in the legion or its impressed labor force that didn't have blisters even on hands calloused to the texture of rawhide. But the fortifications that fenced out the rebels' relief force were now complete, as complete as those that faced inward towards the native citadel. Light came from the towers that studded the Romans' walls, the light of something like pine burning in big metal baskets . . . and from three moons, two of them far too large. Vibulenus looked over his shoulder. The lights on the inner wall would show the bodies of the natives who'd tried to sally . . . and the skeletal forms of the civilians they'd driven out of their lines, to save their remaining food stores for the warriors. The Commander had ordered that any who approached the Roman works were to be killed.

Vibulenus grimaced slightly. He'd have forbidden taking any of them in, too; the Roman force and their auxiliaries had only about thirty days of supplies. But he'd have let them through and into the countryside, at least. None of them were fighting men. At least the stink of rotting meat wouldn't be quite as bad then.

"I think they're having trouble organizing their supply train," he said in a neutral tone, by way of replying to the other's question.

The enemy host sprawled out to the edge of sight was stunning, even in the dark. They'd built bonfires of their own, too. Painted figures in masks and bones

capered and screamed around them, in religious rite
or propitiation or sorcery or some unimaginable alternative. Other figures screamed and writhed in wicker
cages on platforms built above the fires, sacrifices
roasting slowly and then tumbling down as the supports under their containers burnt through. Between
and behind the fires the enemy warriors seethed, like
maggots spilled out of a putrid corpse. The firelight
made the edges of their weapons a twinkling like stars
on a broad lake, eddying and milling as far as sight
could reach.

"Organize their supply train?" Clodius Afer asked.
"Sir, them, they couldn't organize an orgy in a whore-
house. Three gets you one they're starving already, and
it's less than a week since they showed up."

"So, yes, they'll come," Vibulenus said. "Soon, I
think. Tonight. They can signal to the fortress, light
reflected on mirrors."

The eddying and swirling was beginning to take on
a pattern, and drums were beating among the enemy.
A minute later he decided that it was warriors pounding
the butts of their spears or the backs of their axes
against the rawhide inner surface of their shields. For
a while it was discordant babble, and then more and
more of them fell into a rhythm. Tens of thousands
of impacts per second, not all together because the
enemy force was simply too large, but it rippled across
the Romans like thunder echoing in a mountain pass.

The noise was so stunning that Vibulenus missed the
shouts and crashing noises coming from behind him
for a moment. A runner came up, panting.

"Sir," he gasped. "Senior Centurion Rusticanus
reports the enemy in the fort is making sorties—all
three gates. They've got hurdles to fill the ditches, por-
table bridges, and grappling irons and ladders."

Vibulenus felt his mind go cold, into a distant place

where everything moved like stones on a gaming-board. "My compliments to the First Spear, and carry on," he said.

"Hercules," Clodius Afer said. "Here they come."

The numbers of the barbarians charging forward towards the outer face of the Roman works were stunning. Not exactly frightening—not the way standing helpless under the Parthian arrow-storm had been frightening—but . . . impressive.

The light of the fire-baskets extended out as far as the initial deep trench. As the enemy reached it and bunched at the further edge, the catapults and onagers along the line of the siege works opened up. The torsion springs of the smaller devices threw six-foot javelins, or ten-pound rocks. Darts pinned three and four together at a time; rocks shattered torsos into loose bags of blood and splintered bone and exploded skulls with the finality of a hobnailed sandal coming down on a cockroach. The heavier throwing machines were usually used to batter down stone walls; here they threw man-heavy rocks into a target impossible to miss, sending the great rocks bounding and skipping through channels of pulped flesh. The horde ignored it, dropping into the great ditch, handing down ladders, propping them against the inner wall and swarming upward.

A native trumpet shrilled, high and womanish. The towers along the Roman lines were crowded with the local auxiliaries, foot and chariot crews both. Arrows lifted in clouds, driven by the powerful horn-and-sinew bows, their three-bladed steel heads winking in the firelight. Lead bullets whistled out, hard to see in daylight and invisible now. Many of the auxiliaries were using staff slings, with the cord fastened to a yard-long hardwood handle. Lead shot from weapons like those could punch right through a heavy-infantry shield and kill the man behind it through his armor. There was plenty of ammunition.

"I think we underestimated our local allies, a bit," Vibulenus said, looking up. Another sleet of arrows crossed one of the moons—even now the size and reddish cloud-streaked color of it made his spine crawl slightly.

Clodius Afer grunted, shrugging his thick shoulders under the mailcoat. "Easy enough when they're sitting up in them towers, sir," he said.

Vibulenus nodded. The centurion had a point, but it was a bit of a parochial one. Bowmen couldn't slug it out like Roman legionary infantry, granted. But they could be extremely effective when used *properly*; Parthia, and campaigns since, ought to have taught them that.

"They needed something to keep those spearmen and axemen off them," he said musingly, wiping the palm of his right hand down the leather strips that made a skirt under his tribune's cast-bronze armor. "The way . . . the way those Parthians could ride away from us, shooting us up and we couldn't catch them, you see?"

Afer grunted again; by the sound of it, he *did* see. "They're killing a lot of the barbs," the squat man said. "But it ain't going to stop 'em."

Vibulenus picked up his shield. It was lighter than the oval *scutum* of the legionaries, although it didn't give the same degree of protection to the left leg—the leg you advanced in combat. It also had a loop through which he slid his forearm, and a handhold near the rim, rather than the single central handgrip of the line infantry's shield. It was Greek in form, like the rest of his gear. Romans had beaten Greeks all the way from Epiros to Syria, talking less and hitting harder—but when Roman aristocrats went to war, they wore gear that wouldn't have been out of place in Alexander's army. There was an obscure irony to that, he thought.

"You're right," he went on aloud. "They're not stopping for shit."

They did pause on the nearer edge of the ditch, massing before they charged. Arrows and sling bullets were slapping into them in a ceaseless barrage; he could see laborers bringing more ammunition up the ladders that marked the rear faces of the towers, out of the corner of his eye. The screams seemed to be as much rage as pain out there, though.

Hmmm. They're waiting for the ladders to be handed up out of the ditch . . . no, they brought enough to leave those. They're handing fresh ones forward, and bundles of brushwood.

Even dumb barbs learned, eventually. That was one reason his father had approved of Caesar, Crassus's political ally, and his conquest of the Gauls. You had to overrun them before they learned too *much*. Roman politics, more distant than those alien moons . . .

The enemy rushed forward again, the long rough-made ladders in the front ranks. Those dissolved in screaming panic as they ran full-tilt into the "stimulators," covered with hay and invisible in the night anyway. Thousands piled up before that jam, throwing the front ranks full-length into the barbed iron. More hands took up the fallen ladders, walking forward cautiously, or simply over the writhing bodies of their predecessors. The archers and slingers and the ballistae the Romans had made switched their point of aim to the pileup behind the first ranks. Big figure-eight shields went up in an improvised roof, but most of the projectiles punched right through the light leather-and-wicker constructions.

"Still comin'," Afer said expressionlessly, the thick

fingers of his right hand absently kneading the hilt of his sword.

"Not as many," Vibulenus said.

The legion's Tenth Cohort was drawn up behind them, a reaction force ready to rush to any part of the fortifications where the enemy made a lodgment. As they would, as they would . . .

"Holding them up like that in a killing ground, it's really softening them up for us," Vibulenus said. "Wouldn't care to meet all of them in an open field."

Afer grunted again, too proud to say aloud what they both knew; that horde would have overrun a single legion in a single shrieking rush. It could be done—the Cimbri had done it to three consular armies, before Marius caught them and smashed them. You needed a really good commander and enough numbers to keep from being flanked. Then, yes you could kill naked barbs like this all day until your arm got tired from gutting them.

As we're doing right now, Vibulenus thought coldly. The enemy were through the "stimulators" and into the lilies; those stakes were as long as a man's thigh, and they could kill rather than just cripple, but there were fewer of them. Now to the flooded ditch . . .

"Ready!" he said to the signalers.

The bridges that the enemy were manhandling forward were fifteen feet broad and twenty long, platforms of thick plank nailed onto beams to make a floor. They looked like staggering centipedes as they lurched forward towards the flooded ditch, supported on the hands and shoulders of scores of men . . . or at least of creatures very much like men. Very much, when you'd had a *really* broad experience of the possible alternatives. Squads with shields surrounded them on all sides, taking most of the arrows directed at the assault squads carrying the bridges; more crowded forward to take their places as they fell.

"Ready," Vibulenus said again, his eyes wide as memories passed somewhere deep in his mind, far below the level of the consciousness that moved and spoke.

On a distant . . . *planet* was the word the Guild employees used, but that made no sense; how could you walk on a "wandering star"? In a distant land, the legion had fought little furry wogs who had a number of valuable tricks. One of them was a compound of rock-oil, saltpeter, naphtha, pine-pitch, and quicklime. Not all the ingredients had been easy to find here, but something close enough could be cobbled together; vegetable oil would do nearly as well as the black stuff from the ground—

The bridges rose, paused as hands and poles thrust at them from behind—they looked as bristly as a wild hog's skin, with the arrows that thumped into them— and then toppled forward to fall across the water-filled ditch. Even before the massive timber weights stopped flexing and jumping, the first rank of shield-bearing warriors was charging across them, screaming.

"Flame!" the Roman tribune shouted.

The onagers thumped. They had a single thick cable of twisted sinew across the front of their frames, and a vertical throwing-arm fastened in the middle of the cable. Winches hauled it back, a missile was put into the cup at the end of the arm, and the release was slipped. The throwing arm slashed forward until it hit a massive braced and padded bar, supported on timber triangles pegged and mortised into the ground frame of the weapon. This time the cups had been loaded with large clay jugs, wrapped in oil-soaked cloth. Torches were touched to the wrapping, and it took fire with an angry crackling roar.

"Shoot!"

The onagers released, their rear edges kicking up as the throwing arms halted—that gave them their military nickname, "wild donkey." Like meteors, the jugs arched across the night. They wobbled, because the fluid inside them shifted as they flew. The onagers were inaccurate at the best of times, and they hadn't been able to sight them carefully, because there was no telling where the enemy would try to cross the ditch.

They still landed close enough, at least the ones Vibulenus could see. Flame splashed across the massed crowds waiting their turn to storm across the bridge nearest his position. Warriors leapt shrieking into the flooded ditch, but that didn't save them, because the quicklime only burned the fiercer in contact with water. It also burned *on* the water, floating with a redder, milder flame than he remembered from the distant land that had given him the idea. But it was fatal enough. The water was thick with heads, where enemy troops were swimming the ditch with the bundled sticks—fascines—they'd brought to fill the dry ditch beyond. Many of them ducked under the surface as they saw the waves of fire billowing towards them, but the only way for a naked man to keep his body down was to fill his lungs. . . .

"Eat *this*," a legionary behind Gaius Vibulenus screamed as he cast his javelin, pivoting on his left foot and bringing his scutum around to balance the throw.

The Tenth Cohort were charging in line abreast down the ramparts, perpendicular to the parapet on their right hands. Ahead of them was the enemy bridgehead, ladders rearing over the sharpened stakes, feather-skulled figures howling and shaking their weapons at the oncoming Romans. The howls turned to screams as dozens of the heavy *pila* slashed down out of the night.

"*Roma!*" Vibulenus shouted as he ducked under the thrust of a long spear.

His round shield hooked aside a tower-tall one shaped like a figure eight, and his sword of Spanish steel punched upward under a rib cage. There was a crisp popping feeling as things parted under the sharp point and edge. Behind him Clodius Afer punched a native in the face with the boss of his shield, slid nine inches of sword in under a raised arm. The scrimmage was over in seconds; Vibulenus's sword was still making small stabbing motions in the air as he pivoted and looked for another opponent. The forward ranks of the Tenth Cohort spread out to cover the section of wall the enemy had swarmed; cutting the leather cords attached to the grappling hooks sunk in the rampart, pushing ladders over, throwing *pila* down into the crowded mass in the ditch below. They followed that with showers of one-pound stones still piled ready for use, and iron-shod stakes the auxiliaries' smiths had run up.

"Determined bunch," Vibulenus wheezed, letting his shield-arm drop. His bronze corselet squeezed at his ribs, and his mouth was dry and gummy. Somewhere he'd picked up a shallow slash over his left knee that he hadn't noticed until now, and it hurt like Hades himself was retracing it with a red-hot knife.

"They're running!" someone shouted.

Vibulenus pushed himself to the rampart. They were—and the fire from the towers was taking them in the back, now.

"Well, that's that," he said dully. *Now we wait a day or two until the ones in the fort surrender, and then we get back on the ship, and in a few weeks we all go to sleep and wake up for* another *fucking campaign.*

Clodius Afer held out a helmet full of water. "Here, sir," he said, with a quirking smile.

"Thanks," Vibulenus said. *Hercules, how many campaigns ago was it that he gave me that drink, the first time, those eight-foot-tall bastards with the carts?*

They weren't *quite* in the same position as that poor bastard in the old story, the one condemned to roll a boulder up a slope for all eternity and have it slip right down again. He'd been alone. If you were going to be in hell, at least it helped to have some good friends along.

He took the helmet and drank, then upended it over his own head and almost groaned at the feeling of cold water trickling down under his armor into the sweat-sodden tunic and overheated flesh.

"Heads up," Afer said tonelessly.

The Commander was coming, walking along with his giant iron-armored toad-guards. It was a little cramped here for their huge hyena-mounts; of course, this was also a bit closer to the sharp end than Commanders usually came. Tired Romans snapped erect and into their ranks, stepping back for the bubble of space that Commanders always required . . . and the spiked maces of their guards enforced.

The blue-suited figure walked forward, over and among the piled enemy dead. "Congratulations, Gaius Vibulenus Caper," the too-perfect voice said. "Once again, you brave warriors have prevailed over great odds."

The triangular face of the Commander swung forward to peer over the parapet. "*Very* great odds. In fact—"

Clodius Afer was as rigid beside the tribune as a statue cast from bronze. Vibulenus knew why, because his mind was as rigid with the need to control a sudden vision of two swords meeting together in the middle of the inhuman body, scissoring back to leave the torso split nearly in half, whatever the Commander used for guts spilling out on the enemy dead and the soaked dirt. . . . No. Better to go for the skull; two steps forward and he could put the edge right through the thing's temple, right to the central ridge of the blade—

Which neither of them was going to do. Because the guards might well smash them down before their swords were well drawn; the toad-things were *fast*, not just inhumanly strong. Because unless they managed to get the brain or spine, the Commander would be revived just as mostly dead legionaries were. Because although trading their own lives for that of the Commander might be, *would* be perfectly acceptable, the legion would still be there, exposed to the Guild's vengeance and without centurion and tribune.

But it was so *tempting*.

The dead were piled several layers deep against the inner face of the parapet—deeper in the angle than the natural slipperiness of blood-lubricated dead flesh would allow. Not all of that flesh was dead. Vibulenus had let himself relax from the knife-edge concentration of combat, let his muscles feel the trembling exhaustion and stiffen with fatigue poisons. His sword was still rasping from its sheath when the three natives lunged erect, daggers glittering in their hands as they threw themselves towards the Commander.

Clodius Afer's shield slammed one sideways, and the centurion's sword gutted the native while he fought for balance.

Cursing silently, Vibulenus threw himself forward, forcing speed out of abused muscles. He didn't think the Guild would be much concerned with abstract rights and wrongs if the Commander was knifed in the presence of the *assets* who were supposed to absorb the hurt.

Something warm and salty struck him in the face. His vision blurred, but not so much that he couldn't see the follow-through of the Commander's ape-long arm and the track the four razor claws had cut through the native daggerman's neck. The Commander was smiling—Vibulenus saw the expression and hoped it wasn't really a smile—as he dug the claws of both hands under the last assassin's ribs and dragged him forward. Then, with an almost casual motion, he bit off the top of the local's skull.

"Incompatible proteins," he said, after he spat the mouthful out and tossed aside the corpse. "Where was I? Ah, yes. The natives hostile to the interests of the Guild and galactic progress were probably aware that the Federation bans advanced weapons on planets such as this."

He beamed coldly at the Romans. Shreds of matter and feathery not-hair dangled between the multiple rows of teeth. "But as always, they underestimated the organizational skills of the finest trading guild in the galaxy!"

The Commander turned and swept away, followed by his armored guards. Vibulenus smiled wryly as he sheathed his sword. "Good thing we can both resist temptation, isn't it?" he said.

"Sir, yessir," Clodius Afer said, cleaning his weapon and doing likewise. He turned his head to look out over the piled dead that carpeted the ground, to the edge of sight in the dull gray light of predawn.

"Looks like 'e said. They underestimated the fuckin' opposition, all right," he said.

Gaius Vibulenus Caper, military tribune, member of the Equestrian Order and citizen of Rome, put his hand on his fellow-Roman's shoulder. "They underestimated *us*, by the gods of my hearth," he said.

They both looked after the Commander, to where

the blue-suited figure had vanished behind the smaller turtles that brought water to the legionaries, and the greater one that picked up the repairable dead. Far and faint came wailing from the fortress on the hill, as the natives saw their hope receding with the fleeing barbarians.

"And someday—" Afer went on.

Vibulenus smiled, an expression no less sharkish than the Commander's serrated rows of teeth. *Someday, someone in a blue bodysuit is going to underestimate us.*

Everyone made mistakes. But *that* was going to be the last mistake some Commander of the Guild's Roman assets ever made.

CARTHAGO DELENDA EST

Eric Flint

I

"What is the point of this?" demanded Agayan. The Guild Voivode emphasized his irritation by flexing the finger-clusters of his midlimbs.

Yuaw Khta ignored both the question and the cluster-flex. The Guild Investigator was immune to the Voivode's displeasure. The Guild's Office of Investigation had a separate command structure from that of the Trade Web. Although Agayan was its nominal superior in their current mission, Yuaw Khta's career in no way depended on the Voivode's goodwill.

"Again."

The Gha sepoy it commanded twisted the native's arm further. Gobbling with pain, the native struggled furiously.

Its efforts were futile, despite the fact that the orange-skinned biped was not much smaller than its Gha tormentor. It was more slender, true—although much of the Gha's squat bulk was the product of its heavy armor. Still, the native was every bit as tall as the Gha. But the real difference lay beneath the surface. For all the near-equivalence of size, the native was a child in the hands of an ogre.

The Gha were a heavy-planet species. Due in large part to that gravity, theirs was the most inhospitable world that had ever produced an intelligent race. The Gha were few in numbers, but all the great trading Guilds and Combines favored them as bodyguards for their strength and physical prowess.

The native's gabbles reached a crescendo, but they still expressed nothing more than pain—and curses.

"Again," commanded the Guild Investigator. The Gha twisted; the native howled.

Guild Voivode Agayan ceased his finger-flexing. He transformed his mid-limbs into legs and stalked off in disgust. While the native continued to screech, the Voivode stared out at the landscape.

The scene was as barren as their investigation had thus far proven to be. The sun—a green-colored dot in the sky—cast a sickly hue over the gravelly terrain. The land was almost flat, broken only by a scattering of squat gray-skinned plants with long, trailing leaves.

And the bones. Gha bones, and the skeletal remains of the huge carnivores which served as mounts for the sepoys. The bones were picked clean, now, and bleached white by the sun. Every other relic of the battle which had raged across this plain was gone. The natives had buried their own dead, and scavenged all the discarded weapons and armor.

Behind him, Agayan heard a cracking noise. The native shrieked and fell suddenly silent. The Voivode twisted his body, caterpillarlike, and examined the situation. As he had expected, the Gha had finally broken the native's arm. And, still, without the Investigator learning anything they didn't already know.

"Are you quite finished?" he demanded.

Again, Yuaw Khta ignored him. But, after a moment, the Investigator made a gesture to the Gha. The sepoy released its grip. The native, now unconscious, collapsed to the ground.

Satisfied that the charade was at an end, Agayan transformed his forelimbs into arms and reached for his communicator. After summoning the shuttle, he amused himself by watching the Investigator scampering about the area, looking for some last-minute clue.

As always, the Voivode found Yuaw Khta's movements both comical and unsettling. The Investigator, like all members of his species, was a tall and gangling creature. Its long, ungainly head hung forward from its neck like certain draft animals Agayan had observed on various primitive planets. That much was amusing. Yet there was a quick, jerky nature to the Investigator's movements which created a certain sense of anxiety in Agayan's mind. His own species, supple but slow-moving, retained a primordial fear of predators.

He shook the uneasiness off. Ridiculous, really. Even a bit embarrassing. Such atavistic fears had no basis in reality. Agayan's race—like that of the Investigator—was counted among the Doge Species which dominated both the Federation and the great trading Guilds and Combines.

The Doge Species numbered only twenty-three. All other races were subordinate, to one degree or another. Some, like the species which provided the Pilots and Medics for the great trading ships, were ranked Class One. Class One species were privy to the highest technology of galactic civilization, and enjoyed many privileges. But they were still subordinates. Others, specialized laborers like the Gha, were ranked Class Two. Below Class Two species came nothing but indentured servant races, like the quasi-reptilian Ossa whose flexible phenotypes made them useful, or outright slaves like—

The shuttle swept in for a landing. The Investigator joined Agayan as they marched up the ramp.

"I told you the humans did it," he hissed, knotting the finger-clusters of his forelimbs in satisfaction.

II

After their ship left the planet, Agayan pressed the advantage.

"It is the *only* possibility," he announced firmly. "Ridiculous to think those natives were responsible!"

He and the Investigator were in that chamber of the vessel which combined the functions of a lounge and a meeting room. In deference to its multispecies use, the room was bathed with soft indirect light and bare of any furnishings beyond those of use to its current occupants. Each of those two occupants, in his or its own way, was relaxing. For Agayan, that involved nothing more elaborate than draping his body over a sawhorse-shaped piece of furniture and enjoying a tumbler of a mildly intoxicating liquor.

For the Investigator, relaxation was more intense. Yuaw Khta was also positioned on its preferred furniture, in that posture which almost all bipeds adopted when resting. (In their different languages, it was called *sitting*. As always, it seemed peculiar to Agayan—as if a person would deliberately choose to break his body in half.) Yuaw Khta was also sipping at a beverage. A different one, of course. The liquor in Agayan's tumbler would poison the Investigator; and, while Agayan would survive drinking the blue liquid in Yuaw Khta's cup, he would certainly not enjoy the experience.

In addition, however, the Investigator enjoyed the ministrations of a personal attendant. As it leaned forward in its chair, the Ossa behind it subjected Yuaw Khta's long neck to a vigorous massage.

Between grunts of pleasure, the Investigator said:

"No variant explanation can be discounted in advance, Voivode Agayan. Proper investigatory technique is primarily a process of eliminating possibilities, one by one, until the solution finally emerges."

Agayan's forelimb finger-cluster flexed sarcastically. "And are you *now* satisfied? Can we *finally* lay to rest the—variant explanation!—that primitives somehow seized a Guild vessel? *After* they had already been decisively defeated in battle?"

"Your own explanation would also have primitives seizing the ship," pointed out the Investigator.

Agayan restrained his anger. The self-control was difficult, but allowances had to be made. Yuaw Khta, after all, had never personally witnessed the humans in action.

"There is no comparison," he said forcefully. "It is true that the humans were also iron-age barbarians. But their discipline and social coordination were many levels beyond those of any other primitives you may have encountered."

"So you say," grunted the Investigator. Its long, bony face was twisted into an expression which combined pain and pleasure.

To Agayan, watching, the whole process—what Yuaw Khta called a *massage*—seemed as grotesque as the Investigator's seated posture. To the Voivode's soft-bodied species, pain was pain and pleasure was pleasure, and never the twain shall meet. Not for the first time, Agayan concluded that the vertebrate structure which was by far the most common *Bauplan* of the galaxy's intelligent races was a curse on its possessors. A preposterous structure, really. Contradictory to the core.

Still, mused Agayan, it had its advantages.

Strength, for one. The Voivode glanced at the nearest of the sepoys standing silently against the wall of the chamber. Now unencumbered by armor, the Gha's bronze-colored, rangy body was fully visible. Quite impressive, in its own crude way.

Especially this one, thought the Voivode. *He's the commander of the squad, I believe.*

For a moment, Agayan's gaze met the bulging eyes of the sepoy. As always, the Gha's face was utterly expressionless. To humans, that face would seem froglike in its shape. To the Voivode, it simply seemed inanimate.

Gha, he reflected, were the most uninteresting species he had ever encountered. Barely sentient, in his opinion, based on his long experience with the sepoys. The creatures never expressed any sentiments in their faces, and they were as indistinguishable as so many pebbles. This one, for instance—the one he supposed to be the sepoy commander. Agayan thought that the Gha was the same one which had been in his service when he was a mere Guild Cacique. But he was not certain.

He looked back at Yuaw Khta. The Investigator was now practically writhing in the pain/pleasure from its massage. For a moment, Agayan felt genuine envy. The ubiquity of the vertebrate structure, whatever its limitations, meant that vertebrate Guildmasters could enjoy more in the way of personal and intimate service than could members of his own species.

While Yuaw Khta grunted its pain/pleasure, Agayan

took the time to examine its personal attendant. Ossa were particularly favored for that purpose by genetic engineers. The quasi-reptiles lent themselves as easily to phenotype surgery as they did to genetic manipulation. And there was always a large supply of the things. Their sexual and procreative energy was notorious, in their natural state as well as the multitude of bodily forms into which they were shaped by Doge engineers.

Idly, Agayan wondered if this particular Ossa regretted its transformation. It was neutered, now, to match Yuaw Khta's current sexual stage. The Investigator kept two other Ossa on the ship, one male and one female, to serve it/her/him as Yuaw Khta progressed through the cycle.

Agayan did not ponder the matter for more than a few seconds. Ossa, for him, were not much more interesting than Gha.

He decided that he had been polite enough. "Are you going to be distracted by this exercise in self-torture for much longer?" he demanded. "The affairs of the Guild press heavily."

Yuaw Khta's grunt combined satisfaction with irritation. The Investigator made a snapping sound with its fingers and the Ossa attendant immediately departed the chamber.

After taking a long draught from its cup, Yuaw Khta said: "I fail to see your point, Voivode Agayan. Regardless of their social discipline and cohesion, the humans are still primitives."

He made a small waving gesture, which encompassed the entirety of the ship. "Even if they managed—somehow—to seize the ship, they would have no way to fly it anywhere."

"Unless they coerced the Pilot," retorted Agayan. The Voivode spread both his forelimb clusters, to give emphasis to his next words. "Unlike you, Yuaw Khta, I have personal experience with the humans. I was their Commander, for a time, before my promotion to Voivode. As you may or may not know, I passed through the Cacique ranks faster than any Guildmaster on the record. Some of that unprecedented speed in climbing through the ranks, of course, was due—"

He interlaced his finger-clusters modestly.

"—to my own ability. But *every* Commander of the human sepoys enjoyed rapid promotion. The humans were, far and away, the best sepoy troops the Guild has ever had. They were invariably successful in their campaigns, and did not even suffer heavy casualties."

He took a drink from his tumbler. "As these things go," he concluded. "In time, of course, their numbers would have declined to the point where they would have been useless. But there were many, many campaigns which the Guild would have profited from before their liquidation was necessary."

"So?" demanded Yuaw Khta.

Agayan could not control the agitated flexing of his hindlimb clusters, he was so aggravated. But he managed to maintain a calm voice.

"*So?* What do you think accounts for the human success, Investigator? It was not simple physical prowess, I can assure you!"

The Voivode pointed to the Gha commander. "This one—or any of its fellows—could easily defeat a human in single combat. Several of them at once, in fact. But I have no doubt whatsoever that on a field of battle, matched with equivalent weapons, the humans could have defeated a Gha army."

The Investigator was still not convinced.

"Gha are stupid," it grumbled. "Everyone knows that. I am prepared to admit that the humans were unusually intelligent, for a slave race, but—"

The Voivode had had enough. "Do you have any alternative explanation?" he demanded.

The Investigator was silent.

"In that case," stated Agayan firmly, "I now exercise my command prerogatives. If the humans seized their transport vessel, and coerced the Pilot into operating the craft, their most likely destination would have been their original home. Their native planet. Accordingly, this ship will proceed to that same planet. If the humans are there, we will destroy them. This vessel is far better armed than any troop transport."

"*Their native planet?*" exploded the Investigator. "That's ridiculous! The humans were in Guild service longer—*far longer*—than any other sepoy troops. They underwent tens and tens of Stasis episodes. It must be hundreds—thousands—of years since their initial recruitment. I doubt if we even have a record of—"

"The record will exist," stated Agayan firmly. "I have instructed the Pilot to check. You underestimate the care with which the Guild—"

He was interrupted by the appearance of the Pilot herself in the chamber.

"Ah!" he exclaimed. "I presume you have finished your examination of the records?"

"Yes, Guild Voivode." The Pilot belonged to a spindle-shaped species which found bowing impossible, so she indicated her respect by darkening her purple skin.

"The results?"

"The human planet—there is no name for it, beyond the catalog number—is only two hundred and twelve light years distant. The humans were recruited slightly over two thousand Guild years ago."

Agayan turned triumphantly to Yuaw Khta.

"You see, Investigator?" He waved a finger-cluster at the Pilot, dismissing her. To his surprise, the Pilot remained planted on her footskirt.

"There is something else, Guild Voivode."

"Yes?"

"I used a broad-range program in my search, and it brought up all information concerning this planet. In addition to the original sepoy records, there is also a significant—*perhaps* significant—item of meteorological data."

Agayan's finger-clusters began to flex. "What is the point of this?" he demanded.

The Pilot turned a very dark purple, in her attempt to placate the Voivode's rising irritation.

"The Federation's Meteorological Survey has been paying close attention to that region of the galaxy. A Transit storm has been moving down that spiral arm for many thousands of Guild years. The human planet and its environs were cut off from all Transport nodes shortly after the sepoys were recruited. The nodes were only reestablished two hundred Guild years ago."

"Has a Guild vessel returned to that planet since Transit possibility was renewed?"

"No, Guild Voivode. Nor has any Federation ship. But shortly after the nodes re-formed, the Meteorological Survey began detecting oddities in the region, which they eventually pinpointed to that planet's solar system. They didn't know what to make of the peculiar data, until they thought to consult with the Federation's Historiographic Bureau."

Seeing the Voivode's increasingly rapid finger-flexing, the Pilot hurried to her conclusion.

"The data indicate that the natives of that planet have recently developed the capacity to manipulate the electromagnetic spectrum. Radio waves, to be precise."

Agayan's clusters spread wide with puzzlement.

"*Radio?* Of what possible use—"

"It is a primitive technique, Guild Voivode. No advanced civilization bothers with radio, but—according to the Historiographic Bureau, at least—the radio portion of the electromagnetic spectrum is typically the first point of entry for civilizations which—"

The significance of the information finally penetrated. Agayan lurched erect.

"*Civilization?*" he screeched. "Are you trying to claim that these—these human *savages* have reached the point of industrial chain reaction?"

The Pilot scuttled back on her footskirt. Her color was now so deep a purple as to be almost black.

"*I'm* not claiming *anything*, Guild Voivode! I'm just relaying what the—"

"Ridiculous! I know these humans, you fool! They served under me. There is no—no—"

Agayan's indignation overwhelmed him. He fell silent, fiercely trying to bring his fury under control.

The Investigator interjected itself. "No species in the historical record has reached industrial chain reaction in less than two hundred thousand years since initial habitat domestication," it stated ponderously. "And none has done so since the last of the Doge Species."

The Pilot said nothing. She was tempted to point out that the policies of both the Federation and the Guilds were precisely designed to *prevent* such occurrences, but suppressed the whimsy ruthlessly. Foolish, she was not.

Agayan finally restored his calm enough to speak. Icily:

"That is quite enough, Pilot. You may go. This information—this preposterous twaddle, I should say—will be corrected as soon as we reach that planet. Set the course."

"Yes, Guild Voivode. I have already done so. Your instructions, as always, were very clear and precise."

Agayan spread his clusters in acknowledgement of the praise. "Send a message to Guild Headquarters informing them that we are Transiting to the human planet."

The Pilot scuttled out of the chamber as fast as her ungainly form of locomotion permitted.

Agayan resumed his position of rest. "I cannot believe how incompetent some of the Federation's—"

"Ptatti gattokot poi toi rhuch du! Ptatti gatt!"

All six of Agayan's clusters knotted in shock. The sheer volume of the Gha commander's voice had been almost like a physical blow.

The shock deepened. *Deepened.*

Dazed, the Voivode watched one of the Gha sepoys stride forward from its position against the wall and shatter the Investigator's spinal cord with a single blow of its fist. Shatter it again. Seize Yuaw Khta's lolling head and practically twist it in a full circle.

The Voivode could *hear* the bones break.

Ancestral reflex coiled Agayan into a soft ball. He heard the Gha commander bellowing more phrases in the sepoy language. Two of the Gha immediately left the chamber.

Agayan was utterly paralyzed. He could not even speak. Only watch.

His soft-bodied species, some distant part of his brain noted, did not respond well to physical danger.

Standing in front of him, now, he recognized the figure of the Gha commander.

The Gha spoke to him. He did not understand the words.

The sepoy spoke again. The meaning of the words finally penetrated. Oddly, Agayan was surprised more by the *fact* of those words than their actual content. He had not realized that Gha could speak Galactic beyond a few crude and simple phrases.

"I said," repeated the Gha, "do you know my name?"

Paralyzed. Only watch.

The sepoy repeated its question: "Do you know my name, Guild Voivode Agayan?"

The Gha towered above him like an ogre. Immense, heavy-planet muscles coiled over that rangy, vertebrate body. Strength. Leverage. Power.

The other Gha spoke now, also in fluent Galactic: "Just kill him and be done with it."

The sepoy commander: "Soon enough." To the Voivode: "Do you know my—ah! No use."

The monster reached down a huge hand and seized the Voivode by one of his forelimb clusters. A moment later, still curled into a ball, Agayan found himself suspended in midair. The Gha commander's bulging eyes were right before him.

Paralyzed. Only watch.

"My name," said the Gha softly, "is Fludenoc hu'tut-Na Nomo'te. Since I have served you for more years than I wish to remember—a second time, now, when the first was bad enough—I feel that it is only proper that you should know my name."

Paralyzed. Only watch.

"I will even educate you in the subtleties. Some of them, at least. Fludenoc is the familiar. Nomo the family name, with the 'te-suffix to indicate that we are affiliated to the Na clan. Hu'-tut is an honorific. It indicates that my clan considers my poetry good enough for minstrel status."

Paralyzed. Only watch.

"I will not bother explaining the fine distinctions which we Gha make between poets. They would be quite beyond your comprehension, Guild Voivode. Even if you were still alive."

The Gha's other hand seized Agayan's head. Began to squeeze. Stopped.

"On second thought, I'd better not crush your wormface beyond recognition. The Romans are probably holding a grudge against us. If they can recognize your corpse, it may help."

Paralyzed. Only watch. The Voivode saw the two Gha who had left the chamber return. Dragging the Pilot and the Medic with them.

The Gha commander's clawed hand plunged into Agayan's mid-section. Pushing the soft flesh aside until it gripped the vital organs at the center.

"I'm sure you never knew the names of the three Romans you executed, either. To my own shame, I only know one of them. Helvius, he was called."

Squeezed. *Squeezed.*

Paralyzed, even at his death. Only watch.

The Guild Voivode's last thought was perhaps inappropriate. It seemed outrageous to him that there was still no expression on the Gha's face.

III

The Guild official's body made a soft plopping sound when Fludenoc hu'tut-Na Nomo'te finally let it fall to the deck. Around the corpse, a pool of pink blood spread slowly from the Voivode's alimentary and excretory orifices. The Gha commander's incredibly powerful grip had ruptured half of Agayan's internal organs.

"I am *not* cleaning up that mess," announced the Gha who had killed Yuaw Khta. He pointed to the body of the Investigator. "Notice. Clean as a sand-scoured rock. Finesse."

Fludenoc barked humor. "The worm didn't *have* a neck to break. And I meant what I said, Uddumac. His corpse—if they recognize it—may be our passkey with the Romans."

Uddumac made the sudden exhalation of breath

which served Gha for a facial grimace. "All right, Fludenoc. *Explain.*"

The other two Gha in the room flexed their shoulders, indicating their full agreement with that sentiment. The gesture was the equivalent of vigorous head nodding among humans.

Before answering, Fludenoc examined the Pilot and the Medic. The Pilot was utterly motionless. Much like the species which had produced Agayan, the Pilot's race also responded to sudden danger by instinctive immobility. Only her color—pale violet, now—indicated her terror.

There would be no problems with her, Fludenoc decided. He did not think she would recover for some time.

The Medic, on the other hand—

The Medic belonged to a species which would have seemed vaguely avian to humans. *His* instinctive reaction to shock was rapid flight. Yet, aside from an initial attempt to struggle free from the iron grip of the Gha who had captured him, the Medic seemed almost tranquil. His Gha captor still held him by the arm, but the Medic was making no attempt to escape.

Fludenoc stared down at him. The Medic's flat, golden eyes stared back.

"Do not not mind me," the Medic suddenly trilled. "I am just just a bystander. *Interested* bystander."

The Medic gazed down at the corpse of the Voivode. "I always always wondered what the worm's blood looked like." He trilled pure pleasure. "Never never thought I'd find out."

Uddumac interrupted.

"*Explain, Fludenoc.* I obeyed your command because you are the *flarragun* of our Poct'on cartouche. But now that the action is finished, I have a full right to demand an accounting."

Fludenoc decided the Medic was no immediate problem, either. He turned to face Uddumac and the other Gha in the chamber.

"I gave the command because our opportunity has finally arrived."

"*What* opportunity?" asked the Gha holding the Medic.

Fludenoc's whole upper torso swiveled to face his questioner. For all its immense strength, the Gha physique was not limber. Evolved on a heavy-gravity planet, Gha necks were almost completely rigid.

"You know perfectly well *what* opportunity, Oltomar. The same opportunity the Poct'on has been searching for since it was founded."

Oltomar's response was a quick, wavering hiss.

Fludenoc, understanding the subtleties in that hiss, felt a sudden surge of bitter anger. His anger, and his bitterness, were not directed toward Oltomar. They were directed at the universe, in general; and galactic civilization, in particular.

The same evolutionary necessities which had produced the rigid upper vertebra of the Gha species, had also produced their stiff, unmoving faces. The bleak, wind-scoured, heavy planet where Gha had originated was merciless. No soft, supple, flexible animals could survive there—only creatures which presented a hard shield to the world, and thereby withstood its heavy lashes.

Intelligence, when it came to that planet, came in a suitable form. A form which, when other intelligences discovered them—more technologically advanced intelligences, but not smarter ones—could see nothing beyond the stiff shield of Gha faces. And the immense strength of Gha bodies.

The Gha were famed—notorious—among all the intelligent races of the galaxy. They were the epitome of the stolid dullwit. Only the Gha themselves knew of their inner life. Of the subtle ways in which their breath transmitted meaning; their voices, undertones of sentiment.

Only the Gha knew of their poetry. To galactic civilization—to the Doge Species which ruled that civilization—the Gha were nothing more than splendid thugs. The galaxy's premier goons.

Fludenoc shook off the anger. (Literally. His fellows, watching, understood the nuances of that shoulder movement as perfectly as he had understood the skepticism in Oltomar's hiss.)

"I'm quite serious, Oltomar. Even before this incident, I thought the Romans were the best possibility we had ever encountered."

"Too primitive," interjected Uddumac. "We talked it about, you and I, long ago."

Uddumac gestured to the Voivode's corpse on the floor. "The first time we had the misfortune of being assigned to this worm. We talked about it, then, and we reached a common conclusion. For all their astonishing competence, the Romans were simply too primitive. Barbarians, to all intents and purposes."

Oltomar chimed in. Again, literally. The chime-syllable which prefaced his words was a Gha way of expressing agreement.

"Yes. Nothing's changed simply because they managed to seize their troop transport. *If* they seized it. I'm not sure the worm's theory was correct, but even if it is—so what? The Romans are still barbarians. The Poct'on has always known that—"

Fludenoc silenced him with a gesture. Left hand before his face, palm outward, fingers spread. *Stop— I must interrupt.*

"You're missing the significance of the new data," he said. "*That's* why I gave the order to kill them." His next gesture—right hand turned aside, waist high, fingers curled against the thumb—was the Gha expression of apology.

"That's also why I didn't wait until we had an opportunity to discuss the matter, as a Poct'on cartouche would normally do. I had to stop the Pilot from transmitting anything to Guild Headquarters. I'm hoping the Federation itself doesn't understand the significance of the meteorological report. The Guilds may still not know of it at all."

The other three Gha in the room were silent. Their stiff postures, to anyone but Gha, would have made them seem like statues. But Fludenoc understood their confusion and puzzlement.

To his surprise, the Pilot suddenly spoke. Fludenoc had almost forgotten her presence.

"Are you talking about the radio signals?" she asked.

Fludenoc swiveled to face her. The Pilot froze with instinctive fear, but her color remained close to purple. "I'm s-sorry," she stammered, in Gha. "I didn't mean—"

"I did not realize you spoke our language," said Fludenoc.

Then, sadly (though only a Gha would have sensed it in his tone):

"I am not angry at you for interrupting me, Pilot. Among ourselves, we consider conversation a fine art. Interruption is part of its pleasure."

The Pilot's shade developed a pinkish undertone. "I know. I have listened to you, sometimes, when you versified each other in your chamber. I thought the poetry was quite good. Although I'm sure I missed most of the nuances."

Now, all four Gha were staring at the Pilot. And it took no Gha subtlety to realize that they were all absolutely astonished.

"You are not the only people in the galaxy," the Pilot said softly, "who mourn for what might have been."

She shifted her footskirt, turning away from Fludenoc to face the other Gha. "I do not think you grasp the importance of those radio signals. The reason the Voivode was so indignant was because he understood that, if the data is accurate, it means that the Romans—or, at least, the human species which produced them—are no longer barbarians. They have reached industrial chain reaction."

"What in Creation are *radio*?" demanded Oltomar. "And why is it important?"

The Pilot hesitated. Again, Fludenoc barked humor.

"He is not actually an ignoramus, Pilot, appearances to the contrary. It's just that, like most Gha, his education was oriented toward practical matters. His knowledge of history is sadly deficient."

Beyond a mildly irritated inhalation, Oltomar did not argue the point. Fludenoc made a gesturing motion to the Pilot. *Continue.*

"Radio is a part of the electromagnetic spectrum," she explained. "Very far toward the low frequency end. Modern civilization doesn't have any real use for those bands. But in the early stages of industrial chain reaction, it is always the first avenue by which rising civilizations conquer electromagnetism. For a short period of time, such planets project radio waves into the galaxy. The waves are very weak, of course, and undirected, so they are quickly lost in the galaxy's background noise. If the Federation Meteorological Survey hadn't been keeping that portion of the galaxy under close observation because of the Transit storm, those signals would never have been noticed."

Uddumac interrupted. "You are saying that humans have achieved *civilization*?"

"Yes. There can be no natural explanation for such

radio signals. And only a civilized species can project radio signals powerful enough to be picked up at interstellar distances."

"What level of civilization?" demanded Oltomar. "Class One or Two? Or even—Doge?"

"There's no way to tell without—"

"The distinction is critical!" Oltomar's statement was almost a shout. "*It's absolutely critical.*"

The Pilot froze. Fludenoc interposed himself between her and Oltomar. She was actually in no physical danger at all, but her species tended to panic quickly. His protective presence would enable her to relax.

"Stop bullying her, Oltomar," he said quietly. "She has no way of answering your question—without us making the journey to that planet. Which is precisely what I propose to do."

He gestured to the dead bodies of the Voivode and the Investigator. "*Our* journey, not theirs."

Oltomar subsided, but Uddumac was still unsatisfied.

"This could easily be a complete waste of effort, Fludenoc. We need to find a suitable species which can claim Doge status. *Legally.* If the humans are already Class One—*advanced* Class One—we might be able to nudge them over the edge. As long as we could keep hidden the fact that their Transit capability was stolen from already established Doge technology. But if they're only Class Two, there's no way—"

He broke off, shivering his shoulders in that Gha gesture which corresponded to a human headshake.

Fludenoc hesitated before responding. Uddumac's reservations, after all, were quite reasonable. In order for a species to claim Doge status under Federation law, they had to demonstrate a capacity for interstellar travel and commerce. In technological terms,

Transit; in socio-political terms, a mercantile orienta-
tion. An *independent* capacity, developed by their own
efforts, not simply a capacity acquired from already
existing Doges.

Civilized species which lacked that capacity were
considered Class One if they had managed to depart
the confines of their own planet before being discovered by galactic civilization. Class Two, if they were
a society still bound to their world of origin.

As Uddumac had rightly said, it *might* be possible
to give humans a false Doge identity by surreptitiously
handing them Transit technology. Transit technology,
by its nature, was fairly invariant. All the existing Doge
Species used essentially the same method. But the
subterfuge would only work if humans had already
achieved a very high level of Class One civilization.
Nobody would believe that human Transit was self-
developed if the species was still pulling wagons with
draft animals.

"The decision has already been made," Fludenoc
stated, firmly but not belligerently. Again, he pointed
to the Doge corpses. "We have no choice now, brothers.
Let us make Transit to the human planet. The answer
can only be found there."

There was no further opposition. Fludenoc swiveled
to the Pilot.

"Take us there," he commanded.

The Pilot left the chamber immediately. Fludenoc
turned to examine the Medic.

"Do not not mind me," the Medic immediately
trilled. "I am just just a bystander."

All the Gha, now, barked their humor.

"But are you still *interested*?" asked Oltomar.

"Oh, yes yes! Very interested interested!"

IV

Not so many days later, after Transit was made, the Medic was still interested. Fascinated, in fact.

"What what in the name of Creation is *that that that*?"

There was no answer. Everyone in the control chamber was staring at the viewscreen.

Staring at *that*.

The Pilot finally broke the silence. "I think it's a boat," she whispered.

"What is a—a *boat*?" asked Oltomar. He, also, spoke in a whisper.

"I think she's right," muttered Fludenoc. "I saw a hologram of a boat, once. It looked quite a bit like—that. Except *that's* a lot bigger. A whole lot bigger."

"I say it again!" hissed Oltomar. "What in Creation is a *boat*?"

"It's a vessel that floats on water," replied Fludenoc. "Very large bodies of water, such as don't exist on our planet."

Oltomar stared at the screen. "*Water*?" he demanded. "*What* water? We're still in the outer fringes of this solar system!"

A hum from the communication console announced an incoming message.

"I think we're about to find out," said the Pilot. She shuffled toward the console. "Let's hope they speak some language the computer can translate."

Fludenoc was suddenly filled with confidence. *That* was the strangest-looking spacecraft he had ever seen. But, then again, he had thought the Romans were the strangest-looking soldiers he had ever seen, too.

"The computer will be able to translate," he predicted. "Latin has been programmed into it for over two thousand years."

He was not wrong. The Latin phrases which the computer received were spoken in a very odd accent, it was true. Quite unlike the original input. But the phrases were simple enough:

"*Unknown spacecraft: you are ordered to hold position. Any movement toward the inner planets will be construed as a hostile act.*"

"There are more of those—*boats*—coming," said Uddumac. "Lots of them. Very *big* boats."

"*We repeat—hold your position. We are sending a boarding party. Any resistance will be construed as a hostile act.*"

Fludenoc instructed the Pilot: "Send a message indicating that the boarding party will be allowed ingress without obstruction. And tell them we seek a parley."

"These are Romans?" queried Oltomar. His tone wavered pure confusion.

"Pilot," said Fludenoc. "Ask them to identify themselves as well."

The reply came quickly:

"*This is Craig Trumbull speaking. I am the Commodore of this fleet and the Captain commanding this vessel. The CSS* Scipio Africanus."

V

"I feel like an idiot," muttered Commodore Trumbull. His eyes, fixed on the huge viewscreen, shifted back and forth from the sleek, gleaming Guild vessel to the nearest of the newly arrived ships of his flotilla.

The Confederation Space Ship *Quinctius Flaminius*, that was. As she was now called.

Standing next to him, his executive officer grinned.

"You mean you feel like the guy who shows up at a formal ball wearing a clown suit? Thought he'd been invited to a costume party?"

Trumbull grunted. Again, he stared at the CSS *Quinctius Flaminius*. As she was now called.

The USS *Missouri*, in her former life.

"I can't believe I'm trying to intimidate a Guild vessel with these *antiques*."

Commander Stephen Tambo shrugged. "So what if it's a World War Two craft dragged out of mothballs?" He pointed at the ancient battleship on the viewscreen. "Those aren't sixteen-inch guns anymore, Commodore. They're lasers. Eight times as powerful as any the Guild uses, according to the transport's computer. And the *Quinctius'* force-screens carry the same magnitude of superiority."

"I know that!" snapped the commodore. "I still feel like an idiot."

The executive officer, eyeing his superior with a sideways glance, decided against any further attempt at humor. The North American seemed bound and determined to wallow in self-pity.

Commander Tambo shared none of that mortification. True, the Confederation's newly created naval force was—from the standpoint of appearance—the most absurd-looking fleet imaginable. It had only been a few years, after all, since the arrival of the Romans had alerted humanity to the fact that it was a very big and very dangerous galaxy. Proper military spacecraft were only just starting to be constructed. In the meantime, the Earth had needed protection. *Now.*

So—

The Romans had brought the technology. Their captured troop transport's computer had carried full theoretical and design criteria in its data banks. The quickest and simplest way to create an instant fleet had been to refit the Earth's old warships.

By galactic standards, the resulting spacecraft were grotesque in every way. Nor was that simply a matter of appearance. They were not airtight, for instance. Because of the force-screens, of course, they did not need to be. But no proper galactic vessel would have taken the chance of relying on force-screens to maintain atmospheric integrity.

But Tambo did not mind in the least. As a South African, he was accustomed to the whimsies of history.

And besides, there were advantages.

He turned away from the viewscreen and gazed through the window of the bridge. A real window, that was—just plain, ordinary glass—looking down onto the vast, flat expanse where Tambo enjoyed his daily jogging. No galactic spaceship ever built—ever conceived—would have provided him with that opportunity.

The huge flight deck of the CSS *Scipio Africanus*. Formerly, the USS *Enterprise*.

"The boarding party's leaving," he announced.

Commodore Trumbull turned away from the viewscreen and joined him at the window. The two men watched as the boarding craft lifted off from the flight deck—no hurtling steam catapults here; just the easy grace of galactic drives—and surged toward the force-screen. There was a momentary occultation of the starfield as the boarding craft's screen melded with that of the *Africanus*. A moment later, the boarding craft was lost to sight.

"Jesus H. Christ," muttered the commodore. "A *complete* idiot."

Tambo could not resist. He did a quick little dance step and sang, to the tune from *Fiddler on the Roof*: "Tradition!"

Trumbull scowled and glared at the viewscreen. The boarding craft was already halfway to the Guild vessel.

The CSS *Livy*, as she was now called. Naming her after a historian, thought the commodore darkly, was appropriate. He had protested bitterly. *Bitterly*. But the Naval Commissioning Board had been seized by the rampant historical romanticism which seemed to have engulfed the entire human race since the return of the Roman exiles.

The CSS *Livy*. Formerly, the prize exhibit at the Berlin Museum of Ancient Technology. A full-size reproduction—faithful in every detail—of one of the Roman Empire's quinqueremes.

The commodore could restrain himself no longer. *"They could at least stop rowing the damned oars!"*

VI

Gaius Vibulenus shook his head firmly, and turned to Trumbull.

"No, Commodore," he said in his heavily accented English. "I do not recognize them. Not specifically. They *are* the same species as the—we just called them the 'frogs.' Or the 'toads.' "

The Roman looked back at the viewscreen. His eyes were now focused on the corpse of the Voivode. A Confederation Marine lieutenant was holding the creature's head up.

"And I cannot say that I recognize him, either. He is the same type as the Guild Commander who murdered Helvius and the others, yes. But whether he is the same individual—"

Gaius shrugged. "You must understand, Commodore, that we saw many intelligent species while we served the trading guild. But never very many different individuals of any one species. So they all looked much the same to us. Bizarre."

From behind them, Quartilla spoke. "I recognize *him*. The dead one, I mean."

Everyone on the bridge turned toward her.

"You're sure?" asked the Commodore.

Quartilla nodded. "Oh, yes. His species call themselves *Rassiqua*. Their body shapes and—call them 'faces'—are difficult for others to distinguish between, but each of them has a quite distinct pattern of skin mottling." She pointed at the corpse being held up before the viewscreen. "This one has a—"

She leaned over to the historian standing next to her, gesturing with her agile plump hands. "What do you call this, Robert—a thing with six sides?"

Robert Ainsley frowned for a moment, tugging at his gray-streaked professorial beard, before he understood her question.

"Hexagon."

"*Hex-a-gon*," she murmured, memorizing the word. The executive officer, watching, was impressed by the— *woman's*?—obvious facility and experienced ease at learning languages. She and Vibulenus had arrived at the *Scipio Africanus* aboard a special courier vessel less than an hour before. But even in that short time, Tambo had been struck by the difference between Quartilla's fluent, almost unaccented English and the stiff speech of her Roman companion.

"If you turn him around," said Quartilla, "you'll see a hexagon pattern on his left rear flank. Three hexagons, if I remember correctly. All of them shaded a sort of blue-green."

Commodore Trumbull began to give the order, but the Marine lieutenant was already moving the body. A moment later, grunting slightly, he held the Voivode's left rear flank up to the screen.

Three small hexagons. Shaded a sort of blue-green. Gaius Vibulenus hissed. "That stinking *bastard*."

Tambo stared down at the Roman. The former tribune's fists were clenched. The steel-hard muscles in his forearms stood out like cables. For all the man's short size—and Vibulenus was tall, for a Roman—Tambo was glad that rage wasn't directed at him.

By current physical standards, the Romans were not much bigger than boys. The appearance was deceiving. Small they might be, and slightly built, compared to modern men, but the returned exiles' ancient customs were unbelievably ferocious, by those same modern standards. Tambo knew of at least one college fraternity, full of bravado, which had been hospitalized in its entirety after making the mistake of challenging four Roman veterans to a barroom brawl.

"But you don't recognize the frogs?" asked Trumbull. "The—what do they call themselves? The Gha?"

Quartilla shook her head. "No, Commodore. The Gha never demanded service from us Ossa pleasure creatures. We had almost no contact with them."

Her voice was icy with old bitterness. Tambo watched Vibulenus give her hand a little squeeze.

The commodore frowned deeply. Quartilla took a breath and added:

"I can verify everything else the Gha have said, however. I think they must be telling the truth here also. How else could they have known that the Voivode had once been the Roman commander? For that matter, how else could they have learned Latin?"

"He knew Helvius's name, too," muttered Vibulenus. The Roman was frowning very deeply himself, now. Almost scowling, in fact.

Seeing the expression on his face, the commodore stated: "Yet you still seem very suspicious, Tribune."

Vibulenus gave a little start of surprise. "Suspicious?"

His face cleared. "You do not understand, Commodore. I was just thinking— It is hard to explain."

The Roman gestured toward the Gha on the viewscreen. They were standing toward the rear of the Guild vessel's command chamber, closely guarded by armed Marines. "*Guilty,* perhaps. These—Gha—were never anything to us but our masters' goons. It never occurred to me that they might have names. It certainly never occurred to me that they might know *our* names."

The Gha commander in the viewscreen suddenly spoke. His Latin was crude, but quite understandable.

"You Gaius Vibulenus. During period was I assigned guard Cacique, while was your Guildmaster, you tribune command Tenth Cohort."

Gaius winced. "Your name is Fludenoc, am I right?" Quickly, with the easy familiarity of a man accustomed to elaborate ancient nomenclature, he added: "Fludenoc hu'tut-Na Nomo'te?"

The Gha bent forward stiffly.

"I believe him," said Gaius abruptly. The tone of his voice carried the absolutism of a hardened, experienced commanding officer. The Roman returned the bow, and spoke again in Latin.

"I thank you, Fludenoc hu'tut-Na Nomo'te, and your comrades, for finally giving justice to Helvius. And Grumio and Augens."

When he straightened, his face was rigid. "I also declare, on behalf of myself and all Romans, that any quarrel between us and Gha is a thing of the past."

Tambo translated the exchange for the commodore. Like most North Americans, with the creaky linguistic skills of a people whose native language was the world's *lingua franca,* Trumbull had not picked up more than a few phrases of the Latin tongue which had been enjoying such an incredible renaissance the past few years.

The commodore scratched under his jaw. "All right," he muttered. "I'm satisfied these people are who they say they are. But what about their other claims? And their weird proposal?"

Before anyone could respond, the communication console hummed vigorously. The com officer, Lieutenant Olga Sanchez, took the call.

"You'd better look at this yourself, Commodore," she said, standing aside.

Trumbull marched over to the screen and quickly read the message. "Wonderful," he muttered. "Just perfect." He turned back, facing the small crowd on the bridge.

"Well, folks, after two hundred years—and God only knows how much money poured down that sinkhole—the SETI maniacs have finally picked up a signal from intelligent extra-solarians. Wasn't hard, actually. The radio signals are being beamed directly at the Earth from a source which just crossed Neptune's orbit."

He took a breath and squared his stocky shoulders.

"Their findings have been confirmed by Operation Spaceguard, using the radar net set up to watch for asteroids. And Naval Intelligence has spotted them also, with modern equipment. The source is a fleet of spacecraft."

He stared at the Gha in the viewscreen. "It seems they were wrong. About this, at least. Somebody else also realized the significance of the radio signals."

"The Guilds!" exclaimed Quartilla.

Trumbull nodded. "One of them, anyway. They're identifying themselves—in Latin—as the Ty'uct Trading Guild."

Quartilla pointed to the body of the Voivode, still visible in the viewscreen. "That's his guild. The one which bought and used the Romans."

"What do they want?" snarled Vibulenus. His fists were clenched again.

"What do you think?" snorted the commodore. "They say that by right of first contact they are claiming exclusive trading privileges with this solar system. A Federation naval vessel is accompanying them to ensure the correct protocols. Whatever that means."

Tambo translated this recent exchange for the benefit of the Gha. As soon as he finished, the Gha commander spoke.

"What it mean," stated Fludenoc, "is they have right hammer in to the submission anybody objects. But must restrict theyselfs this system existing technology. Federation vessel is watchdog make sure they follow rules."

Again, Tambo translated. The commodore's gloom vanished.

"Is that so?" he demanded. "Is that so, indeed?"

He and his executive officer exchanged grins. The North American often exasperated Tambo with his quirks and foibles. But the South African was glad, now, that he was in command. There was a long, long tradition behind that wicked grin on Trumbull's face.

Trumbull turned back to Lieutenant Sanchez. "Tell Naval Command that I'm deploying to meet this threat. If they have any new instructions, tell them they'd better get 'em off quickly. Otherwise, I will follow my own best judgment."

She bent over the console. Trumbull glanced up at the viewscreen. "Bring that ship aboard the *Africanus*," he commanded the Marine lieutenant. "I want to get it below decks before the Guild vessels arrive."

Seeing Tambo's raised eyebrow, he asked:

"Any suggestions? Criticisms?"

Tambo shook his head. "I agree with you."

The South African waved at the viewscreen, now

blank. "We can decide later what we think about the Gha proposal. It sounds crazy to me, frankly. But who knows, in this strange new universe? In the meantime, by keeping them hidden we leave all our options open."

The sight of the viewscreen flickering back into life drew his eyes that way. Within seconds, a starfield filled the screen. Against that glorious background, little lights could be seen, moving slowly across the stars. The ships were far too small to be seen at that distance, by any optical means. The lights were computer simulations based on information derived from a variation of Transit technology which was quite analogous to radar.

There were fourteen of those lights, Tambo saw. One of them—presumably the Federation observer—was hanging well back from the others. The thirteen ships of the Guild force itself were arrayed in a dodecahedron, with a single ship located at the very center.

"That's a fancy-looking formation," mused Trumbull. "But I don't see where it's worth much. Except for parades."

From the corner of the bridge, where he stood next to Quartilla, Robert Ainsley spoke up.

"Excuse me, Commodore."

Trumbull cocked his head around.

The historian pointed at the screen. "Judging from what I've learned since I was assigned to help the Romans orient themselves after their return—and everything we've just heard today fits in perfectly—I don't—" He hesitated, fumbling for words.

"Go on," said the commodore.

"Well, this isn't my field, really. Not in practice, at least. But—I don't think these Guilds have fought a real battle in—in—Jesus, who knows? Millennia. *Many* millennia."

Trumbull smiled thinly and looked back at the formation marching across the starfield.

"Funny you should say that," he murmured. "I was just thinking the same thing."

Tambo cleared his throat. "According to the computer, sir, there are three classes of warships in that fleet. Eight small ones—about the size of the vessel the Gha seized—four mediums, and the big one in the center."

He issued a modest little cough. "Naval procedure, as you know, recommends that we give enemy vessels a nomenclature. Since we don't know what the Guild calls their own ships, we'll have to come up with our own names."

Trumbull's smile widened. "Do you have any suggestions?"

"Oh, yes," replied Tambo, solemn-faced. "I believe we should name them as follows: small ones, *Bismarcks*; the mediums, *Yamatos*; and the big one—"

He could not restrain his grin.

"—is a *Titanic*."

VII

The bridge was crowded, now, with the addition of the aliens. The Pilot and the Medic huddled against a wall, out of the way. But the four Gha, by virtue of their size alone, seemed to fill half the room.

"Do any of you know the rules of engagement?" Trumbull asked the Gha. Tambo translated his question into Latin.

The Gha were stiff as statues.

"We understand do not," said Fludenoc. "What are—engagement regulations?"

Before Tambo could explain, the Gha commander turned to the Pilot and motioned. Fearfully, creeping on her footskirt, she shuffled forward. Tambo waited while Fludenoc spoke some rapid phrases in a language he didn't recognize.

"That's Galactic," whispered Quartilla. "It's an artificial language, with several dialects designed for the vocal apparatus of different Doge Species. This one is called Galactic Three."

She began to add something else, but fell silent when Fludenoc turned back to the humans.

"Now I understand," said the Gha. "Pilot say she not certain. Doges not fought each other many thousands—*many* thousands—years. But she think there no rules between Guild fight Guild. She—what is word?—strongly says you must not attack Federation vessel."

"Will it attack us?" asked Tambo.

The Gha did not bother to check with the pilot before answering. "No. Federation ship will watch only." He waved a huge, clawed hand at the viewscreen. "This is Guild business. Federation not interfere."

After Tambo explained to his superior, Trumbull nodded. "It's a straight-up fight, then." To the com officer: "How good's your Latin?"

She smiled. "Well, sir—it's just about perfect."

Trumbull grimaced. "Christ," he muttered. "I'm going to have to learn that damned archaic tongue, after all."

Then, with an irritated shrug: "Contact that fleet and warn them off."

"Yes sir. How should I identify us?"

Trumbull hesitated, before turning to the historian.

"Give me some good old Roman term," he ordered. "Something vague, mind you—I don't—"

Ainsley understood immediately. Smiling, he replied: "Just use *SPQR*."

Tambo chuckled. Trumbull said to the com officer: "Use it. Tell them we're the—the *SPQR Guild*—and *we* have already established prior rights to all trade and commerce with this system." Growling: "Way, *way* prior rights."

The com officer followed his orders. Three minutes later, a burst of Latin phrases appeared on the com screen.

Lieutenant Sanchez clucked disapprovingly. "Their Latin's really pretty bad. That's a ridiculous declension of the verb 'to copulate,' for one thing. And—"

"Just give me the message!" bellowed the commodore.

The com officer straightened. "The gist of it, sir, is that our claim is preposterous and we are ordered to surrender."

Trumbull grunted. "I was hoping they'd say that. I've never even met these people, and already I hate their guts." He leaned toward his executive officer. "Any recommendations?"

"Yes, sir. I'd send the *Quinctius*. With an escort of SSBNs."

Trumbull nodded. "I was thinking the same way. We may as well find out now if our lasers are as good as they're cracked up to be. And I'll be interested to see how the missiles work. The galactic computer claims kinetic weapons are obsolete, but I think it's full of crap."

Trumbull began giving the necessary orders to his operations staff. Tambo, seeing the Gha commander's stiffness out of the corner of his eye, turned to face him.

He wasn't sure—Gha were as hard to read as the Romans said they were—but he thought Fludenoc was worried.

"Are you concerned?" he asked.

The Gha exhaled explosively. "Yes! You must careful be. These very powerful Guildmaster craft."

Tambo shook his head. "I think you are wrong,

Fludenoc hu'tut-Na Nomo'te. I think these are simply arrogant bullies, who haven't been in a real fight
for so long they've forgotten what it's like."

He did not add the thought which came to him. It
would have meant nothing to the Gha. But he smiled,
thinking of a college fraternity which had once tried
to bully four small Romans in a bar.

Don't fuck with real veterans.

"We've been doing this a long time, Fludenoc," he
murmured. "All those centuries—millennia—while we
were out of contact with the galaxy, we've been fighting
each other. While these Doges—God, what a perfect
name!—got fat like hogs."

VIII

The battle lasted two minutes.

Seeing the huge ancient battleship sweeping toward
them, with its accompanying escort of three resurrected
Trident missile submarines, the Guild dodecahedron
opened up like a flower. Ten laser beams centered on
the *Quinctius* itself, including a powerful laser from
the "Titanic" at the center of the Doge fleet. The three
remaining Guild vessels each fired a laser at the
escorts—the *Pydna*, the *Magnesia*, and the *Chaeronea*.

Powered by their gigantic engines, the shields of the
human vessels shrugged off the lasers. Those shields,
like the engines, were based on galactic technology. But
the Doge Species, with the inveterate habit of merchants, had designed their equipment with a
cheeseparing attitude. The human adaptations—robust;
even exuberant—were based on millennia of combat
experience.

The *Pydna*-class escorts responded first. The hatches
on their upper decks opened. Dozens of missiles

popped out—driven, here, by old technology—and then
immediately went into a highly modified version of
Transit drive. To the watching eye, they simply disappeared.

"Yes!" cried Trumbull, clenching his fist triumphantly.
Not three seconds later, the Guild fleet was staggered
by the impact of those missiles. As the commodore had
suspected, the Doge Species' long neglect of missile
warfare was costing them heavily. Human electronic
countermeasure technology was vastly superior to
anything the Guild vessels possessed in the way of
tracking equipment. Most of the incoming missiles were
destroyed by laser fire, but many of them penetrated
to the shield walls.

Even galactic shields were hard-pressed against
fifteen-megaton nuclear charges. Four of those shields
collapsed completely, leaving nothing but plasma to
mark where spacecraft had formerly been. The others survived. But, in the case of three of them, the
stress on their engines had been great enough to cause
the engines themselves to collapse. Their shields and
drives failed, leaving the three ships to drift helplessly.

Now the *Quinctius* went into action. Again, there
was an exotic combination of old and new technology.
The three great turrets of the ancient battleship swiveled, just as if it were still sailing the Pacific. But the
guidance mechanisms were state-of-the-art Doge technology. And the incredible laser beams which pulsed
out of each turret's three retrofitted barrels were something new to the galaxy. Human engineers and physi-
cists, studying the data in the Roman-captured Guild
vessel, had decided not to copy the Doge lasers.
Instead, they combined some of that dazzling new technology with a revivified daydream from humanity's
bloody past.

Only a ship as enormous as the old *Missouri* could

use these lasers. It took an immense hull capacity to hold the magnetic fusion bottles. In each of those three bottles—one for each turret—five-megaton thermonuclear devices were ignited. The bottles trapped the energy, contained it, channeled it.

Nine X-ray lasers fired. Three Guild ships flickered briefly, their shields coruscating. Then—vaporized.

Thirty seconds elapsed, as the fusion bottles recharged. The Guild ships which were still under power were now veering off sharply. Again, the turrets tracked. Again, ignition. Again, three Doge vessels vaporized.

More seconds elapsed, while the *Quinctius'* fusion bottles recharged.

The communication console on the bridge of the *Scipio Africanus* began humming. "Sir," reported Lieutenant Sanchez, "it's the Guild flagship. They're asking to negotiate."

"Screw 'em," snarled the commodore. "They're nothing but pirates and slavers, as far as I'm concerned."

Tambo grinned. "You want me to see if I can dig up a black flag somewhere?"

Trumbull snorted. "Why not? We're resurrecting everything else."

The operations officer spoke: "The *Quinctius* reports fusion bottles fully recharged, sir."

Trumbull glared at the surviving Guild ships. "*No quarter,*" he growled. "Fire."

IX

The World Confederation's Chamber of Deputies reminded Robert Ainsley of nothing so much as a circus. He even glanced at the ceiling, expecting to see a trapeze artist swinging through the air.

"Is this way always?" Fludenoc asked quietly. The Gha, towering next to the historian, was staring down from the vantage point of the spectators' gallery. His bulging eyes were drawn to a knot of Venezuelan delegates shaking their angry fists in the face of a representative from the Great Realm of the Chinese People.

The Chinese delegate was imperturbable. As he could well afford to be, representing the world's largest single nationality.

Largest by far, thought Ainsley sardonically, *even if you limit the count to the actual residents of China.*

He watched the bellicose Venezuelans stalk off angrily. Most likely, the historian guessed, they were furious with the Chinese for interfering in what they considered internal Venezuelan affairs. That was the usual bone of contention between most countries and the Great Realm. The Chinese claimed a special relationship—almost semi-sovereignty—with everyone in the world of Chinese descent, official citizenship be damned. Given the global nature of the Han diaspora, that kept the Chinese sticking their thumbs into everybody's eye.

The Gha repeated his question. Ainsley sighed.

"No, Fludenoc. This is worse than usual. A bit."

The historian gestured toward the crowded chamber below. "Mind you, the Chamber of Deputies is notorious for being raucous. At the best of times."

Somehow—he was not quite sure how it had happened—Ainsley had become the unofficial liaison between humanity and the Gha. He suspected that his long and successful work reintegrating the Romans into their human kinfolk had given him, in the eyes of the world at large, the reputation of being a wizard diplomat with weird people from the sky. Which, he thought wryly, was the last thing a man who had spent a lifetime engrossed in the history of classical society had ever expected to become.

On the other hand— Ainsley was not a man given to complaining over his fate. And, fortunately, he *did* have a good sense of humor. He eyed the huge figure standing next to him. From his weeks of close contact with the Gha, Ainsley was now able to interpret—to some degree, at least—the body language of the stiff giants.

"You are concerned," he stated.

Fludenoc exhaled sharply, indicating his assent. "I think—thought—*had thought*"—the Gha struggled for the correct Latin tense—"that you would be more—" His thought drifted off in a vague gesture.

"United?" asked Ainsley, cocking an eyebrow. "Coherent? Rational? Organized?"

Again, the Gha exhaled assent. "Yes. All those."

Ainsley chuckled. "More *Guild*-like, in other words."

The Gha giant swiveled, staring down at the old historian next to him. Suddenly, he barked humor.

Ainsley waved at the madding crowd below. "This is what a real world looks like, Fludenoc. A world which, because of its lucky isolation, was able to grow and mature without the interference of the Guilds and the Federation. It's messy, I admit. But I wouldn't trade it for anything else. Not in a million years."

He stared down at the chaos. The Venezuelans were now squabbling with representatives from the Caribbean League. The Caribs, quite unlike the Chinese delegate, were far from imperturbable. One of them shook his dreadlocks fiercely. Another blew ganga-smoke into the Venezuelans' faces. A third luxuriated in the marvelously inventive *patois* of the islanders, serene in his confidence that the frustrated Venezuelans could neither follow his words nor begin to comprehend the insults couched therein.

"Never fear, Fludenoc hu'tut-Na Nomo'te," he murmured. "Never fear. This planet is as fresh and alive as a basket full of puppies. *Wolf* puppies. The Guilds'll never know what hit 'em."

He turned away from the rail. "Let's go get some ice cream. The important business is going to take place later anyway, in the closed session of the Special Joint Committee."

The Gha followed him readily enough. Eagerly, in fact.

"I want cherry vanilla," announced Fludenoc.

"You *always* want cherry vanilla," grumbled Ainsley.

The Gha's exhalation was extremely emphatic. "Of course. Best thing your insane species produces. Except Romans."

X

After the first hour of the Special Joint Committee's session, Ainsley could sense Fludenoc finally begin to relax. The Gha even managed to lean back into the huge chair which had been specially provided for him toward the back of the chamber.

"Feeling better?" he whispered.

The Gha exhaled vigorously. "*Yes*. This is much more—" He groped for words.

"United?" asked Ainsley, cocking a whimsical eyebrow. "Coherent? Rational? Organized?"

"Yes. All those."

Ainsley turned in his seat, facing forward. Behind the long table which fronted the chamber sat the fifteen most powerful legislators of the human race. The Special Joint Committee had been formed with no regard for hallowed seniority or any of the other arcane rituals which the Confederation's governing body seemed to have adopted, over the past century, from every quirk of every single legislative body ever created by the inventive human mind.

This committee was dealing with the fate of humanity—and a number of other species, for that matter. Those men and women with real power and influence had made sure they were sitting at that table. Hallowed rituals be damned.

Not that all rituals and ceremony have been discarded, thought Ainsley, smiling wryly.

He was particularly amused by the veil worn by the Muslim Federation's representative—who had spent thirty years ramming the world's stiffest sexual discrimination laws down her countrymen's throats; and the splendiferous traditional ostrich-plume headdress worn by the South African representative—who was seven-eighths Boer in his actual descent, and looked every inch the blond-haired part; and the conservative grey suit worn by the representative from North America's United States and Provinces, suitable for the soberest Church-going occasions—who was a vociferous atheist and the author of four scholarly books on the historical iniquities of mixing Church and State.

The Chairperson of the Special Joint Committee rose to announce the next speaker, and Ainsley's smile turned into a veritable grin.

And here she is, my favorite. Speaking of preposterous rituals and ceremonies.

The representative from the Great Realm of the Chinese People, Chairperson of the Special Joint Committee—all four feet, nine inches of her—clasped her hands demurely and bobbed her head in modest recognition of her fellow legislators.

Everybody's favorite humble little woman.

"If the representative from the European Union will

finally shut his trap," she said, in a voice like steel—
Mai the Merciless.

"—maybe we can get down to the serious business."
Silence fell instantly over the chamber.

"We call her the Dragon Lady," whispered Ainsley.

"She good," hissed Fludenoc approvingly. "What is
'dragon'?"

"Watch," replied the historian.

Two hours later, Fludenoc was almost at ease.
Watching Mai the Merciless hack her bloody way
through every puffed-up dignitary who had managed
to force himself or herself onto the Committee's agenda
had produced that effect.

"She *very* good," the Gha whispered. "Could eat one
of those stupid carnivores we ride in a single meal."

"—and what other asinine proposition does the
august Secretary wish us to consider?" the Chairperson was demanding.

The Secretary from the International Trade Commission hunched his shoulders. "I must protest your
use of ridicule, Madame Chairperson," he whined. "We
in the Trade Commission do not feel that our concerns
are either picayune or asinine! The project which is
being proposed, even if it is successful—which, by the
way, we believe to be *very* unlikely—will inevitably have
the result, among others, of our planet being subjected
to a wave of immigration by—by—"

The Chairperson finished his sentence. The tone of
her voice was icy: "By *coolies*."

The Trade Commission's Secretary hunched lower.
"I would not choose that particular—"

"That is *precisely* the term you would choose,"
snapped Mai the Merciless, "if you had the balls."

Ainsley had to fight not to laugh, watching the
wincing faces of several of the legislators. From the

ripple in her veil, he thought the Muslim Federation's representative was undergoing the same struggle.

"What are 'balls'?" asked Fludenoc.

"Later," he whispered. "It is a term which is considered very politically incorrect."

"What is 'politically incorrect'?"

"Something which people who don't have to deal with real oppression worry about," replied the historian. Ainsley spent the next few minutes gleefully watching the world's most powerful woman finish her political castration of the world's most influential regulator of trade.

After the Secretary slunk away from the witness table, the Chairperson rose to introduce the next speaker.

"Before I do so, however, I wish to make an announcement." She held up several sheets of paper. "The Central Committee of the Great Realm of the Chinese People adopted a resolution this morning. The text was just transmitted to me, along with the request that I read the resolution into the records of this Committee's session."

A small groan went up. The Chairperson smiled, ever so slightly, and dropped the sheets onto the podium.

"However, I will not do so, inasmuch as the resolution is very long and repetitive. There is one single human characteristic, if no other, which recognizes neither border, breed, nor birth. That is the long-windedness of legislators."

The chamber was swept by a laugh. But the laughter was brief. The Chairperson's smile vanished soon enough, replaced by a steely glare.

"But I will report the gist of the resolution. *The Chinese people of the world have made their decision.* The so-called galactic civilization of the Guilds and the

Federation is nothing but a consortium of imperialist bandits and thieves. All other species, beyond those favored as so-called 'Doges,' are relegated to the status of *coolies*."

Her voice was low, hissing: "It is not to be tolerated. It *will* not be tolerated. The Great Realm strongly urges the World Confederation to adopt wholeheartedly the proposal put forward by our Gha fellowtoilers. Failing that, the Great Realm will do it alone."

Ainsley sucked in his breath. "Well," he muttered, "there's an old-fashioned ultimatum for you."

"What does this mean?" asked Fludenoc.

Ainsley rose from his seat. "What it means, my fine froggy friend, is that you and I don't have to spend the rest of the afternoon watching the proceedings. It's what they call a done deal."

As they walked quietly out of the chamber, Ainsley heard the Chairperson saying:

"—to Commodore Craig Trumbull, for his unflinching courage in the face of barbaric tyranny, the Great Realm awards the Star of China. To all of the men and women of his flotilla who are not Chinese, in addition to he himself, honorary citizenship in the Great Realm. To the crew of the heroic *Quinctius Flaminius*, which obliterated the running dogs of the brutal Doge—"

When the door closed behind them, Fludenoc asked: "What is a 'done deal'?"

"It's what happens when a bunch of arrogant, stupid galactics not only poke a stick at the martial pride of North Americans, but also manage to stir up the bitterest memories of the human race's biggest nation."

He walked down the steps of the Confederation Parliament with a very light stride, for a man his age. Almost gaily. "I'll explain it more fully later. Right now, I'm hungry."

"Ice cream?" asked Fludenoc eagerly.

"Not a chance," came the historian's reply. "Today, we're having Chinese food."

XI

And now, thought Ainsley, *the real work begins. Convincing the Romans.*

He leaned back on his couch, patting his belly. As always, Gaius Vibulenus had put on a real feast. Whatever else had changed in the boy who left his father's estate in Capua over two thousand years ago, his sense of equestrian *dignitas* remained. A feast was a feast, by the gods, and no shirking the duty.

Quartilla appeared by his side, a platter in her hand.

"God, no," moaned Ainsley. "I can't move as it is."

He patted the couch next to him. "Sit, sweet lady. Talk to me. I've seen hardly anything of you these past few weeks."

Quartilla, smiling, put down the platter and took a seat on the couch.

"Did Gaius tell you that we're going to have children?"

Ainsley's eyes widened. "It's definite, then? The Genetic Institute thinks they can do it?"

Quartilla's little laugh had more than a trace of sarcasm in it. "Oh, Robert! They've known for months that they *could* do it. The silly farts have been fretting over the *ethics* of the idea."

Ainsley stroked his beard, studying her. Quartilla seemed so completely human—not only in her appearance but in her behavior—that he tended to forget she belonged to a species that was, technically speaking, more remote from humanity than anything alive on Earth. More remote than crabs, or trees—even bacteria, for that matter.

And even more remote, he often thought, in some of her Ossa *attitudes*.

The Ossa—whether from their innate psychology or simply their internalized acceptance of millennia of physical and genetic manipulation by their Doge masters—had absolutely no attachment to their own natural phenotype. They truly didn't seem to *care* what they looked like.

To some humans, that attitude was repellent— ultimate servility. Ainsley did not agree. To him, the Ossa he had met—and he had met most of the "women" whom the Guild had provided for the Roman soldiers' pleasure—were simply *unprejudiced*, in a way that not even the most tolerant and open-minded human ever was. Ossa did not recognize species, or races. Only *persons* were real to them.

He admired them, deeply, for that trait. Still—Ossa were by no means immune to hurt feelings.

"What phenotype will you select?" he asked.

Quartilla shrugged. "Human, essentially. The genotype will be fundamentally mine, of course. The human genome is so different from that of Ossa that only a few of Gaius's traits can be spliced into the embryo. And they can only do that because, luckily, the chemical base for both of our species' DNA is the same. You know, those four—"

She fluttered her hands, as if shaping the words with her fingers.

"Adenine, guanine, cytosine, thymine," intoned Ainsley.

"—yes, them! Anyway, our DNA is the same, chemically, but it's put together in a completely different manner. We Ossa don't have those—"

Again, her hands wiggled around forgotten words. "Chromosomes?"

"Yes. *Chromosomes.* Ossa DNA is organized

differently. I forget how, exactly. The geneticist explained but I couldn't understand a word he said after five seconds."

Ainsley laughed. "Specialists are all the same, my dear! You should hear Latinists, sometimes, in a bull session. My ex-wife—my *second* ex-wife—divorced me after one of them. Said she'd rather live with a toadstool. Better conversation."

Quartilla smiled archly. "Why did your *first* ex-wife divorce you?"

Ainsley scowled. "That was a different story altogether. *She* was a Latinist herself—the foul creature!— with the most preposterous theories you can imagine. We got divorced after an exchange of articles in the *Journal of*—"

He broke off, chuckling. "Speaking of specialists and their follies! Never mind, dear."

He gestured at Quartilla's ample figure. "But you're going to stick with your human form?"

"Not quite. The children will have a human shape, in every respect. They'll be living in a human world, after all. Human hair, even. But their skins will be Ossa. Well—almost. They'll have the scales, but we'll make sure they aren't dry and raspy. Gaius says people won't mind how the skin looks, as long as it feels good"— she giggled—"in what he calls 'the clutch.' "

Ainsley raised his eyebrow. "*Gaius* doesn't object to this? I thought—you once told me—"

Quartilla shrugged. "That was a long time ago, Robert. It's his idea, actually. He says modern humans aren't superstitious the way he was. And he doesn't give a damn about their other prejudices."

The last sentence was spoken a bit stiffly. Ainsley, watching her closely, decided not to press the matter. By and large, the Ossa "women" had shared in the general hero worship with which humanity had greeted the Roman exiles. Most of them, in fact, had quickly found themselves deluged by romantic advances. But there had been some incidents—

It was odd, really, he mused. Years after their return from exile, the Roman legionnaires still exhibited superstitions and notions which seemed absurd— outrageous, even—to modern people. Yet, at the same time, they shared none of the racial prejudices which so often lurked beneath the surface of the most urbane moderns. The ancient world of the Greeks and Romans had its prejudices and bigotries, of course. Plenty of them. But those prejudices were not tied to skin color and facial features. The Greeks considered the Persians *barbarians* because they didn't speak Greek and didn't share Greek culture. It never would have occurred to them, on the other hand, that the Medes who dominated their world were *racially* inferior. The very notion of "races" was a modern invention.

It had often struck Ainsley, listening to the tales of the legionnaires, how easily they had adapted to their sudden plunge into galactic society. No modern human, he thought, would have managed half as well. Their very ignorance had, in a sense, protected them. The world, to ancient Romans, was full of bizarre things anyway. Every Roman knew that there lived—somewhere south of Egypt, maybe—people with tails and heads in their bellies. A modern human, dropped onto a battlefield against aliens, would have probably been paralyzed with shock and horror. To the Romans, those aliens had just seemed like weird men—and nowhere near as dangerous as Parthians.

Ainsley, catching a glimpse of Pompilius Niger across the room, smiled. Only an ancient Roman would have so doggedly tried to make mead by following something that might be a funny-looking bee. A modern human would have understood the biological impossibility of the task.

And, in that wisdom, died in the hands of the Guild.

He looked back at Quartilla.

And so it had been with her and Gaius. The ancient Roman had been frightened and repelled by her scaly reptilian skin, when he first met her. But he had never thought she was anything but a—person.

"I am glad," he said quietly. "I approve of that decision. You understand, of course, that your children will face some difficulties, because of it."

Quartilla shrugged. It was a serene gesture.

"Some, yes. But not many, I think. If other children get too rough on them, Gaius says he will put a stop to it by simply crucifying a couple of the little bastards."

Ainsley started to laugh; then choked on his own humor.

He stared across the room at Vibulenus. The tribune was standing in a corner of his villa's huge salon, wine glass in hand, in a cluster of veterans who were having a vigorous and friendly exchange of war stories. With him were Clodius Afer, Julius Rusticanus—and all four of the Gha.

Good Lord. That's probably not a joke.

He caught Quartilla watching him closely.

"No, Robert," she murmured. "He is a Roman. He is not joking at all."

XII

An hour later, Gaius Vibulenus called the meeting to order.

There were almost sixty former legionnaires sprawled everywhere in the great salon. Fortunately, Gaius owned an enormous villa. The entire estate—not far

from Capua, to his delight—had been a historical
museum before it was turned over to him by the Italian
regional government, following the dictates of popu-
lar demand.

Many more legionnaires had offered to come, but
Gaius had kept the invitations reasonably small. Too
many people would make decisions impossible. Besides,
the men in the room were, almost without exception,
the surviving leaders of the Roman legion. All of the
centurions were there, and almost all of the file-closers.
Whatever decision they made would be accepted by
the rest of the legionnaires.

"All right," began Vibulenus, "you've all heard the
Gha proposal. In its basic outline, anyway."

He waved his hand airily. "I have it on the best
authority that the Confederation government will give
its backing to the scheme. Unofficially, of course."

Clodius Afer sneered. "Those *politicians*? Be serious, Gaius! They're even worse than that sorry lot of
senators we left behind."

Several other legionnaires grunted their agreement
with that sentiment. Ainsley, watching, was amused.
With few exceptions—Vibulenus, for one; and, oddly
enough, Julius Rusticanus—the Romans had never been
able to make sense out of modern politics. They tended
to dismiss all of it as so much silly nonsense, which
could be settled quick enough with just a few cruci-
fixions.

Much as the historian admired—even loved—the
Romans, he was glad not to have lived in *their* political
world. True, much of modern politics was "so much
silly nonsense." But, much of it wasn't, appearances to
the contrary. And, modern man that he ultimately was,
Ainsley thoroughly approved of the world-wide ban on
capital punishment—much less torture.

"You're wrong, Clodius," rumbled Julius Rusticanus.

The first centurion set down his wine goblet, almost ceremoniously, and stood up. Trained in the rhetorical traditions of the ancient world, he struck a solemn pose. His audience—just as well trained—assumed the solemn stance of listeners.

"Listen to me, Romans. Unlike most of you, I have paid careful attention to modern politics. And I do not share your contempt for it. Nor do I have any desire to listen to puling nonsense about the 'glories of Rome.' I remember the old politics, too. It was stupid Roman politics—the worst kind of personal ambition—that marched us all into that damned Parthian desert. Whatever folly there is in modern men—and there's plenty of it—they are a better lot than we were."

He glared around the room, as if daring anyone to argue with him. No one, of course, was foolish enough to do so. Not with the *first centurion*.

"No children starve, in this modern world. No old people die from neglect. No rich man takes a poor man's farm by bribing a judge. No master beats his slave for some trifling offense. There *are* no slaves."

Again, the sweeping glare. The silence, this time, came from more than respect. Whatever their crude attitudes, the legionnaires all knew that in this, at least, Julius Rusticanus spoke nothing but the plain and simple truth.

"So I'll hear no sneering about 'politicians.' We humans have always had politicians. Our old ones were never any better—and usually a lot worse. I know why Gaius is confident that the Confederation will support the proposal. I don't even need to know who his 'best authority' is. All I have to do is observe what's in front of my nose."

He laughed heartily. Theatrically, to Ainsley; but the historian knew that was an accepted part of the rhetoric. The ancients had none of the modern liking for subtle poses.

"The simple political reality is this, legionnaires," continued Rusticanus. "The people, in their great majority, are now filled with anti-Galactic fervor." Again, that theatrical laugh. "I think most of them are a bit bored with their peaceful modern world, to tell you the truth. They haven't had a war—not a real one, anyway—in almost a hundred years. And this is what they call a *crusade*."

"Won't be able to fight, then," grumbled one of the file-closers. "They're all a pack of civilians."

"Really?" sneered Rusticanus. "I'll tell you what, Appuleius—why don't you explain that to the Guild fleet? You know—the one that's nothing more than gas drifting in space?"

The jibe was met with raucous laughter. Joyful, savage laughter, thought Ainsley. For all their frequent grumbling about "modern sissies," the historian knew the fierce pride which the Romans had taken in Trumbull's destruction of the Guild fleet.

The first centurion pressed home the advantage. He gestured—again, theatrically—to one of the Medics standing toward the side of the salon. This was the "old" Medic, not the "new" one—the stocky, mauve-skinned, three-fingered crewman from the ship the Romans had captured years earlier. A few months after their arrival on Earth, the troop transport's Pilot had committed suicide. But the Medic had adjusted rather well to his new reality. He had even, over time, grown quite friendly with many of the legionnaires. Vibulenus had invited him to this meeting in order to take advantage of his Galactic knowledge.

"Tell them, Medic!" commanded Rusticanus. "Tell them how long it's been since an entire Guild fleet was annihilated."

The Medic stepped forward a pace or two. All the Romans were watching him intently, with the interest of veterans hearing the story of an unfamiliar campaign.

"As far as I know, it's never happened."

The legionnaires stared.

"What do you mean?" croaked one of them. "What do you mean—*never*?"

The Medic shook his head, a gesture he had picked up from his long immersion among humans. "Not that I know of. I'm not saying it *never* happened—way, way back toward the beginning of the Federation, sixty or seventy thousand years ago. But I know it hasn't happened in a very long time."

The Romans were practically goggling, now.

Again, the Medic shook his head. "You don't understand. You all think like—like *Romans*. All humans seem to think that way—even modern ones like Trumbull. The Guilds—and their Federation—are *merchants*. Profit and loss, that's what sets their field of vision. The Guilds fight each other, now and then, but it's never anything like that—that *massacre* Trumbull ordered. After one or two of their ships gets banged around—they hardly ever actually lose a ship— the Guild that's getting the worst of it just offers a better deal. And that's it."

The room was silent, for over a minute, as the Roman veterans tried to absorb this fantastical information. Ainsley was reminded of nothing so much as a pack of wolves trying to imagine how lapdogs think.

Suddenly, one of the legionnaires erupted in laughter. "Gods!" he cried. "Maybe this crazy Gha scheme will work after all!" He beamed approvingly at the huge figure of Fludenoc. "And at least we'll have these damned giant toads on *our* side, this time."

Fludenoc barked, in the Gha way of humor.

"Only some of us, you damned monkey shrimp," he retorted. "In the beginning, at least. All the members of the Poct'on will join, once they learn. But most Gha do not belong to the secret society, and it will take time to win them over."

"That doesn't matter," interjected Gaius. "The new legions are the heart of the plan. They'll have to be human, of course. There aren't very many Gha to begin with, and half of them are scattered all over the galaxy. Whereas we—!"

He grinned and glanced at his watch. "Let's stop for a moment, comrades. I want you to watch something."

He nodded at Rusticanus. The first centurion picked up the remote control lying on a nearby table and turned on the television. The huge screen on the far wall suddenly bloomed with color—and sound.

Lots of sound.

Wincing, Rusticanus hastily turned down the volume. In collusion with Gaius, he had already set the right channel, but he hadn't tested the sound.

The legionnaires were transfixed. Gaping, many of them.

"This scene is from Beijing," said Vibulenus. "The small square—the one that *looks* small, from the camera's height—is called Tien-an-Men."

The scene on the television suddenly shifted to another city. "This is Shanghai," he said.

Another scene. "Guangzhou."

Another. Another. Another.

"Nanjing. Hangzhou. Chongqing."

China was on the march. Every one of those great cities was packed with millions of people, marching through its streets and squares, chanting slogans, holding banners aloft.

"It's not just China," said Rusticanus. His voice, like that of Gaius, was soft.

Another city. More millions, marching, chanting, holding banners aloft.

"Bombay."

Another. "Paris."

Another. Another. More and more and more.

Sao Paolo. Moscow. Los Angeles. Lagos. Ciudad de Mexico.

On and on and on.

A different scene came on the screen. Not a city, now, but a hillside in farm country. The hillside itself— and everywhere the camera panned—was covered with an enormous throng of people. Speeches were being given from a stand atop the ridge.

"That is called Cemetery Ridge," announced Rusticanus. "It is near the small town of Gettysburg in the North American province called Pennsylvania. These people have gathered here to participate in what they are calling the Rededication."

Harshly: "Most of you ignorant sods won't understand why they are calling it that. But you can find out easily enough by reading a short speech which a man named Lincoln gave there not so very long ago. He was a 'stinking politician,' of course."

None of the legionnaires, Ainsley noted, even responded to the jibe. They were still utterly mesmerized by the scenes on the television.

The historian glanced around the room. Its other occupants, mostly aliens, were equally mesmerized— the Gha, Quartilla, the two Medics and the Pilot.

But only on the faces of the legionnaires did tears begin to fall.

They, like the others, were transfixed by the unforgettable images of sheer, raw, massive human *power.* But it was not the sight of those millions upon millions of determined people which brought tears to Roman eyes. It was the sudden, final knowledge that the world's most long-lost exiles had never been forgotten.

One thing was common, in all those scenes. The people varied, in their shape and color and manner of dress. The slogans were chanted in a hundred languages, and the words written on a multitude of banners came in a dozen scripts.

But everywhere—on a hillside in Pennsylvania; a huge square in China—the same standards were held aloft, dominating the banners surrounding them. Many of those standards had been mass-produced for the occasion; many—probably most—crafted by hand.

The eagle standard of the legions.

Gaius rose. Like Rusticanus, he also adopted a theatrical pose, pointing dramatically at the screen.

"There are twelve *billion* people alive in the world today," he said. "And all of them, as one, have chosen that standard as the symbol of their new crusade."

The tribune's eyes swept the room, finally settling on the scarred face of Clodius Afer.

"Will history record that the first Romans failed the last?" he demanded.

Rusticanus switched off the screen. For a moment, the room was silent. Then, Clodius Afer rose and (theatrically) drained his goblet.

Theatrically, belched.

"I never said I wouldn't do it," he announced. With a dramatic wave at the screen:

"Besides, I couldn't face my ancestors, knowing that all those innocent lads went off to war without proper training from"—dramatic scowl—*"proper legionnaires."*

Very dramatic scowl: "The poor sorry bastards."

XIII

"Is this where you died?" asked Ainsley.

For a moment, he thought Gaius hadn't heard him. Then, with no expression on his face, the former tribune shrugged. "I don't think so, Robert. I think we pretty much razed that fortress after we took it. I don't remember, of course, since I was dead when it happened."

Gaius turned his head, examining the walls and crenellations of the castle they were standing on. "It was much like this one, though. Probably not far from here." He gestured toward the native notables standing respectfully a few yards away. "You could ask them. I'm sure they remember where it was."

Ainsley glanced at the short, furry beings. "They wouldn't remember. It was so long ago. Almost two thousand years, now. That was one of your first campaigns."

"They'll know," stated Gaius firmly. "They're a very intelligent species, Robert. They have written records going back well before then. And that was the battle that sealed their fate."

He scanned the fortress more carefully, now, urging Ainsley to join him in that inspection with a little hand gesture.

"You see how well built this is, Robert? These people are not barbarians. They weren't then, either. It was a bit of a shock to us, at the time, coming up against them. We'd forgotten how tough smart and civilized soldiers can be, even when they're as small as these folk."

His face grew bleak. *"Two thousand years,* Robert. For two thousand years these poor bastards have been frozen solid by the stinking Doges. The ruinous trade relations the Guild forced down their throat have kept them there."

"It wasn't your fault, Gaius," murmured Ainsley.

"I didn't say it was. I'm not feeling any guilt over the thing, Robert. We were just as much victims as they were. I'm just sorry, that's all. Sorry for them. Sorry for us."

Suddenly, he chuckled. "Gods, I'm being gloomy! I'm probably just feeling sorry for myself." With a grimace: "Dying *hurts*, Robert. I still have nightmares about it, sometimes."

Ainsley pointed down the wooded slope below them. "Look! Isn't that Clodius Afer?"

Gaius turned and squinted at the tiny figure of the horseman riding up the stone road which led to the castle. After a moment, he chuckled again.

"Yes it is, by the gods. I will be damned. I never thought he'd let the legion fight its first real battle without him there to mother his chicks."

Ainsley raised his eyes, looking at a greater distance. In the valley far below, the legion was forming its battle lines against the still more distant enemy.

"How soon?" he asked.

Gaius glanced at the valley. His experienced eye took only seconds to gauge the matter. "Half an hour, at the earliest. We've got time, before we have to go in."

The horseman was now close enough for Ainsley to see him clearly. It was definitely Clodius Afer.

Fifteen minutes later, the former centurion stamped his way up the narrow staircase leading to the crenellated wall where Vibulenus and Ainsley were waiting. His scarred face was scowling fiercely.

"I couldn't bear to watch!" he snarled. He shot the historian a black, black look. "I hold you responsible, Ainsley. I know this whole crack-brained scheme was your idea."

The centurion strode to the battlements and pointed

theatrically toward the valley. "In less than an hour, thousands of witless boys—and girls, so help me!—will lie dying on that field. Crushed under the heels of their pitiless conquerors. *And it will all be your fault.*"

He spit (theatrically) over the wall.

Ainsley's reply was mild. "It was the Poct'on's idea, Clodius Afer, not mine."

"*Bullshit.* Fludenoc and the other Gha just had a general plan. *You're* the one put flesh and bones on it—I know you were!"

There was just enough truth in that last charge to keep Ainsley's mouth shut. Vibulenus filled the silence. "So we've no chance, Clodius Afer? None at all?" The placid calmness of his voice seemed utterly at variance with the words themselves.

"None," came the gloomy reply. "Might as well put sheep—*lambs*—up against wolves. You should see those frightful brutes, Gaius! Fearsome, fearsome. Ten feet tall, at least, maybe twelve. Every one of them a hardened veteran. I could tell at a glance."

Gaius shook his head sadly. "Such a pity," he murmured. "Throwing away all those young lives for nothing."

He pushed himself away from the wall, shrugging with resignation. "Well, there's nothing for it, then, but to watch the hideous slaughter. Come on, Robert. They should have the scanners in the keep set up and running by now. We can get a much better view of the battle from there."

As he strode toward the stairs, he held up a hand toward the centurion. "You stay here, Clodius Afer! I know you won't want to watch."

The centurion sputtered. Ainsley stepped hastily aside to keep from being trampled as Clodius Afer charged past him.

✧   ✧   ✧

The room in the keep where the viewscanners had been set up was the banquet hall where the local clan chiefs held their ceremonial feasts. It was the largest room in the entire castle, but, even for Romans, the ceiling was so low that they had to stoop slightly to walk through it. Ainsley, with the height of a modern human, felt like he was inside a wide tunnel.

The poor lighting added to his claustrophobia. The natives normally lighted the interior of the castle with a type of wax candles which human eyes found extremely irritating. So, for the occasion, they had decided to forgo all lighting beyond what little sunlight came through the narrow window-slits in the thick walls.

"I still say we could have put in modern lighting," grumbled Vibulenus, groping his way forward. "Temporarily, at least. The Guild command posts always used their own lighting."

"We already went through this, Gaius," replied Ainsley. "The Federation observers are going to watch us like hawks. Especially here, in our new Guild's first campaign. They'll jump on any violation of the regulations, no matter how minor—on our part, that is. They'll let the *established* Guilds cut every corner they can."

"You can say that again," came a growling voice from ahead.

Peering forward, Ainsley saw Captain Tambo's face raising up from the viewscreen.

"Come here and take a look," grumbled the South African. "The Ty'uct are already deploying their Gha. The battle hasn't even started yet, for Christ's sake— and they've got plenty of native auxiliaries to begin with. They don't need Gha flankers."

Gaius reached the viewscreen and bent over.

"That's it!" cried Clodius Afer. "Gha flankers? *The legion's doomed!*"

Vibulenus ignored the former centurion's dark prediction. Silently, he watched the formations unfolding on the large screen in front of him.

After a minute or so, he looked up and smiled. "Speaking of Gha flankers, you might want to take a look at this, Clodius Afer. After all, it was your idea in the first place."

The centurion crowded forward eagerly. "Did Fludenoc and his lads move up?"

He stared at the screen for a moment. Then, began cackling with glee. "*See? See?* I told you those stinking hyenas were just a bunch of turbo-charged jackals! Ha! Look at 'em cringe! They finally ran into something bigger than they are. A *lot* bigger!"

Ainsley managed to shove his head through the small crowd and get a view of the screen.

"I will be good God-damned," he whispered. He patted the former centurion on the shoulder. "You're a genius, Clodius Afer. I'll admit, I had my doubts."

Clodius Afer snorted. "That's because you modern sissies never faced war elephants in a battle. The great brutes are purely terrifying, I'm telling you."

"As long as they don't panic," muttered Gaius.

"They won't," replied Clodius Afer confidently. "These are that new strain the geneticists came up with. They're really more like ancient mammoths than modern elephants. And they've been bred for the right temperament, too."

He pointed to the screen. "Besides, the Gha know just how to handle the damn things. Watch!"

The scene in the viewscreen was quite striking, thought Ainsley. The main body of the Ty'uct army was still milling around in the center of the field, whipping themselves into a frenzy. On the flanks, Gha bodyguards had pushed forward on their "turbocharged" giant quasi-hyenas. But they were already falling back before Fludenoc and the other Poct'on members who were serving the legion as a special force. There were thirty-two of those Gha, all mounted on gigantic war elephants, all wielding the modified halberds which human armorers had designed to replace the traditional Gha maces.

The Poct'on warriors loomed over their counterparts like moving cliffs. The giant "hyenas" looked like so many puppies before the elephants. Bad-tempered, nasty, snarling puppies, true. But thoroughly intimidated, for all that. Despite the best efforts of their Gha riders, the hyenas were slinking back toward their lines.

Ainsley could hardly blame them. Even from the remoteness of his televised view, the war elephants were—as Clodius Afer had rightly said—"purely terrifying." These were no friendly circus elephants. They didn't even *look* like elephants. To Ainsley, they seemed a perfect reincarnation of mammoths or mastodons. The beasts were fourteen feet high at the shoulders, weighed several tons, and had ten-foot-long tusks.

They also had a temperament to match. The elephants were bugling great blasts of fury with their upraised trunks, and advancing on the hyenas remorselessly.

"Jesus," whispered Tambo, "even the Gha look like midgets on top of those things. They seem to have them under control, though."

"I'm telling you," insisted Clodius Afer, "the Gha are wizards at handling the brutes." He snorted. "They always did hate those stinking hyenas, you know. But with elephants and Gha, it was love at first sight."

Tambo glanced up. "Whatever happened to their own—uh, 'hyenas'? The ones they had on the ship they seized?"

Gaius whistled soundlessly. Clodius Afer coughed, looked away.

"Don't rightly know," he muttered. "But Pompilius Niger—he raises bees now, you know, on his farm— told me that Uddumac asked him for a couple of barrels of his home-brewed mead. For a private Gha party, he said."

Tambo winced. "Don't let the SPCA find out."

The centurion mumbled something under his breath. Ainsley wasn't sure, but it sounded like "*modern sissies.*"

"The hyenas are breaking," announced Gaius. "Look at them—they're completely cowed."

Tambo slapped the heavy wooden table under the viewscreen. The gesture expressed his great satisfaction.

"It'll be a straight-up fight, now! Between the legion and those—what in the *hell* are they, anyway? Have you ever seen them before, Gaius?"

The tribune grinned. So did Clodius Afer.

"Oh, yes," he murmured. "These boys were the opposition in our very first Guild campaign."

"Sorry clowns!" barked the centurion. "Look at 'em, Gaius—I swear, I think those are the same wagons they were using two thousand years ago."

The Ty'uct mercenaries started their wagon charge. Clodius Afer watched them on the screen for a few seconds before sneering: "Same stupid tactics, too. Watch this, professor! These galloping idiots are about to—"

He scowled. "Well, if they were facing a *real* Roman legion."

Deep scowl. "As it is—against these puling babes—?" Low moan of despair. "It'll be a massacre. A *massacre*, I tell you."

"Actually," murmured Gaius, "I think the puling babes are going to do better than we did."

He glanced over at Tambo, who was sitting to one side of the big screen. The naval officer's eyes were on a complex communication console attached to the viewscanner. "Are we secure?" asked Gaius.

Tambo nodded. "Yeah, we are. Our ECM has got the Federation's long-distance spotters scrambled. Everything in the castle is out of their viewing capability."

He sat up, sneering. "And, naturally, the lazy galactics never bothered to send a personal observer. Even if they shuttle one down now, it'll be too late. The battle'll be over before they get here."

"Good." Gaius turned and whistled sharply. A moment later, several natives appeared in the main doorway to the great hall. Gaius gestured, motioning for them to enter.

Somewhat gingerly, the natives advanced into the room and approached the small knot of humans at the viewscreen.

"You watch now," said Gaius, in simple Latin.

"Is safe from Federation?" asked one of the natives, also in Latin. Ainsley recognized him. The Fourth-of-Five, that one was called. He was a member of the clan's central leadership body, as well as the clan's warchief.

"Safe," assured Gaius. "They can not see you here with"—he groped for a moment, in the limits of the simplified language—"high-raised arts. But must keep this secret. Not tell them. Not tell anyone."

"Secret be keep," said the Fourth-of-Five. Still a bit gingerly, the warchief leaned forward to examine the scene on the scanner.

"Battle start?"

"Yes," replied Gaius. "Now you watch. I explain what we do. Why we do."

Two minutes later, the battle was joined in earnest. As it unfolded, Gaius followed the action with a running commentary for the benefit of the Fourth-of-Five, explaining the methods and principles of Roman tactics. The warchief was an attentive student. A very knowledgeable one, too, who asked many pointed and well-aimed questions. His own people had never been slouches, when it came to warfare; and now, hidden miles away in a forest camp, the warchief's own native *legion* had already begun its training.

Commander Tambo watched some of the battle, but not much. He was a naval officer, after all, for whom the tactics of iron-age land warfare were of largely academic interest. He was much more concerned with keeping a careful eye on the ECM monitors. By allowing the natives to follow the battle with the help of modern technology, the humans were breaking the letter of Federation law.

The *spirit* of that law, of course, they were trampling underfoot with hobnailed boots.

Ainsley simply watched the battle. Quite transfixed, he was; oblivious to everything else.

Ironically, *his* interest was purely academic. But it was the monomaniacal interest of a man who had spent all but the last few years of his adult life studying something which he was now able to see unfold before his own eyes. *A Roman legion in action.*

A purist, of course, would have been outraged.

Such a purist, in his own way, was the legion's expert consultant and field trainer, the former centurion Clodius Afer. Throughout the course of the battle, Clodius Afer danced back and forth between the viewscreen and the far wall, to whose unfeeling stones he wailed his black despair.

Roman legion, indeed!

Smiling, Ainsley leaned over and whispered to Gaius: "Is the rumor true? Did Clodius Afer really call Colonel Tsiang a 'slant-eyed bastard'?"

Gaius grinned, though his eyes never left the screen. He was keeping a close watch on the legate commanding the legion, in order to provide him with expert consultation after the battle.

That legate was a former colonel in the Chinese Army. Of the ten tribunes commanding the legion's cohorts, four were Chinese, three North American, one German, one South African and one Pakistani. True, there was one Italian centurion, and three Italian file-closers. But the overall national and racial composition of the legion was a fair reflection of modern Earth's demographics, except that it was skewed toward Chinese and North Americans. This, for the simple reason that all the legionnaires were former soldiers, and only the North Americans and Chinese still maintained relatively large standing armies.

"Oh, yes," murmured Gaius. "Fortunately, Tsiang's a phlegmatic kind of guy. Good thing for Clodius. The colonel has a black belt in at least five of the martial arts."

He turned his head. "You might want to watch this, Clodius Afer! They're getting ready for the first volley of javelins!"

Two seconds later, the former centurion's face was almost pressed to the screen. "They'll screw it up," he groaned. "Damned amateurs think they're throwing darts in a tavern."

Silence ensued, for a few seconds. Then:

Gaius grinned. Clodius Afer scowled and stalked off. Robert Ainsley hissed, face pale.

"God in Heaven," he whispered shakily. "I had no idea."

The former tribune's grin faded. "A good javelin volley is like the scythe of death, Robert. It's pure butchery."

"Was this one good?"

"As good as you'll ever see. I knew it would be."

Ainsley studied Gaius for a moment.

"You've never shared Clodius Afer's skepticism. Why?"

Gaius snorted. "The old bastard's just jealous, that's all."

The former tribune jabbed his forefinger at the screen. "Every single one of those legionnaires, from the legate down to the last man in the ranks, is a hand-picked volunteer. The cream of the crop—and it was a huge crop of volunteers. Every one's a soldier, and every one's dedicated to this cause. Not to mention the fact that, on average, they're probably half again as strong and twice as fast as the average Roman legionnaire of our time. So why shouldn't they do well?"

Ainsley rubbed his chin. "It's still their first real battle."

Gaius shrugged. "True. And it shows." He nodded at the screen.

"They're sluggish, right now. They're not reacting as quickly as they should to the success of their javelin volley. That's inexperience. A blooded legion would already be down the enemy's throat. But—*see*? Tsiang's already bringing the line forward. Good formations, too. The spacing's excellent."

He glanced over his shoulder at the figure of Clodius Afer, wailing against the wall.

"Clodius forgets. How good do you think *we* were in the beginning? A bunch of ignorant kids, half of us. Marched off to slaughter in the desert and then sold to aliens. I had no idea what I was doing, at first. *This* legion's already doing well. Give them three more campaigns and they could have chopped us up for horse meat."

He turned back to the screen. "Trust me, Robert.

There's never been a better Roman legion than the one down there on that field today."

Again, he cocked his head and bellowed at Clodius Afer. "They've almost closed with the enemy! Oh—*and look*! The Tenth Cohort's going to bear the brunt of it!"

"*That bitch!*" shrieked Clodius Afer, charging back to the screen. "She's going to get 'em all killed!"

Silence, for two full minutes. Then:

Gaius laughed. Clodius Afer spit on the floor and stalked back to the wall. Spit on the wall. Ainsley wiped his face.

"I thought the Tenth Cohort was supposed to be the legion's shield, not its sword arm," he muttered.

Gaius's grin was cold, cold. "Yeah, that's the tradition. But traditions are meant to be broken, you know. And Tribune Lemont is *not* the phlegmatic type."

"Is it true?" whispered Ainsley. "Did Clodius Afer really call Shirley Lemont a—"

Gaius laughed. "Oh, yes! Then, after he woke up, he insisted on a formal rematch. He didn't quit until she threw him six times running, and told him she was going to start breaking his puny little bones."

Ainsley stared at Clodius Afer. The former centurion was studying the stone wall with a deep interest which seemed entirely inappropriate to its bare, rough-hewn nature.

"I guess it took him by surprise, seeing women in the legion's ranks."

Gaius started to reply but broke off suddenly, rising halfway out of his seat. "Gods, look at them rolling up the flank! This battle's already won, Robert." Turning his head, he bellowed:

"Hey, Clodius Afer! You might want to see this! The enemy's pouring off the field! The legion's hammering 'em into mash! And—guess what?—*great news!* It's our old Tenth Cohort that turned their flank! God, what a maneuver! I'm telling you, Clodius Afer—*that Shirley Lemont's the best tribune I've ever seen!* Come here! You don't want to miss it!"

In the next five minutes, Gaius Vibulenus went over the battle with the Fourth-of-Five, patiently answering the native warleader's many questions. Robert Ainsley simply sat, recovering from the experience—simultaneously exhilarating and horrifying—of finally seeing the Roman war machine in action.

Clodius Afer leaned his head against the stone wall. Banged it once or twice. Wept bitter tears for the lost legacy of ancient Rome.

Ruined—*ruined*—by modern sissies. *Girls.*

XIV

As he watched the troop transport settle its enormous bulk into the valley, Ainsley found it impossible not to grin.

"Travelling in style, I see," he chuckled.

Gaius gave him a stern look. "I beg your pardon? The *Cato* is an official SPQR Guild transport vessel, properly registered as such with the Federation authorities."

Ainsley snorted. "She's also the former *Queen Elizabeth*, luxury liner."

Gaius grinned. "So? It could be worse, you know. They're already talking about raising the *Titanic* and retrofitting her."

A voice from behind them: "It's already been decided. Damn fools are going to do it."

The two men turned to face Tambo. The naval officer was just climbing off the stairs onto the stone ramp behind the castle's crenellations. A few steps behind him came the Second-of-Five.

The South African and the native clan leader joined them at the battlements. Tambo scowled.

"I think it's pure foolishness, myself. The whole point of refitting old naval vessels is to re-arm the Earth as fast as possible. *Stupid.* It'll take twice as long—and twice the money—to fix up that shipwreck than it would to build a brand-new transport."

Ainsley's reply was mild. "Humans are a bit swept up in historical sentiment, you know. All things considered, I have to say I'm rather in favor of it."

Tambo grimaced but didn't argue the point. Instead he went straight to his business.

"I've just gotten word from the escort vessels. The Federation ship and the Guild transport have left the system, so there are no observers left. The colonists can debark before the legion boards the transport."

"Any threats?" asked Gaius.

"From the *Ty'uct*?" sneered Tambo. "Not likely—not after we smeared their second invasion fleet in less time than the first. No, no threats. But they are definitely in a foul mood after yesterday's whipping. They're complaining about the elephants."

Gaius shrugged. "Let 'em! Elephants were a regular feature of Roman warfare."

"Not genetically engineered semi-mastodons," pointed out Ainsley.

Again, Gaius shrugged. "So what? The Guild can hardly complain—not when *their* Gha ride mounts that have to be turbocharged to even breathe the air."

Tambo smiled. "They're still going to complain about it. Demand a full Federation hearing, they say." His smile broadened. "God, would I love to be there! Did you hear? Mai the Merciless has been appointed Earth's official representative to the Federation."

"Heaven help them," murmured Ainsley. Then:

"I thought you *were* going to be there."

Tambo's smile was now an outright grin. "Change of orders." He squared his shoulders. Struck a solemn pose.

"You have the honor of being in the presence of the newly appointed commodore in charge of Flotilla Seven."

The false pomposity vanished, replaced by a cheerful rubbing of his hands. "The campaign against the Ssrange is on! And I'm in command!"

Ainsley's eyes widened. "They decided to do it? I thought—"

Tambo shook his head. "No, it seems good sense won out over timidity, after all. Christ, I should hope so! We've got a tiger by the tail. Last thing we can afford to do is let go. If the Guilds and the Federation ever figure out how vulnerable we are—will be, for at least twenty years—they could slaughter us. *Keep the bastards cowed*—that's the trick!"

Gaius nodded. "I agree. Bloodying the Ty'uct Guild's nose in a couple of small ship battles will only win us a couple of years. Before one of the bolder guilds decides to mount a real armada."

"Unless we show the galaxy how rough we are—by wiping out the nest of pirates that the whole Federation's whined about for thirty millennia." The South African's voice took on a whimpering tone. *"What can we do? Best to reach an accommodation with the Ssrange. They're businessmen, too, after all, in their own way."*

Gaius's eyes were icy. "They held Quartilla, for a time. Did you know that?"

Both Tambo and Ainsley nodded.

"What's your plan, Stephen?" asked the historian. "You're the commander."

For a moment, Tambo's eyes were as cold as the Roman's. "It's been named Operation Pompey. That should give you the idea."

Ainsley sucked in his breath. Gaius grinned like a wolf.

As well he could. In 67 B.C.—just fourteen years before Crassus's ill-fated expedition against the Parthians had resulted in Gaius's enslavement to the Guild—the Roman republic finally lost patience with the pirates who had plagued the Mediterranean for centuries. Pompey the Great—one of the three members, along with Caesar and Crassus, of the First Triumvirate—was charged with the task of exterminating piracy.

He did it. In exactly three months.

"The *Roman* way," growled Gaius.

"Here come the colonists," murmured Tambo. He raised the binoculars hanging around his neck and studied the small crowd of people filing from the *Cato*. Then, after a minute or so, passed them to the Second-of-Five. The native clan leader immediately—and with obvious familiarity with the eyeglasses—began examining the scene in the valley below.

Ainsley spent the time studying the binoculars themselves. He was rather fascinated by the simple, obsolete device. Modern humans, when they wanted to view something at a distance, used computer-enhanced optical technology. But such technology would be far beyond the capacity of the natives who had just entered a new trading agreement with the galaxy's newest guild.

The *SPQR Guild*, as it was formally known—and so registered, officially, with the Federation.

The "guild" had other, unofficial names. Many of them, in many human languages. The names varied, depending on each human subculture's own traditions. Some called it the Tea Party, others the Long March.

Others, Francophones, *la Resistance.* Most people, though, simply called it the Liberation.

Ainsley's attention shuttled back and forth between the binoculars and the small, furred figure of the native holding them.

They've started their first lens-grinding works, Tambo tells me. They already knew how to make good glass.

He looked away, smiling. The occasional Federation observer who scanned from orbit, now and then, would have no way of seeing the technological and social revolution that was exploding across the surface below. This planet—and its people—were frozen no longer.

The "SPQR Guild" had set up quite different trade relations than the ones which had dominated here for two millennia. The Doge guilds, had they known, would have been utterly shocked.

These trade treaties would not bleed the natives dry. Quite the opposite.

Ainsley looked down into the valley. He could not see the individual faces of the colonists who were now making their way toward the castle, escorted by elephant-mounted Gha. But he knew what those faces would look like. Human faces, in their big majority—although some of those faces concealed Ossa. But there would be a few unreconstructed Ossa among them, the first contingents of what was already being called the Underground Railroad. And, here and there, a few members of other species. Freed slaves, some. Others, people from Class One planets—like the Pilot and the Medic—who had decided to throw in their lot with the rising new human "Doge Species."

On every planet which the SPQR Guild's legions cleared of their former guild masters, such small colonies would be set up. Scattered like seeds across the starfields, to intermingle with the natives and create a multitude of new, vibrant societies.

He caught Tambo's warm eyes watching him.

"Twenty years, Robert," said the naval officer softly. "Twenty years. By then, Earth's navy will be too strong for the Guilds—even the Federation—to defeat us."

He made a sweeping gesture which encompassed the valley and, by implication, the entire universe. "And, by then, we'll have created an army of allies. A *host*, Robert, like this galaxy's never seen."

Ainsley smiled crookedly. "You're not worried, Stephen? Not at all?"

Before answering, Tambo studied him.

Then, he shook his head. "God, I'd hate to be a historian," he muttered. "Worry about everything." Again, he made the sweeping gesture.

"You're concerned, I assume, that we'll screw it up, too? Set up a new tyranny?"

Ainsley nodded. Tambo chuckled.

"Don't worry about it, Robert. I'm *sure* we'll screw it up. Some. Badly, even, here and there. So what? It'll sort itself out, soon enough."

He grinned widely. "We humans have always been good at sorting out that kind of thing, you know."

Tambo stretched out his muscular, light-brown arm.

"*Look at it, historian*. There's all of Africa—half the world—in that arm. Bantu, Boer, Khoisan, English. A fair chunk of India, too." He lowered the arm. "When I was a boy, growing up, I was thrilled as much by the Trek as I was by Isandhlwana, Moshoeshoe and Mandela. It's all part of me. Now that it's been sorted out."

Tambo pointed his finger at the great banner flying above the castle. The banner of the new guild, proudly announcing its trade dominance of the planet.

"We'll sort it out. And wherever we screw up, there'll

be others to kick us in the ass. We humans are just as good at learning from a butt-kicking as we are at delivering one. Better, probably."

Ainsley stared at the banner. Then, smiled as broadly as Tambo. "Poor Doges," he murmured. "Merchants have never been worth a damn, you know, historically speaking. Not, at least, when they try to run an empire."

Emblazoned atop the banner, above the eagle standard, were the simple letters: *S.P.Q.R.*

Below, the Guild's motto:

Carthago delenda est.

XV

Some years later, a great crowd filled the villa near Capua owned by Gaius Vibulenus. The occasion was the ninth birthday of Gaius and Quartilla's first child. The boy they had named Ulysses, but called simply Sam.

Clodius Afer, one of the boy's four godfathers, had been disgruntled by the name. "Sissy Greek name," he'd muttered, speaking of the official cognomen. And he had even less use for the nickname.

Pompilius Niger, the second of the godfathers, also thought the name was a bit odd, for a Roman. But, unlike Clodius Afer, the simple farmer rather liked the simple "Sam."

Julius Rusticanus, the third godfather, was delighted by the name. As well he should be—it was his suggestion in the first place. Unlike his two fellow legionnaires, Rusticanus knew that the boy had not been named after an ancient Greek adventurer. No, Rusticanus had become quite the student of world history—as befitted a man who had recently been elected, by an overwhelming majority of Italians, to the

Confederation's most august legislative body. The former first centurion, born a peasant, was now—what would his father have thought, he often wondered?— a senator.

Ulysses had been named after another, much later man. The man who led the armies which destroyed chattel slavery. Ulysses "Sam" Grant. Rusticanus had great hopes for the boy. Especially now, watching the child bouncing in the lap of his fourth godfather, demanding an explanation for the new toys.

The boy, though large for his age, was almost lost in that huge Gha lap.

"What do you do with them, Fludenoc?" demanded Sam. "How do you play with them?"

Rusticanus grinned. Fludenoc hu'tut—*No*. He was now Fludenoc *hu-lu-tut*-Na Nomo'te. His epic poem— the first epic poem ever written by a Gha—had won him that new accolade, from his clan. Fludenoc now belonged to that most select of Gha poets, those considered "bards."

The epic had been entitled the *Ghaiad*. Rusticanus had read it, twice. The first time with awe, at the Gha's great poetic skill, which came through even in the Latin translation. The second time with amusement, at the Gha's wry sense of humor. It was all about a small band of Gha, long ago, who had been driven into exile by rapacious conquerors. Wandering the galaxy—having many adventures—until they finally settled on a new planet and founded Rome. (With, admittedly, a bit of help from the local natives.)

Fludenoc, like Rusticanus, had also become an avid student of human history.

"Tell me, Uncle Fludenoc, tell me!" demanded the boy. The child pointed at the new toys which the Gha had brought him for his birthday. "How do you play with them?"

Fludenoc's huge, bulging eyes stared down at the tiny Ossa/human child in his lap. As always, there was no expression in the giant's face. But the boy had long since learned to read the subtleties of Gha breathing.

"Stop laughing at me!" shrilled Sam. "I want to know! How do you play with them?"

"I was not laughing at *you*, Sam," rumbled Fludenoc. "I was laughing at the Doges."

Sam's slightly iridescent, softly scaled face crinkled into a frown.

"When you grow up," said the Gha, gently, "you will know how to use them."

Sam twisted in Fludenoc's lap, staring down at the peculiar toys sitting on the floor.

A small plow.

A bag of salt.

The following is an excerpt from

Paying the Piper
by David Drake

Baen Books, hardcover, July 2002

===

CHOOSING SIDES

The driver of the lead combat car revved his fans to lift the bow when he reached the bottom of the starship's steep boarding ramp. The gale whirling from under the car's skirts rocked Lieutenant Arne Huber forward into the second vehicle—his own *Fencing Master*, still locked to the deck because a turnbuckle had kinked when the ship unexpectedly tilted on the soft ground.

Huber was twenty-five standard years old, shorter than average and fit without being impressively muscular. He wore a commo helmet now, but the short-cropped hair beneath it was as black as the pupils of his eyes.

Sighing, he pushed himself up from *Fencing Master's* bow slope. His head hurt the way it always did just after star-travel—which meant worse than it did any other time in his life. Even without the howling fans of *Foghorn*, the lead car, his ears would be roaring in time with his pulse.

None of the troopers in Huber's platoon were in much better shape, and he didn't guess the starship's crew were more than nominal themselves. The disorientation from star travel, like a hangover, didn't stop hurting just because it'd become familiar.

"Look!" said Sergeant Deseau, shouting so that the three starship crewmen could hear him over the fans' screaming. "If you don't have us free in a minute flat, starting *now*, I'm going to shoot the cursed thing off and you can worry about the damage to your cursed deck without me to watch you. Do you understand?"

Two more spacers were squeezing through the maze of vehicles and equipment in the hold, carrying a power tool between them. This sort of problem can't have been unique to *Fencing Master*.

Huber put his hand on Deseau's shoulder. "Let's get out of the way and let them fix this, Sarge," he said, speaking through the helmet intercom so that he didn't have to raise his voice. Shouting put people's backs up, even if you didn't mean anything by it except that it was hard to hear. "Let's take a look at Plattner's World."

They turned together and walked to the open hatch. Deseau was glad enough to step away from the problem.

The freighter which had brought Platoon F-3, Arne Huber's command, to Plattner's World had a number rather than a name: KPZ 9719. It was much smaller than the vessels which usually carried the men and vehicles of Hammer's Regiment, but even so it virtually overwhelmed the facilities here at Rhodesville. The ship had set down normally, but one of the outriggers then sank an additional meter into the soil. The lurch had flung everybody who'd already unstrapped against the bulkheads and jammed *Fencing Master* in place, blocking two additional combat cars behind it in the hold.

Huber chuckled. That made his head throb, but it throbbed already. Deseau gave him a sour look.

"It's a good thing we hadn't freed the cars before the outrigger gave," Huber explained. "Bad enough people bouncing off the walls; at least we didn't have thirty-tonne combat cars doing it too."

"I don't see why we're landing in a cow pasture anyway," Deseau muttered. "Isn't there a real spaceport somewhere on this bloody tree-farm of a planet?"

"Yeah, there is," Huber said dryly. "The trouble is, it's in Solace. The people the United Cities are hiring us to fight."

The briefing cubes were available to everybody in the Slammers, but Sergeant Deseau was like most of the enlisted personnel—and no few of the officers—in spending the time between deployments finding other ways to entertain himself. It was a reasonable enough attitude. Mercenaries tended to be pragmatists. Knowledge of the local culture wasn't a factor when a planet hired mercenary soldiers, nor did it increase the gunmen's chances of survival.

Deseau spit toward the ground, either a comment or just a way of clearing phlegm from his throat. Huber's mouth felt like somebody'd scrubbed a rusty pot, then used the same wad of steel wool to scour his mouth and tongue.

"Let's hope we capture Solace fast so we don't lose half our supplies in the mud," Deseau said. "This place'll be a swamp the first time it rains."

KPZ 9719 had come down on the field serving the dirigibles which connected Rhodesville with the other communities on Plattner's World—and particularly with the spaceport at Solace in the central highlands. The field's surface was graveled, but there were more soft spots than the one the starship's outrigger had stabbed wasn't working. Well, that was par for the course.

Trooper Kolbe sat in the driver's compartment, his chin bar resting on the hatch coaming. His faceshield was down, presenting an opaque surface to the outside world. Kolbe could have been using the helmet's infrared, light-amplification, or sonic imaging to improve his view of the dimly lit hold, but Huber suspected the driver was simply hiding the fact that his eyes were closed.

Kolbe needn't have been so discreet. If Huber hadn't thought he ought to set an example, he'd have been leaning his forehead against *Fencing Master*'s cool iridium bow slope and wishing he didn't hurt so much.

Platoon Sergeant Jellicoe was at the arms locker, issuing troopers their personal weapons. Jellicoe seemed as dispassionate as the hull of her combat car, but Trooper Coblentz, handing out the weapons as the sergeant checked them off, looked like he'd died several weeks ago.

Unless and until Colonel Hammer ordered otherwise, troopers on a contract world were required to go armed at all times. Revised orders were generally issued within hours of landing; troopers barhopping in rear areas with sub-machine guns and 2-cm shoulder weapons made the Regiment's local employers nervous, and rightly so.

On Plattner's World the Slammers had to land at six sites scattered across the United Cities, a nation that was mostly forest. None of the available landing fields was large enough to take the monster starships on which the Regiment preferred to travel, and only the administrative capital, Benjamin, could handle more than one twenty-vehicle company at a time. Chances were that even off-duty troopers would be operating in full combat gear for longer than usual.

"What's that gas-bag doing?" Deseau asked. "What do they fill 'em with here, anyway? If it's hydrogen and it usually is . . ."

Foghorn had shut down, well clear of the starship's ramp. Her four crewmen were shifting their gear out of the open-topped fighting compartment and onto the splinter shield of beryllium net overhead. A Slammers' vehicle on combat deployment looked like a bag lady's cart; the crew knew that the only things they could count on having were what they carried with them. Tanks and combat cars could shift position by over 500 klicks in a day, smashing the flank or rear of an enemy who didn't even know he was threatened; but logistics support couldn't follow the fighting vehicles as they stabbed through hostile territory.

"Aide, unit," Huber said, cueing his commo helmet's AI to the band all F-3 used in common. "Tatzig, pull around where that dirigible isn't going to hit you. Something's wrong with the bloody thing and the locals aren't doing much of a job of sorting it out."

Sergeant Tatzig looked up. He grunted an order to his driver, then replied over the unit push, *"Roger, will do."*

There was a clang from the hold. A spacer had just hit the turnbuckle with a heavy hammer.

A huge, hollow metallic racket sounded from the field; the dirigible had dropped its four shipping containers. The instant the big metal boxes hit the ground, the sides facing the starship fell open. Three of them did, anyway: the fourth container opened halfway, then stuck.

The containers were full of armed men wearing uniforms of chameleon cloth that mimicked the hue of whatever it was close to. The troops looked like pools of shadow from which slugthrowers and anti-armor missiles protruded.

"Incoming!" Huber screamed. "We're under attack!"

One of the attacking soldiers had a buzzbomb, a shoulder-launched missile, already aimed at Huber's face. He fired. Huber reacted by instinct, grabbing his two companions and throwing himself down the ramp instead of back into the open hold.

The missile howled overhead and detonated on *Fencing Master*'s bow. White fire filled the universe for an instant. The blast made the ramp jump, flipping Huber from his belly to his right side. He got up. He was seeing double, but he could see; details didn't matter at times like this.

The attack had obviously been carefully planned, but things went wrong for the hostiles as sure as they had for Huber and his troopers. The buzzbomber had launched early instead of stepping away from the shipping container as he should've done. The steel box caught the missile's backblast and reflected it onto the shooter and those of his fellows who hadn't jumped clear. They spun out of the container, screaming as flames licked from their tattered uniforms.

A dozen automatic weapons raked *Foghorn*, killing Tatzig and his crewmen instantly. The attackers' weapons used electromagnets to accelerate heavy-metal slugs down the bore at hypersonic velocity. When slugs hit the car's iridium armor, they ricocheted as neon streaks that were brilliant even in sunlight.

Slugs that hit troopers chewed their bodies into a mist of blood and bone.

The starship's hold was full of roiling white smoke, harsh as a wood rasp on the back of Huber's throat in the instant before his helmet slapped filters down over his nostrils. The buzzbomb had hit *Fencing Master*'s bow slope at an angle. Its shaped-charge warhead had gouged a long trough across the armor instead of punching through into the car's vitals. There was no sign of Kolbe.

The tie-down, jammed turnbuckle and all, had vanished in the explosion. Two pairs of legs lay beside the vehicle. They'd probably belonged to spacers rather than Huber's troopers, but the blast had blown the victims' clothing off at the same time it pureed their heads and torsos.

Slugs snapped through the starship's hatchway, clanging and howling as they ricocheted deeper into the hold. Huber mounted *Fencing Master*'s bow slope with a jump and a quick step. He dabbed a hand down and the blast-heated armor burned him. He'd have blisters in the morning, if he lived that long.

Huber thought the driver's compartment was empty, but Kolbe's body from the shoulders on down had slumped onto the floor. Huber bent through the hatch and grabbed him. The driver's right arm came off when Huber tugged.

Huber screamed in frustration and threw the limb out of the vehicle, then got a double grip on Kolbe's equipment belt and hauled him up by it. Bracing his elbows for leverage, Huber pulled the driver's torso and thighs over the coaming and let gravity do the rest. The body slithered down the bow, making room for Huber inside. The compartment was too tight to share with a corpse and still be able to drive.

Kolbe had raised the seat so that he could sit with his head out of the vehicle. Huber dropped it because he wanted the compartment's full-sized displays instead of the miniature versions his faceshield would provide. The slugs whipping around the hold would've been a consideration if he'd had time to think about it, but right now he had more important things on his mind than whether he was going to be alive in the next millisecond.

"All Fox elements!" he shouted, his helmet still cued to the unit push. Half a dozen troopers were talking at the same time; Huber didn't know if anybody would hear the order, but they were mostly veterans and ought to react the right way without a lieutenant telling them what that was. "Bring your cars on line and engage the enemy!"

Arne Huber was F-3's platoon leader, not a driver, but right now the most critical task the platoon faced was getting the damaged, crewless, combat car out of the way of the two vehicles behind it. With *Fencing Master* blocking the hatch, the attackers would wipe out the platoon like so many bugs in a killing bottle. Huber was the closest trooper to the job, so he was doing it.

The fusion bottle that powered the vehicle was on line. Eight powerful fans in nacelles under *Fencing Master's* hull sucked in outside air and filled the steel-skirted plenum chamber at pressure sufficient to lift the car's thirty tonnes. Kolbe had switched the fans on but left them spinning at idle, their blades set at zero incidence, while the spacers freed the turnbuckle.

Huber palmed the combined throttles forward while his thumb adjusted blade incidence in concert. As the fusion bottle fed more power to the nacelles, the blades tilted on their axes so that they drove the air rather than merely cutting it. Fan speed remained roughly constant, but *Fencing Master* shifted greasily as her skirts began to lift from the freighter's deck.

A second buzzbomb hit the bow.

For an instant, Huber's mind went as blank as the white glare of the blast. The shock curtains in the driver's compartment expanded, and his helmet did as much as physics allowed to save his head. Despite that, his brain sloshed in his skull.

He came around as the shock curtains shrank back to their ready state. He didn't know who or where he was. The display screen before him was a gray, roiling mass. He switched the control to thermal imaging by trained reflex and saw armed figures rising from the ground to rush the open hatch.

I'm Arne Huber. We're being attacked.

His right hand was on the throttles; the fans were howling. He twisted the grip, angling the nacelles back so that their thrust pushed the combat car instead of just lifting it. *Fencing Master*'s bow skirt screeched on the deck, braking the vehicle's forward motion beyond the ability of the fans to drive it.

The second warhead had opened the plenum chamber like a ration packet. The fan-driven air rushed out through the hole instead of raising the vehicle as it was meant to do.

The attackers had thrown themselves flat so that the missile wouldn't scythe them down also. Three of them reached the base of the ramp, then paused and opened fire. Dazzling streaks crisscrossed the hold, and the *whang* of slugs hitting the *Fencing Master*'s iridium armor was loud even over the roar of the fans.

Huber decoupled the front four nacelles and tilted them vertical again. He shoved the throttle through the gate, feeding full emergency power to the fans. The windings would burn out in a few minutes under this overload, but right now Huber wouldn't bet he or anybody in his platoon would be alive then to know.

Fencing Master's ruined bow lifted on thrust alone. Not high, not even a finger's breadth, but enough to free the skirt from the decking and allow the rear nacelles to shove her forward. Staggering like a drunken

ox, the car lurched from the hold and onto the ramp.
Her bow dragged again, but this time the fans had
gravity to aid them. She accelerated toward the field,
scraping up a fountain of red sparks from either side
of her hull.

The attackers tried to jump out of the way. Huber
didn't know and didn't much care what happened to
them when they disappeared below the level of the
sensor pickups feeding *Fencing Master*'s main screen.
A few gunmen more or less didn't matter; Huber's problem was to get this car clear of the ramp so that *Flame
Farter* and *Floosie*, still aboard the freighter, could
deploy and deal with the enemy.

Fencing Master reached the bottom of the ramp and
drove a trench through the gravel before shuddering
to a halt. The shock curtains swathed Huber again; he'd
have disengaged the system if he'd had time for non-
essentials after the machine's well-meant swaddling
clothes freed him. Skewing the stern nacelles slightly
to port, he pivoted *Fencing Master* around her bow
and rocked free of the rut.

The air above him sizzled with ozone and cyan light:
two of the tribarrels in the car's fighting compartment
had opened up on the enemy. Somebody'd managed
to board while Huber was putting the vehicle in
motion. *Fencing Master* was a combat unit again.

There must've been about forty of the attackers all
told, ten to each of the shipping containers. Half were
now bunched near *Foghorn* or between that car and
the starship's ramp. Huber switched *Fencing Master*'s
Automatic Defense System live, then used the manual
override to trigger three segments.

The ADS was a groove around the car's hull, just
above the skirts. It was packed with plastic explosive
and faced with barrel-shaped osmium pellets. When
the system was engaged, sensors triggered segments

of the explosive to send blasts of pellets out to meet and disrupt an incoming missile.

Fired manually, each segment acted as a huge shotgun. The clanging explosions chopped into cat food everyone who stood within ten meters of *Fencing Master*. Huber got a whiff of sweetly-poisonous explosive residues as his nose filters closed again. The screaming fans sucked away the smoke before he could switch back to thermal imaging.

An attacker aboard *Foghorn* had seen the danger in time to duck into the fighting compartment; the pellets scarred the car's armor but didn't penetrate it. The attacker rose, pointing his slugthrower down at the hatch Huber hadn't had time to close. A tribarrel from *Fencing Master* decapitated the hostile.

A powergun converted a few precisely aligned copper atoms into energy which it directed down the weapon's mirror-polished iridium bore. Each light-swift bolt continued in a straight line to its target, however distant, and released its energy as heat in a cyan flash. A 2-cm round like those the tribarrels fired could turn a man's torso into steam and fire; the 20-cm bolt from a tank's main gun could split a mountain.

One of the shipping containers was still jammed halfway open. Soldiers were climbing out like worms squirming up the sides of a bait can. Two raised their weapons when they saw a tribarrel slewing in their direction. Ravening light slashed across them, flinging their maimed bodies into the air. The steel container flashed into white fireballs every time a bolt hit it.

Huber's ears were numb. It looked like the fighting was over, but he was afraid to shut down *Fencing Master*'s fans just in case he was wrong; it was easier to keep the car up than it'd be to raise her again from a dead halt. He did back off the throttles slightly to bring the fans down out of the red zone, though.

The bow skirt tapped and rose repeatedly, like a chicken drinking.

Flame Farter pulled into the freighter's hatchway and dipped to slide down the ramp under full control. Platoon Sergeant Jellicoe was behind the central tribarrel. She'd commandeered the leading car when the shooting started rather than wait for her own *Floosie* to follow out of the hold.

Jellicoe fired at something out of sight beyond the shipping containers. Huber touched the menu, importing the view from Jellicoe's gunsight and expanding it to a quarter of his screen.

Three attackers stood with their hands in the air; their weapons were on the gravel behind them. Jellicoe had plowed up the ground alongside to make sure they weren't going to change their minds.

Mercenaries fought for money, not principle. The Slammers and their peers took prisoners as a matter of policy, encouraging their opponents toward the same professional ideal.

Enemies who killed captured Slammers could expect to be slaughtered man, woman and child; down to the last kitten that mewled in their burning homes.

"Bloody Hell . . ." Huber muttered. He raised the seat to look out at the shattered landscape with his own eyes, though the filters still muffled his nostrils.

Haze blurred the landing field. It was a mix of ozone from powergun bolts and the coils of the slug-throwers, burning paint and burning uniforms, and gases from superheated disks that had held the copper atoms in alignment: empties ejected from the tribarrels. Some of the victims were fat enough that their flesh burned also.

The dirigible that'd carried the attackers into position now fled north as fast as the dozen engines podded on outriggers could push it. That wasn't very fast, even with the help of the breeze to swing the big vessel's bow; they couldn't possibly escape.

Huber wondered for a moment how he could contact the dirigible's crew and order them to set down or be destroyed. Plattner's World probably had emergency frequencies, but the data hadn't been downloaded to F-3's data banks yet.

Sergeant Jellicoe raked the dirigible's cabin with her tribarrel. The light-metal structure went up like fireworks in the cyan bolts. An instant later all eight gunners in the platoon were firing, and the driver of *Floosie* was shooting a pistol with one hand as he steered his car down the ramp with the other.

"Cease fire!" Huber shouted, not that it was going to make the Devil's bit of difference. "Unit, cease fire *now*!"

The dirigible was too big for the powerguns to destroy instantly, but the bolts had stripped away swathes of the outer shell and ruptured the ballonets within. Deseau had guessed right: the dirigible got its lift from hydrogen, the lightest gas and cheap enough to dump and replace after every voyage so that the ballonets didn't fill with condensed water over time.

The downside was the way it burned.

Flames as pale and blue as a drowned woman's flesh licked from the ballonets, engulfing the middle of the great vessel. The motors continued to drive forward, but the stern started to swing down as fire sawed the airship in half. The skeleton of open girders showed momentarily, then burned away.

"Oh bloody buggering Hell!" Huber said. He idled *Fencing Master*'s fans and stood up on the seat. "*Hell!*"

"What's the matter, sir?" Learoyd asked. He'd lost his helmet, but he and Sergeant Deseau both were at their combat stations. The tribarrels spun in use, rotating a fresh bore up to fire while the other two cooled. Even so the barrels still glowed yellow from their long bursts. "They were hostiles too, the good Lord knows."

"*They* were," Huber said grimly. "But the folks living around here are the ones who've hired us."

The remaining ballonets in the dirigible's bow exploded simultaneously, flinging blobs of burning metal hundreds of meters away. Fires sprang up from the treetops, crackling and spewing further showers of sparks.

Huber heard a siren wind from somewhere deep in the forest community. It wasn't going to do a lot of good.

The dirigible's stern, roaring like a blast furnace, struck the terminal building. Some of those inside ran out; they were probably screaming, but Huber couldn't hear them over the sound of the inferno. One fellow had actually gotten twenty meters from the door when the mass of airship and building exploded, engulfing him in flames. He was a carbonized husk when they sucked back an instant later.

Huber sighed. That pretty well put a cap on the day, he figured.

excerpt from *Paying the Piper*, by David Drake available from Baen Books, hardcover, July 2002